A MAN FOR THE MOMENT

"This isn't right," he said brusquely. "It's yesterday's passion and it will disappear just as fast. I can't give you more."

She bit her lip and looked away from him, blinking away the pain his words inflicted. "How can such a wondrous feeling, such a miracle, pass and leave no memory or longing for more?"

"Miracles," he muttered as he raked his hand through his hair. "It's lust, not a miracle."

"I like it," she said artlessly, no longer fooled by his protestations.

"Well, I sure as hell don't," he shouted. "It's damned uncomfortable trying to tumble a rosebud. You have too many thorns for my taste, Cameo, and you require too much tending. Find yourself a man who will enjoy being permanently staked out in your garden."

"You're lying, Zach. You want me."

CONNIE RINEHOLD

MORE THAN JUST A NIGHT

A DELL BOOK

Published by
Dell Publishing
a division of
Bantam Doubleday Dell Publishing Group, Inc.
666 Fifth Avenue
New York, New York 10103

The trademark Dell® is registered in the U.S. Patent and Trademark Office.

ISBN: 0-440-21195-6

Printed in the United States of America

Published simultaneously in Canada

February 1992

10 9 8 7 6 5 4 3 2 1

RAD

A true friend unbosoms freely, advises justly, assists readily, adventures boldly, takes all patiently, defends courageously, and continues a friend unchangeably.

—William Penn

To my husband, Sam, for all of the above, and for making a special moment last twenty-seven years.

To Mary Lee Billings and Diana & Russ Logan, special friends who are always there, always supportive, always loving.

To Kathryn Falk and Carol Stacy, for believing everyone should be a winner.

With special thanks to Jay Acton and Tina Moskow for making it so.

And to my children, special one and all—
Sam III for generous spirit and Don Quixote.
Eric, for sensitivity and challenging "discussions."
April for hanging on when Mom was going over the edge.

Legend

An End . . . and a
Beginning . . .

In the twelfth century A.D. a prince of Wales gathered his followers into ships and sailed on the night sea to escape a war with his brother. They knew not where the winds would carry them. To an endless plunge over the edge of the world? To a new life of freedom and destiny? Or to a watery oblivion merely postponed by their flight? It mattered not. His choices were incontrovertible, unalterable. And so he chose probable death in an unknown future rather than face certain death at the hands of a brother who hated him.

Winds filled the sails and the tides surged, carrying the fugitives away until their silhouettes were swallowed by the night. Setting his course to the south and west, the rogue prince bade farewell to the land of his forebears as he watched the horizon with eyes as silver as the moonpath on a stormy sea.

In the centuries to come, legends were born, telling of a race of people in the new land whose ways were apart from those of the natives and whose tongue was like no other spoken there. They moved freely among the nations and tribes, their knowledge and peaceful ways accepted out of fear or respect or reverence, for some thought them to be the children of gods.

They were known as the "Others."

More men came from across the big waters to claim the land and destroy its bounty, to rule the "People" and taint their blood with disease. They were men like the Others in countenance, with fair skin, strange languages, and hair upon their faces. Men who recognized the Others, yet did not accept their shared pasts.

And the Others, knowing peace could no longer thrive between themselves and the People, moved across the land until they found an empty place and made it their own. For they also knew they belonged to neither culture. Many of their ways were of the People while their past was that of the first prince, the place from which he came. They knew, too, that their appearance was a curiosity, neither of the People nor of the newcomers, but somewhere in between. Each carried the mark of his ancestor—a streak of light in the hair, a stature grown taller with each generation, a fineness and strength of feature, and eyes gleaming like the silver moonpath on a stormy sea . . . twilight eyes.

And the legends lived on, legends only, because the Others chose to walk a hidden path, alone, untouched by a war that swept the land. A war between brothers.

—— Prologue ——
Hero with a Thousand Faces

Colorado–New Mexico Territory—February 20, 1862

A subtle tension hung in the air. The Confederate camp grew quiet as men sat around fires and spoke in hushed tones. Seasoned fighters watched the darkness and tried to hear above the sluggish rumble of the Rio Grande, knowing that night merely concealed danger rather than postponed it. Less experienced soldiers joked and bragged and waited impatiently for the sun to bring death into the open, certain that it couldn't possibly single them out.

Zachary McAllister crouched among the bushes that huddled on the riverbank, keeping one eye on the Rebels and the other on the adobe walls of Fort Craig across the river. He yawned and forced his eyes to open wide. Boredom had set in with the damp chill from the ground. At times like this, he felt as if he were waiting for his turn to play in a senseless game. A game dreamed up by President Lincoln, Jefferson Davis, and their respective Departments of War. Zach couldn't help but wonder why he'd had the lousy luck to be the subject of one of the most asinine legends that ever resulted from war.

A grim smile tugged his mouth as he thought of what had recently been written about him.

He is a shadow, anonymous, barely noticed when present, easily forgotten when not—a drifter who lives each moment as if none had gone before and the next might never come. Always "just passing through," he has a different name for each place, a different look, even a different horse. For each person he meets, he alters his manner and way of speaking so that no two memories of him are the same. He moves among the enemy like a shadow on the wind and leaves thunder and lightning in his wake.

To the Northerners, he is a hero, a rogue warrior who steals secrets from the enemy to give to the cause of justice and liberty for all. To the Confederates, he is death with a thousand faces, a thousand names. . . .

It's enough to make you puke, Zach thought. In polite society, actors weren't considered to be *real* men. Yet now, because he was employing his talents to spy on the enemy, legends were being written about him. The President had told him that stories of his deeds were painstakingly developed and embellished by the Secretary of War to give the fighting men an example of bravery to follow and the encouragement to dance with death just one more time.

So who in the hell was supposed to encourage him? he wondered. This was no way to fight a war—in isolation, surrounded by mysticism, being feared by friend and foe alike. At times the very separateness he so skillfully cultivated made him wonder if he would ever again recognize the man he saw in the mirror.

It was his own fault—first because he'd agreed to it, and

second because he'd trusted Paddy Graydon with the secret of his double life.

Years earlier, boredom with his studies at Harvard had led him to indulge his love of theater. An introduction to the leading lady had resulted in indulgences of another kind, and her performance in bed had held him captive for three years. During those three years, she'd discovered in him a skill for bringing the prose to life. He'd trod the boards every chance he had and learned well the nuances of greasepaint and costume.

Paddy Graydon had known both the lady and the role she'd played in introducing Zach to a life in the theater. No confidence was sacred when Paddy was exercising his elbow more than his discretion. Before the first shots had ever been fired at Fort Sumter, Zach had been summoned by President Lincoln. It had seemed so simple then, so right for him. He hadn't had the sense to say no. It probably wouldn't have done him much good if he had, thanks to Paddy's powers of exaggeration. Ironically, Paddy was now the captain of a Union 'spy' company serving here in the territories of New Mexico and Colorado.

Out of the corner of his eye, Zach caught movement on the opposite bank of the river. A rock dug into his knee and a tree branch scraped his cheek as he shifted slightly for a better view. A Confederate soldier tossed the remains of his coffee into the bushes. Closing his eyes, Zach willed himself to remain still as cold liquid hit him in the face. Unable to move enough to dry himself, he turned his head just enough to see Fort Craig across the river.

A group of shadows slipped away from the thick adobe walls of the fort. He counted four men, two leading the patrol and two leading mules that looked scarcely able to carry the boxes of howitzer shells tied to their backs. It didn't take much imagination to figure out what was happening. It took even less to know who was leading the raid. Only Paddy Graydon, whose men—and mules—would follow him anywhere, had the balls to think this up.

Graydon led his men across the river to within a hundred yards of Zach's hiding place. Recognizing the mules, Zach clenched his teeth and fought the impulse to cover his eyes. The beasts were too old for this, too accustomed to their stalls and feed troughs at the fort.

Near the picket lines of the Reb camp, Graydon gestured to his men. The sound masked by a breeze sweeping through the trees, they struck matches and touched flame to fuses attached to the howitzer shells. At least Paddy had the sense to run for cover as soon as they'd pointed the animals in the direction of the enemy.

Being Union property, the mules had the same idea. With brays of contempt for the primitive corral of the enemy camp, the beasts lazily turned to follow the Union soldiers stealing back to the fort.

"Shit!" Zach didn't bother to stifle his whispered curse. All hell was about to break loose anyway. His muscles tensed for action, he thought fast, then muttered another curse. There wasn't a damn thing he could do except duck and hope Paddy and his men did the same.

The fuses made contact. A heartbeat passed. Howitzer shells exploded from the crates, lighting up the sky. Horses screamed in fear. Men jumped and ran in every direction as they grabbed their weapons and looked for targets. One rambunctious fool shot at the sky and shattered what was left of a box that had flown straight up upon explosion. Another—obviously a hardened veteran who knew the difference between diversion and destruction—leaned against a tree and rolled a smoke.

. . . full of sound and fury, signifying nothing, Zach thought cynically as he raised his head to see Paddy and his companions fly over the water and race into the safety of the fort. Never one to allow opportunity to pass untried, he flattened himself to the ground and belly-crawled through the chaos in the Rebel camp.

The guards posted on the walls of Fort Craig leaned over the ramparts and cheered as they watched a herd of horses stampede across the river, a single rider driving them toward the walls. Orders flew to open the gates. The rider herding the horses veered away from the fort and disappeared into a stand of cottonwoods on the bank of the Rio Grande. President Lincoln had lost two old mules, but —thanks to Zach—had gained over two hundred head of Confederate horses.

For the second time that night, men crept out of the fort, only two this time: Paddy Graydon and Kit Carson. Zach dismounted and leaned back against a tree, waiting for them to reach him.

"You trying to make me look bad, Zach?" Paddy asked mildly.

"My pleasure, Paddy."

"Seems to me, you did a fair job of it without help, Paddy," Kit said, his expression deadpan.

Zach's mouth quirked as he looked back across the river. "You ought to recommend those mules for a citation. The Rebs were laughing so hard, they didn't notice me sneaking in to cut loose their mounts."

Paddy's eyes narrowed on his old friend. "What's it going to cost me for you to keep this quiet?"

Pushing away from the tree, Zach settled his rifle in the crook of his arm. "I figure this one is worth a good rip-roaring drunk when the war is over—on you." His gaze scanned the area as he picked up the reins of his horse. "Be seeing you, Paddy. Kit, better send the Rebs packing soon."

"I don't have much choice, Zach. Canby has it in his mind that I can do more by commanding the New Mexico Volunteers than"—Kit snorted in disgust—"'playing nursemaid to a bunch of trouble-making Indians,'" he quoted, clearly frustrated by the general attitude of the U.S. Government.

"Aren't you staying around for the battle tomorrow? Should be fun since the Reb cavalry will be on foot." Paddy grinned.

"Nope."

"Why not?" Paddy grimaced. He knew better than to ask.

"I'll be somewhere else," Zach said laconically as he mounted his horse. "Keep your head down and watch out for mules bearing howitzer shells."

Wincing at the dig, Graydon held out his hand. "I'd like to think it's a woman and not business. One of us ought to have some *real* fun."

Zach's mouth tightened as he returned the handshake. If Paddy knew how close to the mark he was, he'd laugh his head off. Then he'd let everyone in the territory in on the joke: Zach McAllister, Union spy, was going to play nursemaid to a scrawny girl barely out of the schoolroom, act as caretaker of a ranch so big it claimed several mountains, *and* run a business he knew nothing about. It was bad enough that Sam Fielding had instigated the whole thing with his crazy request, even going so far as to bring up the matter of an old debt, but now President Lincoln had made it an order.

There ought to be a law against civilians meddling in a war.

Hell, there ought to be a law against old friends dying and willing their daughters to suckers like him.

1
Rogue Warrior

Colorado–New Mexico Territory—February 1862

"Don't make any moves you'll regret," commanded a soft, deadly voice.

Cameo froze in her crouched position between the mewling calf and the still-warm carcass of its dead mother. Imperceptibly she twisted her head to sneak a glance over her shoulder. The sun hung low in the sky behind the stranger, silhouetting him on the rise above her so that all she saw was a tall, forbidding shadow against the sky. He didn't move a muscle, but held his stance—loose-limbed, almost casual—and kept his gun pointed at her head.

With the instincts developed by life in the territories, she quickly reviewed her situation. She was partially concealed by brush, giving him a restricted view of her hat and maybe part of her fringed leather jacket. Her gaze darted to the bloody knife on the ground next to her. Had *he* left it there?

The unmistakable click of a gun being cocked told her all she needed to know. In this country a man didn't cock his gun unless he meant to pull the trigger.

She remained still, barely breathing as she fought a

surge of panic. Her fingers itched to grab the knife, take
aim, throw it. All she needed was enough time. . . .

Gunfire echoed in her ears as dirt sprayed in all directions and the knife flew sideways away from her.

"No more tricks, friend. Stand up and turn around—
slowly."

That whispery voice meant business. Energy pumped
through Cameo's veins, urging her to act, to run, to fight,
to scream, anything to ease her tension and fear. Cautiously she inched her hand upward from her lap to her
waist, trying not to give herself away.

Her hat blew off, releasing a single long braid that
whipped across her face as she drew and cocked her own
gun, twisted, and landed belly down in the dirt, facing him.

Her aim wavered, following a blur as he threw himself
to the side and flattened himself on the ground with lightning speed. Before she could draw a bead on him, the
stranger recovered his aim and unerringly pointed the barrel of his pistol at her head.

She blinked and swallowed. "Who gets the first bullet,
mister? You or me?"

She couldn't believe what she was doing.

"I'll call your bet, ma'am," he said, his voice calm as the
air before a storm. If he was surprised to find himself aim-
ing at a woman, he didn't show it. She squinted against the
glare, trying to get a better look at his face.

What now? Cameo wondered, mesmerized by the dark,
malevolent eye of his gun. *"Do* something, curse you," she
said, her voice grating.

"I will, soon as I figure out what, ma'am."

"What are you doing here?"

"Passing through."

"Are you a deserter?" The knowledge was never far

from her mind that General Sibley's Texas rebels had marched into New Mexico and now fought their way north with plans to take over Denver City. They always left a trail of deserters in their wake.

"Nope," he answered.

"A miner?" They too strayed into her valley, wearing defeat like old age, willing to do the most menial labor for enough money to return home.

"Nope."

"Did you kill my cow?"

"*Your* cow, ma'am? Last I heard, this was Sam Fielding's land."

Cameo squinted harder upon hearing her father's name. The stranger angled his head a little to the side and she had the odd sensation of being studied in a very thorough manner. "Do you know him?"

"Maybe—" He lowered his gun a fraction. "Ma'am?"

"What?" Cameo snapped, feeling more absurd with every word that passed between them.

"Don't move . . . there's a snake sidling up to your gun hand."

"That's an old trick—" She felt it, then—a slight pressure and the sinuous glide over her arm. Fear turned to stark terror. Her throat closed around a scream. Dimly she recognized the markings and knew what would happen if she did move—a rattle, then swift attack.

Pressing her lips together, she swallowed down a whimper as the snake stopped, then slithered its way over her other arm. Her blood ran cold as the stranger watched her, his gun tracking the snake. His voice reached her, a soothing whisper she barely heard above the roaring in her ears.

"That's right, sweetheart, don't move. Don't even breathe. I'm going to shoot in a second . . . keep still

. . . let that sidewinder clear your arm. That's it. Let him get out of striking range in case I miss."

In case he missed? The cords in her neck felt as if they might snap. From the corner of her eye she saw the snake's tail move out of view, its rattle blessedly silent. A loud crack drowned out the stranger's voice and deafened her ears to any other sound.

Cameo still didn't move. Her body felt cold, unable to function.

"Ma'am? You're safe. Put down your gun . . . let me help you."

She shook her head and held her gun steady.

"I'm not going to hurt you, ma'am." He paused, then sighed as he glanced around. "Fair enough. I don't blame you. I wouldn't trust me either."

She didn't answer.

"Cameo?" he said, his voice still soft and soothing. "I'm not too inclined to trust your judgment right now, so I'll just get on my horse. . . ."

The barrel of her gun followed him as he cautiously rose to his feet and inched toward his horse. "My gun is holstered, Cameo." He lifted a foot into a stirrup.

"What . . ." Her voice was a scratch in the air. After swallowing several times, she again tried to speak. "What are you doing?"

He stopped dead and held his hands away from his body and the holstered gun at his waist. "Frankly, ma'am, it scares the piss out of me to have a woman point a gun in my direction. If you don't mind, I'll just ride out." Reaching for the reins, he mounted and settled into the saddle. "The ranch house is close—only about a mile." He stared at a cloud of dust moving toward them. "Your *vaqueros* must have heard the shot. They're on their way."

Cameo blinked against the spots growing larger before her eyes. Her stomach felt like a clenched fist. Swallowing, she found her voice. "Just keep riding, mister. You stop and I'll shoot."

"Yes, ma'am. I don't doubt it for a minute." He touched his fingers to the brim of his hat. "My compliments, Miss Fielding. You've got more grit than any ten men I know." With that, he turned his horse and urged him down the other side of the rise.

Cameo watched him disappear, then looked over at the dead snake and shuddered.

The Sangre de Cristo Mountains cradled the Empress Valley Ranch like cupped palms, holding the unseasonable warmth and sunshine lest they slip away too soon. Shadows gripped mountain folds, extending from clustered ranch buildings and people hurrying to finish late-afternoon chores.

A gnarled old man hurried out of the stables as Cameo Fielding rode in with a newborn calf across the front of her saddle and a half dozen *vaqueros* flanking her. *"Patrona,* there is a visitor. Your father waits for you inside. We will take care of your horse and the little one."

A young stable hand ran over and relieved Cameo of the calf as he listened to Jorge's instructions for its care.

"Thank you, Jorge." Still dazed by what had happened, Cameo slid off her horse and smiled her thanks at the *vaqueros.* Thank God they had been working close enough to hear the stranger's shot. Once he had disappeared, she discovered she hadn't the strength to lift the calf onto her horse, yet she'd been reluctant to give it up. As they had ridden for home, she'd been so lost in thought that she hadn't watched where she was riding. One of the men had

finally taken her reins and led her horse, explaining tact-
fully that she needed both hands to hold the calf steady.
The hands had assumed her feeble state of mind and lack
of strength were due to her narrow escape from the snake.
They'd also assumed that she fired the shots. Too busy
fretting over the familiar manner of the stranger, she
hadn't bothered to tell them otherwise.

He had called her Cameo and, later, Miss Fielding. He'd
known who she was, had known, too, who her father was.
Yet she knew nothing about the man who had threatened
her life, saved it, then disappeared as suddenly as he'd
appeared, a man with a voice that still seemed to vibrate
through her body.

"Patrona?"

"What?" She focused on Jorge and realized that all the
other men had left for their homes a little farther up the
trail. Her brows drew together in concern. "Save the calf if
you can, Jorge. The mother is dead."

Jorge's clouded gaze sharpened; his rheumy shoulders
tensed. "The same as before?"

"Yes. The cow's throat was cut."

"It is a warning. You must tell the *Patrón.*"

"No, Jorge. Papa's heart is weak enough as it is. As
before, he is not to know—"

"Your father has a right—"

"Whose right is greater, Jorge? His right to know, or
mine to protect him?" Removing her hat of indeterminate
age and style, Cameo frowned at the burrs sticking to the
floppy brim. "I won't have him worried. His heart is not
strong enough to handle the strain and he would confine
me to the house if he knew of the threats."

"I do not like it. This thing happens too often—"

"Neither do I, Jorge, but the notes left on the carcasses

threaten only Papa. All we can do is guard him carefully and keep him from worrying. I will lose him soon enough without hastening the process."

"That is much to do, *Patrona.*"

"I know, Jorge," she said on a sigh, and, considering the subject closed, she headed toward the sprawling adobe ranch house.

Her arms ached and her hands stung from cuts inflicted by stubborn brush. The smell of horse and cow mingled on her cotton blouse and old riding skirt that pulled taut across her full hips. Soil and grime were smeared on her leather jacket. Crimped strands of hair had escaped her braid and fell around her face. Her mouth felt gritty with dust and the aftertaste of fear.

The cow's body had still been warm when she found it. She should have known better than to leave herself wide open for attack. Jorge was right. The senseless murder of cattle was a threat she couldn't ignore when notes were left on the bodies warning of more gruesome consequences if her father didn't cease his investigations into the gold shipments missing from Fielding Freight wagons.

And then there was the stranger who had acted as if he held women at gunpoint every day. Only one thing was clear to her. He hadn't killed the stock. If he had, he would have shot her right away. He had known her name, had spoken it with gentleness and compassion.

He'd called her "sweetheart."

Stopping at the roofed porch of the house, Cameo frowned at the unremarkable chestnut mustang hitched to the post, the worn saddle and trail gear hanging over the rail—the same mustang that had been ground-tethered near the stranger.

The wretch had been on his way to the valley all the

time. She'd been scared witless and he'd been having fun at her expense. Or, she wondered, would he have told her the truth if the snake hadn't appeared?

She looked down at her clothes. Botheration. Nothing was going to keep her from the fancy bathtub her father had imported for her. Nothing would make her face that man again until her person was clean and her composure well starched. If she could just sneak past the office undetected . . .

Sighing, she sat on the steps to tug off her mud-caked boots. After brushing the worst of the dried mud off the soles, she carried both boots in one hand as she rose and slipped quietly into the house.

"Neither commander was present on the battlefield? Where in bloody blazes were they?" The sound of her father's agitation, punctuated by his precise, British accent, drew her to the partially closed door of the office. The mention of a battle captured her attention. The familiar voice of a stranger drove all thoughts of bathing from her mind.

"General Sibley passed the time in a hospital wagon and, from what I hear, drank himself senseless with the Rebs' supply of medicinal whiskey. Canby didn't leave Fort Craig until late afternoon."

The voice was the same—deep with a slow, easy drawl, both soothing and disturbing, like distant thunder, charging the air, filling it with expectations. And it was familiar, yet not, teasing her in unfamiliar ways, touching her in unmentionable places. How extraordinary. She felt as if she were being confronted with something long awaited yet unexpected and all the more shocking for its sudden appearance.

Something? Or someone? The peculiar turn of her

thoughts unsettled her. She wasn't expecting anyone she hadn't met many times before. Officers from Fort Union often passed through the valley to buy livestock for the army and any number of her father's cronies such as Kit Carson, Seamus Casey, and Alexander 'Pigeon' Valle, who had missed the last gathering of old mountain men. They all came here to spend the winter and spin yarns of days gone by. But no other visitor to the ranch had disturbed her like this. Certainly none of their other visitors had threatened to shoot her.

Hearing Sofia, their housekeeper, knock on the other door to the office, Cameo scowled in annoyance and sank down on the deacon's bench in the hall, her boots still clutched in her hand. She told herself she only wanted to hear more about the war. The stranger with a deadly aim and a voice that stirred up every restless thought she'd ever had didn't have a thing to do with her curiosity. It was the war that worried her, kept her awake nights, not knowing which frightened her the most—the darkness or the threat of invasion into her valley.

The Confederates had been advancing closer and closer to the Colorado border in a campaign to secure a route through which to channel California and Colorado gold to the South, as well as the vast stores of munitions stocked in the Union forts.

Gold, in her opinion, was truly the root of all evil. It was a disease, consuming the desperate and greedy, afflicting them with a blindness for anything that didn't shine yellow and buy dreams by the ounce. In his paintings, her father had faithfully rendered the squalor and despair the miners lived with. She'd been appalled at their willingness to sacrifice everything of value for a handful of color that slipped through their fingers in exchange for a bottle to ease their

misery or a woman to fill the night. Gold fever had destroyed families and men's lives. Gold itself financed wars.

In the last few months, an army had invaded the territory, killing and destroying in order to finance more death
and destruction. If they succeeded, her home would be
forfeit.

Cameo wryly acknowledged the contradiction of her
thoughts. Gold might be the root of evil, but it was also the
reason she enjoyed the luxury of polished wood floors,
metal hinges, glass windows, and an indoor water closet.
Few homes in the territories boasted such amenities. Her
father had made a fortune in the China Trade and increased it with the ranch and freight business. His discovery of gold in some unnamed place had insured their
future.

Cameo heard a soft shuffle down the hall and glanced up
to find Sofia watching her. Putting her finger to her lips,
she shook her head, a warning for the housekeeper not to
give her away. Sofia rolled her eyes and threw up her
hands as she stalked off in the opposite direction.

Cameo immediately turned her attention back to the office and the conversation the men had resumed, drawn by
the stranger's voice rather than by what was actually being
said.

"What amazes me," Samuel said, "is that we lost the
battle, yet still occupy Fort Craig."

"Defeat is in the eyes of the beholder," said The Voice.
"Those Texans are meaner than a herd of horny bulls. Our
troops were the ones to retreat first, but . . ." He chuckled. "The Texans decided they didn't want the fort when
they saw how many cannon we had mounted on the
walls."

"I don't recall Fort Craig having a large number of cannon."

"It doesn't. What the Rebs saw were Quaker guns—logs painted to look like cannon."

Cameo angled her head so she could peek through the sliver of space between door and frame, squinting with one eye while focusing through the space with the other. The doorjamb pressed uncomfortably against her cheek. The men sat in matching wingbacks in front of the fireplace. All she could see of the stranger were his long legs stretched before him and a lower body that seemed lean and fit under fringed buckskins and knee-length moccasins crisscrossed by rawhide thongs around his calves. She remembered how tall he had appeared standing on the rise above her, a dark, menacing shadow against the blazing sky. At the time, she had noticed little else but his voice and his gun.

She shifted, hoping to obtain a better view and gritted her teeth in frustration. Tentatively, she inched her hand along the smooth wood and nudged the door so the space widened a fraction. She angled her head even more. The wing of the chair concealed his face. His sleeve pulled tight over a well-muscled arm as he lifted his glass, paused a moment, then completed the action. Draining it quickly, he bent his knees and pulled forward, allowing Cameo a partial view of his face.

All thought vanished. She forgot about the crick in her neck and the press of wood on her cheek. A tremor began in her throat and raced downward, leaving tingling shocks in its wake. Her body felt as if it were liquid . . . and hot. So hot.

Planes and angles harshly defined a wide brow and a slightly hawkish nose. Light and shadow played amid high cheekbones and widely spaced, deep-set eyes. A short, black beard and moustache obscured the lower part of his face and his black shoulder-length hair was held back by a strip of Indian beadwork tied around his forehead. Taken separately, his features seem cast from irregular molds. Together, they formed a countenance attractive in its roughness.

The muscles in his broad back and shoulders appeared to tighten and swell. His manner was more alert, as if he were ready to pounce. He turned his head.

Her heart tumbled. His eyes—all the more startling against his tanned skin—were of a hue between the blue of day and the silver-gray of winter twilight, compelling eyes that missed little and revealed even less. His bold, finely shaped brows arched.

Still she stared, watching his eyes change from the hardness of tempered steel to amusement, and something more, something that made her think of midnight restlessness and forbidden yearnings. She had a tingly sensation of being watched, as if he could see her as clearly as she could see him, and the solid wood was no barrier. Still she couldn't move—didn't want to move. He was so fine, and she felt so incredibly . . . unlike herself.

He resumed his former relaxed position as Samuel stood up and carried their empty glasses to the desk to refill them from a decanter of his best whiskey. Jerking completely away from the door, Cameo knocked her hand against the bench and dropped one of her boots. She stooped awkwardly, trying to catch it before it thumped on the floor. The boot slipped her grasp and she stumbled against the bench, banging her knee in the process.

"Cameo? Is that you?" Samuel grinned widely around

his cigar as he walked toward the door. "Come in. We have a guest."

"Oh curses," she muttered. Shaking her head vigorously, she pointed to her clothes.

"Nonsense," Samuel said. "The last time Zachary saw you, you were playing with the chickens and making little mud plates for their feed."

Cameo groaned and considered throwing her remaining boot at her father as *Zachary* joined him with a solemnity that was obviously forced. With her chin held high, Cameo marched into the room, her shoulders squared, her dignity hanging by a thread. Her face burned as she felt his gaze sweep over her from head to foot, linger, then shoot up to a place above her shoulder. Those twilight eyes were sparkling and she just knew he was biting the inside of his cheek. Curious, Cameo dropped her gaze to the place his suddenly seemed to be avoiding and saw one pink toe protruding from a hole in her brown woolen sock. "Oh, dear," she mumbled as she rubbed a smudge on her cheek.

"Cameo, I'm sure you don't remember Zachary McAllister," Samuel said. "You were only five when he was last here."

"I'm sorry, I don't recall . . ." Her brow wrinkled. The only McAllister she knew was Jacob, mountain man, explorer, and her father's friend until he'd been killed in the Pueblo rebellion in '47. Comprehension dawned as Cameo's gaze moved up Zachary's length. "Jacob's son?"

Zach nodded warily as she glared at him with challenge and anger sparking in her jade-green eyes. She might not have recognized him from his previous visits, but she remembered plenty about their confrontation earlier that afternoon. Obviously, he hadn't made a good impression. He waited for her to mention their stalemate and the dead cow, but she didn't. He met her stare and wondered just how much she was keeping from her father, and how well she was succeeding.

Because of their earlier encounter, he knew better than to underestimate Cameo. Not only did she have courage and a quick, intelligent mind, she was also a beautiful, voluptuous woman. Her eyes gave everything away as she looked him over—relief and wariness, curiosity, attraction . . . innocence.

This was going to be a real bitch of an assignment.

"But the last I heard, you were at Harvard," Cameo said as she concentrated on old memories, finding only one, barely an hour old. Surely she should remember such a man.

Samuel chuckled. "Time has no meaning for the young."

"I finished my studies there nine years ago," Zachary said.

"Oh." Feeling gauche, Cameo focused on his Colt revolver tucked under the flap of a holster. His large hand slipped beneath hers, raising it in courtly fashion for an almost brush of his lips.

Cameo's boot dropped from her tingling fingers. All of a sudden there was too much air in the room, hot and heavy as a summer day when everything seemed more vivid and alive. "I'm pleased to meet you *again,* Mr. McAllister," she managed to reply without stuttering or otherwise sounding like a porridge-headed adolescent.

"Zach . . . after all, we're almost family." He said it firmly, knowing the phrase was trite, yet stressing it anyway, suddenly needing a reminder of who Cameo was and why he was here. Somewhere along the way he'd forgotten that little girls grew up.

"Really?" she said tartly, irritated at the commotion he had started in her body. "Almost counts only if you miss a target, or a bullet misses you . . . Zach." Cameo pulled her hand away, wincing as the callouses on his hand scraped over the cuts on hers.

Zach's mouth slashed upward at one corner as he leaned back against the desk.

Samuel frowned as if her dishevelment had just come to his attention. "I thought you were going to Spirit Canyon to read."

"I found a calf tangled in the brush, Papa," Cameo said quickly, then turned to aim a warning look at him. "Your horse isn't stabled. Aren't you staying?"

"I just stopped to pay my respects on my way up north," he said, playing his own game of deception.

"I've been trying to persuade him to stay for a week or so," Samuel said.

A week. Cameo didn't know whether to feel excitement at the prospect or annoyance. It was clear from his expression that before he left—in a week or an hour—he was going to demand explanations, as if he had the right. And clearer still was the tangle of responses he inspired in her. She felt like a mess, inside and out. She wondered if a week would be too long or not long enough.

She decided that the only way to sort herself out was to take first things first—find out what he was and why he wasn't in the army like every other able-bodied young man. His body certainly looked able and though he had to be a dozen or so years older than herself, he was still young. She jerked her gaze back to his face. "Are you a trapper, Zach?"

After a pause, he answered grimly. "You could say that."

"Isn't February a strange time to be trapping?"

"Depends on the prey."

Cameo's mouth turned to dry cotton at the memory of their earlier meeting when *she* had been his prey. "I see," she said casually. "Since the beaver are played out and no longer fashionable for apparel in Europe, what is it exactly that you hunt?"

"Buffalo," Samuel said hastily.

Zach just stood there, his thumbs hooked in his belt, his mouth quirked in amusement.

"Buffalo? What do you do with them?" she asked.

"He sells the meat to the army, Cameo. And the hides make excellent robes." Samuel cleared his throat at the wry look Zach slanted his way.

"How interesting," Cameo said, her ironic tone mocking Zach's silence and her father's sudden gift of gab. "How do you transport a buffalo after you kill it? Or do you simply talk it into following you to the nearest fort and then shoot it?"

Zach sobered, his mouth as straight as the barrel of his gun. "I shoot the critter, bind it up good, put one end of the rope in my teeth and drag it behind my horse." He rubbed one hand over his chin. "Course, I try to find herds close to Union forts. Saves me trips to the barber to have my teeth pulled."

Samuel sputtered into his drink.

Cameo glared at her father, then back to Zach, whose smile stretched lazily across his face. That smile turned her knees to butter and made her heart turn somersaults. And it was as infectious as the measles. Suddenly Cameo smiled too. Being raised on a ranch populated mostly by men, she had learned early to take teasing in the spirit in which it was given.

"Then perhaps you should hunt beaver, Zach. You might one day have need of *their* teeth."

Shaking his head, Zach studied her appreciatively. "I don't know why I expected to see the same little terror who stole eggs from the henhouse and spit in the dirt like the men." He tried to match that vision with the one standing before him. Her eyes were the same: large and tilted slightly upward, clear jade shot with gold. He remembered, too, the widow's peak dipping gently toward her forehead, the hair as dark and richly brown as good coffee. She wasn't beautiful by the present-day standard of soft and pale and oversweetened. Her features were unique, her coloring healthy, and he sensed that though she might have a sweet nature, it was liberally laced with spice.

She blushed as his perusal continued down her body. His gaze lingered over full breasts and hips, a graceful turn of waist. Even smeared with half the dirt in the territory, she was exotic, arresting, compelling in the extreme.

"She favors Chai, don't you think?" Samuel said. "Except for her quick tongue." Samuel refilled the glasses he'd forgotten when his daughter appeared.

Zach thought of the delicately exquisite woman for whom Sam had left his beloved England and given up his way of life. Chai Fielding had been half–Chinese by birth and anglicized by the missionaries who had adopted her. A quiet, unassuming woman, she had preferred to move in the background until people tended to overlook her existence. Except Sam, whose mind and heart had never been far from his wife regardless of the physical distance separating them.

"No. She is uniquely Cameo Regine." Accepting his

glass, Zach raised it in toast to her, his gaze locked with hers.

As her name rolled off his tongue in a continuous blending of sounds, breath snagged in her throat. Time passed, a mere whisper of moments while Cameo stood captive to his stare. His eyes darkened, silver-blue to smoldering ash, burning her skin wherever they touched. She turned away, disconcerted by the intimacy of his appraisal and the boldness of her thoughts.

Cameo's lack of guile intrigued Zach. He was a practical man, disdaining whimsy, but Cameo inspired his imagination . . . and his body. He had a strange sense of being captured by her, imprisoned in this single moment by the force of her presence.

Cameo made him think of warm beds, smooth linen sheets, and soft whispers in the night.

He'd be better off facing her gun.

Needing a diversion, Cameo focused on the rifle propped against the desk. "Is this a Henry Repeater? May I see it?" The words tumbled out in a breathless rush.

Zach cleared his throat. "Yes. Do you like guns, Cameo?" he asked with devilment in his eyes.

His deliberate query relaxed Cameo, made her see the afternoon in a different light. He wasn't taking it seriously, so why should she? They had both simply been doing what came naturally on the frontier—protecting themselves from possible danger. "They're very . . . handy," she answered with a straight face and twinkling eyes. "You never know when you'll meet up with a polecat, or a two-legged snake."

Staring at her over the rim of his glass, Zach shared the memory with her. "I have no doubt, Cameo, that you'd know how to manage either one," he said quietly, a solemn tribute to the way she had handled herself in a dangerous situation even though it had been obvious that she'd been scared out of her bloomers.

Flushing with pleasure and not knowing what to say, Cameo picked up the weapon and balanced it in her hands before lifting it to her shoulder and sighting it on the far wall. "Does it really fire fifteen shots without reloading?" she asked, amazed that she remembered such trivial details when all she could think of were Zachary McAllister's details.

"Yes," Zach answered, his mouth twitching at her fierce concentration on the sight. In spite of her obvious familiarity with firearms, she had a white-knuckled hold on the rifle. He set his glass down on the desk and stepped nearer to her, ready to take the weapon before she dealt a mortal wound to the wall.

She glanced brightly at Samuel. "Papa, we really should have one of these."

"Will a dozen do?" Zach asked.

Wide-eyed, Cameo lowered the rifle. "A dozen? How? I thought the army received all available weapons."

Zach rubbed his hands down the sides of his thighs, resisting the desire to touch her, "The war won't be won or lost for a dozen rifles that never would have found their way to the army anyway."

"Why not?"

"A couple of deserters were trading them to the Indians."

Cameo shivered. His eyes were focused on something other than the office or its occupants. His expression was hard, uncompromising, dangerous.

"Zachary persuaded them to retire," Samuel said, staring into his glass as if he saw his own youth and brave deeds mirrored there.

Cameo stared at Zach curiously, then nodded her head. "Good for you, Zachary McAllister. And thank you for the rifles." Her nose wrinkled impishly. "To legitimize our possession of them, we'll call ourselves the Empress Valley Dragoons. Maybe I can persuade Jorge to retire his old blunderbuss."

Winking at his daughter, Samuel set his glass down. "Sofia will have dinner ready soon. I, for one, am going to clean up and change. Since we have accepted your gift, you have no choice but to accept our hospitality."

Cameo held her breath waiting for his answer. Men seldom questioned Papa's authority, but Cameo suspected Zach had more than his fair share of implacability.

"Please stay, Zach." She laid her hand atop his, then snatched it away again.

Heat shot through Zach and a deep, burning desire flared in his groin. Cameo's touch kindled more than his lust, and he experienced a sudden eruption of the obsessive need for family and belonging that he'd long ago smothered beneath the weight of duty. From the moment she'd held her gun on him and kept right on holding it though a snake was slithering over her arm, he'd felt a warmth that had nothing to do with physical passion.

He hesitated, listening to Cameo's voice, the sounds of the valley, people living harmoniously. He was growing emotionally deaf, listening to the death rattle of a nation and knowing that he was one of the murderers. Sadness shaped his smile as he reflected that a man should enjoy his work.

Cameo watched Zach's hand tighten, then release the

Henry. He smiled, a self-deprecating quirk as if he'd been bested in a silent battle.

"My bedroll could use an airing out."

Her emotions leaped with an exuberance that staggered her at his agreement to stay. If she remained in the room one moment longer, she just knew she'd make a fool of herself. "I'll . . . uh . . . go clean up. Excuse me."

Cameo maintained a sedate pace out of the office, past one fallen boot and then the other. Once out of sight, she broke into a run down the hall to the water closet Samuel had imported from Europe.

Shedding her clothes quickly, she stepped into the waiting tub of heated water and blessed Sofia for anticipating her need. She wanted to lie back and soak, relax, and restore at least some of her equilibrium, but restlessness overcame her. Her nerve ends trembled at being so suddenly brought to life by unfamiliar emotions. The warm water caressed her bare skin, reminding her of the sensations Zach evoked with a word, a simple touch, a look that reached into her soul.

A wanderer. The words came unbidden into her thoughts, an unwelcome warning. He was probably a man who would always be more interested in where he hadn't been than where he was. A man to whom home and family were simply a place to visit and people to see between adventures, as her father had been until failing health had decreed that this winter would likely be his last. Now, for the first time in her life, her father was home to stay. She finally felt as if she were part of a family years after she'd learned to live without one.

Sighing at the bitter irony of it all, Cameo stepped out of the tub and reached for a towel to dry her hair. Oh, yes, she knew exactly what kind of man Zach was. A man more dazzling than gold dust and just as difficult to hold for more than a moment.

Giving up on useless thoughts of what might have been, Cameo absently rubbed a fresh towel over her body, then donned fresh bloomers, camisole, and petticoat. Zach's appearance had robbed her of common sense. With his continued presence, she would need all her wits about her. Her childhood had taught her one very important lesson: better to live alone than to live with loneliness. Cameo had a feeling that Zach was capable of leaving an empty trail of loneliness through a woman's life that would lead her nowhere.

A voice drifted through the air outside the window. "All right, Manolito. You can let out the plug again."

Determined not to yield to the curiosity luring her to the window, Cameo yanked a hairbrush through her hair. She knew what Zach was doing. A man had a right to privacy while bathing. He laughed, the deep rumble reaching inside to pluck at her weak resolve. The hairbrush clattered to the dressing table. As she drew the curtains aside, she peered cautiously through the glass panes, angling her body to better see toward the side of the house.

A large wooden tank was built off the ground to catch and store rainwater. When removed, a peg near the bottom released water down a trough into a stall made of planks, four deep, nailed crosswise around tall fence posts. Not twenty feet away from her window, Zach stood within the structure rinsing soap from his body, which was hidden only from lower chest to above his knees. She stared intently, wishing that she could see through the wood planks.

"Close it up, Manolito. *Gracias.*"

The boy inserted the peg, driving it home with a mallet as Zach dried with a linen towel.

Cameo bent over to rest her elbows on the sill and propped her chin in her hands. When he moved, the sunset light gilded his body, shading his skin with the play of his muscles. A gentle wind ruffled his hair, evaporating the moisture from the black curls on his head and chest. Her admiring gaze moved downward, her imagination filling in what was hidden by the stall. The burnished copper hair sprinkled on his well-formed calves caught golden sparks from the setting sun—

Questioning what she saw, her gaze flew back to his head . . . his chest . . . his legs . . .

Two colors of hair?

He stepped out of the stall, arresting her thoughts. Her breath caught; her heart hesitated over a beat, then pounded like the hooves of stampeding horses. Nothing, not even her imagination, had prepared her for the view of Zach unclothed. *So that is what* it *looks like,* she thought. The way her classmates at the Academy for Young Ladies in Santa Fe had talked, *it* was the source of all pleasure, not to mention the subject of late-night conversations that kept everyone awake for all the giggling and sighing.

Cameo centered her attention on that part of Zach's anatomy, studying it carefully. As it was now, it certainly didn't look like anything worth losing a night's sleep over. But then she thought of the bulls and stallions on the ranch. How much, she wondered, could it grow?

Guilt at her actions—and her thoughts—urged her to pull away. She complied reluctantly, but not before taking a final sweeping look. He was so pleasing to the eye— broad here, narrow there, with strength and grace as he moved with deceptive laziness.

Zach paused, with an almost imperceptible tensing of his body before picking up his clothing and stepping back into the enclosure. Casually, he turned around, folded his arms over the siding . . .

And winked at her.

2

The Seeds Are Sown

Cameo frowned at her image in the mirror and turned one way and then another, trying to see herself as Zach might, then trying to figure out if what she was seeing would be good or bad from his point of view. She wasn't even sure what she wanted him to see.

Certainly not a young woman who had enjoyed the sight of him so much that she couldn't quite summon up shame for spying on him. Certainly not a young woman who was mortified to her back teeth only because she'd been caught.

Concentrating fiercely on her image from neck to décolletage, she tugged the bodice of her dress downward to reveal the rise of her breasts. Too much? Zach probably already thought her the most brazen of women. Impatient at the lengthy process of preparing to impress a man, Cameo pulled the neckline up again and tore out the pins holding her mass of hair up in a sophisticated cluster atop her head.

She'd seen the style on a fashion doll wearing a ball gown. Though it was her most feminine frock, the deep-rose silk was definitely not a ball gown. Her frown deepened as she studied her hairstyle, and decided that it was definitely not proper for the dress or the occasion. Her gaze strayed to the window. Proper or not, she mused, there were times when no attire was the best of all.

"Cameo?"

Startled at her father's voice, Cameo jerked her gaze away from the window and looked about her room, as if there might be evidence of her thoughts lying around to incriminate her. "Yes, Papa."

"I've poured you a glass of wine. Are you coming soon?"

There was no help for it. She couldn't hide in her room. Zach would find it too amusing, and she'd provided him with quite enough amusement for one day. "Yes, Papa. I'll be along shortly."

With a sigh of resignation, she tugged on her bodice—down, then up, then down again—adjusted the satin rose sewn into the vee of her neckline, and smoothed the deeply flounced hem. Standing back, she appraised her appearance. The dress with its gathered wrist-length sleeves and sash was demure, yet—she thought—just the teeniest bit tantalizing. The rose concealed her décolletage. The snugly fitted waist showed some curves while the full skirt hinted at others.

Naughty thoughts aside, she *looked* like a lady. Perhaps Zach would overlook her indiscretion in gentlemanly fashion.

As soon as she entered the large parlor, Zach picked up a glass of ruby liquid and met her just inside the portal. The wretch had obviously been waiting for her. She accepted the glass warily. "Thank you."

"You're welcome," he whispered. "Shall we have a toast?"

Her gaze shot to the settee where her father seemed to

be contemplating the fire. She sighed in relief to see that he gave no evidence of hearing the conversation between herself and Zach or even of knowing that she had finally made an appearance. "By all means," she replied and held up her glass.

Zach touched the rim of his glass to hers and whispered, "Drink to me only with thine eyes."

His use of poetry startled her. Embarrassment heated her face as she stared at Zach's expression of patient expectation. Just what in blazes was he expecting? she wondered. Cameo forced herself to stand her ground and brazen it out. The words he had uttered were familiar—a quote from Ben Jonson.

"And shall you pledge to me with thine?" she asked with false bravado, changing the next line in the poem to suit her purpose. It pleased her to see it suited just fine. Zach's gaze had dropped to his glass and he broodingly contemplated its contents.

"Or leave a kiss but in the cup," he quoted accurately and gave her a heavy-lidded look, ripe with suggestion.

"I'd rather have the wine," she retorted and sipped from her glass.

"I would have thought otherwise."

With her customary practicality, Cameo sighed and took a slow, measured breath. She had just plumbed the depths of her sophistication. "I deserved that. Papa says I have yet to learn to temper impetuosity with discretion."

"He's right."

"Are you going to be boorish about this, Mr. McAllister?"

"I wouldn't dream of it, ma'am," he drawled, catching her arm as she tried to move past him. The teasing glint faded from his narrowed eyes. "Tell me, do you issue similar invitations to every man who comes here? You were barely covered yourself."

She smiled. Mischievous lights danced in her eyes. "I have no predilections as a Peeping Tom and no desire to study the forms of most men."

"Should I take that as a compliment?"

"That, or simply curiosity about a man who has two distinct colors of body hair."

Zach choked and sputtered into his glass, loosing his hold on her arm as his mind raced, wondering which of his hair-covered body parts she referred to. He hadn't done a thorough job of dying all his hair, thinking it wasn't necessary for a visit to the valley. He sure as hell hadn't expected to be seen in the altogether by a woman with more sass than sense.

He watched Cameo grin smugly as she turned on her heel and casually sashayed across the room. Her smile became gentle and a little sad as she discovered that her father had fallen asleep on the settee.

Damn it! It had been Sam's idea for him to show up with an altered appearance so they could gauge Cameo's recall of the last time he'd been here. The next time he came into the valley, he'd be staying for an indeterminate length of time and it would be more difficult to maintain a disguise. Personally, Zach thought that Cameo was too smart to be fooled for long, if at all. He'd much rather let her in on the whole scheme, but Sam and Secretary Stanton were dead set against it. Didn't they realize that Cameo was no scatterbrained ingenue who believed everything she was told simply because it was easier than arguing about it? More importantly, he and Sam and even the President were playing dangerous games with her life.

Making matters worse was the information that the

Confederacy knew that the Shadow was now operating as a spy in the western territories. The only thing in his favor were his many identities, which had the enemy confused. For the time being he was safe, but eventually he'd be pegged and his effectiveness would be at an end. The way he was feeling right now, that would be a blessing. God knew he was tired of waking up every morning and having to remember which part he was playing that day.

Zach tossed back his drink and wondered why he was standing by himself in a corner when everything he craved was across the room by the fire. Family. Warmth. Belonging. Things he hadn't known in a long time. Surrendering to the attraction of more than domesticity, he sauntered to the fireplace. Just this once, he was going to be selfish and forget the rules he'd lived by for so long. If miracles really did happen, he might forget, for the space of an evening, exactly what role he was to play in Cameo's life.

Cameo watched Zach approach, fascinated by his prowling walk, grace and power in a slow stroking of the floorboards. She couldn't help wondering if his hands would be that way on her skin. Drawn by the memory of his nakedness, she let her gaze travel downward to that place below his belt—

"Cameo," Zach said softly, nodding toward her father. "The furniture is going to burn."

A flush moved up her body, the color clashing with the rich color of her gown. Fascinated at the way the fabric rose on her bodice moved as she took a deep breath, Zach watched the play of light on the satin petals. She looked like a rose in that gown, fresh and soft and just beginning to bloom in her womanhood.

Prying his attention from the exposed flesh above her neckline, he watched her eyes cloud as she leaned over to remove a smoldering cigar from Samuel's fingers and stub it out in a dish set on the table for that purpose.

"Papa?" Her frown deepened as she gently tapped Samuel's shoulder.

Samuel snapped awake and straightened in his seat. "Cameo, you finally joined us." Noticing his daughter's concern, he directed a silent plea to Zach and spoke heartily. "Zachary was telling me about the fiasco at Fort Fillmore."

Zach stared grimly at his host. In their conversation before Cameo had arrived, they had been arguing about Sam's determination to keep his impending death from his daughter. One more secret that would lead to a hundred more lies. Dammit, Cameo had a right to know Sam's heart was failing under the strain of too many years of hard living.

"Horace Greeley said that the commander panicked and ordered an evacuation. Is it true that most of the soldiers filled their canteens with whiskey instead of water?" Cameo looked at Zach with a silent plea in her expression.

He saw many things in her eyes just then: vulnerability, fear, comfort. *Comfort?* Did she know Sam was dying or was he imagining things? It wouldn't surprise him. He'd been imagining a lot of things since he'd met Cameo.

Clearing his throat, he followed her lead. Evidently, it was what Cameo wanted no matter what she did or didn't know.

"It's true. The Rebs caught up with them on the Fort Stanton road. Our men were drunk. They threw down their weapons and begged for water." He snorted. "The three hundred troops at Fillmore could have defended the fort from a force of three thousand. They surrendered unconditionally instead."

Cameo shook her head. "It shouldn't have happened."

"No," Zach agreed and braced an arm on the mantel.

"War shouldn't happen," she said vehemently.

"No."

"I heard that Governor Gilpin is sending a detachment of Colorado Volunteers to help," Cameo said as she stared down into her glass.

"Mmm. It's Acting Governor Weld now. Governor Gilpin was dismissed for issuing government drafts without proper authority. Seems the government took exception to him trying to pay the troops."

"Damn cheeky of him," Samuel said sarcastically, "to actually pay soldiers when they've already been given the honor of fighting and dying for their country. The next thing we know, someone will try to give them decent weapons and warm uniforms." Rising from the sofa, Samuel picked up his cigar and clamped it between his teeth. "Fools. Patriotism is a fine thing, but it doesn't fill the belly or warm the flesh."

Watching her father's agitated pacing, Cameo broke in as soon as he stopped to take a breath. "Zach, are the Colorado Volunteers on their way yet?"

"The last I heard, three companies had moved south to Fort Wise and the remaining seven companies were still at Camp Weld under Major Chivington. That was last autumn. They should have been here by now."

"Chivington. Papa, didn't we meet a man by that name on our last trip to Denver City?"

"Yes, Cameo. He was elder of the Methodist Church there. I understand he was offered the position of army chaplain, but he declined. Said he wanted to fight."

"A most forceful man, if I recall correctly." She received no argument from her companions. "What do you suppose possesses a man of the cloth to choose killing bodies instead of ministering to souls?"

Zach held his tongue. He knew Chivington. Unable to gainsay the man's dedication, he was nevertheless uneasy about him. Maybe it was the extreme of dedication Chivington displayed. Zach wouldn't relish meeting the major in battle. Chivington wasn't the type to show mercy or take prisoners.

Like Cameo, he thought as his gaze strayed back to the swell of her breasts rising above her bodice and framing the silk rose. If the flower didn't match her gown so precisely, he'd wonder if she'd put it there deliberately just to torment him.

"*Patrón,* dinner is ready," Sofia announced from the doorway, then silently retreated to the kitchen.

"Zach?" Cameo said softly.

Ripping his gaze away from her cleavage, he saw that Samuel had risen from the settee and had offered Cameo his arm.

She smiled and held out her other arm. "Zach?"

A delicate scent of roses and spice wafted around him as he tucked her hand into the crook of his elbow. Her touch was warm through the fabric of his sleeve. The rose mocked him as he looked down at Cameo and caught a glimpse of what the ornament concealed: skin the color of light honey, a crease between full breasts, a delicate vein disappearing into her gown. He wondered what she would taste like in that particular spot—

"I hope you're hungry, Zachary," Samuel said from Cameo's other side. "Sofia always prepares a feast when we have guests."

"Mmm," Zach said. "Starving."

* * *

MORE THAN JUST A NIGHT

A discussion of the war progressed throughout dinner. Cameo ate little, preferring to encourage the conversation just so she could hear Zach's voice and, when she could get away with it, openly watch him. Only when she spoke and he answered did she feel as if he was aware of her presence. Otherwise she might be a speck on the wall for all the notice he seemed to take of her.

Sighing, she poured coffee into his cup and searched her memory for bits and pieces of information about the outside world. "How sad for Colonel Canby to have to engage in battle against General Sibley, his own brother-in-law." She held up the creamer and set it back down again when Zach shook his head without directly meeting her gaze. "I hate to think what their wives are going through."

"The same thing all wives are going through, Cameo," Samuel said. "Women are the true victims of war. They have to survive and rebuild with what is left, if anything is left."

She searched Samuel's face while handing him a cup of coffee. He had been listening with few offerings of his own, increasing her worry over him. It was a rare day he remained passive when war and politics were being discussed. "Do you think the Confederates are in the territories to stay, Zach?" she asked.

"No. The Confederacy has neither the men nor the means to maintain an occupying force in the territories. Hell, our own army is spread as thin as cheesecloth out here."

Holding her cup with both hands, Cameo thoughtfully stroked its rim with her finger. "There is a lot of pro–South feeling here," she mused. "The group of sympathizers who met in Mesilla last spring to declare New Mexico and Arizona for the Confederacy, and the Bummers in

Denver City. They're reportedly disbanded, but still . . ." She turned her gaze on Zach. "You don't think the Rebs will gain a military foothold here, but you do believe the war will be fought in other ways, don't you?"

At his indulgent look, she carefully set her cup down and met his gaze head on. "Don't bother with 'You're a woman and can't be expected to understand these things.' I understand very well," she said mildly.

Angling himself more comfortably in his chair, Zach stretched out his legs and abruptly drew them back as his feet encountered Cameo's beneath the table. "I don't doubt it. In fact . . ." A grin slashed crookedly across his face. "I was disappointed when you didn't bring it up sooner."

Nonplussed, Cameo searched his expression for amused tolerance, boredom, irritation that she should dare to speak of "man things." All she saw was sincerity and attentiveness. The only man who had ever asked her opinion was Papa. The idea that Zach might actually be serious tied knots in her tongue. She took a deep breath and swallowed. Serious or not, this was too good an opportunity to miss, and he *had* asked.

"There are secret societies and pockets of Confederate supporters forming everywhere. Then there are the deserters, renegade bands, and men who don't want to fight but aren't averse to profiting from the war. We have spies. So do they. It won't be difficult for them to obtain information on gold shipments and such." She paused to sip her coffee.

"Actually, it seems more sensible in the end. Why expend valuable fighting men, livestock, and supplies on the battlefield when a network of civilians can reach the same objective with fewer restrictions to slow them down?"

Samuel pushed his cup and saucer across to Cameo to be

refilled. "Better to let the more unsavory elements of society take the risks, eh, Cameo?" He winked at his daughter as he accepted the steaming brew.

"Exactly, Papa. And if a portion of the booty is redirected into private coffers, who is to know or care? Mr. Davis and the Confederacy can disavow any nefarious activities and look the other way. It's still less costly than supporting an occupation force over so much land."

"Don't tell President Lincoln about my daughter, Zachary. He'll want her on his staff."

"That will be the day, Papa. Women can have brains and even use them if they are discreet about it. If it were common knowledge we were more than decorative vessels to bear children and simper on command, men would feel . . ." Her voice trailed off as a flush rose up her cheeks.

"Gelded?" Zach supplied in a silken voice, his brows arched over glittering eyes.

Her mouth opened, then shut again. *Drat.* Why did her mouth always run a mile ahead of her brain? She shrugged her shoulders. Ah, well, she was already in for a penny. "In truth, I had another word in mind, Zach, but yours will do," she said tartly, then changed the subject. "Can we expect more than the usual trouble from Indians?"

Zach relaxed his fingers. As long as she kept talking about fighting, Indians, and guns, he could force his attention away from the hot, driving ache in his groin, the surge of need every time he looked at her, beguiling thoughts of—

His mind skidded to a halt and reared in protest at the direction of his musings. Running his hand over his face, Zach searched his memory for another war story, a tall tale—anything to keep his mind off the urges of his body.

"Zach?"

Self-mockery twisting his lips, he answered her. "You might, although the Indians seem to like Sam." His gaze went to a painting on the wall of an Apache woman and child beside their dwelling. And he thought of another tribe—a people who didn't belong in either the white or the Indian world—living in dwellings borrowed from ancient spirits, borrowing the customs and mode of dress from the culture that had given them refuge, and hiding from the rest of the world, belonging nowhere—his mother's people, *his* people—roaming for six hundred years, a secret that would never be told.

He exchanged a quick, understanding look with Samuel as he picked up the conversation. "The areas farther west will see more activity, but there are always raids so it won't hurt to be prepared."

"And be pleasantly surprised if it doesn't come," Cameo added.

Zach chuckled, then sobered as his eyes traveled over her shoulders, her neck, her breasts rising above the scoop of her bodice. The honey tan of her skin tantalized his imagination. Did she swim naked and then dry herself in the sun? Her hair fell in silky waves to her waist, contained only by the sides braided and draped around her head to meet in the back. Enough hair to clothe a man's bare skin in sensual delight, it shimmered in the candlelight, moved vibrantly with every breath she took.

Cameo glanced up as she felt Zach's perusal. Not by word or deed had he displayed an awareness of her this evening. Until his total lack of reaction over her altered appearance, she hadn't thought that approval could mean so much or be so devastating in its absence. Now, even though he hadn't said a word, she felt his admiration with every visual touch, saw that and more in his eyes as they darkened to an intimate shade of night. A shade of night that suggested bright dreams rather than a lonely void.

Zach didn't miss her reactions—her caught breath released in a shuddering sigh, the soft glow suffusing her skin, the quickening pulse in her throat. Curving his fingers, he pressed them into his palms. He was as randy as an old tom and there wasn't a cathouse in sight.

Panic kicked him from the inside out. Survival instinct prodded him to stand abruptly and push his chair away from the table. Without meeting Samuel's eyes, he cleared his throat and spoke hoarsely to his host. "Sam, I've been sleeping in the saddle for over a month. If you don't mind . . . ?"

"No, of course we don't, Zachary. I didn't realize it was so late. We have all week to talk."

Cameo looked from her father to Zach. "You're staying a week?"

Giving her a brooding look, Zach nodded. He'd been a damn fool for making that particular promise, not to mention another more binding one he had made to Sam. Oddly enough, he worried more about Cameo's reaction than his own inconvenience when she found out. His commitment was supposed to be temporary, a few years at worst, giving him a good cover for his next assignment and costing him nothing.

Nothing? A woman like Cameo could wring every emotion out of a man and make him enjoy every minute of it.

Offering a polite if strained good-night, he stood and turned quickly, before Cameo and Samuel could catch sight of the growing hardness of a certain part of his body.

The irony of his predicament didn't escape him. He was to act as Cameo's guardian and business partner until she

either reached twenty-five or married. Well, pray she married soon and rid him of the burden. Until then, he would
honor his promises with an impatient eye on the next trail
he would follow.

Alone.

Ignoring the reasons why he qualified his assertion, he
entered his room and restlessly paced its length. *Guardian.*
The word taunted him with its absurdity. Who would protect Cameo from him? Or him from Cameo?

Sam didn't know what he was asking.

There was no way in hell Zach could tell him.

You horny fool, he berated himself as he pulled off his
clothes, arranging them by rote at the side of the bed for
easy donning should the need arise. *Cameo is nothing but a
vision conjured by the heat of desires too long denied. With
the expert ministrations of a certain madam in Taos, your
ardor will cool, the vision fade.*

With a heavy sigh he stretched out on the feather bed
and savored the feel of clean linen sheets and the mattress
pillowing his body like a cloud. He covered himself and the
heavy quilt likewise molded to his contours, sheathing him
in softness and warmth. Only one thing could feel better
than this.

He heard Cameo bid her father good night in the hall
and move past his door humming a lilting tune. Clasping
his hands behind his head, he grinned at her off-key rendition of an old sailor's ditty. The door to the room next to
his opened, then clicked shut. His amusement faded as the
rustle of cloth reached his ears . . . her dress? More rustling, a frustrated "drat." A stubborn petticoat tape? The
humming continued . . . a whisper of cloth. Bloomers?
Camisole? Water pouring into a basin. Washing her face?
He winced as she switched to another song, slow, dreamy,

and flat. Was she brushing that glorious hair? Next came the creak of bed ropes, a sigh, silence.

Damn. What had Sam used to build the walls in this house? he wondered. Paper? Forcing his muscles to relax, his jaw to unclench, Zach shifted, searching for a cool spot on the sheets. The bedding rubbed against him delicately, tormenting his already strained nether regions, which had risen to new heights and made a tent of the linens. Even that slight pressure intensified the ache. Muffling a groan, he kicked off the offending covers to let the air cool his skin.

He cursed himself for being susceptible to her. Why her? Why not a woman sophisticated and shallow enough to expect only mutual physical pleasure and a short visit whenever he passed through?

He cursed Sam for being so trusting.

He cursed Cameo for being, and took it back again.

Bolting out of bed, Zach strode to his saddlebags and the bottle of Taos Lightning stowed there. The first swallow set fire to his gullet; the second gagged him. The third made his eyes stream. He sank to the side of the bed and stared at the luxury of civilized trappings set about the room: a tin of biscuits lest he hunger in the night, braided rugs on the floor, lace doilies on polished wood furniture, damask curtains across the windows, Sam's painting of a trapper's rendezvous. Women's touches symbolizing permanence and the end to a man's freedom.

The end of loneliness.

Zach glared at the bottle in his hand. Loneliness, hell. He wasn't lonely. Striding to the window, he threw the bottle into the night with all his strength. Just as easily would he toss Cameo out of his mind. He didn't need her. Again, his gaze swept the room. He didn't need any of this.

The chains forged by lace doilies and feather beds, a woman's sunshine smile and sweet perfume were not for him. A woman like Cameo would imprison him within her silken walls and never more would he roam.

Drawing in gulps of air, he glowered at the moonlight glistening on the bottle that had landed at the base of a tree. With a succinct curse, he hitched one leg over the window sash, then the other, and dropped to the ground outside. The frosty night air nipped his skin exposed above and below his brief undergarment, yet he felt no relief from the heat of his thoughts. He dashed to the tree, retrieved the bottle, and turned back toward the house.

His gaze shot to the house, drawn by the gentle light glowing from a window. Cameo's window. His first thought was that she'd heard him and was again watching him. Warily, he stared at her window, but he saw only the dim light. He shook his head and climbed back into his own room to drop the empty bottle into a woven basket on the floor by the bureau. No sound came from the next room. Maybe she had fallen asleep with a candle burning.

It galled him that she could find rest so easily.

Pinching out the flame of his own candle, Zach angrily spread his bedroll on the floor and sprawled on its unyielding length. This was all he needed. Uncomfortable, cold, empty; it was all he needed to survive.

But what good is survival without a purpose?

At the end of the week, he would ride away without a backward glance. For the moment, he refused to think of when he'd have to return.

Weariness and Taos Lightning washed over him. Gratefully he gave himself into their keeping. His eyes closed, only to snap open at the sound of stirring in the next chamber. Groaning, he reached for a pillow off the bed and pulled it over his head. He was acting like a demented fool. Praying for numbing sleep, all he could think of was Cameo, resurrecting all the dreams he'd had once upon a time. Cameo, reminding him that women were more than a physical necessity. Cameo, her eyes staring so openly into his, sowing seeds of yearning in his fallow heart.

He had seen too much in those eyes.

He had seen home.

3

Gathering Rosebuds

Cameo and Zach were silent as they entered a passage carved by the restless flow of an ancient river. The solid rock walls of the twisted corridor rose fifty feet on either side, their time-smoothed surfaces marked with the sacred symbols of an elusive people.

Cameo had never seen the Indians who claimed Spirit Canyon. It was generally believed that the race was long departed from life and only their spirits remained here, nurtured and protected within the mountain folds. Oddly, she'd never known a fear of this place. The Mexicans on the ranch crossed themselves whenever she mentioned it and refused to come anywhere near the canyon. Because of superstition and the gruesome nature of the rock paintings, this secret nook in the world had become a very private retreat enjoyed solely by the Fieldings and, before his death, Jacob McAllister.

Today, with a peculiarly intense look passing between the men, her father had suggested she bring Zach here for a picnic. Without resentment, Cameo had readily agreed. She hated to think of just anyone coming here, but Zach was as special as the place.

In the six days since he had come to the valley, they had talked, laughed, and endured some awkward silences together. At those times, he had stared at her with brooding intensity, as if she were a mystery he needed to solve. Uncomfortable under his steady regard, Cameo had chosen those moments to voice an outrageous thought or flirt with every skill in her limited repertoire, thus startling him from his contemplation. Her outrageous behavior was simply a game, but the flirting was serious and she counted every response as a victory. After several such incidents, he'd lifted his shoulders in a what-the-hell shrug and relaxed, allowing her intriguing glimpses into the depths beneath his roughhewn visage. Zachary, she realized, had decided that they would be friends.

She had other ideas.

She hadn't failed to notice the way his gaze wandered over her, with admiration and—she hoped—with desire. She had always loved dresses and lace and ribbons. Now she reveled in the special excitement of wearing them to catch a man's eye.

She'd also made some surprising discoveries about Zachary. The man who gave the impression of merely being a passerby through other people's lives was a thinker, a reader, a dreamer. If confronted about it she had no doubt that he would deny an interest in pursuing anything but the horizon. Yet at times, when they had ridden through the high pastures or talked while performing some mundane chore, he would say something completely at odds with his usual demeanor. Something that came from the heart rather than the mind—poetic, full of rhythms and dreams and yearnings. And at those times she had been very still, hardly daring to breathe, afraid she might distract him while she listened to words set down by others hundreds of years ago. Words brought to life by the emotion in Zach's voice. And then he would shake his head as if he had given away a secret too precious to share.

That was what gave her hope that perhaps he, too, valued permanence and continuity.

As they rounded the final curve, the trail widened into a canyon boxed in by multi-layered stone ramparts, striated in a vividly hued chronicle of time itself. A waterfall streamed from a high granite peak, feeding three terraced pools surrounded by verdant earth. Budding aspens grew everywhere, their fragile heart-shaped leaves trembling with the kiss of unseasonably warm breezes. Wildflowers nestled in the grasses, prematurely awakened after a winter's sleep. Boulders lay where they had fallen when a tantrum of nature had tumbled them from loftier perches.

Cameo pointed to the mouth of a cave opened in a long narrow yawn with two smaller openings spaced some feet above. "The Old Man of the Mountains. I used to think he made thunder with his snores. Have you been here with your father, Zach?"

"Mmm. The first time when I was about nine."

"Did you go into the cavern?" Cameo led the way to a shaded spot by the middle pool.

"Hell, no. I was too scared."

"Scared of this place?" Her eyes widened.

Zach studied the cliff, the pigment of native dyes caked in its weathered lines, a ghostly face painted for war. "The colors were brighter then and he looked a lot bigger. Your sleepy old man seemed pretty fierce to me. I thought he'd eat me alive." Lowering himself to the ground, Zach stretched out on his side.

"Well, don't worry, Zach. The spirits won't hurt you as

long as you're with me." Smoothing her riding skirt, she sat next to him, an impish grin on her face.

"You'll protect me, huh?" His eyes swept her form outlined in the dark-green poplin skirt, fitted bolero jacket over a cream silk shirtwaist, and knee-length boots. "I don't think I'd fit behind your skirts."

There was a look about him that hinted at what he would like to do with her skirts, making her heart skip several beats. "Since you came back, you must have decided he wouldn't devour you."

Zach rolled onto his back, folding his hands beneath his head. "I was with Pa and Sam during the Pueblo revolt in '47 when I was fifteen. Pa was killed and I'd been shot. Sam brought me here to dig the bullet out. When I came to, I thought this was a piece of Eden in the middle of hell."

"Papa didn't tell me about that."

"He wouldn't. He saved my life. My wounds were infected. Four or five times a day, he stuck me in the hot springs in the cave. The warm water drew out the poisons, I guess."

Cameo scowled in mock affront. "All these years I thought it was my own private bathing chamber."

His eyes narrowed as he turned his head to look at her. "You go in there to bathe? Alone?"

"Do you think I should invite one or two officers from Fort Union to accompany me?" she asked sweetly. "Of course the gringos are as frightened by Spirit Canyon as the Mexicans and Indians. Chivalry might not prevail over superstition."

"You have a sassy mouth, Cameo," Zach growled.

Opening her saddlebags, she laid out their meal of cold ham, cheese, bread, and dried fruit. "Oh, for heaven's sake, Zach, this is silly. I've been coming here for years. Haven't you seen the paintings in the cave? If the ones out here don't scare people off, those certainly will."

"I saw them," he said grimly. "Aren't you afraid of anything?"

Cameo removed her Green River knife from a sheath secured to the back of her belt and began slicing the food. "I'm afraid of quite a few things and terrified of others. But not Spirit Canyon. As you said, a bit of Eden in the midst of hell."

"Eden had a snake."

"I've been bitten by a snake. I survived."

"Where?" He already knew the story, had heard all of it from Sam, along with Sam's fears because of her stubborn I'll-take-on-anything attitude. He was curious to know Cameo's version of the story and anxious to confirm his impression that she could keep a confidence even if she didn't understand why. He needed to know how far she could be trusted.

"My leg," she said wryly. "Here in the canyon."

"If you'd been alone, you might have died."

"I was alone." The memory of that day and night were fragmented, bearing a sense of unreality, questions without answers.

She had fainted after burying her knife in the rattler, awakening to dark figures moving against the night . . . three men in breechclouts and feathers . . . a strange language unlike any Indian dialect she had ever heard . . . gentle hands tending her, strong arms carrying her home on the back of a horse . . . Papa's voice uttering more strange words . . . phantoms riding into the darkness . . . her own bed and the *curandera* giving orders . . . safety.

"Alone?" Zach asked with a skeptical look.

"Of course," she said without hesitation, then whispered, "Who else would there be?"

He stared at her with a solemn expression.

She had never spoken of her rescuers after she'd asked her father about the three men. He had patted her head and told her she'd made her way home alone; her fever had given her hallucinations. She'd known better.

Within the privacy of her own thoughts, she'd named her rescuers the "Others." That they were real she never doubted, though she'd never actually seen them again. At odd times since then, she'd sensed a benevolent presence watching her from a distance. To this day she hadn't questioned her memory or accepted her father's blithe dismissal of the subject. She'd spent too much time alone, accepting without question the responsibility for her own survival, to fabricate such a tale. And since then, Cameo had never spoken of the Others and wouldn't now, even to Zach. If her gentle guardians—for that was how she thought of them—wanted anonymity, she owed them that and more.

"You shouldn't come here alone, Cameo," Zach said gruffly, both pleased he hadn't been wrong about her trustworthiness and disappointed that she hadn't confided in him. There was a newly discovered part of him that wanted—needed—to share secrets of the mind as well as those of the body with her. And there was the rub. He'd been going crazy trying to establish a platonic relationship with her, even going so far as to mention in casual ways that her eighteen years compared to his thirty-one invited friendship and filial interest, but nothing more. Cameo had, for the past week, taken his efforts just as casually.

Cameo laid her hand over his and bent to kiss his cheek.

His beard tickled her chin. She fought the desire to nibble her way to his mouth. "I like thinking you're worried about me, Zach, but there is nothing here other than an old legend or two. Out there"—she nodded toward the passageway—"people are doing their best to kill each other. You'll be in the line of fire."

Zach sat up abruptly and bit into the sandwich she handed him. "I'm not a soldier."

"You're not a trapper, either, or a buffalo hunter."

"No?"

Cameo settled back on her heels. "No. You're leaving even though I don't think you want to. That sounds like duty to me." Staring into a distant thought, she whispered, "But men insist on their comings and goings, and women are always patient in waiting for them to come back."

"But not you."

"Not me," she said quietly. "The first good-bye is free. After that, if my man leaves me, he won't be welcomed back."

Her man. The idea aggravated his digestion. "What about love?"

"What about it? If I love a man enough to wait for him, shouldn't he love me enough to stay with me? Does love mean that I should stay at home, work the land, raise the children, and defend both while he enjoys his freedom? Shouldn't love, its responsibilities and hardships and rewards, be shared equally? Anything else makes home nothing more than a boarding house, laundry, and brothel."

"Those are some dangerous sentiments you're spouting, Cameo. I've seen people tarred and feathered for less."

"What about your mother, Zach?" Cameo asked. "She used to follow the beaver with your father and mine. I remember hearing the old trappers say that she was a better mountain man than they were."

"She was," Zach agreed as he munched his sandwich. "That's probably why I'm not boiling tar and plucking feathers." Carefully controlling his expression, Zach thought there was a lot to be said for brainless women. Right now he wished Cameo was one of them. Her talk of love and forever brought his dreams too close for comfort. Her observations made his convictions squirm with unease. He believed in doing his duty. He also believed that lying to Cameo would have disastrous consequences. When the war was over and his duty done, he knew he'd come back to the valley as a man looking for a home, a future, a dream.

The thought brought him up short. He was thinking like a man in love. When had that happened? How? He'd only known Cameo for six days—

"If you're not a soldier or a trapper, what is it calling you to the trail, Zach?"

Zach sighed. He had to tell her something. "I'm a cartographer. I make maps for the government." At least his explanation was based on honesty. Scattered among his studies in literature and language, he had taken some classes in mapmaking and surveying.

Why, he wondered, did it bother him to tell her less than the truth? Lies, both spoken and silent, were his stock in trade.

"I see." Standing, Cameo picked up an enameled coffee pot. "Will you start a fire for the coffee while I fetch the water?" There had been too many things suggesting more ominous possibilities as to his occupation: his well-honed alertness, the stealth that controlled his every movement, the way his gaze constantly seemed to be piercing the surfaces of what he saw. His explanation did nothing to reassure her that death would not trample him in its path across the country. Another question died in her throat. Zach's answer had sounded final, like a door being slammed in her face.

Zach turned his back to her as he arranged kindling and a few larger logs, then struck a match. "Cameo, promise me you'll carry one of the Henrys and a revolver whenever you're away from the house."

Not—stay home and follow womanly pursuits or take a man along to protect you—but a simple acknowledgment of her survival skills and the ability to use them wisely. Stunned, Cameo froze in her position kneeling by the uppermost pool and stared at Zach as if he had grown an extra head. She glazed moisture over her lips with her tongue. "All right, Zach. I always do."

"You didn't today," he pointed out as he stretched out again. Leaning back on his elbows he watched her walk toward him with a surefooted grace he found infinitely more attractive than the seductive sway most women cultivated.

"I'm not alone today," she countered.

A teasing breeze carried a fine mist from the waterfall to bathe their faces gently; leaves stirred and rustled in the air. The coffee boiled, weaving tendrils of enticing aroma around them. Aside from the quiet movements to pour, sip, and swallow, the only sounds came from the natural tenants of the land.

Recently, silence had not been a habitable condition for Cameo. It was too much the prophecy of what was to come; loneliness, emptiness, a void where love and family used to be.

Zach was leaving soon.

"Papa is dying, Zach." Her voice was dull and quiet with a pain so intense, she had no energy left to express it.

Zach flinched. "How did you know?"

Glancing down, she traced a pattern in the grass. "I saw the doctor from Fort Union come from Papa's office. I asked him if anything was wrong and he told me. He . . . thought I had a right to know."

Zach nodded, his expression grim. "I was debating whether to tell you myself."

Her head jerked as if she'd been slapped. "I could have lived the rest of my life quite happily without knowing Papa told you and not me."

Zach felt lower than a snake's belly for not being more careful of his phrasing. He knew better. Cameo had the tough flexibility of a frontier woman and walked right into a subject without the subtleties of drawing room conversation. She was forward and sassy and too damned curious for her own good, but she had a tender, vulnerable heart. She was too young and vital to be holed up in the valley with nothing but memories and another grave to tend.

Wanting to comfort and knowing he couldn't, he picked up her hand and pressed it to his mouth. "Sam told me you're the one thing he hates leaving. I don't think he could handle a long good-bye."

Blinking rapidly, she raised her eyes to the sky. "That doesn't help. When I think of how many good-byes I've said over the years. It was my first word, you know."

"I know." And he did. He'd had said more than his share of farewells to a father he had idolized. "Sweetheart, this one will be for keeps. There will be no homecoming when the snows fall."

"Zach, out here a woman learns to think all good-byes are for keeps or she could go mad with the waiting. A promise to return is nothing but a wish, or a prayer. How many frontier women have you seen whose spirits starved to death on wishes and prayers? How many times has loneliness eaten away a mind?"

She stared at his thumb rotating over her palm, felt comfort in having her hand held in one larger and stronger than hers. "You never offer promises, do you, Zach?"

"No." He frowned at the mingling of their fingers and released his hold. "And you never ask for them."

"No," she agreed tightly, the yearning strong to give lie to her words. Hope for his return or no hope at all—either, she knew, would follow her days like a starless night. A darkness that gave no offer of dawn. She couldn't accept that possibility. All her life she had spent her nights thinking ahead only as far as the sunrise. It had always been better to believe only in now. Happiness and despair were easier to manage in small amounts, and one moment of happiness, she'd discovered, could make the darkness bearable.

But she couldn't say that to Zach, couldn't share her weaknesses so readily. Leaning over him, she traced the firm contours of his mouth with her fingertips. "Zach, kiss me."

Kiss her? It was a simple enough request—loaded with dynamite and lit with a short fuse. Before he could talk himself out of it, he clasped the back of her head to guide her down and pressed his mouth to her brow.

Reproach showed in her eyes as she settled her breasts against his chest and ruffled her hands through his hair. "A real kiss, Zach. A lover's kiss."

For one brief moment he gave in to his need to the temptation of her plea, but his better nature met what was left of his noble intentions. Grasping her arms, he lifted her away from his body and moved her aside, ignoring the chill that cut through him at the absence of her touch. In one motion he rolled to his side and gained his feet, a string of vivid curses filling the air in his wake. "What in unholy hell do you think you're doing?"

"Seducing you," she said gravely as she sat back on her heels. "Aren't I doing it right?"

"Oh, you're doing just fine." Agitated, he presented his back to her, then spun around to face her with glowering disapproval. "Didn't anyone ever tell you it isn't proper to seduce a man?"

"I'm less concerned with doing what is proper than I am with doing what is necessary."

"What?" His shout ricocheted off the canyon walls.

"You're leaving in a few days."

Wariness crept into his eyes. "Yes."

"Would you have done what you've been wanting to do since the first day? Would you have seduced me before you left?"

"Hell, no. Sam—"

"Papa has nothing to do with this. Unless you plan on telling him about it. In that case, he might think it was his concern."

Zach reached for the coffee pot, needing to occupy his hands before he either throttled her or made love to her until they were both senseless. Both prospects offered satisfaction. The handle seared his fingers. Cameo brushed him aside and used one of her gloves to pick up the pot.

Accepting the tin mug from her, he took a large swallow, scalding his tongue. He muttered under his breath and tossed the rest of his coffee on the ground. "Do you do this often?"

"No."

"Why me?"

"How should I know? It simply is. I would have preferred feeling this way about almost anyone else. I don't even know what you really look like. You could have warts on your chin, or no chin at all."

Zach ran his hand over his beard. "Woman, you sure have a way of shortening a man's pride by several inches."

"That's right, Zach . . . *woman,*" she said with satisfaction as she rose to her feet. "Papa told me emotion should never be saved for a rainy day. Each feeling has a time to be spent and a person it belongs to. Unused, it becomes cold and worthless."

That did it. Cameo had a knack for finding the last word and using it as a weapon, and he had an embarrassing lack of armor to ward off her brand of reasoning. With anger and desperation, Zach twisted his hand in her hair to pull her closer and drew her mouth under his. Her lips parted for him. Her arms wound around his neck as her body drifted into his, burning him at breast and hip and thigh, branding him. His arousal grew and pressed against her belly, harder and harder, insisting on more. Never had he wanted with such painful intensity. Never before had he lost control, burned so hotly from a simple kiss . . .

Not simple at all.

It was all wrong—the time, the place, the dream.

He strengthened his assault, demanded before she could offer, took before she could give, deliberately hurting her before she could find pleasure in the embrace. He had to stop this before he completely forgot the war, the disguise, the lies.

Through mists of beginning passion, Cameo felt his anger. His mouth plundered hers without commitment to pleasure or sharing. His fist held her hair in a brutal grip, his body tensed as if in battle against hers. Her response died. She opened her eyes and lowered her arms to pry his bruising fingers from her waist. When he tore his mouth away from hers, she spoke in a flat, even voice. "Keep your anger to yourself, Zach. I haven't asked for your heart, your soul, or your promises. All I wanted was to hold the moment close. Nothing more."

"Nothing more? You're just gathering rosebuds, is that it? And if I feel *obliged* to come back, so much the better. That's an old trick, Cameo. It takes more experience than you have to pull it off."

She shrank back as his rejection ran icy fingers over her, inside her, draining her of feeling and leaving a cold and bitter misery where vivid emotion had been a few moments ago. Some other part of herself responded in a distant voice that was steady, precise, stiff with pride. "That didn't occur to me in my inexperienced zeal. An *obligation* is the last thing I would wish to result. . . ." Disgusted by the catch in her voice, she turned away to pack the remains of their meal.

"Oh, hell." Zach stalked over to the pool and crouched down to sort through the pebbles scattered on the bank. Satisfied with a handful of flat stones, he straightened and skipped one over the water.

Cameo closed the saddlebags and mounted her horse. There seemed little to be gained from tossing comments back and forth like hot coals. They would both be burned, but in the end it would be her more tender skin that carried the scars.

Absently, she sifted her horse's mane through her fingers. "Papa said you wanted to explore a bit. I'll leave you to it." Her gaze barely flicked over him, but it was enough to show her the rueful lift of his mouth and the bleak gray of his eyes.

Twilight—the moment before darkness fell.

"Wait." Zach shot to his feet and reached her in a few long strides. His hand grasped the reins of her horse. With his other hand he freed the Colt Army Revolver from his belt and offered it to her while studying the shadows cast over her features. "Take this."

Wordlessly she took the gun and tugged on the reins.

Zach held fast. "You're crying," he said with a note of dread in his voice.

"I'm not in the habit of using tears to oil a man's conscience, Zach," she said with an air of dignity and genuine affront. With her thumb she pushed her hat to the back of her head and stared down at him, dry-eyed and expressionless.

"Guilt usually satisfies a woman when a man won't," he said harshly.

"Satisfaction doesn't apply."

Perplexed, he frowned up at her. "You want to explain that?" he asked, though he knew he'd regret it.

"Only love and promises will satisfy me, Zach . . . and I stopped asking for them when I was ten." She glanced down at her hands and sighed. How could she tell him that she wanted his love, not his guilt? She wanted dreams when all life offered was reality.

Though she choked on the effort, she summoned a friendly smile. "You were right. I was gathering rosebuds." She glanced around the canyon and lifted her shoulders. "Unfortunately, it's too early in the season for them to grow."

Wordlessly, Zach released her reins and stepped back,

his expression closed and guarded by the utter blankness in his eyes, as if he'd already dismissed her from his thoughts.

And that said it all.

"I'll see you at dinner." With his rejection and scorn painfully sticking like burrs in her feminine pride, she managed to sit tall in the saddle as she turned her horse and rode into the corridor leading out of Spirit Canyon.

If only she could escape herself as easily.

The sense of inadequacy that had plagued her all through childhood was again making itself known. For years she'd wondered why her father always seemed to be away more than he was at home, and she had naturally believed that it was some failing of hers urging him on his way. She'd learned independence and realized that her father's wanderlust was something inside him and had nothing to do with her. After years of anguished self-doubt, Cameo had found a familiar yet wary comfort within herself.

Until she had tried on her womanhood for Zach and seen in his manner how little she filled it out.

She shouldn't care so much for a rogue wanderer who craved adventure as if it were the ultimate lover. But she did care—so much so that all else paled in comparison. And it hurt so terribly, terribly much.

A sob disturbed the silence, then another, wrenched from Cameo against her will. Angry at herself, she clamped her lips together and swiped at the tears running down her face.

A shadow crossed the ground in her path. Instinct overcame emotion as she wrapped her fingers around the butt of her pistol and scanned the ridge above. Something moved, then disappeared. She blinked and looked again, seeing nothing but ragged peaks piercing the sky. Her gaze moved back to the trail. Nothing.

She knew it had been there; a horse and rider, a smooth flow of lines in the silhouette unbroken by the bulk of a white man's clothing and tack. Since she was still within the corridor of Spirit Canyon, it could not have been an Apache or a Pueblo. Had it been the shadow of one of the Others crossing her path once more, or simply her imagination summoning up the gentle spirits of her memory? It wouldn't be the first time today that she'd been carried away by fantasies.

Leaving the entrance behind she rode into more open ground and directed her mind to watchfulness of the terrain and its inhabitants. Whatever rosebuds awaited her gathering lay strewn in her future. The present demanded she have a care to avoid the hidden dangers of her surroundings.

And the more threatening ones of an undisciplined heart.

4

Rags of Time

*S*he's an assignment, Zach told himself as he watched
Cameo ride out of the Canyon. *She's an obligation. A pain
in the . . .*

Plagued by a nagging ache rather than actual pain, Zach
walked back to the pool, his body tense and too hard and
swollen for comfort. Ripping open the laces of his buck-
skin shirt, he jerked it over his head, then dropped his
pants and kicked them away. Spring had come early this
year, but he knew the water was barely warmer than the
ice that had recently been crusted over the surface. In his
present condition, he hoped it was cold enough to turn his
cock as blue as his balls and numb the ache he'd had since
meeting Cameo.

If he was lucky, it would numb his mind as well. Ever
since Cameo had withdrawn from his anger, he'd been
chewing on an expanding bite of humility, and it had been
all he could do not to negate the effects of his behavior by
doing something about it.

His work didn't allow him more than a nodding ac-
quaintance with his conscience. A man in his position who
let himself argue with his principles usually wound up dis-

tracted and dead, in that order. So why, as a man who had learned to meet only the needs of the moment, had he denied himself the body so temptingly offered? She'd known what she was doing. And why, in the face of his supposedly remorseless nature, did he so bitterly regret the manner in which he'd accomplished it?

Because, you jackass, Cameo is more than a "body" to you. And because you just found out how much an unfeeling bastard can feel.

Having answered himself to complete dissatisfaction, Zach found other questions presented for his flinching attention. How in the hell was he going to come back here and carry out his mission as planned? What shining inspiration would give him the means to prevent Cameo's involvement? Failing that, in what manner could he keep her safe?

Why was he standing naked as the day he was born on the bank of the pool? He took a step forward and stared at the water, his thoughts dragging at him like chains locked around his ankles.

How could he leave here with hostility so thick between them? His plans would come to naught if she hated him. If she hated him, he'd feel like only half a man, emotionally crippled by the loss of all that Cameo offered. Home. Family. Belonging . . .

Love.

He'd known her for six days—long enough for God to create a universe. Long enough to fall in love. Long enough to create a dream.

His skin prickled and he sensed a subtle change in his surroundings, a nuance rather than anything definite. He paused for a heartbeat, drew air slowly into his lungs, and imperceptibly shifted his weight. Like a flash of lightning, he lunged for his Colt, rolled, and righted himself into a low crouch, his gun aimed at the waterfall.

Streaming ribbons of water poured over a tall, menacing figure appearing out of the mist. The man was lean and bronzed by the sun, his garb a breechclout and moccasins, his weapons a pistol, a shotgun, and a bow and arrow, which presented an image at odds with itself. The descending sun cast a glow on the blond slash in his dark hair. His blue eyes twinkled. The clothing spoke of Indian culture, the shadow of whisker growth and keen silver-blue eyes testament to other origins. His speech and the mind behind it, Zach knew, were enhanced by a university education. It was these very qualities that would save a people from extinction and allow them to rejoin the race from which they had been exiled six centuries ago.

The curtain of water closed behind the figure as he made his way toward Zach over a narrow ledge, unconcerned that Zach's gun was aimed right between his eyes. His gaze lowered.

"Relax, cousin," he said with a serious look at Zach's still-swollen privates. "Trigger-happy men make mistakes."

"A little more trigger-happy and I'd be relaxed by now," Zach grumbled as he holstered the gun and dived into the pool. When he emerged and shook his head like a wet dog, droplets of frigid water hit Cloud Walker in the face.

Cloud Walker jumped back. "Damn! Stay in the water much longer and you won't have to worry. It'll freeze and fall off." He grinned. "You should have dumped Cameo in here."

"The thought crossed my mind," Zach said, unsurprised that Cloud Walker had witnessed the scene between himself and Cameo. There were no secrets between Zach and his only remaining blood relative. In some ways, his cousin knew far more about Cameo than either he or Cameo's father.

Zach emerged from the pool and lay spread-eagled on a warm rock. "That woman is a pain in the ass."

"Granted," Cloud Walker said. "God knows she's kept us busy over the years." Bending over, he picked up Zach's clothes and tossed them onto the rock.

"Sam should have named you and the others her guardians. You have a hell of a lot more experience in watching out for her." Rolling to his side, Zach sat up and pulled on his pants.

Cloud Walker sobered and shook his head. "Sam chose the right man, Zach. Our people are beginning to scatter. In another year or so, all that will be left of us here is the dust of our dead." He shook his head again, clearing it of matters already decided. "From the way things were heating up between you and Cameo, I'd say it's a good thing you're leaving soon."

"How soon?" Zach asked, instantly alert, all else forgotten.

"A week or so—when I bring word that the Colorado Volunteers are on the move again."

Zach sat facing Cloud Walker and worked his feet into his knee-length moccasins. "Again? Last I heard they *were* on the move."

"Hell, you know the army, Zach. It can't go a step forward unless it takes two steps back first," Cloud Walker answered. "The Pike's Peakers are better fighters than most and that's the problem. The frontier doesn't breed followers. There's so much dissension in the ranks that those buzzards will be seasoned veterans before they ever see battle."

Guessing that the officers of the newly formed regiment of volunteers from Colorado had their hands full maintaining order among men who ranked discipline with abstention—of any kind—Zach smiled faintly. "How many officers have been visiting the hospital wagons?"

"Plenty. Insubordination has been a big problem. Also disturbing the peace, petty larceny, and mutiny. Denver City will never be the same." Cloud Walker scratched the stubble on his chin. "Tappan ordered them to Fort Wise just in time to prevent mayhem." He sighed heavily. "Things are bad, Zach. If reinforcements don't come soon, we'll all be singing "Dixie.""

"Santa Fe?" Zach asked sharply.

"The Stars and Bars is flying over the capitol building. Albuquerque, too. The Rebs will be marching on Denver soon."

"Shit!" Restlessly, Zach began to pace, his thoughts grim. Since Cloud Walker had temporarily set aside his medical degree to act as a scout and courier for the Union Army, Zach knew he was getting the best and most recent information available. Suddenly the Confederate invasion had become a personal issue. For the first time in years, he felt a need to protect more than his own skin. "Then why in the hell am I supposed to sit tight for another week?" Another week of Cameo and that part of his anatomy that she so profoundly affected probably would fall off.

"Because Kit Carson said so. We're watching the Rebs' movements. When we know exactly what they're doing, you'll have to move faster than Sibley chasing down a bottle of whiskey. The Colorado hell-raisers are camped at Pueblo and Bent's Fort. They'll be leaving in a week, and if they don't make some fast time, Colonel Paul is going to be hard put to defend Fort Union. I reckon you'll be or-

dered to intercept them at Raton Pass with their orders."
Cloud Walker rose to his feet. "Time to be moving on.
Watch your back, cousin." He grinned, his gaze once again
traveling downward. "And keep your pants buttoned.
Cameo may be a pain in the ass, but she can cause an
intolerable amount of swelling up front."

Zach's head jerked up. "Personal experience, cousin?"
he asked in a quiet, deadly voice.

Cloud Walker's smile was lopsided, wistful. "Every man
who knows her has seen her in his dreams, but that doesn't
mean she's seen them in hers." Pausing, he looked down at
his feet. "It would be a good idea if you stayed out of her
dreams, Zach. A woman like her complicates a man's life."

"Shadows don't have lives." Zach said bitterly as he
tugged on his shirt and tied the laces. "We just drift
through everybody else's." A sense of foreboding descended on him like a cloud of smoke after a battle as he
stood and clamped a hand on Cloud Walker's shoulder.
"I'm glad you're here instead of in some surgeon's tent on
the other side of the Mississippi. You remind me that I'm
real."

Cloud Walker lowered his head to stare at the ground.
"It'll be over soon," he said wistfully.

"You really miss it—practicing medicine."

"Mmm, well, I'm sure I'll get tired of it fifty years down
the line." Raising his head, he smiled. "In the meantime,
I'm here, close enough to help our people make the transi-
tion, and to do what I can for Cameo and Sam. After all,
charity begins at home."

Home. A word that encompassed every dream Zach and
Cloud Walker and all their people shared. With a jerk,
Zach held out his hand to his cousin and sighed. "I guess
that says it all."

"I think it's beginning to say even more to you," Cloud Walker said as he grasped his hand. "Your orders are to stick with the army—advise them and scout out intelligence for the battle. You're going to be in the thick of it, Zach."

Angling his head back, Zach looked at Cloud Walker. "As who?"

Cloud Walker grimaced. "Your choice, cousin. As long as it isn't as Colonel McAllister. I'll be bringing your marching orders. Pick a name and I'll fill it in then."

"Zachary McAllister, scout."

"You weren't listening—"

"I heard you, Walker. I said scout, not colonel."

Cloud Walker shot him a puzzled glance. "I don't see—"

"Walker, no one knows that Zachary McAllister has anything to do with the army or the war," Zach explained. "If . . . nothing happens to me, then I'll be coming back to the valley as myself. Who is going to put a retired army scout who has taken on the trusteeship of someone else's property together with the Shadow?" There were other reasons, but Zach wasn't ready to explain them fully, even to himself.

Cloud Walker rubbed his chin. "Makes sense, I guess. The closer you stay to the truth, the fewer lies you'll be caught in. Do you think Cameo will appreciate it?"

"It'll just be easier," Zach mumbled.

"Okay, cousin. I'll take care of it." Looking down at their clasped hands, Cloud Walker pulled Zach into a brotherly embrace.

Relieved that Cloud Walker wasn't going to pursue the subject, Zach accepted his cousin's embrace, knowing there might never be another opportunity to experience the bond of friendship and brotherhood they had always shared. They held one another for seconds, holding, too, their memories of childhood and deep affection, knowing that each good-bye might be the final one.

"Vaya con Dios, compadre," Cloud Walker whispered. "And for the love of God, remember that you're supposed to be a shadow and keep your hide in one piece. Kit said to remind you that scouting and spying are all you're supposed to do. Dead heroes don't get the job done." With that, he climbed the rocks to the waterfall and was quickly hidden by the spray. As he and Zach and all their people had done for centuries, he didn't look back.

Zach also turned and began saddling his horse. He could think only of the time he had in the valley before all hell broke loose. An extra week. An hour ago, Zach would have sworn that he couldn't wait to be on the trail, had in fact been planning to leave that very night.

Cameo was getting under his skin and sprouting roots. He was becoming too attached to peace and the soothing routines of everyday life. Instead of being irritated that Kit Carson had commanded him, via Cloud Walker, to remain in the valley a while longer, Zach was relieved to have the matter taken out of his hands. He latched on to Kit's directives like a kid looking for a reasonable excuse to sneak away to the fishing hole instead of going to school. Worse yet, he was looking forward to playing hooky regardless of the consequences.

A week, give or take. His time left in paradise was nothing but a rag compared to the blanket he needed to keep life from freezing him out.

The ranch yard was empty as Zach rode in two hours later. He glanced at the sun and judged that the *vaqueros* were in their homes, enjoying their families and hot meals. But that didn't explain the eerie silence of the house, the lack of light, and old Jorge's absence. Jorge was always on hand, never seeming to take time to eat or sleep.

His head jerked toward the front door as it slammed. Sofia bustled across the wide porch carrying a pail of steaming water and a basket filled with a large bar of lye soap and several towels.

"Sofia," Zach called. "Where is everyone?"

"Jorge is visiting the shepherds and the *Patrón* is sleeping," she said as she maintained a steady pace toward the stables. "The *Patrona* does not wish him to know she is in great trouble." She lumbered onward, hot water sloshing over her skirts.

Zach didn't wait to ask more questions. Panic started in his chest and rushed through his body as he vaulted off his horse and took off at a dead run for the stable, leaving Sofia huffing behind him.

"Sofia, hurry!" Cameo's voice reached him, full of urgency and fear. Zach slid to a halt outside a stall door.

Dark stains covered Cameo's skirt, and her once white camisole was now grimy and brown with the same stains. Her shirtwaist lay in a heap in a corner of the stall, as if she'd discarded it in a hurry. She knelt on a bed of fresh hay, her face white and drawn, her hands shaking as she stroked the distended belly of her prize Andalusian mare.

He barreled into the stall, grasped her upper arms, laid her back on the straw, and began wiping her face and chest with the hem of her skirt. "Dammit! Hold still and tell me what happened."

Cameo struggled against him, her arms and legs flailing for leverage. "Not now, Zach. Let me go!"

Not now? Holding her wrists in one hand, he straddled

her legs and took a good hard look. He saw no cuts, no bruises, no fresh gushes of blood. "You're not bleeding," he said flatly.

Cameo looked up at him with wide, tragic eyes. "It's Diamond's water, Zach. It's been too long."

He sat back, still straddling her and ran his gaze over the mare, seeing what he'd missed in his fear for Cameo's safety. Diamond's belly convulsed, knotting and unknotting in violent spasms. Her coat was matted with patches of sweat. The mare looked spent and grunted weakly with each new contraction. If it wasn't already too late, it soon would be. He released Cameo and pulled away from her. "We'll have to work fast."

"No," Cameo said, sitting up. "*We* won't. I can take care of her."

Zach glared at her in disbelief. "Cameo, nature isn't going to take its course. She needs help, not someone to pet her."

Crawling over to the mare, Cameo didn't even spare him a glance. "Get out of the way, Zach. I don't need you."

"You can't—"

"Here is the water, *Patrona,*" Sofia gasped as she hurried into the stall and set down the basket and pail.

Zach's hand shot out, grabbing Cameo's wrist a mere inch above the water as he realized what she was going to do. "You'll burn yourself and that soap will eat off your skin."

"I don't care," she shouted, twisting her arm out of his hold. "The water has to be hot and the soap strong to kill the bacteria."

"This isn't a goddamn surgeon's tent. It's a horse, not a man," he shouted back.

"Go away, Zach. I don't need you here."

"The hell you don't. This is hard enough for a man. It takes strength."

Cameo lowered her head and wiped her brow with her forearm, leaving another streak of fluid. "I have as much strength as I need, Zach—always. Now, please, let me take care of my mare."

Before he knew what she was doing, she plunged her arms into the pail and began scrubbing her skin with the soap, her teeth clenched, her eyes wide and fixed. He could feel it himself—the hot water, the abrasive soap, her almost tangible determination to take care of her own.

Acting quickly, Cameo worked her arm into Diamond's birth canal and winced as another contraction seized the mare.

"Cameo, be careful, dammit. You'll break your arm."

"It's breech!" Cameo gasped, then a low moan escaped her. Her body jerked and she gripped Zach's leg with one hand while trying to wrap her fingers around the unborn foal's hind feet with the other.

"Are the hind feet presented or the rump?" he asked sharply.

"The feet. Give me a towel. They're too slippery."

Zach thrust a towel into her hand, then anchored her with his hands grasping her waist and his feet braced against the wall. At least the foal wouldn't have to be pushed back in an effort to locate the feet and push the rump down. From the looks of Diamond's belly, Zach guessed that the foal was large and it would take more muscle than Cameo possessed to pull it free.

Cameo said nothing, but used the cloth to maintain a better hold on the foal. A hoof appeared, then two, then nothing more.

She groaned in frustration and rolled to her stomach.

"Grab my legs, Zach." she ordered between breaths, as if she were in pain.

Registering nothing but the desperation in her voice, Zach groped under her skirt and cursed the smooth, bulky surface of her boots. He jerked them off without care, and winced at Cameo's involuntary cry of pain, again acknowledging only the urgency of pulling the foal before it smothered for lack of air. Cameo's Andalusian breeding stock was her pride, and her dream for the future of the ranch. She'd risk just about anything to preserve her breeding stock. Damn fool woman. She was lucky that her arm hadn't been trapped in the mare's birth canal and broken by the pressure.

Her ankles were fast in his grip and he felt her calf muscles straining. "Don't wait for another contraction, Cameo—pull now!"

Cameo was way ahead of him as she angled her body so that she could ease the foal down toward its mother's legs as it emerged, her hands wrapped around the hooves and she pulled with all her strength. "Damnation, Diamond, *help me.*"

As if she understood, the mare flexed her legs and reared up her head, giving a mighty push. The foal slipped free.

And lay still.

Cameo rose to her knees and leaned over the foal. "No, curse you. You will not die." Quickly she wiped away mucus from its mouth and nostrils. Nothing. Again she reached into the foal's mouth, deeper this time. The foal gagged. With a sob of relief, Cameo grabbed a clean towel and began to rub it briskly over the foal's matted black coat, then kneaded its chest, willing the blood to flow and warm the foal. Its nostrils quivered and a soft whuffle followed. Diamond snorted and turned her head to nuzzle her offspring.

While she was occupied with the foal, Zach dealt with the afterbirth and made sure Diamond hadn't suffered any damage during the birth.

Cameo exhaled and sat braced against the wall as she wiped her eyes with the back of her hand. Her right arm lay in her lap.

After barking at Sofia, who hovered in the yard, to bring him a bucket of cold spring water, Zach swallowed down the lump that had been damn near choking him since Sofia had said Cameo was in trouble. Every gruesome picture he'd conjured of her possible fate replayed in his mind one more time, making him shudder. Sweat beaded on his forehead, his upper lip, down his back.

"He's black," he said inanely, as rattled by his panic as by the reason for it. He glanced from the foal to Diamond's mottled silver coat.

"Andalusians are born black or dark gray," Cameo said on a sigh. "They usually turn to silver as they mature."

"Here is the water, *Señor* Zach." Sofia set two buckets inside the stall and disappeared down the aisle.

Zach hooked a bucket of water with his hand and scooted closer to Cameo. Without ceremony, he grasped her wrists and dunked her arms into the cool water.

She cried out and lifted her right arm by cradling it with her left. He saw it then—the swelling and the bruises that distorted her arm from wrist to elbow. He let out his breath slowly. "Stubborn, contrary woman," he muttered as he leaned forward to gently probe and examine. "I told you to be careful. I've seen arms crushed during this kind of delivery."

"Oh," she said, staring down at his hands.

His head jerked up. *"Oh?"* Suspicion narrowed his eyes. "You didn't know what the hell you were doing, did you?"

"I knew enough."

"Not enough to keep from getting your arm mangled," he shot back. Cursing under his breath, Zach reached for two towels, soaked them in the water, and wrapped them around her hands and forearms to cool her reddened skin. "Why I listened to you—" He broke off and shook his head. "I should have taken over whether you liked it or not. This was too much for you."

"Because I'm a woman?" Cameo's glare was as challenging as her voice.

Zach sat back on his heels and glared back. "Because a man is stronger," he shouted. "Where's Sam and Jorge? Why weren't they here to help you?"

Cameo held her injured arm close to her body. "Papa is napping and Jorge went to visit his son at the high pasture. They couldn't have helped anyway. Papa is weaker than I am and Jorge is full of rheumatism."

Zach removed the towels, wet them again and wound them back around her arms. "It isn't proper for a woman to do this." He gestured toward the mare and her newborn.

"Proper? What would happen next time when you're gone and Papa's gone and Jorge is the only one here because all the other men are out working? Am I to sit in a corner and weep and do nothing because there isn't a man here to help me?" Cameo looked away, the tears she refused to shed threatening to add one more humiliation to a day full of humiliations.

She wanted to hate Zach for causing it all—her foolishness, the rejection she obviously hadn't yet learned to handle, the helplessness that had suddenly caught her in its grip. But she couldn't hate him. He was too close and her memories too fresh and sharp. For just an instant this afternoon in Spirit Canyon, she'd known his passion, and it had been far stronger than the anger that followed.

Zach's eyes narrowed at her blank expression. Her voice had been flat, final, as if she'd accepted an inescapable fate of loneliness and self-sufficiency, as if it were final and forever.

I have as much strength as I need—always. It was a bold statement coming from any woman, but from Cameo it amounted to a declaration of independence. *I don't need you, Zach.* And then she'd gone ahead and done a job that most men would find difficult, without fussing over the mess or the pain she'd inflicted on herself in order to do it right.

She not only had a way of shortening a man's pride, but she could do a hell of a job of chopping it up and scattering it on the ground like so much chicken feed.

Cameo's face softened as she watched Diamond blow soft breaths on her foal's body and nuzzle it as if she were checking the number of legs, ears, and eyes to make sure everything was put together right.

With his forefinger crooked beneath her chin, Zach urged her to look at him. He saw it then, the sheen in her eyes, her smile of joy and relief.

"I did it," she whispered, a soft smile curving the corners of her mouth. "I really did it."

"Proving what?"

"That I *can* do anything I have to do," she answered honestly, not aware that she was exposing her fears to him in that simple statement.

Zach saw and heard her vulnerability in the determination shining out of her eyes, the forced steadiness of her voice. That first day when he'd faced her gun while she faced the snake, he'd admired her grit. Now he knew that her true courage lay in her resolve to *be* brave and endure whatever life threw at her.

"What else do you have to do, Cameo?" he asked gently. He knew her strengths. For some reason it seemed important that he know her weaknesses as well.

"I have to get through the nights," she said absently. "I used to keep a candle in the window so Papa could find his way home. One night I forgot and realized that I needed the light so that I would know where *I* was."

The revelation shocked Zach. Night after night, he'd seen the dim light reaching out into the darkness from her window, but had thought that she liked to read herself to sleep as he did. It hadn't occurred to him that—

"It's silly—a child's fear," Cameo said, the words coming fast and running together. "Actually, I'm getting over it. If there's moonlight and I can see even a little bit . . ." She swallowed and shook her head. "I don't know why I'm telling you this."

"Because being alone in your fear is too much like being in the dark." His scalp prickled at the sudden insight.

"Yes," she said, then tilted her head. "Who said that?"

"I did. We all have fears, Cameo."

"You, too?"

"Too numerous to mention." He closed his eyes as he experienced the despair of forever wandering, forever being a stranger even to himself. Warmth and softness touched his face as Cameo's hand cupped his jaw, smoothed over his eyelids, then was snatched away. He opened his eyes and saw the sadness in her expression, the regret as she lowered her hand to her lap and looked away.

In that moment, he wanted her as never before, right

then while they were both vulnerable and full of thoughts of new life and miracles. Rubbing his hand down his face, he focused on wringing out the towels again and gently cleaning her hands and arms.

His original purpose got lost as he eased a corner of the cloth between each of her fingers in turn and felt the way they curled around his, as if he were a fence and she were a wild rose conforming to his support and strength. Her soft sigh ruffled through his hair.

His frigid bath in the pool had been a wasted effort.

With another wet towel, he cleaned her face, her neck, the perspiration dampened skin bared by her camisole. Her breasts heaved; her body trembled. His fingers brushed her skin and lingered—at the hollow of her throat, the dip in her shoulder, the soft, sensitive skin beneath her ears and jaw.

Cameo's breath caught and shivered at the pleasure of his touch. She could feel the fine tremors in his hand, hear his own careful breathing. She wanted more—his hand trailing lower into her bodice to discover the swelling, the expectation and need that burst through her.

His face was set in hard lines, his eyes without expression, and she knew that his mind was equally set against giving in to the desire she'd sensed in him that afternoon. She hated it—that look and manner of his that seemed to rob him of humanity, as if he were only the shadow of a man. "Thank you, Zach," she said, willing him to look at her.

"For what?" he asked, glancing up at the utter weariness he heard in her voice.

"Groping under my skirts and giving me a bath?" she said, forcing mischief into her tone, wanting to see him as he'd been in the past week—real and warm and animated.

He threw the towel into the water and gave it a savage twist. "Stop it, Cameo. Just. Stop."

Her breath snagged again as he caressed her with the towel, the tips of his rough fingers, his eyes. Sensations, sharp and invasive, reached deep inside her as the cool dampness of the linen and the heat of his hands stroked and stroked, a prelude to the pleasure she'd yearned for in the canyon. *Stop?* It was his hand lingering just above her camisole, his touch doing more than wiping away grime. She felt more naked than if she were completely unclothed.

Stop.

Feeling shriveled inside her as the evening air flowed over her skin, chilling, numbing . . . Her hand grasped his wrist, forced it away. "Gathering rosebuds, Zach?" she asked, throwing his accusation back in his face.

It hit him like the cold, wet linen he dropped into her lap. *I don't need you.* He had a nasty feeling that she'd be saying that to him a lot in the future. Rising, he stared down at her, his jaw working, his body protesting yet another rejection of its own needs. "Why should I settle for roses when there are so many wildflowers by the side of the road?" He wiped his hands on the sides of his pants. "Better get Diamond on her feet," he said as he tossed her silk blouse into her lap. "And put on the rest of your petals, Rosebud, or some poor blind bastard is likely to mistake you for a wildflower." He walked away from her without looking back.

5
House of Air

The false spring had surrendered to the winter storms besieging the southern Colorado Territory. Though it was barely past noon, gray clouds cast a grim light over the valley and fell away to the horizon. All the ranch inhabitants had been going about their duties with urgency, their heads cocked to watch the slightest change in the sky. Jorge mumbled about great winds and predicted the amount of snow that would fall by the ache in his gnarled joints. Sofia had recruited anyone who lingered in the ranch yard to chop extra wood, and she'd added extra quilts to the beds in the house. Cameo was busy stocking the line shacks with extra provisions for the shepherds and men riding the boundaries.

Damn fool woman, Zach thought as he drove a buckboard loaded with firewood out of the forest and onto a badly rutted track that intersected with the main road to the ranch. Cameo refused to allow the trees surrounding the ranch to be cut and insisted that the forests be culled of diseased and dead ones instead. That her notions made sense failed to soothe his temper. She had too many notions. Why couldn't she flounce around in righteous indignation and cut him to ribbons with that sawtooth tongue of hers? God knew he deserved some kind of retribution from her. He'd been crude and cruel. But no, she was too damn contrary to make things easy for him.

He'd be better off fighting in the war, Zach decided as he clenched his teeth against the jarring ride. He preferred battlefields with cannon fire and clouds of gunsmoke hovering overhead. Even the back alleys and hideouts where any movement could mean danger and one wrong turn could lead to death were better than the battle of wiles he'd found himself in with Cameo for the last five days.

He'd expected silence, animosity, a case of the sulks. He'd prayed for it every time he had to face her. At least then he could have reverted to seeing her as a willful, temperamental *girl.* That was something else he'd expected when he rode into the valley almost two weeks ago—a girl who did not live up to the unusual and very feminine name she bore. Growing up the way she had, she should have preferred pants to skirts, flannel shirts to silk and lace blouses. She should have been offensive rather than feminine, refreshingly honest, artlessly innocent, and world-wise practical.

By all rights, she should have been the same obnoxious, swaggering child who had spit in the dirt like the men, trying so hard to fit in to the only society she knew.

Oh, hell. Now he was understanding why she had been such an obnoxious child. Too bad he couldn't figure out how to deal with her. He wanted her to be the enemy, convince him that she wasn't worth the tight control he'd been exerting over his body and his emotions.

Hell hath no fury like a woman scorned. It was one of those absolute rules that men were raised to believe, such as: There's nothing more dangerous than a woman with a loaded gun. Or: All cats look alike in the dark. Such truths were passed from generation to generation as being Wisdom of the Ages. At least that's what Zach had always thought. A man should be able to trust the Wisdom of the Ages. Only none of the old poets and philosophers had met Cameo.

She couldn't be trusted at all. He'd never seen a scorned woman act like Cameo, as if he hadn't rejected her twice in the space of one afternoon. Evidently she'd been taught an entirely different set of rules to live by. More likely, she'd made up her own. Her version of fury was to be friendly as they came—the perfect hostess, the perfect lady—serving him steady doses of honey sweetness from the tip of an imaginary pole that was at least ten feet long. What really rankled was that he'd been treated like one of the family that first week. Now she was treating him like a guest. It was enough to make a preacher swear.

Distracted by his thoughts, Zach almost ran the buckboard into a ditch. He sawed on the reins, wiped his forehead with his arm, and automatically glanced up at the sky.

She was smarter than the old sages who had written the Rules. Everything Cameo did seemed to magnify his loneliness, his lack of belonging. She'd put a vase of dried wildflowers in his room with a single silk rose in the center of the arrangement. The same rose that had teased him so unmercifully his first night in the valley. The wildflowers had shed all over the lace doily until nothing was left but a few withered leaves and brown stalks, but that blasted rose had still been there, a message he couldn't ignore. After he'd dumped the lot into the basket by his bed, he'd missed the sight of it, until she'd shown up at the dinner table with it sewn back into her dress. He'd tried to ignore it, but the fool thing had been nestled into the valley between her breasts, like a surveyor's flag marking unexplored territory.

The woman had no mercy in her soul.

He pulled the horses up short as he almost overshot the main trail, a two-rutted track that led into the ranch yard over a mile away. Logs rolled off the top of the pile in the wagon as he urged the team into a precariously sharp turn, then cursed and stopped the big workhorses again. In the distance the ranch looked deserted and dreary in the pewter light. A gust of bitter wind whined through the valley and caught him full force. Tendrils of smoke rose from the chimneys in the distance and faded into the sky as flakes of ash drifted on the air, nothing more than memories of warmth and security.

As he jumped down to retrieve the fallen firewood, he caught movement out of the corner of his eye. A quarter mile or so behind him on the main trail, he saw Cameo dismount and lead her horse forward a few steps, then stop to stare down at something. Her hand dropped the lead rope of her pack mule and the reins of her mount. Both beasts took the opportunity to bolt for home. Cameo didn't appear to notice or care. It wasn't right how she didn't move, but stood stiffly as the wind plucked her hat into the air and carried it away. Her favorite hat and she didn't move.

It wasn't right. . . .

Disregarding the heavy wagon and weary horses, he loped toward Cameo. A few feet away from her he stopped and cursed under his breath. Her face was chalky, her eyes wide and glazed, and her body swayed.

"It's a calf," she said matter-of-factly. "I found the mother a mile back." Her breath shuddered in and out.

"They didn't leave a note this time, but then the message seems clear enough without it."

Her body was stiff, as if she had to tighten all her muscles and joints or crumple to the ground. Zach took the remaining steps toward her and wrapped his arm around her waist to lead her away.

"That makes thirteen," she whispered, her gaze drawn back toward the dead calf. "And one of our bulls."

Zach nodded to himself at the confirmation of his information. Jorge had shown him the notes that had been attached to the carcasses with a knife. The rest of his knowledge he had gained by his own careful inquiries. Unfortunately he had a lot of facts but no answers to speak of.

Cameo allowed him to walk her back to the wagon, but she couldn't tear her gaze from the murdered calf. "They mutilated her. The cow, too. Did you see what they did to her, Zach? They want to do that to Papa, and now me. How could anyone hate like that?"

"I don't think it's personal, Cameo," he said softly, and placed his hand over hers. Her skin was clammy with shock, and beneath the rigid discipline she'd imposed on her body he felt the fine tremors of fear. Or was it his own apprehension for Cameo and Sam that he felt? The other cows' throats had been slit—a relatively quick and clean death—but this was different, sadistic.

"Not personal?" she said, her voice tinged with hysteria. "The other times were warnings, Zach. That"—she pointed at the calf—"that isn't a warning, but a promise. And it is hate. How could anyone want to do that to another human being unless hate is involved? They want to torture us, Zach. They want us helpless and suffering and—"

She felt Zach's hands encircle her waist and urge her

toward the wagon. "No," she said, resisting. "I have to leave extra provisions with the shepherds in the high pasture."

"You're coming home with me."

"I can't." She looked around wildly. "Where's my pack mule . . . and Boston?"

"They took off for home. You have nothing to deliver." Ignoring her struggles, Zach began to lift her onto the seat and heard her moan.

"Oh, no . . . don't." She closed her eyes as she swayed against him, her hand clamped over her mouth.

"You're going back with me whether you like it or not, Cameo."

Suddenly she bent over and heaved. Her skin broke out with beads of moisture. He firmly held her around her middle, flinching at the dry spasms that wracked her after her stomach had emptied. There was a defeated quality to the way she sagged in his arms afterward, and somehow he knew that it had been fear rather than the actual carnage that had made her sick.

Breathing deeply, she pried his fingers from her waist and moved away from him to walk circles around the wagon. "It's not right. We're being terrorized. And the worst of it is the waiting for something to happen, always watching, always having to make excuses to Papa for carrying extra weapons and sending men to watch over him, hoping they will be enough, always wondering where they will strike next and how, always being afraid." On her third circuit around the wagon, she whirled toward the place where the calf lay. "Look at that. They come boldly to wreak their havoc, practically to our doorstep, not two miles from the house. And they leave no signs, no tracks or clues, only those vicious notes, and their cheap knives, as if they had an arsenal full of . . . It's as if they were phantoms, or demons."

Hearing the shrill edge in her voice, Cameo breathed deeply and closed her eyes. She didn't want Zach to see her like this—babbling and frightened and on the verge of asking him for help. He had already stayed five days longer than the initial week, and more often, she caught him staring toward the entrance to the valley. She couldn't mistake the way he stared at the horizon so intensely, his head cocked as if he were listening to a ritual call only he could hear.

Zach caught her arm and pulled her close, smoothing her hair away from her face. "Don't be afraid, Cameo. It'll be all right, I promise."

"Of course it will, Zach," she agreed flatly. "And knights in shining armor will be here within the hour to—"

"You'll have to settle for me—"

"No!" she shouted and tore away from his hold. "No," she said more calmly. "I can handle this. I will handle this." She lifted her head and spread her hands in a gesture of finality as she continued to back farther away from him. *I must handle this,* she told herself firmly. Defiantly, she faced Zach. "I can take care of my own and fight my own battles, Zach. You have no obligations here and are quite free to gather wildflowers."

His mouth straightened into a flat, grim line at the way she'd rallied. He knew what it was like to face danger, knew, too, what it took to keep fear at a distance and go on as if it weren't hot on his trail. It was hell, staying ahead of it or trying to guess from which corner danger might confront him. He couldn't imagine how it was for a woman when they were taught from the beginning that they were weak and unequal to the strength and capabilities of men. Only through his mother and the women of his race did he know that women were neither weak nor simpleminded.

Even so, he didn't like the idea of Cameo's being forced to wage a man's battle. He hated the knowledge that soon he would be leaving her to do just that—even if just for a short time. Unsettled by the feeling that he was failing her, he shook his head and spoke harshly. "Get in the wagon, Cameo."

She glanced at him, mistaking his manner for anger at her caustic rejection of the comfort he had offered. Too tired to fight Zach and the panic that wouldn't stop clutching at her belly, she gave in without protest, willing to accept, for the moment, any comfort and protection she could get, even from a lone knight wearing buckskins.

Zach watched her climb up onto the plank seat, then took his place beside her. The wagon lurched forward as he slapped the reins over the horses' rumps, and they began a steady walk toward home. "Are you all right?" he asked gruffly, his gaze focused ahead.

"Yes."

He snapped the reins and urged the horses into a faster pace. He didn't like her control. It was too tight and brittle. With a devilish smile he began to whistle off-key and steer the wagon over every bump and rock on the rutted trail.

Cameo tensed against the jarring ride. With every flat note he whistled, her nerves coiled a little bit more. She shot a venomous glare at him. "Keep that up and I'll sew your lips shut," she said.

He glanced at her, saw her rigid posture, her fists clenched in her lap. Her eyes blazed with a mixture of determination and rage. He sighed dramatically. "You're feeling ornery," he said, careful to keep the satisfaction out of his voice. Anger was the only emotion he knew that could overcome fear and panic. He wanted her mad enough to spit nails, but he wouldn't tell her that. She was contrary enough to go back to being white-knuckled scared just to spite him.

"You're doing it on purpose," she said accusingly.

"Doing what?" He smiled to himself as he noted the flush in her cheeks, the challenging spark in her eyes, her little flounce as she turned away from him. From the way she was balanced at the very end of the plank seat, she looked as if she were ready to jump off at any moment.

"The bumps, that infernal whistling, your high-handed attitude."

"I'm always high-handed. And most things people do are on purpose."

"Why?"

"Because, Rosebud, now is the time for you to do what's necessary—What the hell?"

Suddenly Cameo leaned over him to snatch the reins from his hands and stop the team, pushing him back against the narrow plank that made up the back of the seat. Before he could recover his balance, she stretched farther across him to set the brake, then lost her balance and landed face down across his lap.

He hauled her up and over his knees and splayed his hand across the small of her back to hold her down.

"Let me up, Zach."

He exerted more pressure against her struggle to get up.

She turned her head to look up at him. "Let me go," she ordered as she twisted her body in an attempt to free herself.

"I'm thinking about it."

"What?" She bucked once, hard, but to no avail. His hand felt as heavy on her back as the foot of an elephant and his other hand had come to rest on her backside. Divining his intention, she ceased her struggles.

"Seems to me I've got you right where you deserve to be."

"Papa—" she licked her suddenly dry lips.

"If he knew that you had just done your damnedest to turn us over, he'd probably cut the switch . . . hell! Cameo, be still," he barked as she redoubled her efforts to escape his hold. She slipped farther down until her face was pressing against his groin, alerting his body to more than anger. With a last oath flung at the heavens, he flipped her back onto the seat. "Don't ever do that again, little girl," he said between clenched teeth.

Stung, Cameo straightened her jacket and smoothed her skirt, then averted her face. "I apologize, Zach, for taking the reins from you." *Little girl. Hah!* She'd felt that telltale swelling of his body, the way his hand had so briefly stroked her bottom before he'd jerked it away. It was a victory of sorts to know that she was not, after all, lacking in feminine appeal. Yet it was defeat, too, because he'd made it clear that to a man, one flower was much like another unless he took the time to know its essence. She peeked at him from beneath her lashes.

Zach clenched his hands, sensing there was an unspoken "but" dangling from her apology.

"But," she said as she picked up the reins and draped them over his knee. "I cannot regret stirring your complaisance." She smiled with a woman's knowledge, a woman's triumph.

Zach spoke as if she were slow-witted. "If I thought you knew what you were talking about, I'd wash your mouth out with soap. Now if you have something to say about damn near getting us killed, spit it out before Sam gets the idea that we're in trouble." Zach nodded toward the lone figure standing tensely in the ranch yard, watching their progress. Beside him, Cameo's mount, Boston, and the pack mule were tethered to the corral fence.

Her eyes widened and her gaze flew to Zach, then to her father in the distance. Standing up, she waved, letting him know all was well. "Papa is why I did it, Zach. I wasn't thinking when I let my horse and mule go."

Zach raised his brows.

Sighing, Cameo sat back down and stared at her hands. "It felt good not to think for a few minutes," she whispered.

"Your few minutes are up," he said curtly.

She scooted closer to Zach and spoke quickly. "Listen, Zach. These threats—they're because Papa has been investigating missing gold in our freight shipments to Denver City. I've been terrified for him, but I've not been able to do much. He thinks the extra guards and weapons are because I'm afraid of deserters from the Confederate Army. He humors me."

"He knows about the murdered cows, Cameo, and the bull."

Somehow the revelation didn't surprise Cameo, but it still made her sag back against the narrow plank behind the seat. "How? No, never mind. It had to be Jorge. No one else knew." She closed her eyes. "From now on, I vow I'll never trust anyone."

"Never is a big word, Cameo," he said, wishing it were enough to banish the cynicism and defeat in her voice, her posture. She was too vital, too full of dreams. He didn't want her to be stripped of her illusions.

Her eyes snapped open. "I'll do whatever I must to keep Papa alive as long as possible." She took a deep breath. "That's why I'm going to tell him about the calf."

Zach began to understand what she was up to. It made him sick to realize that his mind was already chewing on possibilities and consequences as they applied to the U.S. Government rather than to Cameo and Sam. No matter how he tried to think in more personal terms of people and places he cared about, his mind kept following the same track—cold and straight and infinite.

Puzzled by his frown, she quickly explained. "The threats haven't discouraged Papa from his course. If he knows that I'm being threatened, maybe he'll stop his investigation." She swallowed. "Maybe then he'll be safe."

His mouth slanted in a parody of a smile. Cameo's idea would suit the Secretary of War just fine. He'd ordered Sam to "cease and desist" his probing into the missing gold shipments, but Sam was as stubborn as his daughter and had refused in less than diplomatic language.

Zach stared at Sam, leaning against the corral fence now that he'd seen that his daughter was safe. Cameo was right. Sam probably would quit his investigation to keep her safe. But Sam had a streak of patriotism for his adopted country second to none and he had a strong sense of right. The conflict between protecting his daughter and doing his part for his country would add one more complication to his life that he didn't need—not when so little of his life was left to him. Sam felt useful.

For the first time in his career, Zach overcame his instinct to live and breathe his job. "It might worry him into an early death," he said harshly and saw Cameo shrink away at his words. "Think carefully, Cameo. Why do you want to tell him now after working so hard to keep it from him?"

The question gutted Cameo, as if with one swipe of a blade Zach had exposed her good intentions as something ugly and self-serving. It hurt all the more because she was forced to think about it, doubt herself and her purpose. She did want to share the fear and be free to huddle in her father's arms when it became too great to bear alone. Fear, she'd discovered in the last few months, was like falling into a black, bottomless chasm that tore at the body as well as the soul. It hadn't been the carnage she'd witnessed that had made her sick; it had been the panic. Was she so desperate to escape that place that she would take her father's hand and pull him in with her?

She gazed at Zach with wide, unblinking eyes. "Of course, you're right. Papa's heart might not withstand that kind of distress," she said smoothly, and then because the rage of absolute helplessness had begun to fill her, she lashed out at him, not caring that it was spiteful and cruel. "Of course, my silence very neatly saves you from concern that my selfishness might precipitate a sudden crisis. You wouldn't want to be detained—"

"That's right, Cameo, I wouldn't," he interrupted with an edge to his voice. "And I'd damn well better ride out soon before you convince me that you're as shrewish as you sound." Jerking the reins, he snapped them against the horses' rumps and drove on.

Vaqueros ran out to unload the wagon and distribute the extra stores of firewood among the many households that made up the ranch. Samuel pushed away from the fence and walked straight to his daughter, extending his hand to help her down from the high seat. A stranger walked out of the barn leading a milch cow and stood quietly a few feet away.

"What happened?" Samuel asked, his face pale, his eyes anxious.

"Nothing, Papa. I'm sorry I worried you. I met Zach on the trail and since—"

"Boston and the pack mule got away from her, Sam," Zach broke in smoothly after seeing her ineptitude at lying. A flush was climbing her face and she'd dropped her gaze to the toes of her boots. "We met on the trail and I talked her into riding back with me."

"Yes." Cameo shot Zach a stiff smile. "Zach's persuasions are irresistible." She nodded at the stranger, who was dressed in the garb of a prairie farmer. "We have company, Papa . . . ?" she prompted as she took a second, more thorough look at their visitor. He was tall and striking, his bearing relaxed. She frowned at the pistol strapped to his waist, the rifle—a Henry Repeater—in a scabbard attached to the well-worn saddle of his horse. A fine horse, she noted—a mustang, to be sure, but larger, more sleek than most, as if it had been specially bred for speed and endurance.

The man's build reflected hard physical labor, but his woolen pants, suspenders, and laced-up calico shirt were clean, almost new. He didn't have the shoe-leather skin and stooped shoulders of a farmer, either, or the weary, almost defeated look that came from battling the soil and the weather year after year. His eyes were sky-blue, penetrating, intelligent, appearing to miss nothing. A wide streak in his dark hair reflected the color of the weak afternoon light shining behind the light-gray clouds.

Never had she seen a prairie farmer such as this.

"Walker McCloud," Samuel said, interrupting her

thoughts. "He has recently come to the territory from the East, and stopped by to inquire about purchasing a milch cow."

"Oh. Hello, Mr. McCloud. You chose well. Philadelphia comes from good stock."

Samuel smiled at his daughter. "Philly for short. Except for her Andalusians, Cameo insists on naming our home stock for cities and countries. We have, over the years, literally had the entire world at our fingertips. I think she harbors a secret wish to see exotic places."

Zach watched Cameo rub the side of her nose, frown, and scrape the toe of her boot in the dirt. She seemed uncomfortable with Samuel's comment, as if her deepest secret had been discovered, and he wondered if she did, indeed, have a deeply buried wanderlust.

"I doubt that Philadelphia is exotic, Papa." She smiled at Walker McCloud. "You're from the East, Mr. McCloud? Is there any news of the war?"

He shifted and glanced at Zach, passing a subtle message as he did so. "Ah . . . your father and I were about to retire to his office for a glass of brandy."

"Yes," Samuel said cheerfully. "You'll need a bill of sale for the cow. Zach, will you join us?"

Cameo's body jerked as if she'd been struck with a whip. She was being dismissed, her request ignored as if she neither had the right nor the brains to understand what would be said. Her father had never excluded her from the business of the ranch before or dismissed her from a conversation. She didn't know what to do, what to say, where to look. Things were happening too fast, changing too dramatically.

"Is the news so terrible that I can't hear what is threatening my home?" someone croaked and Cameo realized that it was her own pitifully voiced question. Her gaze flew from her father to Walker McCloud, seeing that they wouldn't quite look at her. Blindly, she turned her head and stared at the wall of the barn. A gust of wind brought a biting chill that remained with her, intensifying until it soaked her with cold.

Warmth came from behind her, closer and closer, solid and sheltering, and then she felt strength from large hands taking her arms, holding her when she would have run. Calloused fingertips snagged on the fabric of her blanket-cloth coat as they reassured her with a slow circular stroke. *Zach.* He was standing at her back as if he knew the severity of the blow she'd been dealt and would protect her.

"She's right, Sam. She has a right to know *about the war,*" Zach said.

Cloud Walker cleared his throat. "From what I hear, it looks bad for us. The Colorado Volunteers are marching over forty miles a day, but it's not enough. They don't know that the Rebs have taken Santa Fe and Albuquerque. There's talk of sending a courier to intercept them at Raton Pass . . ."

"But there's a storm brewing," Cameo said. "A bad one from the looks of it. What if they're caught by the weather and can't advance?"

Cloud Walker fidgeted with his suspenders, his gaze seeming to be directed at Zach rather than at her as he replied. "With all due respect, ma'am, those Pike's Peakers are crazy sons of bitches. If they find out that the Texans are marching toward the Colorado border, they'll wade through snow ten feet deep to stop them."

"Is a courier on his way, then?" she asked.

"Yes, ma'am . . . at least that's what I hear. He should reach them within a few days if he rides hard."

Cameo felt Zach's hands tighten and tilted her head to look at him. His expression appeared calm and only mildly concerned, but she could have sworn that his body had changed somehow, become more tense, alert.

"Thank God!" Samuel quipped. "For a moment there, Cameo looked as if she would take her swiftest mount and warn our men herself."

"Me, Papa? How can you say so?" Cameo said as she stepped away from Zach's hold, still smarting from the many blows she'd received that day. "I am but a simple woman to be wrapped in cotton wool and protected from the harshness of life. Why, such horrors might drive me mad." With that, she walked over to the team of horses and began to unhitch them from the wagon. "You gentlemen go on to your business and brandy. I'll take care of the stock."

The three men frowned in unison.

"Cameo—" Samuel stepped toward her, his arm outstretched.

"It's all right, Papa. I'm being a shrew." She didn't look up from her task as she wished the men would leave so she could behave foolishly in private.

Thankfully, caring for the horses was one of those mindless tasks that allowed thoughts to stray and become lost in the rhythm of grooming and feeding. In this way she was able to forestall thoughts of the humiliations she'd suffered.

Unable to find another chore, she strolled out of the barn in time to see Walker McCloud riding away. She blinked and squinted after him. He was not leading the milch cow he had purchased. Zach and her father were strolling toward her, their conversation hushed, serious.

With a fixed smile, Cameo walked toward them, determined to salvage the remains of her pride. If Zach wished to find her wanting again, he would find no just cause in her own behavior. As for her earlier panic, it would change nothing, and would solve even less. Never again would she allow herself to lose control. . . .

Her step faltered as her gaze met Zach's across the yard, and her hand rose to her throat. The intensity of his expression unnerved her, stopped her in her tracks, held her there as surely as if she were encased in ice. He appeared to her now as a stranger full of suspicion and menace, the man who had confronted her with his gun, a man who would do whatever he had to do to survive without remorse. He stared at her as if she were his deadliest enemy.

Zach watched Cameo halt suddenly, her expression confused, her eyes suspiciously bright, as if she might have been crying. The events of the day gave her the right to cry, yet he begrudged her those tears. They reminded him of his own callousness in the past week and all the times in the future when he would no doubt be responsible for causing her misery. His mouth twisted in a sneer as he muttered a curse under his breath and abruptly veered away from her.

Cameo's head jerked at the blow from that single, blunt look from Zach. He'd shunned her with that silent curse and bitter expression, the way he'd hastened from her presence. She glanced at her father, then quickly lowered her gaze to the ground, feeling shattered and wondering if she would find all the pieces of herself lying at her feet. If Zach had made her feel spurned, then her father's obvious pity and avoidance of her gaze made her feel abandoned. Without a word, she walked past him and into the house.

Distressed by what he had witnessed, Samuel let her go. Troubled by the information Cloud Walker had elaborated upon in the privacy of the office, he had not immediately noticed the tension between Cameo and Zach. He'd known that a bond was growing between them and had foolishly thought it to be a good thing. It had eased his conscience over his decisions concerning Cameo's future, decisions she would never forgive him for. But he hadn't envisioned their attraction for one another and the complications that would arise as a result. It was one thing to entrust Zach with Cameo's inheritance and her life, but quite another to entrust him with her heart.

Samuel closed his eyes. Had all his careful planning, his confidence that he had insured Cameo's protection and guaranteed her future, come to naught? He raised his head to stare at the barn, a single certainty echoing louder and louder in his head.

Instead of securing his daughter's future and protecting her home with his schemes and deceptions, he had done nothing more than build her a house of air that could never support her needs.

6

Yesterday's Passion

Shrill winds wrapped around the house, whined through the chimneys, and shuddered over the buildings, a bitter announcement that winter would not die without giving the world something to remember it by. Slivers of luminous gray light shone between the shutters of Cameo's bedroom as she lay beneath the counterpane, unable to sleep for the sinister shadows that crept into her dreams, blotting out thoughts of her father and Zach and the valley. Apprehension that chilled her from the inside out. Every time she closed her eyes, specters of the carnage on the prairie tortured her. Whenever she allowed her mind to wander, it carried her down lonely, deserted paths where only she existed.

At least it wasn't completely dark.

Sounds from the chamber next to hers filled her with another, more substantial source of dread. Wide-eyed, she lay rigid in her bed, listening, her hands clenched tightly around the covers drawn up to her chin. Bed ropes creaked in the next room, then a floorboard groaned. The rustle of clothes . . . footsteps. A door opened, its hinges squeaking as it was pulled shut . . . a pause and the hinge again as the door was once again opened . . . footsteps back into the room . . . another pause . . . a final click of the door, closed all the way this time . . . more footsteps down the hall toward the front door.

She squeezed her eyes shut, willing herself not to listen, not to think about what those sounds portended, but in her mind, she followed the progress of a tall figure walking across the yard, entering the barn, speaking in a low, soothing voice to the animals.

The moment had come. He was leaving. She wished she could walk away from her feelings as easily as Zach was walking away from her.

She turned onto her side and buried her head in the pillow. Somehow she'd known it that he would leave tonight. She'd known, too, that the last memory he'd leave her with would be of his callous treatment of her in the canyon, his forced disregard of her since then, the way he'd swerved away from her earlier in the day as if she were the most distasteful of companions. Zach had become a different man from the one who had held a gun on her, then restored her dignity by riding away, pretending that he hadn't witnessed her fear. A man whose behavior had been inconsistent, to say the least—

Forced . . . pretending . . . inconsistent.

Cameo fought her way out from the smothering bedclothes and sat bolt upright. It had all been deliberate. Her sensitivity to rejection and criticism had betrayed her and given him the perfect weapon with which to fight her. It made an odd kind of sense and explained the incongruities in his manner. She remembered his physical reactions to her body lying over his in the wagon, and in Spirit Canyon . . .

She sighed and her shoulders slumped. What did it matter now? It was over. Another good-bye to survive. Except that there would be no good-bye. Zach would deny her even that.

If she allowed it.

Tossing the quilts back, she sprang from the bed and ran from her room without donning robe or slippers. That afternoon Zach had wanted her to be angry. Well, he had succeeded admirably. He would not, however, succeed in fading from her life like a shadow at dusk.

Dim light shone from the stable, and as she slipped inside the door, she heard the soft whickers of Horse, the mustang Zach had ridden into the valley two weeks ago. She had teased him about being too lazy to give his mount a proper name—

"Go back in the house, Cameo." Zach didn't look up from saddling Horse. His voice was cold as the winds ripping through the valley.

The cloth whipped about her legs as she stood in the open doorway watching Zach's movements. Cameo hadn't felt the cold as she ran to the stable, but now it seeped into her as her body heat melted the snow clinging to her nightgown.

He glanced up and raked her figure with eyes as dull as his voice. "Close the door—from the outside." Horse reared and sidestepped, nudging Zach into a corner of the stall. He shoved the animal away and stepped into the aisle that ran down the center of the building. "Go back to bed, little girl."

The soft folds of her gown settled around Cameo as she shut the door—from the inside—and leaned back against the rough wood, her mouth set with determination, her gaze pinning him, daring him to look away. "Say it,

Zach," she demanded. "Just say it so I'll know it's real, and final."

His silence was thick, choking out the sounds of creaking leather and the impatient dance of hooves. "I'm leaving," he said, as if it didn't matter at all.

Cameo struggled not to ask, struggled against the weakness making her ask, "And when the snows fall?"

"You don't ask for promises, remember?" Zach strolled back into the stall to tighten the cinch and adjust a stirrup.

She shrugged. "Either you'll be back or you won't. There's no harm in asking." Zach stood so still, it seemed as if he had become one with the night, a shadow in the darkness. Cameo sensed that it was natural to him, a defense, a leaving though he hadn't moved a muscle.

"Don't watch for me, Cameo."

She walked over to a pillar and lit the lantern hanging on a nail. Soft, yellow light glowed over the stall and aisle, giving her confidence, chasing away her shivers even though she still felt chilled. "And break a lifetime habit?" Her laugh was choked and angry as she stormed into the stall. "Watching the trails is what I do best," she said, her voice anguished.

All he gave her in return was a wretched silence that told her nothing, left her with nothing to believe.

"Damn you! Tell me. You owe me that much. Tell me you won't *ever* be back, that you don't *want* to come back." She breathed deeply and advanced toward him. "Make it easy for me, Zach."

"Shit!" He jerked on the cinch one more time, then swung about and smashed his fist into the wall.

Startled by his sudden violence, Cameo blanched, but recovered quickly. "I didn't think you were a coward, Zach."

Before she knew what had happened, he grasped her arms and slammed her back into the wall. Zach's body pressed into hers, big, warm, hard. His thumb and forefinger cupped her jaw and turned her face toward his until only a breath separated his mouth from hers. A dark and turbulent storm raged in his eyes. His voice was harsh and strained.

"Who's going to make it easy for me, Cameo? Who is going to convince me not to—" His mouth crushed down on hers, bruising and desperate with fury, yet not like the last time, not purposefully, not calculated to discourage. Her lips parted for him under the pressure, taking his rage and matching it with her own. This time she would not be fooled or goaded into indignant withdrawal. This time she would not merely try on her womanhood, but wear it until it fit as well as her skin.

He wanted her—she knew that now. He'd always wanted her. That first day, she had mused on the nature of his manhood. Now she knew. It pressed into her belly and brought moisture to her most secret places as Zach rotated his hips, closer, more tightly against her, then from side to side. Instinct dictated her response, her movements that matched his. She wrapped her arms around him, encouraged him with long, urgent strokes on his back. Her eyelids drifted shut, closing out the light. Zach became her beacon, chasing away her fear of the dark. His tongue plunged wildly into her mouth, sought every crevice, tasted and drank from her, until she could no longer inhale, but drew breath from Zach as he groaned into her mouth.

She didn't know what to do with her tongue. It seemed to be in his way, colliding with his, obstructing his progress. She thrust her hips into his and heard him groan again in a mixture of pleasure and pain.

He lifted his head, just a fraction, not really separating from her at all. "Follow me, Cameo," he whispered and took her mouth once more, without mercy for her lack of experience.

She obeyed his command, copying his movements, plunging her tongue into his mouth, equaling him in passion and demand. Unafraid, she accepted his hands as they molded her neck, her breasts, then her stomach and thighs with primitive desire, fierce need. Her own hands began a frantic journey over his body: to knead his chest, grip his buttocks, then sweep around to touch that male place of fascination and—

He lifted his head and shoved her away, holding her at arm's length. She cried out in denial of the sudden cold, the emptiness. She opened her eyes, needing the light.

Zach's breath rasped in his throat, and his heart pounded as if there suddenly wasn't enough room in his chest. He shook his head to rid his mind of the weight of his recklessness. As Cameo opened her eyes to stare into his, Zach fought the worst battle of his life. Cameo was his. They both knew it, though only she accepted it. He could not. Not until he was free to fulfill her needs and recognize his own. Not until he could allow Zachary Sloane McAllister to become more than a shadow that was just passing through.

"This isn't right," he said brusquely.

"Of course it is." Cameo stated without a shred of doubt. "We would have to be dead to believe otherwise."

He shook his head again, a quick, savage jerk. "No! It's yesterday's passion, Cameo, and it will disappear just as fast. I can't give you more than that."

"Can't or won't?"

"Either. Both. What the hell difference does it make?"

She smiled up at him. "It's a new day, Zach, barely an hour old. What is happening between us belongs to today."

"It'll pass."

"Will it?" She bit her lip and looked away from him, blinking away the pain his words inflicted. "Tell me how, Zach. How can such a wondrous feeling, such a miracle, pass and leave no memory or longing for more?"

"Miracles," he muttered as he raked his hand through his hair. "It's lust, not a goddamn miracle."

"I like it," she said artlessly, no longer fooled by his protestations.

"Well, I sure as hell don't," he shouted. "It's damned uncomfortable trying to tumble a rosebud. You have too many thorns for my taste, Cameo, and you require too much tending. Find yourself a man who will enjoy being permanently staked out in your garden."

"You're lying, Zach." Her gaze strolled down his body and lingered on the swelling beneath his pants. "It's quite obvious that you want me."

"I want a woman—any woman." He paced the length of the stall, then halted in front of her and ran his hand down her body. "Yours is a woman's body, little girl." His hand cupped her breast, kneaded it, flicked her nipple with his thumb. "Your breasts are ripe and tender." Trailing his fingers downward, he traced a circle around her navel, skimmed her belly, reached around to grip her bottom and pull her hips into the hardness of his. "Your hips were made for a man's attentions, a perfect cradle to rock him into sweet oblivion and bathe him in your scent."

A shudder wracked her at his bold explorations and even bolder words. She swayed toward him. "You're not shocking me, Zach." Wrapping her arms around his neck, she stood on tiptoe and parted her lips. "You find me as pleasing as I find you. I would like to know more of this kind of pleasure—with you."

He didn't move, didn't respond, but simply gazed down at her impassively. "Do you believe that would make me stay?" Before she could answer, he spoke again. "It would take more wiles and sophistication than you offer to hold me captive. You have a woman's body, Cameo, but that's nothing rare. And when I take a woman's body, I make sure that I have the price for its use in my pocket."

Cameo smiled at him, a purely feminine smile of knowledge and newly found power. That knowledge twisted her heart; that power gave her a heady sense of fulfillment. In that moment she felt wise and bold and confident. "You're trying so hard to hurt me, Zach, yet still you hold me tenderly and your hands tremble on my body."

He snatched his hands away from her hips, gripped her upper arms and shook her until her teeth rattled. "What do you expect from me?" he asked savagely. "You flaunt yourself like a whore and use your clumsy wiles to attempt seduction."

Cameo flinched. "Clumsy?" she said weakly, then clenched her fists and wrenched out of his grasp. *"Clumsy."* she repeated, her voice hard as bedrock. "Of course I'm clumsy. What did you expect of a virgin who doesn't even know what to do with her tongue?"

"Your tongue is the problem. You wield it like a goddamn tomahawk and bury it in a man's back when he least expects it."

"I speak my mind."

"Your mind could crowd a man out of bed, Cameo."

"Whereas a man's mind will leave a vast space unfilled,"

she retorted. "Papa told me that men would rather follow a man with a bulge in his pants than a woman with brains in her head."

"That's because a woman will talk him to death and nothing would get done. You've detained me long enough." He grabbed the reins and led Horse out of the stall. As he pushed open the heavy door, the wind yanked it out of his hand and flung it against the side of the building with a mighty bang.

"You didn't say good-bye, Zach," Cameo whispered to his back.

His step hesitated, then stopped abruptly, as if he had run into a solid barrier. She watched him as he stood there, unmoving and silent, staring out at the world that awaited him, a world of adventure and discovery that she could not hope to match. All she had to offer was a paltry valley and an overzealous heart.

Above the keening wind, Zach heard her soft whisper and the patient silence that followed. *The first good-bye is free.* She was offering him a way out, a blessing of sorts for the steps he was about to take away from her. *After that, my man won't be welcomed back.* Free. The word rang in his head and he knew it to be a lie. If he took her gift, the price would be all he could lay claim to—his dreams of once again recognizing the man he saw in the mirror as well as the faces he saw around him.

"Rosebud." The name was wrenched out of him, tormented and full of regret. He turned, knowing it was far more cruel to Cameo than any words he had used to diminish her feelings—and his own. Yet he knew, too, the transience of life, the sorrow of words left unsaid. Gently, he reached out to her, smoothed her hair, straightened her gown, fastened the buttons he had freed. "You're a woman for years, Cameo, not just a night from time to time. All I can offer is hours—not enough for either of us."

"I have learned to accept hours, Zach. They're better than nothing at all." She smiled at him without bitterness for the robberies commited on her heart. A smile that was painful to give, yet she would not have him remember her as sniveling and without spirit.

He swallowed hard as his thumbs skimmed her eyelids, her cheeks, her lips. The touch of her tongue on his palm was tentative, quick, as if she were sneaking a taste of a forbidden delicacy, or poison. And he was poison, the kind of man who would deal a slow, lingering death to her dreams. He saw the knowledge in her eyes, the acceptance of her own needs, and his inability to fulfill them. Yet he could not foreswear the recklessness any more than she, and renounce the need to taste the forbidden, to hold the dream. Just once. Just for a moment.

Cameo watched his face, the naked emotion he dared to show her as he lowered his mouth again, gently, his kiss telling her what she most wanted to know and what she least needed to know. He did want her. He cared. That awareness meant doom to all her logic and conviction. She would watch the trails for him, and spend too much of her life gathering rosebuds, only to have them turn to dust when the snows fell.

He pulled away from Cameo, deeply regretting that his return would be cloaked in lies. "Cameo, forget that I was ever here," he whispered, his voice rough. He cradled her chin in his hands. "For both our sakes, forget me and *forget my name,*" he added so softly it might have been a secret he was sharing with her. It was all he could do to warn her, to ask for forbearance in the times to come. Before he could succumb to the temptation to take her down into the sweet, fresh hay of an unoccupied stall, he turned his back to her and walked out of the barn.

"Till the snows fall, Zach."

He jerked as if she had struck him and raised his face to the sky, feeling the stinging pelts of wind-driven ice. "The snows are falling," he said. It was all wrong. The world was askew. This was the time when wanderers sought their rest in the comfort of homes and families, not the other way around.

Horse snorted and tossed his head, anxious to be away. For a reason Zach couldn't name, he gripped the reins and walked beside his mount, delaying the moment when he would take the final step out of paradise.

Cameo stood in the middle of the yard as he bent into the gale and walked farther and farther away from her. The wind cut through her nightgown, blew it against her body so that it outlined her form, making her feel more than physically naked. Snow stung her face and whipped around her. Tears froze on her cheeks as she watched him fade into a shadow in the storm, then even that was swallowed by swirling plumes of snow and Zach became another memory that ended in good-bye.

7

A Riddle of Destiny

Hell had frozen over. Gone were the roads of brimstone and walls of fire, replaced by endless vistas leached of color, barren peaks, naked trees. Zach stopped Horse and wrapped a woolen scarf more tightly around the lower part of his face as he squinted into the glare of unrelieved white. It took him a minute to identify the column of Colorado Volunteers plodding toward him, their snow- and ice-coated bodies blending with the land like feet moving restlessly beneath a blanket. With a sweeping glance, Zach saw that they had lost some of the animals that had been pulling the supply wagons to overwork and lack of food. Zach guessed that the men weren't much better off. Hell, he wasn't much better off. His belly was gnawing at his backbone, he'd forgotten what it was like to breathe without the cold searing his lungs, and he was so tired that he'd probably fall off Horse if his butt weren't frozen to the saddle.

After two and a half days of hard riding, he had found the Pike's Peakers at the apex of Raton Pass, a ragged, poorly provisioned, and exhausted group who had left behind all but the most necessary items of survival in order to march forty miles a day—mostly uphill. In the last thirteen days, Zach knew, they had covered over four hundred miles, fighting the mountain hurricane most of the way. They hadn't been riding boldly—only a few were mounted —but had trudged against driving winds, sometimes digging their way through man-high drifts on their way to meet the enemy. He'd been with them all the way from Raton until Colonel Slough had sent him out to scout ahead. No one had known for sure how far they were from the shelter of the next fort or, for that matter, how far Sibley's Texans had advanced toward them. With no sun to guide them, they hadn't even been sure if they were going in the right direction.

Zach watched with a mixture of fascination and awe as a man stumbled, his fall knocking over several others. One by one, they labored to their feet and carried on as if there had been no interruption in their forward movement. As far as he was concerned, heroes weren't necessarily made on the battlefield but by their sheer doggedness to plow through hell to get there.

The Pike's Peakers were a shock to the regimented system of Fort Union, and Zach decided to place his bedroll as far from the chaos as possible without giving up a view of the action. He lay there now, his hands behind his head and his ankles crossed as he watched them brawl, steal, and fire their guns at the slightest provocation. If there was a drop of liquor to be found, the men from Colorado drank it. If there wasn't a reason to fight, they made one up. Since the Rebels weren't within striking distance of the fort, officers, civilians, and their own compatriots became convenient targets. Zach didn't flinch when a sergeant shot a lieutenant in the face—thankfully not a mortal wound—

because the officer dared to arrest him for being drunk and disorderly. It would take nothing short of a cannon to intimidate any of these men.

Their contrariness reminded him of Cameo.

"Sir?"

Zach grunted in reply as he shifted his cigar from one side of his mouth to the other and glanced at the boy standing above him with a bedroll slung over his shoulder and a knapsack in his hand. For some reason, Private Calvin Boyd had attached himself to Zach's heels and had been his shadow since Raton Pass.

Calvin was a likable boy, but his habit of addressing him as "sir" annoyed him. "Ma and Pa taught me to show respect to my elders, sir," had been the boy's reply when Zach informed him that he was simply a scout for the army. He wasn't ready to think of himself as an "elder."

"Mind if I join you?" The boy shifted his feet, watching them as if he were afraid he might trip himself up.

"Got caught in the crossfire, huh?" Zach said, indicating the boy's black eye and swollen jaw.

"Yup . . . I mean yessir. Ever'whur I go, I'm gittin' in the way. One old fart told me to go to bed without supper. I went into the tradin' post for a drink and the barkeep said I couldn't have hard likker 'lessen I showed him that I got hair growin' 'round my balls."

Zach bit the inside of his cheek to keep from laughing at the boy. "Pick a place, soldier. The ground is free."

"Thankee, sir." He spread out his bedding and sprawled in an imitation of Zach's pose.

Calvin was a year younger than Cameo, and Zach was uncomfortably aware that he'd become involved with the stripling because he was—like Cameo—too young and naïve to be caught in the middle of a war he didn't even understand, and he was too reckless and stubborn to watch out for himself. Though Calvin's lips were chapped and split from the cold march from Denver, his skin was soft and smooth—not a whisker in sight on a childish face that was homely as a mud fence. His voice still cracked in the middle of words, and Zach doubted if he had hair under his arms, much less in his crotch.

"Sir?" Calvin held out a bottle of cheap whiskey. "Wanna drink?"

"Where'd you get that?"

"Stole it, sir, when the barkeep warn't lookin'." Seeing Zach's frown of censure, he hastily added, "I lef' money on the bar afore I lit outa there . . . and if'n I'm old 'nough to fight, I'm old 'nough to drink."

Zach remembered making a similar statement to his father when he was fifteen and fighting in the Pueblo uprising. "You have a reason for wanting to get drunk?" he asked, remembering, too, that his pa had passed a jug of Lightning over to him, saying that every man had need of a little Dutch courage now and then. Zach hadn't found much courage in that jug, but he'd sure felt good until he threw up his socks the next morning.

"Women, sir," Calvin gasped as he swallowed a healthy draught and tried not to gag.

"More than one?"

"Ain't one 'nough?" Calvin passed the bottle to Zach.

Not wanting to make the boy's pride suffer any more than it already had, Zach took a drink. "Anyone I know?"

"Mebbe. Name's Melanie—Mellie. Met her outside the tradin' post. Thought she was from one o' the families here, ya know? We took a walk 'round the fort."

"You'd better ask her daddy before you step out with her again," Zach advised.

"She ain't got no daddy. No ma either. She . . . ah
. . . works fer a livin'. Tol' me she'd let me kiss her fer a
penny. If'n I wanted to toss her in the hay, it 'ud cost me
four bits, two bits if'n I pleasured her real good. I never
had me no fancy lady before."

The last thing Zach would call one of the girls who
serviced the soldiers at the fort was a fancy lady, but he
didn't say so. "Did you?"

"Nope." Calvin sat up and stared at the ground between
his outspread knees. "Sure would like t' toss her in the hay,
though."

"No money, huh?"

"I got money," the boy said wistfully, his words beginning to slur. He didn't offer Zach another pull at the bottle, but kept drinking as if it were water.

"Private, you'd be better off spending your two bits on
that girl than draining that bottle."

"Cain't, sir."

"Why not?"

"Don't know how." Belching loudly, Calvin turned to
Zach. "I watched my brother once, but all he did was stick
it in and pull it out a couple times, and she looked kinda'
. . . well . . . bored. Ma always sang and Pa whistled
mornin's after we heerd the bed creakin' in their room."

Zach thought of Cameo's kisses, her touch, the innocent
yet lusty response she'd so freely given. After hearing her
sing, he couldn't say that he'd want to wake up to that in
the morning, but it would be better than the hollow look
she had in her eyes when he walked away from her.

"D'ya know how, sir? If'n I'm gonna do it, I wanna do
it right." Calvin turned to face Zach, his expression earnest, his eyes crossed. "I'd sure like to make a woman sing
b'fore"—his voice broke and his Adam's apple bobbed as

he swallowed—"b'fore them Johnny Rebs start shootin' at me."

A memory stopped Zach from offering the boy some platitude about doing what comes naturally. *Of course I'm clumsy. What did you expect of a virgin who doesn't even know what to do with her tongue?* And he remembered the brief flash of hurt in her eyes, the humiliation staining her cheeks even as she had torn into him. If she'd been any more clumsy, he might have embarrassed himself. *I simply wanted to hold the moment close, Zach.* It wasn't right for eighteen-year-olds like Cameo and this beaver-faced youth to be forced into living moment to moment because that might be all they ever had.

"Sir? Is a woman's pleasure 'portant?"

You are trying so hard to hurt me, Zach, yet still you hold me tenderly and your hands tremble on my body. "Depends on whether you want to just relieve yourself or whistle in the morning, Private."

"Cain't whistle, sir. It's my teeth, Pa says. All they're good fer is eatin' corn and chewin' down trees."

Zach bit back a laugh at the boy's description of his buck teeth. Calvin Boyd drew him, made him feel protective, made him want to help him gather rosebuds instead of weeds. Suddenly it seemed necessary not to turn this boy away with pallid answers. New to the art of advisor, Zach gave the matter some thought, then cleared his throat. "Every woman is different, Calvin—"

"Jes' a minute, sir." Fumbling in his knapsack, Calvin produced a tattered scrap of paper and a stub of pencil. "Got to write this down so's I kin 'member it all." With his tongue sticking out of the side of his mouth, he painstakingly wrote and recited at the same time. "Ever' woman's diff'rent . . . does that mean there's more'n one way to pleasure? I ain't got time to learn more'n a couple. Ain't there jes' one surefire way?"

Zach shook his head and sighed. What in the hell had he gotten himself into? He pushed his hat farther down over his eyes as visions drifted through his mind: of Cameo, and what he had wanted to share with her. He spoke without thought, describing what he'd wanted to do to her, with her, for her. The fantasy caught and held him as his thoughts became full of Cameo, how he wanted to taste and tease her, inhale the womanly fragrance of her skin, hear her sounds of pleasure, her imperious demands for the same release he'd craved since that first day. He gave no names except in the memories that carried him away, the dreams that gave rise to his hopes for the future—

Zach heard a thump followed by a snore. He tipped his hat up to glance at Calvin. The boy had passed out cold, the paper and pencil still clutched in his hand. Shaking his head, he sat up and groaned as he became aware of an aching pressure between his legs. His dreams for the future weren't the only thing on the rise.

Breathing deeply, he jackknifed up from his bedroll and went in search of the nearest well to dump a bucket of cold water over his head.

Calvin Boyd remained Zach's shadow as they left Fort Union to march on a collision course with the Confederate Army. It was a mistake, Zach told himself over and over again, to let anyone get so close to him. He'd always worked alone, a necessity that kept his mind on two things —doing his job and living to report his actions to the powers that be. Distractions like Calvin Boyd and Cameo could get him killed, yet he couldn't seem to shake either one of them, in his thoughts or otherwise. When Calvin wasn't near him, Zach worried about what kind of trouble he might be getting into just by being too young and tender a soul to hold his own against his ornery compatriots.

"Sir?"

Zach looked down to find Calvin walking beside Horse. "Thought you'd gotten yourself lost, Private."

"No, sir. I was bringin' up the rear for a while. I was late gettin' back." Calvin grinned, his mouth appearing to have four more teeth than he needed.

"You were with Mellie?" Zach asked. Calvin had spent most of his time with the camp follower while they were bivouacked at Fort Union.

"Yep. We borrowed a horse and went to the mission."

"You have any money left?"

"No, sir. I gave it all to Mellie."

Zach's eyebrows rose. "You have any energy left?"

Calvin grinned. "Yessir. We got hitched."

"You *what?*"

"Now don't you say it, sir." Grabbing the reins to Zach's mount, Calvin brought him up short and glared at Zach with as much ferocity as he could muster. "Don't you tell me what I already know—that Mellie's a whore and all."

Crossing his arms over the saddle horn, Zach leaned over. "You love her, son?"

Calvin nodded solemnly. "That's part of it, sir."

"Better tell me the rest, then." Visions of a smart opportunist playing on the innocence of one such as Calvin Boyd set Zach's teeth to grinding.

"She didn't sing, sir. She cried and cried and I thought I'd hurt her powerful bad, but that warn't it. She said she'd never had real pleasure 'afore and warn't likely ever to agin. I didn't like the sound of that. She's just a little thing, and she ain't no older'n me." Calvin kept talking, fast, with his eyes straight on Zach. "I wondered what it'd been like if'n Ma had never sung or Pa had never whistled in the mornin's. An' I thought to myself that it ain't right for a body to go through life like that with no . . ."

"Love?" Zach asked, thinking of Cameo and how alone she would be when Sam was gone, how alone she'd been most of her life.

"Yessir." Calvin's expression cleared. "You know what I mean cuz you're always alone. You ain't got nobody, but you're a man and kin take care of yerself. Fer a woman— well, it's diff'rent. I left Mellie with the padre, paid him to take care of her till I git back and kin take her to my ma."

Zach straightened in his saddle and nudged Horse onward. But for the grace of God and Sam's money, Cameo's fate might have been as grim as Mellie's. Calvin was right, and for some reason Zach couldn't name, he felt pride and respect for the boy. "Will the padre take care of her, Calvin?" he asked softly.

"Yessir. He's always tryin' to save the who—the girls like Mellie. If'n I don't come back from this here battle, he'll git her to my folks in Denver."

The idea of Calvin's not making it back brought a lump to Zach's throat, something that felt like fear. The boy had become important to him. "You'll make it back, Calvin. I promise."

Calvin bent his head as he trudged along beside Horse. "No, sir. Don't do that. I had this dream t'other night. It was real, sir. I even felt it when the bullet went in my chest an' I got real cold like."

A chill traveled up Zach's spine at the way the boy spoke, certain and accepting of whatever fate had in store for him. "Soldiers have dreams like that, Calvin, even when they're awake."

"Mebbe. I sure hope you're right, sir, but I got this *feelin'*, like there's a lump of that snow we come through in my chest. It just won't go away. I think the Almighty is mebbe tellin' me to make my peace and take care of my business afore my number comes up." He looked up at Zach and his chin was quivering. "That's why I took care of Mellie. If'n I can't live, then I wanted her to—" His voice wavered. "I'm so scared, sir."

"I know, son," Zach said. "Me, too." He'd be in the thick of things whether the Secretary of War liked it or not. The honorable Secretary seemed to think that Zach's skills and services couldn't be risked to bullets flying across the battlefield. Only his emotions were expendable. But his orders to stay out of the line of fire weren't worth shit in this situation. There hadn't been a battle this big in the western territories. The terrain was a real bitch and both sides were fighting for high stakes. He couldn't do his job and stay uninvolved at the same time.

He wondered what it would be like to fight on someone else's terms rather than his own. He'd always faced death eyeball to eyeball, always knowing the face of the man who might take his life. For the first time since the war started, Zach wouldn't know the names and faces of the men he shot at or who shot at him. He wouldn't be in control. He hadn't lied to Calvin. He was scared shitless.

For the first time in years survival mattered. *Living* mattered.

He wasn't prepared for death anymore. Not since he'd ridden into a fertile valley and gotten himself all tangled up with a wild rose who had taken root in his dreams and wrapped herself around his heart.

* * *

Make peace and take care of business.

Zach walked out of the commandant's tent with a feeling of urgency nipping at his heels. He didn't know much about peace; it seemed as if he'd been fighting in one war or another all of his thirty-one years. But business he had in plenty and it was time to do what he could.

He'd found the Rebel forces at Apache Canyon and Johnson's Ranch south of Glorieta Pass and had just pried himself loose from the meeting of officers over their battle plan. Once the intelligence he'd gathered had been passed on and he'd put in his two cents' worth as to the lay of the land and the best ways for the Union forces to gain an advantage and keep it, he was dismissed with the order to reconnoiter further.

So much for living legends, he thought wryly as he rode out of camp. His two cents might as well have been dropped into a pocket full of holes. The officers had listened politely, then turned their backs on the "civilian" who dared to meddle in their business. As far as they knew, he was just a scout and courier, not a seasoned veteran. Zach laughed as he turned Horse onto a familiar track. They'd never know that he was himself a colonel and technically outranked most of them.

Pigeon's Ranch was located on the Santa Fe Trail on the way to Glorieta—a pretty piece of country to ride through, but a real bitch of a battleground, and Zach had the feeling that's what it would be within the next few days, or close enough so that his old friend Alexander Valle, the owner, deserved some warning. It was a lucky bit of fate that the rancher was also one of the very few people Zach could trust.

Alexander, otherwise known as Pigeon for his peculiar

manner of dancing, squinted up at him as he trotted Horse into the yard. "That face. I know that face," he said, standing on tiptoe to get a better look through Zach's beard.

"Pigeon," Zach said as he remained in the saddle waiting for Pigeon to decide whether he was welcome or not.

Pigeon's face cleared and broke out in a wide smile. "But I know that voice even better. Zachary, *mon ami* . . ." Pigeon's smile faded. "The only time I see you is when you have news." He shook his head. "And it is always bad." Without waiting for a reply, he motioned Zach to follow him and turned toward the main house, talking all the while.

"I have seen the campfires in the distance—near Johnson's Ranch to the west. Then I see more light from Kozlowski's in the east."

Zach dismounted and slung his saddlebags over his shoulder. "The Rebs are at Johnson's."

"*Oui.* And the crazy men from Colorado are on the other side." Pigeon gave a fatalistic shrug. "Of course, I am in the middle where no self-respecting Frenchman should be. My land will be a battlefield and later a burial ground. I have said I want to fight, but the Major Chivington say I am too old. Bah!" He bent his arms outward and bobbed his head as he jigged in a circle. "I can still dance and move quickly to dodge the bullets. I am brave. What more does he want?"

"Pigeon, every time you do that I want to scatter feed on the ground," Zach said, changing the subject, relieved that Chivington hadn't taken Pigeon up on his offer.

"Bah!" Clasping his hands behind his back, Pigeon stalked into the house. "You have brought your bad news.

Now you will go to fight the Texans without sharing a drink with this *old* man?"

"You pour, I'll drink."

"It is serious, then—this visit." Keeping his gaze on Zach, Pigeon lifted a bottle and poured his own version of Taos Lightning into a glass without spilling a drop.

Light from the window struck crystal lights through his glass as Zach lifted it in a silent toast, drank, and shuddered as it seemed to explode in his stomach. "It's serious," he gasped. "What in the hell did you put in this shit —gunpowder?"

"This was not a good year for my brew, but still it warms your gullet, does it not?"

"What's left of it," Zach agreed, then set the glass down, his expression sober. "Pigeon, I need you to do me a favor."

"But of course. What else would you come here for? The army wants to shoot cannons on my land and use my home for a hospital, but they will not let me defend it with a gun in my hands—" He sighed dramatically. "What is one more *favor?*"

Zach turned toward the window, his hands in his back pockets, his head thrown back to catch the warmth of sunlight through glass. "If anything happens to me, I want you to tell Sam Fielding—personally and privately."

"But you will be gone—poof, like smoke—when the war comes to Glorieta, will you not? Always you are as they say . . . a shadow driven by the wind." Pigeon shrugged again as Zach glanced at him sharply. "My ears are always pressed to the ground, *mon ami.* I know these things, but I do not tell."

Not bothering either to ask how Pigeon knew or to deny it, Zach strode to the table and rifled through his saddlebags. "I have a letter for you to give Sam . . ." His hand paused over a worn leather-bound book before he pulled it out and handed it to Pigeon. "And this goes to Cameo." He stared at the book, feeling as if he had just given his life, the essence of himself into the old man's keeping. It was the only personal item he carried with him and even that gave no clues to his identity. The irony struck him that his most intimate possession wasn't even his own, but the words of others that he'd copied on sheets of paper and bound himself in soft deerskin.

Never a slave to propriety or subtlety, Pigeon blatantly displayed his curiosity by leafing through the book. At a page three quarters of the way through, he paused to read the entry and stare at the object pressed between the sheets of parchment. "So you have seen her," he said and glanced shrewdly up at Zach. "Cameo is a beautiful young woman. Each time I see her, she has grown a little more . . . here," he placed his hand over his heart, "and here." His hand moved up to his head. "I never see such spirit in a *jeune fille.* I have wondered what kind of man can live with her spirit and walk through her fire and know he is blessed."

"Mmm." Zach muttered, then shook his head as if to shake free of his thoughts.

"She is a rose among women," Pigeon said as he watched Zach's expression.

"Yes." Zach stared at the rose that he'd found frozen on a bush at the settlement outside the Empress Valley. A wild rose, forced to bloom early by the unseasonable warmth that had preceded the storm.

"Non. It is not right. You fight alone, not with the army. I have heard the stories about the rogue warrior, the

Shadow. And you must watch over Cameo when Sam is gone."

"Cloud Walker can take over," Zach said as he reached into his saddlebags once more to pull out a scrap of fabric edged with lace. His thumb brushed over the raised threads of the embroidery as he tucked it into his shirt. A lingering hint of fragrance clung to the doily, Cameo's fragrance, clean and fresh like everything in the valley.

"Zachary, why do you do this? You are needed—"

"Wherever, whenever, and however is necessary." Zach clapped his friend on the shoulder. "It's time to come out of the shadows and become a man."

"Bah! Only fools like me wish to prove their manhood on the battleground. And, what good is a man with a bullet in his heart—to anyone?"

"I don't plan on catching any bullets, Pigeon." Zach shook his friend's hand and left without another word. He'd had a bellyful of good-byes.

Zach spurred Horse to a brisk canter back to headquarters, his mind clearer than it had been in days, the scrap of soft fabric he'd tucked inside his shirt offering a soothing comfort against his skin. Since he'd confessed his fear to Calvin, the emotion had settled into a calm acceptance and the fight to come held a curious appeal. Oddly enough, Zach was looking forward to action—out in the open, knowing what to expect. Anger had been burning in his gut for months, a slow, steady blaze waiting to flare. Frustration had fanned the flames since he'd left Cameo. Pigeon's words had threatened to consume him in one devastating burst of fury.

He was sick of moving in the shadows, feeling little better than a criminal whose activities were sanctioned by a desperate government. Battle was more straightforward, no deceptions. The enemy would shoot at him; he'd shoot back. He would feel real, a part of the world rather than a member of a strange cast of men who each had his own role to play, of soldier and victim, hero and survivor.

It was a riddle of destiny that if he did not survive, he would be tossed into a mass grave . . . anonymous.

8

To Die and Live
. . . Anonymously

Hell exploded in a flood of sound and fury. Amid billows of smoke and bursts of fire, opposing armies roared and charged in chaos that only man could create. Fear and self-doubt were lost to primal instinct. Thought surrendered to the lust and passion for life as each man performed the violent act of survival.

From a rocky ledge overlooking the scene, Zach sat on Horse, watching the insanity of war with the commanders and Pigeon flanking him as if they were in a box seat at the theater. It had been going on for hours, a brutal show on a stage that gave no quarter to those who would violate it with blood and fratricide. He was standing by for the next situation, which would require his special skills and knowledge of the territory. At least Calvin was safely away, escorting prisoners back to Kozlowski's Ranch.

Two days before, they'd fought the Texans in Apache Canyon. In spite of the enemy artillery and the narrow canyon with its deep gulches and tricky arroyos, the Union forces had won. The Confederates had lost about two hundred men while Union forces had suffered only thirty casualties. Zach had kept one eye on Private Boyd and seen the boy charge recklessly closer to the Reb howitzers set up in the middle of the Santa Fe Trail that cut through the canyon floor.

That night Calvin had the same dream as before. Zach had returned from a meeting in the commander's tent to find Calvin staring wide-eyed at the sky, his hands clutched tightly around his blanket.

Zach hadn't pried, but had simply passed over a bottle of Pigeon's brew with an order to drink. Calvin gulped it down like so much water.

"I dreamed it agin, sir," he whispered. "I got shot right in the chest and died." He shivered violently. "It scared me so bad I—" Shaking his head, Calvin rummaged in his pack, then stumbled off toward the trees with a spare pair of pants rolled up in his hands.

As soon as Calvin disappeared, Zach had gone back to headquarters and jeopardized his position by pulling rank to get the boy an assignment away from the fighting—

"Bah!" Pigeon spat on the ground, interrupting Zach's train of thought. "That Chivington. Look at him. If a preacher can fight, why not an old Frenchman?" he grumbled. "In the canyon, he fight with a gun in both hands and under each arm. The Rebs were all firing at him and his fancy uniform. The bullets don't hit him. He put his head down and fight like a mad bull."

Zach shifted in the saddle restlessly, hating the inactivity, the feeling that he was missing his own cues. . . .

Suddenly he stood in the stirrups and squinted at a rocky bluff where a group of Coloradans were picking off the enemy. Private Calvin Boyd was square in the middle of the action. A knot of dread threatened to choke him as he watched one of Calvin's companions point out a mounted Confederate officer. Cursing Calvin for not staying away as ordered, Zach jumped off Horse and hit the ground running, his gaze fastened on Calvin, and leaped from rock to rock.

Calvin raised his rifle and took careful aim at the enemy officer. He fired, one explosion among many, yet it seemed to vibrate in Zach's ears. Zach ran faster, slipped, regained his balance, and pressed on. The officer fell. To the side, Zach saw a Texas sharpshooter cock his own rifle and fire at the group on the bluff . . . at Calvin.

No! Damn you to hell! No! He jumped across a space separating him from the bluff, fell short, his hands catching onto an outcropping. A bullet whizzed by his ear, struck the rock, and ricocheted with a whine. Something hit the side of his thigh just above his knee. He swung his body and pulled himself onto the bluff.

Another bullet flew past and rebounded off Calvin's gun before it struck flesh. Calvin reeled, but didn't fall. He glanced down at the small hole in his shirt to the side of the buttons, then up at Zach. "Ya see, sir. I told ya this'd happen."

Zach reached for him, cradled his body as he lowered him to the ground and ripped his shirt open. No blood— just an ominous gurgle that passed for breath. Zach knew what it meant. The bullet had pierced Calvin's lung and blood was being sucked inward.

Calvin's mouth moved, but no words came. He gripped Zach's shirt, pulled him down. His whisper was liquid and red bubbles foamed from his mouth. "Mellie . . . take care . . . of . . . Mel—" His head fell back and he stared at the sun, unseeing, drowned in his own blood.

His growl obscured the sounds of fighting as Zach rose and looked wildly in the direction of the man who had shot Calvin. The Texan was crawling toward him on his belly. Zach crouched and waited calmly, oblivious of the carnage around them. Only they existed. A drum throbbed in Zach's ears, his own heart, beating . . . beating . . . beating. He remained still, seeming to blend with the rocks and bushes, a mere shadow, waiting. . . .

Then he struck, his hands reaching out for the Texan, taking hold of his shirt, pulling him upright, his expression a cold mask of doom. His words were a grating whisper in the air. "Goddamn you to bloody hell."

Zach saw the man through a haze and didn't realize that moisture clouded his eyes. All he knew was that this man was warm and alive while Calvin Boyd lay on the ground, staring sightlessly, his chest cold, as if a lump of mountain snow were lodged there. He wrapped his arm around the Texan's neck, squeezed, twisted, then released him to fall from the bluff.

He turned, as if he expected the damage to be undone by his act of retribution. Calvin lay unmoving, fear forever engraved on his face. At his feet Zach saw the rifle that the Texan had dropped. He bent to pick it up, every move deliberate, slow, painful. The red of his own blood flowing from the wound in his leg caught his eye. He frowned. Funny, he didn't feel anything. Later, he knew, it would hurt like the devil. He straightened and stared at the rifle in his hands as he smoothed his hand over the butt, then took hold of the barrel and, with a furious roar, smashed it against a boulder.

His hand jerked. A shot sounded, unnaturally close. He felt a sting, a liquid warmth run down his face, a floating sensation in his head. Blinking, he saw smoke curl from the muzzle of the rifle. He smiled at the irony of it. Damn if he hadn't shot himself.

Darkness seemed to descend suddenly. He fell forward

and heard the crack of his head on stone. Grainy roughness pressed into his cheek. Closing his eyes, Zach smiled
again as he saw a vision of Cameo standing in the middle
of the ranch yard, her white nightgown pressed against her
body by the wind, her arm raised—No, that wasn't right.
She hadn't waved to him. There had been no good-byes,
spoken or otherwise. He'd been careful to avoid that. *The
first good-bye is free, Zach.*

He opened his eyes wide, trying to dispel the false image,
but they fell shut again. She was still there, her hair flowing behind her, her hand raised, waving. *Say it, Zach, so
that I'll know it's real.* It was another riddle. She hadn't
waved, but had held her arms across her middle tightly,
refusing as he had, to say good-bye. Her image grew small
and misty and faded into the darkness that bled into his
mind.

Darkness. Sound grew distant and he felt as if his body
had left him. He sighed, his last thought of Cameo.

She wouldn't have to fear the dark again. He would be
there, waiting for her . . . always waiting.

"Here's another one, Cap'n."

The dimly heard voice called him back, but he couldn't
seem to move. It was the cold, numbing, paralyzing cold.
His face, his limbs, even his eyelids—frozen shut. But they
had found him and would wrap him in a blanket to warm
him.

"Damn! It's that scout. Too bad. He was a sharp one,"
another voice said. *One of the officers,* Zach thought, but
couldn't focus beyond that.

"Whur do we put 'im, sir?"

A pause followed by a heavy sigh. "With all the others."
Zach struggled harder to open his eyes, but all he saw

was darkness. The voices and shuffling around him faded
in and out. He was floating above the ground. Pain lanced
through his leg and his head as he felt a lurch . . . falling
. . . then jerked back up again. He realized that he was
being carried by the legs and shoulders. His middle sagged
and a sharp rock scraped his butt. Didn't they have litters
to carry the wounded?

Why couldn't he speak? Or move? Why was it so cold?
He heard another set of footsteps approaching and heard
another voice.

"Our scout?"

Yes!

"Yessir. He got it in the leg and the head. Hit his head
on the way down, too."

It only grazed my head. Are you blind?

"Damn fool—risking his neck like that. We'll not find
another to replace the likes of him."

Replace?

"He was the best we had."

Was?

"Uh, sir? Should we bury him separate?"

Bury? The cold became sharper, more invasive. He tried
to swallow, to speak, to shake his head. He couldn't be
dead. He hurt too much. *Dammit, I'm breathing. I know I
am.*

"No. Everyone gets buried in the mass grave, Private—
no exceptions."

Mass grave. The words stopped his thoughts and held
him in horror. *Replace. Was. Bury. Mass grave. Oh, God.*
His body jerked. Fresh waves of pain rushed over him,
through him, surrounding him, drowning out everything
else.

"He moved, sir. He's alive!"

Yes!

Zach heard footsteps, felt a suggestion of warmth on his face, a hand on his chest.

"Sorry, son. No heartbeat."

"But—"

"What'd ya expect?" the third voice said. "Ya drag his butt over the rocks, the body jerks. Now pick up yur end, Private, an' hold it high. He won't move no more."

No heartbeat. It must be true. I'm dead. He would have smiled at the irony of it. Dead, just when he'd discovered there was more to life than survival. Dead and buried in a mass grave—anonymous. Not even a false name on a wooden cross. A man who never was. Zach felt himself lifted again, and then a sensation of falling, drifting, as if he had become a part of the wind. He sighed in relief. He was free.

Everyone knew that the wind had no shadow.

A man crouched beneath the trees on the fringes of the field, watching the burial detail. The moon slipped out from behind a cloud and struck the golden vein running through his hair.

Cloud Walker had returned from delivering a dispatch and had watched in agony as a man leaped over rocks and boulders to get to a young boy stricken by an enemy bullet. He had felt the rage, and then the pain, as if they were his own, as Zach had fought and fallen. And then, as if nothing important had happened, the colonel had sent him out with another dispatch for Major Chivington, who was attacking the Confederate supply train. He'd followed orders, then sneaked back at nightfall. All he could do was wait for the opportunity to steal the body and make sure that his cousin's spirit found a place with those of his own people.

When the last burial detail had left for a cup of coffee before shoveling dirt back into the grave, Cloud Walker broke from the trees and ran toward the pit. A sentry appeared, rolling a smoke as he strolled by. Cloud Walker hit the ground and rolled into the large grave. By the light of a capricious moon, he crawled among the fallen, gently moving limbs as he searched the faces and bodies, tears slipping unheeded down his cheeks.

Soft light streamed through the trees of a thicket and danced on the ground as a chill dawn breeze rustled the branches overhead. Judging himself far away from the paths of both armies, Cloud Walker dismounted his horse and lowered Zach to the ground, gently, as if his cousin were only sleeping and should not be disturbed. Methodically he unsaddled Horse, having retrieved him from the hilltop, and brushed him down. He built a fire, made a pot of coffee, sat before Zach's body, and stared.

Sometime during the three hours since he'd found Zach and pulled him from the grave, he had made the decision to take the body to the Empress Valley for burial. But that would take time, and he would have to prepare Zach and wrap him well. At least winter was still breathing in the air. The cold would make the task possible. Cloud Walker did not bother to wonder about his actions. All he had done had come from his heart, though he was one of a race that prided itself on being brutally practical in all things.

He blinked and focused on his cousin's face. Zach didn't look dead. But then, Cloud Walker wasn't ready to accept or believe that this man who had been his friend, his brother, and at times, his protector, could be gone. Zachary of the strong heart and brave spirit—a man who loved beauty, yet had known so little of it, a man who'd had enough dreams for all his people.

He blinked again and leaned forward. Something didn't seem right. He stared and tried to concentrate, to understand the significance of what he saw. Zach's face was ashen, his eyes closed, his mouth unmoving. Startling against his pale skin, fresh blood trickled from the gash on the side of his head, the wound in his leg. . . .

He shook his head and called on his medical training, but nothing penetrated his exhaustion and grief. Rising to his feet, he picked up a canteen and walked to the stream for water. He would have to clean Zach up and get moving again soon—

He paused, turned his head back toward camp, his mouth agape in disbelief. A smile broke across his face. He jumped in the air and shouted.

Fresh blood.

He ran for the stream, slid down the embankment, and fell into the water in his haste, breaking the thin crust of ice. Like a fool, he sat in the frigid water and filled the canteen. *Fresh* blood!

Zach lay exactly as Cloud Walker had left him. With great care, Cloud Walker stripped him down and bathed the wounds. A bullet had lodged in his thigh, but the head wound was a deep crease above his temple—the kind of injury that bled like hell, but wasn't usually fatal. The bullet had ripped through skin but left the bone intact. Cloud Walker remembered that Zach had struck his head on a rock as he fell. A concussion would explain his unconsciousness. The cold would have slowed down his heartbeat and breathing.

"Fool," he muttered under his breath. "Just because you

saw him pitched into a grave, you had to go and assume he was dead."

Using both his own bedroll and Zach's, he wrapped Zach up and then piled on another layer of warmth with the saddle blankets. The fire blazed with the extra wood Cloud Walker had added. After boiling his knife, a needle, and thread, he removed the bullet from Zach's leg, then stitched the gash in his head. His smile never faded.

Nothing happened. Cloud Walker waited patiently, adjusting the blankets from time to time, trickled warm water into Zach's mouth, and rubbed his throat to urge him to swallow. Before night fell, he built a lean-to. The air grew damp, colder. Cloud Walker lay beside Zach and wrapped himself around him, giving warmth, praying it would be enough.

A twitch. A shudder. A sound like sand against metal. He was being watched. Cloud Walker opened his eyes and stared into Zach's. They were fever-glazed, confused. His lips moved, but no sound came. Cloud Walker rolled to his hands and knees and reached for his canteen. He wet his fingers with the water and rubbed them over Zach's mouth.

"Cold."

Cloud Walker smiled. "Quit your bellyaching, cousin. The cold saved you from bleeding to death."

"Dead."

"Not this time around."

"Grave."

"You were just passing through."

"Alive?"

"As far as I can tell."

"Who knows?"

"Nobody."

"Home."

"We're on our way."

Zach gave his cousin what passed for a smile. Alive. He fell into feverish slumber with the thought that he had died and lived anonymously. It seemed to be the story of his life.

9

Twilight Dreams

The Empress Valley—August 1862

Cameo stood on the rim of a grassy plateau, watching the entrance to the valley as she had every afternoon since Zach had gone. Every afternoon ended the same way with twilight blurring an empty trail with ephemeral silver light.

It had to stop—the waiting, the hoping, the memories that kept her from living in the present.

She'd been so sure that he would return, so sure that he would keep in touch somehow. She had taken his refusal to say good-bye as an unspoken promise when she should have been taking what he had actually said seriously. *Forget me. Forget my name.* Zach wasn't the type of man to say what he didn't mean or give promises he wouldn't keep.

Today would be the last time she would watch and wait for a dream that was too far away to touch, a dream that would never become real.

Zach had been gone for almost five months. Twenty weeks without word as to where he was, or what he might be doing. Every day that passed without sight or word of him intensified the sense of foreboding that plagued her unmercifully.

At the end of March she had awakened from a nightmare. *Zach, walking away without looking back. Zach and pain. Zach and soul-deep cold.* There had been no clear pictures in the dream—only sensations and a shadow being swallowed by darkness. Since that night, she'd felt empty, as if hope had been wrenched from her with devastating finality.

Resolutely, she tore her gaze away from the trail and saw—really saw—the changes that five months had wrought. All around her, the land was lush with summer greens and fertile scents, a vivid calico of wildflowers and brightly colored birds. Aspens in a crescent-shaped grove swayed gracefully in the breeze, their leaves catching the light and fluttering like spangles on a new gown. In their midst, the light caught and shimmered on tiny particles of rock imbedded in her mother's gravestone.

Nearby, Samuel sat on a stool in front of his easel, painting Cameo, stroking color and texture and a part of his soul onto canvas. He worked swiftly to capture the moment as the sun met the horizon, light melting into the earth, casting shadows until Cameo and the land became one, silhouetted against the fire colors that radiated across the sky.

Memories approached and, finding welcome, lingered to pass the time.

Remember? Cameo glanced over her shoulder at him, the silent question in her eyes.

Look, Papa! God is painting a sunset, too.

Just for you, Cameo Regine. And if you wish for dreams at twilight, the angels will sprinkle them like diamonds across the sky.

Voices and images from the past soughed through Samuel's mind. Every year on her birthday, he'd brought Cameo to this place, telling her about Chai as he preserved Cameo's image on canvas, building new memories, reliving old ones.

At ten she'd sat among the trees next to her mother's grave, her head leaning against the headstone, her arms wrapped around her knees, her thoughts wrapped in dreams. The pants and shirt she'd worn had been too short on gangling arms and coltish legs. Hair the color of rich coffee had been braided and looped above her ears with strips of rawhide. At ten, she'd disdained feminine frills and furbelows.

But Cameo had just turned nineteen, a woman who had mastered the womanly arts and gloried in the trappings of her sex. Odd how he hadn't really noticed the changes until he'd witnessed the admiration and hunger in Zachary's eyes. It had frightened him, seeing his daughter that way—as a beautiful and desirable woman. Until then, he'd had absolute faith in Cameo's strength and common sense, her abilities to run the ranch and the freight business once the danger was past. Until then, he hadn't considered that she might one day be ruled by her heart rather than by her head.

Upon reflection, Samuel knew that he should have foreseen it. Zachary was the kind of man who spun reality from a maiden's dreams. His strength matched Cameo's as did his intelligence, and because of his mother—the way she had commanded respect by rivaling the skills and endurance of the mountain men—Zachary viewed women as equals rather than as workhorses and brood mares. In a perfect world, Cameo and Zachary would have been perfect mates for each other. If only their dreams had matched as well.

Applying his signature to the lower corner of the canvas, Samuel squinted, his gaze traveling from the painting to his daughter and back again. With the passing of years, she had grown, becoming so much a part of the valley that her roots spread throughout every acre of their holdings, possessing and being possessed by the land in a way no piece of paper could define. Soon it would all be hers. This, he knew, would be the last of Cameo's birthdays that he would record.

It was fitting, then, that he had painted her in silhouette, a memory without definition that would never change, never grow old, but remain as perfect and elusive as the carved ivory cameo locket he had given Chai when Cameo had been born. A memory that would remain as mysterious as her future.

He smiled as Cameo walked over to the grove of aspens that embraced her mother's grave.

But I have so many dreams, Papa. Which should I choose?

Take as many as your imagination can hold, Cameo.

What do I do when I have my dream, Papa?

You polish it and look deep inside it, then decide if you want it badly enough to work for it.

"I chose the wrong dream, Papa," she said wistfully.

Samuel blinked and dropped his gaze to the painting. He had failed her so many times in the past, never being there when she needed him to fuss over a scratch or praise an accomplishment. When she'd begun to favor lace and ribbons and fine gowns over linsey-woolsey and suspenders, he should have invited young, bright men to the ranch, encouraged her to make a choice rather than depriving her and Zachary of their individual freedoms, robbing them both of choice in order to satisfy his own conscience.

"There will be others, Cameo." *And better times. Another man who will be happy to entangle his roots with yours.*

"I don't think another would suit me quite so well." Her voice was absent as she stroked the bark of a tree. "How can it be wrong, yet feel so right?" Swallowing a sob, she stared at the grass and flowers that carpeted the little grove. Her throat convulsed; a tear found its way to the corner of her mouth as she watched the shadow of her mother's headstone lengthen and reach out for him, as if it were anxious to hold him in its embrace.

She couldn't doubt the signs that had been piling up on each other, demanding her acceptance. Time had eroded his health and stamina, weighing him down as his once robust body shrank in on itself. He'd been sharing his memories with her more and more often of late, gathering them as he'd gathered herbs and roots for his special paints, giving them to her in a bright mural of life fulfilled, distracting her from thoughts of Zach and the dread that never left her.

Panic welled as she thought of the missing gold and the murdered cows. Then there was the war, a raging inferno of hate-filled causes, lost to the control of reason. Oh, dear God, what was happening in the war? And Zach? Somehow, in spite of his protestations to the contrary, she knew that he was involved, that whatever trail he followed was rutted by the wheels of artillery wagons and the feet of soldiers.

Twilight crept across the sky, night bleeding into day. Samuel stowed his paints and canvas into a box anchored to the wagon bed for that purpose.

"Are you finished, Papa?" Cameo joined him by the wagon. "May I see it?"

"After it's framed, Cameo." Samuel smiled, seeing his mind's image of the painting: woman and land, a cameo against an enchanted sky. A frame and a gold plate engraved with his chosen title awaited at home. . . .

Twilight Cameo.

A man stood on the porch as Cameo drove the wagon into the yard. She leaned forward and squinted, a smile spreading as she recognized the short figure with the bandy legs. "Pigeon!" She jumped down from the wagon and ran up the steps to place her hands on his shoulders and kiss his cheeks in the French fashion that never failed to please him. "How wonderful to see you." She gazed at him in reproach. "You never come unless you have news. . . ." Her voice trailed off as cold dread settled in the pit of her stomach.

Pigeon was silent as his arms slowly wrapped around her, hesitantly, as if he weren't sure of his welcome. She drew back and searched his expression. If doom had a countenance, it would be Pigeon's—here, now. He didn't meet her eyes. Anxiety enveloped her like a smothering blanket, and she grasped at any reason for Pigeon's demeanor but the one she feared most. "Pigeon—the Confederates—have they taken Fort Union?"

"Non. They are leaving. We beat them good. I have seen the battle, and buried the dead on my land."

"They fought at Glorieta?" Samuel asked as he led the way into the house.

Cameo reluctantly followed the men into her father's office, apprehension holding her back even as she listened carefully to the conversation. Absently she watched her father perform the social courtesies, offering Pigeon a drink, asking if he would like food, waiting with barely concealed impatience for their guest to settle into a chair.

Pigeon accepted a snifter of brandy and one of Samuel's cigars. *"Oui,* they fight. And they drink. Government man was at my ranch and fill his canteen with my whiskey, and government never pay me for that whiskey. Texas man come up and surprise them and they fight six hours by my watch, and my watch was slow!"

"Only six hours?" Samuel swirled the liquid in his glass. "That's all it took to decide the fate of the territories?"

"Non, non." Pigeon shook his head vigorously. "That was the second day of fighting. First, they fight in Apache Canyon. Then, after the killing, they have a truce and share medicines. Then, they fight again." Pigeon set down his glass and picked up the bundle he'd set on the tea table between the chairs in Samuel's office. "Then they bury the dead in one big hole."

At Pigeon's second mention of graves, fear grew solid in Cameo's throat, strangling her, preventing speech. With careful, deliberate movements, she walked over to the desk, poured herself a draught of brandy, and then just stared at it without drinking.

Samuel drained his glass and clenched his hands around the delicate stem.

Rocking on his heels, Pigeon drew in a breath that puffed out his cheeks and let it out slowly. "I have the letter for you, Sam, from Zachary." He pulled it out of his bundle and held it out to Samuel. "He say to give it to you if—"

Dark . . . cold . . . empty.

The snifter slipped from Cameo's fingers and crashed to the floor. She looked down at the fragments of glittering glass, counting them, as if that alone would keep her from screaming. "It became real, didn't it?" she said dully, her head shaking back and forth as she spoke without awareness of what she said or who listened. "I tried not to think about it. I was so afraid that if I thought about it too much, or talked about it—"

"What became real?" Samuel asked.

"Zach's death. I dreamed of him walking away, over and over again." She laughed bitterly. "As if once weren't enough. I didn't really see anything, just feelings, sensations. Zach was a shadow, then nothing but death everywhere." Her eyes were glazed as she stared at her father, seeing nothing. "I felt it, Papa, the emptiness and the cold. My body jerked as if I had been tossed into an open pit."

"Pigeon didn't say that—"

"Zach is dead."

Pigeon shifted uncomfortably.

"Tell me," Cameo whispered. *Tell me good-bye, Zach, so that I'll know it's real.* Oh, dear God, why had she made such a demand?

"Oui, Zachary is dead, little one," Pigeon said, his own gaze downcast. "I see it all—how he ran to try and save a young boy, and the Texas man's gun shoot him in the leg and another bullet hit him in the head and then he hit his head on the hard rock."

"Wh—" Samuel cleared his throat. "When did this happen?" Every fear he had ever had concentrated into one overwhelming sense of panic and hopelessness. Zachary, who was—had been—like a son to him . . . gone. Zachary, the only man capable and ruthless enough to ensure Cameo's future, her life . . . lost. Not lost, he amended, refusing to think in such terms. He knew that Cloud

Walker would take Zachary's place as trustee. And Cloud Walker, in his own way, could be just as ruthless as Zachary. Blinking away the moisture that gathered in his eyes, Samuel lowered his head and let the conversation drift around him, unnoticed. What did it matter when Zachary had died?

"March twenty-eight—at Glorieta, on the last day. I had to wait until the government mans leave and I clean up the mess." He shrugged again. "Then it was the time for much work before I could come."

"Did he save the boy?" Cameo asked, wondering why it mattered, except that it must have been important to Zach. A boy, Pigeon had said.

"The boy is dead. Zachary try very hard to keep him safe. He had the colonel send the boy away, but that foolish fellow come back to fight. Zachary charge like the wounded bear when he see the boy get the bullet in the chest."

Numbly Cameo listened to Pigeon's account of how Zach had fallen, though the details didn't matter—not really. She heard nothing but the sound of a single bullet, felt nothing but the chill of a March night, saw nothing but the darkness of a hastily dug hole in the earth.

How ironic that just this evening, she'd finally accepted his absence—accepted, too, that she might never see him again. As long as she'd known that he was alive and following some unknown trail, she might have convinced herself that her life would go on without him.

"Zachary leave this for you, little one." Pigeon placed something in her hands, wrapped her fingers around its edges. Glass crunched under his feet as he stepped back.

Soft doeskin gave beneath her fingers. Fine parchment

crackled as she opened the handmade book, saw the neat, angular script on the first page:

> Cameo—
> *"And the soul of the rose went into my blood . . ."*
> *As everything in my life, the words are borrowed, but I*
> *could not have said it quite so well as Tennyson.*
> —Zachary

Her finger traced the writing, memorizing it, as she read and reread the words. No wonder she felt so empty. Zach had refused to take her body and her heart, but he had taken her soul with him to forever wander unknown realms. A soft rustle was followed by a dry wispy sound of something falling to the floor. She stared down to see a dried rose lying in a pool of spilled brandy and shards of glass.

Samuel bent to pick up the blossom, only half-opened when it had been plucked and pressed between the pages of the book. "It appears to be fairly new. I wonder where he found a wild rose at that time of year?" he mused as he held it out to Cameo, but she didn't seem to notice. With a sigh, he tucked it into the crease formed by the cover and the first sheet of parchment. "Cameo? Are you all right?"

She looked up at him, her breath shuddering, her eyes wide. "No, I don't think so. I can't feel anything. Shouldn't I be sad or angry? Shouldn't I feel *something?*" Not waiting for an answer, she clutched the book to her chest and walked away.

She didn't go to her own room, but instead entered the one Zach had occupied. Shutting the door firmly, she locked it and climbed up onto the high feather bed where

Zach had slept, the book still held against her breast. It
seemed to weigh more with every passing second as she
gazed around the room—at the painted tin he had emptied
of biscuits, no matter how often she had refilled it, the
bowl and pitcher where he had washed his face and
trimmed his beard, the bare table where a gaily embroidered doily had rested.

She imagined that his scent still lingered in the air,
though in truth all she smelled were the mingled odors of
beeswax and sun-fresh linens. The room was wiped clean.
No matter how hard she tried, she could not find the ghost
of his presence, could not recall his face or the exact way
his feet stroked the floorboards when he walked across a
room. Yet still she felt with sharp clarity the touch of his
hands on her skin, his mouth hotly, insistently, pressed
against hers, his tongue speaking to her in a language without words.

Breathing deeply, she opened the book and began to
read. On yellowed parchment, Zach had written poetry—
not of his own composition, but borrowed from the mas-
ters of the art: Byron and Shelley, Merrick, Shakespeare,
Tennyson, and Ben Jonson, whom he had quoted that first
evening. The care with which he had copied them told her
of reverence and love for these works, emotions she had
guessed at but had refrained from asking about.

Silent tears coursed down her face as she looked up at
the mirror above the bureau and stared at the image of
Zach she imagined she saw reflected in the silvered glass. It
was indistinct, illusory, more shadow than man—a twilight dream whose substance existed only in her thoughts.

A noise intruded, a loud counterpoint to the sound of
dreams shattering and hopes being crushed. Tilting her
head, she listened to her father's footsteps: an uncharacter-

istic shuffle down the hall, a pause, then the shuffle again, dragging, like a funeral march.

In silence and tears, Cameo grieved and discovered that worse than saying good-bye to the man you love was losing the hope that he would come back.

10

Travelers Between
Life and Death

Southwestern Colorado—Mid-August 1862

Perspiration glistened on Zach's bare chest as he forced himself to walk, then run to work the damaged muscles in his leg. Bouts of dizziness still plagued him since he'd fully regained consciousness seven weeks ago. Impatience drove him to recover his strength in spite of Cloud Walker's warnings not to push beyond his limits.

But his cousin didn't know that if Zach didn't get back to the valley soon, he was going to drop from lack of sleep rather than overexertion.

From the moment he'd awakened after Cloud Walker had pulled him from the grave, visions had plagued Zach as he hovered in the twilight between life and death. Tormenting dreams—of Cameo turning away from him, leaving him, over and over again. Haunting dreams of her soft mouth and jade eyes, her arms holding him tightly, making him stay when he would give himself up to darkness and the peace of death. Feverish dreams where he saw himself standing alone, the wind blowing around him as he watched her walk away.

Like mist, other images had drifted through his awareness—of a land of legends and secrets, a mesa with a hidden entrance undiscovered by all save an elusive people. One race had come and gone, faded into a past life that left behind no descendants to inhabit the dwellings that remained. Another race had taken shelter there, sequestered from a world that had no place for them, living in harmony with the spirits of the vanished.

When he'd awakened for short periods, he had found himself in those familiar surroundings, the borrowed home of his mother's people. He'd heard their voices, felt their presence, seen hazy outlines of men and women as they cared for him, determined that he survive as their race had survived for centuries in a foreign land.

Seven weeks ago, in June, he'd recovered enough to see more than hazy forms, feel as if he was more than a traveler between life and death.

He'd opened his eyes to slits and winced at the bright ribbons of sunlight streaming through the windows of the structure built from native sandstone. Memories had filled his thoughts, bringing him back to reality, back to himself. He had given up to them, reliving moments of the past in order to reacquaint himself with the present.

Familiar items soothed him, spoke to him. In a corner stood an old rocker his maternal grandfather had purloined from an abandoned soddy many years ago: *This will be the first step back to where we belong, the first move back to the ways of our own people.* An enameled tin coffee pot steamed on the grate his father had fashioned in the firepit: *Your pa bought me a fancy cookstove, and then he couldn't figure out a way to get it up here.* Hanging on the wall was a quilt made by him and his mother when he'd been but a boy.

Ah, Ma, that's woman's work. I'm not gonna sew a quilt or anythin' else.

You'll sew if you want to go on the trail with me and your pa come spring. And you'll learn to cook, too. How else will you take care of yourself in the wilderness?

I'll find me a woman like you.

What if she got sick? How would you take care of her? Pa doesn't sew.

Your pa makes his own clothes from deerhide, son. And when I was birthin' you, he cooked and cleaned.

A figure sat cross-legged beside his bed, watching him calmly. "Where's Ma?" The words felt like spurts of fire coming out of his throat.

Cloud Walker leaned forward and studied Zach's face. "What's your name? How old are you?" he asked as he pried Zach's lids wide to check his eyes.

"Wind Shadow, thirty-one," Zach croaked, giving his tribal name. He turned his face away from his cousin's probing and swallowed. "Ma's dead. Pa, too," he said dully, puzzled by the low rasp of his voice. His arm felt leaden as he lifted his hand to his head, felt the ridge of a healing scar. "I died, too." As he shifted, pain thrust sharply down his leg.

"I'm sure several of our women wished you had over the last couple of months. You've been sheer hell to—"

"Months?"

"Give or take."

"Why?"

"I don't really know. You've been drifting in and out. The crack on your head was bad. Frankly, I'm amazed that you're alive at all." Cloud Walker sighed. "Aside from that, you caught a bullet in the leg and another plowed a furrow above your temple. The cold kept you from losing a lot of blood, but that and the lack of immediate care and the filth of the grave brought on infection, lung fever, too. Do you remember waking up at all?"

Zach frowned as he struggled with a mixture of dreams and memories. "I remember being fed." He closed his eyes and his face flushed. "The women had to help me piss in a bucket."

"Yep," Cloud Walker said lightly. "You gave them hell. One of them threatened to diaper you and be done with it." His expression sobered. "Remember anything else?"

"The battle . . . *Calvin.*"

"The boy that died?"

Zach nodded weakly. "I was too late. Too damn late."

"Your fool stunt nearly made you the 'late' Zachary McAllister."

"Oh, God, why Calvin? Why do children have to be braver than their leaders?" Zach's voice cracked and broke. His throat felt like a rocky track heated by the sun.

"I heard that neither Colonel Canby nor General Sibley were there." Cloud Walker held a cup of lukewarm broth to his mouth, pressing until he drank.

"Tastes like shit."

"At least you *can* taste, and complain. It's taken you a hell of a long time to decide whether you wanted to live or die."

"No choice. You wouldn't let me go quietly." Fragments of time fell into place, giving Zach a clearer memory of the concerted efforts of his people to keep him alive. He remembered wanting to give up, but something had always pulled him back from the shadows. "Neither would Cameo."

Cloud Walker watched him warily. "Cameo wasn't here, Zach."

Cameo walking away without looking back, without saying good-bye. He'd had to stop her. "Damn contrary woman would've haunted me into the next life." Zach swallowed again. His voice was coming easier with use; the fiery pain became a straining ache. "If I'm going to be robbed of peace, I might as well stick around and let her torment me in person."

"Cousin, I don't care what pulled you back, as long as you are back. Every time you went to sleep, I was afraid you'd never wake up again."

"Too much noise around here to sleep."

Cloud Walker glanced at him sharply. "You could hear us?"

Zach nodded. "Enough to wake the dead."

"Sweet Jesus," Cloud Walker muttered. "I've heard that the senses are still alert even if the patient is unconscious." He shook his head. "The more I know about medicine, the less I know."

"You didn't give up."

"We shoved enough nourishment down your gullet to keep you alive, but I figure you did the rest with God's help."

"He had me and threw me back." Zach licked his lips. "How did you find me?"

A grim smile gave Cloud Walker a savage look. "I pulled you out of that hole they called a grave. Thought you were dead until I saw fresh blood running out of your leg and head."

"Feels like a cracked melon."

"Yup. It was a cracked melon."

"My voice—"

"It'll come back. You're lucky to have a voice, the way you hollered in your sleep, fighting the war and cussing out

Cameo. After the bout of lung fever, I'm surprised you can still breathe." Seeing the fatigue that weighted down Zach's eyelids, Cloud Walker kept talking. "You have a lalapalooza of a scar on your temple and another on your thigh. If that bullet had hit a little higher, you'd be a eunuch."

Zach's hand felt as if it weighed a ton as he inched it downward and probed. "The Rebs? Win?" Zach slurred, satisfied that he hadn't lost any valuable body parts.

"The Union flag is flying over Santa Fe, and the Texans are on their way home. Major Chivington destroyed their supply train and even slaughtered their pack animals. It was downhill from there for the enemy."

"The war's over?"

"Nope. It's a good thing I've been assigned to keep an eye on things at the valley or I'd be shot for a deserter."

"Why aren't you there now?"

"You needed me more. We have a dozen of our best watching out for the Fieldings. Now that you're on the mend, I'll head out."

"Do Sam and Cameo know?"

"About you?" Cloud Walker shook his head. "Nope. I kept quiet until you could decide how to handle things."

"Wish I knew . . ." Zach's voice faded as he drifted into sleep.

Cloud Walker watched Zach's eyes drift shut and listened to his breathing before quietly slipping from the room.

True to his word, Cloud Walker had left that very night. In the two months since, he had returned periodically to check on Zach's progress and give him instructions on how to pace his recuperation.

Zach hadn't been inclined to listen. Between his nightly

dreams of Cameo and the reports Cloud Walker brought back of more cattle mutilations, he knew he wasn't going to have peace until he himself was doing all he could to solve the problem.

He'd taken the first step back to the valley by telling Cloud Walker to deliver a message to Sam.

Slowing to a walk, Zach wondered how Cameo had reacted to the news of his "death."

And he wondered how she would react to the news of his "replacement."

The Empress Valley—September 1862

He came again, an illusion that carried her beyond life and death to a place of shadows and sensations. In her dreams, he lingered at her side, caressed and stroked her, filling her with sensation upon sensation. Fine dew misted her skin as her legs opened, her body writhed. A breeze drifted over her, warm like breath, a sigh of words.

> *I arise from dreams of thee . . .*
> *In the first sweet sleep of night . . .*

She moaned and her breasts tingled, swelled, responding to the touch of her dreams. A sweet and urgent ache built between her thighs. Her hands fluttered, brushed her body, pressed against her nipples, skimmed downward, finding readiness, a desperate plea for more, and always, the words whispering through the darkness:

> *And a spirit in my feet*
> *Hath led me—who knows how?*
> *To thy chamber . . .*

Her arms straightened, reaching out in need, in hope—

She cried out at the emptiness, once, a sharp sound of sudden, bitter knowledge. On the fringe of her lost dream, she heard the words again, familiar now from many readings of Zachary's book.

> *My cheek is cold and white, alas!*
> *My heart beats loud and fast;—*
> *Oh! press it to thine own again,*
> *Where it will break at last.*

Cameo lay in her bed, unmoving and stiff, willing her body to hush its tortured demands as she recited the truth to her treacherous mind. Zach was dead. He would never hold her in the night as he whispered words borrowed from Shelley in her ear and over her skin. He was lost.

And, dear Lord, she feared that she was lost, too, for she could almost hear his heartbeat, his breathing softly in sleep, rather than in death.

She had to forget. Somehow.

Again, as she had done every night in the two weeks since Pigeon's visit, Cameo stared at the candle burning on the bedside table and recalled the memory of Zach walking away from her, becoming a part of the night and the wind. With a cry, she turned up the lantern by her bed and leaned over to pick up her sewing basket from the floor. Needlework always soothed her, occupying her hands and emptying her mind of everything but the task at hand. All her nights ended this way now, with her embroidering a doily to replace the one gone missing in the chamber next to hers, a measure of her insistence that things return to normal.

As dawn lit the way for a new day, Cameo put away the

colorful silk threads and plucked a skein of heavier cotton thread from the basket. By the time she finished the lacy crocheted edging, several hours had passed without notice. Muffled voices in the entry at the front of the house brought her out of the trance imposed by counting stitches in the intricate pattern.

Two voices, she thought absently. One was Sofia's; the other sounded vaguely familiar. Cameo shrugged in unconcern. The prospect of company no longer excited her. Three men had ridden into the valley in recent months, each bringing news of disaster and loss. She would rather have the existence of a hermit than hear any more news.

"Patrona?" Sofia called as she tapped on Cameo's door.

"Yes, Sofia. Come in."

The housekeeper walked in, an envelope in her hand. "A message is delivered for the *Patrón*. The man say it is *muy importante."*

"All right, Sofia. Where is Papa?"

"He go to find paint in the forest. You take this to him?"

Muttering in exasperation, Cameo pulled her riding skirt and boots from the wardrobe. Why did Papa insist on courting danger by going out alone?

"Patrona? You will take this to him?" Sofia repeated.

"Yes, I'll take it to him. Who delivered it?"

"I not know this man. He has the light in his dark hair . . ." She spaced her thumb and forefinger an inch apart and indicated a streak in her own hair.

Cameo's blood turned to ice. A man with a streak in his hair. The prairie farmer . . . but no, Sofia had met Walker McCloud. Yet, who else would have such a distinctive feature, and why would he be delivering an urgent message to her father? She rushed through her toilette. Sofia still stood in the doorway as if to make sure Cameo didn't tarry. "Sofia, I'd like a cup of coffee, *por favor,* and something I can eat on the way—a muffin, perhaps. You'd best pack a lunch, too."

"Sí, Patrona." Nodding vigorously, Sofia bustled down the hall calling to the cook to pour a cup of coffee, *pronto!*

The letter seemed to burn through Cameo's pocket as she rode to her father's favorite place to gather roots and plants for his paints. Worry for her father's safety dogged her tracks. Curiosity was an itch in her mind and an impatience for every rock and tree root that slowed her progress. Had the enemy returned? Had more gold been stolen from the Fielding Freight wagons en route to Denver City? She forced her speculations into brighter possibilities. Perhaps the war was over.

It was late afternoon by the time she found her father wandering around in a small clearing, bent over slightly, his gaze fixed on the ground as he searched for certain plants. Her nagging worry dissolved, and she gazed at him fondly as she watched him examine a root. He glanced up at the sound of hooves crushing the ground cover, and his expression lightened. "Cameo. You're just in time to help."

"I'll be happy to, Papa, as soon as you read this message." Dismounting, she thrust out the envelope.

He broke the wax seal and unfolded the single sheet inside. A frown crossed his features. He looked up, then down, then up again, his throat convulsing as he swallowed hard. His eyes blinked rapidly several times before he squeezed them shut. "A miracle. I prayed for a miracle." His voice was musing, private, as if he'd forgotten Cameo's presence beside him.

He blinked again and his mouth spread into a smile of absolute joy. "I'll be damned. I'll be bloody well damned," he said exuberantly, and Cameo thought he might dance a jig on the spot.

"Good news, Papa?" she asked dryly.

"Good!" he shouted. "It's—" His smile faded with his voice. The frown returned. He reread the message and looked up at her, a heaviness in his features that alarmed her. Her father was not given to displaying emotional extremes, yet he was swinging between moods like a madman swinging from treetop to pit. Without ado, Cameo snatched the paper from his hand and read the two brief sentences:

Accept your offer of position as manager and trustee. Will arrive soonest to assume duties.—Sloane

Manager and trustee. Cameo focused on the words, feeling as if she'd been hit in the stomach. "What does this mean, Papa?"

He exhaled and drew himself up. "I've made arrangements for your future, Cameo." He held up his hand to forestall her questions. "And before I explain that message, I'd best tell you what I've done."

"What have you done, Papa?" she asked, suspecting that she really didn't want to know. The letter in her hand struck her as a warning of sorts, as threatening in its way as murdered cows and notes written in blood.

"I have grown old and tired, and I am going to die," he stated baldly.

"I know."

Sighing, Samuel nodded again. "Then you should know that your future is in question. I had named Zachary as your guardian and manager of our holdings until you married or—if the war had ended—when you turned twenty-five, whichever came first. That was why he came to the valley—to sign the agreements."

"You did what?" Cameo asked, stunned as much by her father's revelation as by her sudden laughter. Since Pigeon's news of Zach's death, she had been bereft of emotion. Life had become existence, a forcible effort to make it through each day without remembering, each night without dreaming.

"I expected anger," Samuel said.

"I'll be angry as soon as I recover from the absurdity of it all."

"Absurd?" Indignantly, Samuel paced around the clearing.

"Of course. You named Zachary as manager of the ranch and Fielding Freight and my guardian. *Zachary!*"

"I fail to see—"

"How on earth did you imagine that he would remain here any longer than it would take to air out his bedroll?" Cameo stared down at her hands as she felt mirth replaced by the anger her father expected. "Aside from that, I take exception that you think I couldn't—can't—manage my own affairs."

"That wasn't why I did it, Cameo."

"No? Then, please, Father, tell me why you feel that I need a keeper?"

"The reasons are obvious. Surely, you haven't strayed so far from reality that you can't see them." Samuel's voice was deliberately harsh and goading. Finally he was seeing signs of the old Cameo, after weeks of unnatural silence and suppressed tears.

"I'm not removed from reality at all, Father." She saw him wince at her formal address. Always she had called him "Papa." "I have known for quite some time that you are dying. I will be left alone and unprotected; therefore, you chose Zachary to tend me and my affairs. What I can't credit is that he agreed." Her eyes narrowed. "Or did you force him in some way?"

Samuel flushed and looked away.

"You blackmailed him, didn't you?"

"That is not at issue here, Cameo."

"No, you're right. What is at issue is that the two people I cared most about took *my* life, *my* future, and reduced it to an agreement written in precise legal terms." She crushed the letter in her hand and waved it at him. "Neither of you gave a moment's consideration to what was important to me. No one gave me a choice."

"You would have chosen badly, Cameo. I did what I thought was best, what with the war and stolen gold shipments."

Chosen badly. Sighing, she smiled stiffly, her eyes hard. "Yes, you're probably right. Recently, I've made a habit of choosing badly." She tried to close her mind to all but the matter at hand. Her own misguided heart had robbed her of all control—over her thoughts, her body, and now her tongue. Admitting to poor judgment wasn't going to further her cause.

She smoothed out the sheet of paper still crumpled in her hand and read the message one more time. "So you've found someone to take Zach's place—again without discussing it with me."

"There was nothing to discuss, and I haven't the time to waste in useless arguments."

"Hardly useless, Papa. I will not have you or any other man deciding my future unless I choose the man and the reason," she said firmly, her thoughts running far ahead of her for solutions and arguments her father would understand and agree to. "We will sell Fielding Freight and I will manage the ranch. It's all I care about anyway."

Samuel shook his head and urged her to sit on the soft carpet of wild grass. At her compliance, he sank down beside her. "The Secretary of War has all but ordered me not to sell. He wants no disruptions of present shipping until the why, how, and—more importantly—the who of the missing gold is discovered."

"What does the honorable Secretary know? We can't continue to deal with this. If he wants to control the situation, then let him send an expert, a spy."

"There is no one for him to send."

The odd quality of her father's voice struck Cameo, as if his simple statement of fact had a more complex meaning. His absolute certainty made Cameo's heart drop to her feet, her nerves jump in fear. Not only had she found several more dead cows, but two of the carcasses had been tossed into one of the wells they used to water the stock, fouling it. "Then the War Department will have to work something out. The army, for instance. They could—"

"Do nothing." Samuel sighed. "Cameo, the army is spread too thin to take on the investigation unless it is a matter of war."

"All right, Papa. If we are to be left to our own devices by the government, then we'll sell to Butterfield or Wells Fargo or close it down entirely, regardless of what the Secretary says. That is really our only problem. I can manage the ranch."

"I forbid it!" Samuel hit the ground with his fist for emphasis. "The rebels might come back. Even you can't fight a war—"

"I'm perfectly capable—"

"Capability has nothing to do with it. You're a woman,

Cameo. Even if the *vaqueros* are willing to work for you, the teamsters won't be. They will either walk out or rob you blind, or both."

"Then it will be no one's fault but my own. I would rather pay for my own mistakes than those of another, Papa."

Samuel shook his head. "Cameo, you don't know what you're dealing with."

"Yes, Papa, I do," she said quietly.

"You bloody well don't!" he roared. "A few murdered cows and a bull?" He smiled grimly at her lack of surprise. "I see that Zachary must have told you that I knew. I suspected it when you stopped giving me such weak reasons for not wanting me to ride out alone." He touched her cheek in reassurance and comfort. "No doubt Zachary told you that I refused to be a prisoner on my land."

Cameo lowered her head and whispered, "No, Papa, he told me nothing."

Samuel cleared his throat, shifted uncomfortably, and changed the subject. "Yes, well, I've known for quite some time about them, the notes left on the carcasses, and your efforts to keep it from me—which proves my point. If given a choice, our people will give their loyalty to a man —me or a manager—before trusting a woman to solve problems."

"Their loyalty is to you because you are my father and you're here. But later, when . . . you're not, they will trust me."

"If you're here, Cameo, they might—if nothing more happens." Samuel took her hands in both of his. "You're forgetting that we've both been threatened with a similar fate and we're not sure of the exact motive. I'd hazard a guess that they are trying to wait me out, hoping that I will die and save them the trouble of murdering me. After that, you would be easy pickings."

"Not so easy. Why, I even held a gun on Zach and made him back down." Cameo's gaze skipped from her father's as she embroidered the truth to suit her purposes. "I'm not a fool."

He allowed her comment to pass about Zach. Zachary had already told him of their first meeting. At the time, he'd been inordinately proud of his daughter, but now that same behavior terrified him. "No, not a fool, Cameo. But you are too young, inexperienced, and impetuous to recognize, much less accept, your own limitations." Samuel rose to his feet and paced the clearing in agitation. "We are not dealing with common criminals or gentlemen. Our enemies possess cold, calculating minds with no reserve as to the means they use to gain success. For all your abilities, you haven't the understanding of those who tread the dark edges of life."

"And Zach did?"

Samuel paused, choosing his words with care. Zachary's use of the name "Sloane" was an explicit message for Samuel not to use his true name. The man who would appear as Sloane would have a very different appearance. He had no illusions that it would fool Cameo for long, but perhaps it would give Zach some time before she began interfering.

"Zachary's experiences in the Pueblo uprising as well as his gift for survival made him the logical choice. Despite his easy manner with you and his dedication to the written word, he was a sinister man with skills you know nothing about." Afraid he had said too much, Samuel changed the course of his argument. "He was also a loyal friend who harbored no desire for your wealth. When the trouble ended or you found a suitable husband, he would have left you to continue your own life."

"It seems, Papa, that Zachary was precipitate in doing just that," she said bluntly. Plucking at her skirt, Cameo conceded a point in the hope that she would win others. "I might have accepted his trusteeship, but I will not accept a stranger." A sudden thought made her narrow her eyes suspiciously. "Who is Sloane? You've never spoken of him and he's never come to the valley."

"He's an old friend."

"No, Papa. I know all your friends. I would remember—"

"As you remembered that Zachary had previously visited us?" Samuel interrupted smoothly. "Believe me, Sloane is a man I trust implicitly."

Cameo frowned and stared down at the ground. Of course it must be true since she couldn't imagine her father trusting a stranger. Still, she didn't like it.

"You can either promise right now to accept Sloane and his counsel or I will sell the ranch and send you to England," Samuel said wearily. "I'd rather you were landless, rich, and safe than die worrying that you might come to harm, perhaps even losing it all and ending up penniless to boot."

She looked at her father with wide, uncomprehending eyes. Her breath caught and held in her throat, and she had to concentrate on forcing it out. "Papa, never have you robbed me of choice. Never have you shown such disregard—" She shook her head, unable to speak.

"We are fighting a war, Cameo, and that robs us all of choice. We do what we must to survive, to make sure those we love survive."

Samuel held up his hand before she could interrupt.

"Make no mistake, America is a land of freedom—if you're a man. A woman has few rights and only as much independence as the man who happens to be in control allows her. I've done the best I can to find someone who will protect your freedom as well as your property. Property that many would kill for. I will take any steps necessary to insure your safety."

Cameo had no doubt that he meant everything he'd said. He would sell the ranch rather than leave her to cope alone. Necessity was something Cameo had understood from the cradle. Having the wisdom to accept it was more difficult, yet it, too, had become a necessity.

Rising, she brushed off her skirt and took up the reins of her mount. "All right, Papa. We will both do what we must to preserve that which we love." She paused as she put her foot in the stirrup, unable to resist airing a final grievance. "I find our society to be quite distorted. If a nation must war with itself to emancipate slaves, what, I wonder, will it take to free its women?"

Samuel swung into his saddle as Cameo did the same. "I don't know, but I suspect that a woman's weapons of war are far more subtle and effective than cannon."

As they turned their horses toward home, Cameo slanted a glance at Samuel. "I've read about Lysistrata, Papa. I simply can't believe that women hold so much power over their men."

Samuel chuckled. "Women have power, Cameo. Enough power to drive a man to do anything, if she knows how to wield it judiciously."

"Well, I certainly have seen no evidence of it," she said tartly, then drew her brows together in concentration. Something wasn't right . . .

"You won't see it, but you will feel it—" Samuel broke off and cocked his head. "Cameo . . . listen."

"I know, Papa. It's too quiet all of a sudden." She ignored the fluttering panic rising in her throat and settled more deeply into the saddle. "Papa—"

The trees exploded in sound and flashes of light in the fading dusk. Birds shot into the sky, shrieking in protest. Leaves rained down on them, tattered by sprays of buckshot. The smell of gunpowder rose on wisps of smoke.

Instinctively, Cameo dived for her father, knocking him off his horse and following his descent into the creek. Their horses bolted. Her shoulder jerked back, and she twisted to avoid falling on him. Water splashed around them. Bits of thought broke through frantic reaction. *Surrounded. Shotguns and pistols. We're dead. Our guns . . . with the horses . . . gone.*

Cameo tried to reach for the knife secured in her belt. A burning pain caught her by surprise. Her arm wouldn't obey her commands to move. Looking down, she saw blood spreading across her shirt, a hole in the cloth at her shoulder.

Another volley of shots were fired, closer this time. She grabbed the knife with her other hand and threw herself across her father's body. He lay beneath her, silent, unmoving. Raising her head, she searched for a form, a face —anything—to satisfy her instinct to fight back. There were so many ominous shadows moving toward her, faceless in the twilight. One fell, a stain of red growing on his midsection, as if he'd been shot. How could that be? Their rifles were gone—

A figure separated from the pack, charging straight at her. She held her knife by the blade, took aim, and threw.

Light splintered in her head as a fist crashed into her

jaw. Pain erupted, enshrouding her, smothering her in darkness.

She heard a voice—her voice—distantly, as if it came from another world. "No, damn you. I will not let you win. . . ."

11
Shadowy Recollections

The hushed voices were hauntingly familiar, speaking in a language Cameo knew, yet didn't understand. Gentle hands turned her. Strong arms lifted her, carried her, held her cradled on the back of a horse. She had no desire to see or question. She felt safe and protected. It was enough.

She heard Jorge and Sofia speaking rapid Spanish. Softness cushioned her; warmth enveloped her. Familiar scents of fresh linen and beeswax surrounded her. Home. Her own bed. It was all right. Everything would be fine, now. Other voices intruded into her thoughts, in English this time, voices she recognized—almost. "Shot in the shoulder . . . bleeding too much . . . can't stop it."

Cameo felt detached from it all: the pull of cloth away from her skin; the probing of her shoulder; the jostling as her wet clothing was cut away.

"Cameo, can you hear me?" a man asked, unnaturally loud.

Yes, I can hear you. She should open her eyes, speak, but she felt weighted down, lethargic, unconcerned by her lack of good manners. So tired. So weak.

"She's unconscious. Just as well."

A new voice intruded. The *curandera*. Papa always called her a witch doctor. . . .

Papa! She struggled to remember, to open her eyes, and ask someone why she suddenly felt lost, abandoned. Weakness crept through her and she gave in to it, inviting darkness for the first time in her life.

Icy wet. Bone-deep cold. Good-bye, Zach.

"No!" His limbs jerked. Zach sat upright on his bed, suddenly wide-awake after such a deep sleep. His gaze swept his surroundings, finding the thick darkness of a moonless night. He shivered as cool air washed over his sweat-drenched body.

A sense of urgency twisted in his gut, a feeling of danger and loss. It had been the dream, disturbing for its lack of images and intensity of sensation. Sound. Fear. Desperation. Pain.

He flexed his shoulders, his arms, then worked each part of his body in turn, a ritual he had established since awakening that first day and finding Cloud Walker by his side. He'd been steadily getting stronger, though he still walked with a limp that became more pronounced when he was tired. The dye had faded from his skin and hair. His body was leaner, harder than before, from the work of reawakening his muscles. In another week or two, he'd be ready to return to the Empress Valley, and Cameo.

Cameo. The dream. Fear, renewed and growing. His heart beat like a march, steadily, growing louder, more urgent. He cocked his head, listening. Not his heart at all, but hoofbeats, pounding hard through the settlement of outcasts. No one rode that fast on the mesa. It was too dangerous with the open pits in the ground and the crumbling ruins—

Unless something was wrong.

Zach stood quickly and strode to the door, pulling it open in time to see Cloud Walker rein his horse and leap to the ground.

He ran to the doorway and stopped abruptly as he nearly mowed Zach down in his haste. His eyes were bleak, his voice hollow with despair. "How do you feel?" he asked Zach with forced calm.

"What happened?"

Cloud Walker's mouth opened, then closed as he looked away.

"Sam?"

A bleak nod. "And Cameo."

The chill was back, penetrating beyond bones to settle in his heart. "Tell me while I pack." Zach didn't stand still for the explanations, but walked over to the rough table and lit a lantern, then barreled around the single room to gather his clothes and stuff them into his saddlebags.

"Ambush. Sam's paralyzed, but he's lucid and hanging on. He won't last long. Cameo got it in the shoulder, but she's lost a lot of blood, and her lungs are full of water."

"Where in the hell were our watchers?" He stuffed food and ammunition in with the clothing.

"We were there. We got three of them and chased off the rest. Cameo nailed one with her knife before—"

"When?"

"Five days ago."

"Five days? Where in the hell have you been?"

"With Cameo. It's bad, Zach. I couldn't leave her till day before yesterday. The *vaqueros* are spooked. I stuck around to keep things going. When Kit Carson and Seamus Casey arrived, I figured it was safe—" At Zach's sharp glance, Cloud Walker held up his hands and explained, "Sam asked that they be notified. He knew I'd have to leave and wanted them to be there for Cameo. Our people are still there—hiding out, of course"—he added as Zach shot him a glare—"to keep an eye on things."

"Why in the hell weren't you able to prevent the ambush?"

Cloud Walker met his challenging glare. "We were trying to give them some privacy. Sam was telling her about Sloane."

Cursing under his breath, Zach tossed his saddlebags over his shoulder and stalked out of the dwelling. "Did you get a look at the men who attacked them?"

"It was almost dark and they were wearing bandannas over their faces. We killed two of them, but I didn't recognize them. One was wearing a Confederate hat."

Horse snorted as Zach approached the lean-to attached to the hut. Zach reached for his saddle, then drew back. "I can't take Horse. Cameo knows him."

Cloud Walker nodded. "I'll get Pegasus."

Within a few minutes he returned with a piebald stallion in tow. Like Horse and Cloud Walker's Storm Runner, the piebald was short on looks and long on speed, endurance, and surefootedness, especially at night. Zach jumped into the saddle and reached down to take his cousin's hand in a firm shake.

"I'll ride with you a ways," Cloud Walker said casually.

"I'll be making time, cousin."

"Me, too. You think all I have to do is nursemaid you?"

Zach wheeled Pegasus around and rode as fast as a horse without wings could take him.

The dream came to her again, like a lover, closer with each passing night, a cruel visitor that took shape and sub-

stance, making her relive the night in the stable, adding
fuel to needs she didn't quite comprehend, bringing her to
a peak of longing she could barely stand. It hurt, and she
was afraid that it would never end, and Zach was the only
man who would ever make her feel as she had—still did—
for him. She might as well love a shadow. Why couldn't
she forget, even now, when her father lay dying and her
own body was racked by pain and fever?

As she had the past three nights, she left her bed,
donned her plaid woolen robe, and tiptoed to her father's
room, not wanting to alert the men who had come to keep
vigil over their old friend. She loved Seamus Casey and Kit
Carson, but the endless conversations of politics and war
jarred her nerves as much as their fond reminiscences of
the exploits they had shared with Sam Fielding. Hearing
about a past she had not shared with her father was more
than she could bear.

She opened the door and peeked into Samuel's room. He
was awake, watching the door as if he'd known she would
come. His brows rose in question. All he could move was
his head and arms.

"I couldn't sleep, Papa."

"Come in." His voice sounded as fragile as his life.
"More bad dreams?"

"I . . . no, not really." Bad dreams—oh, dear God,
they were horrible, but how could she tell her father that
Zach came to her while she slept, becoming more alive to
her with every dream? "I didn't tell you about—"

"No," Samuel said gently. "But I've heard your distress
more than once. I would have come to you, but I'm
trapped in a body that has already died. I'm sorry, Cameo.
It seems that I've never been there when you've needed
me."

"Papa—"

"Tell me about your dream," he interrupted. "Is it about Zachary?"

She nodded miserably.

"It's only natural, Cameo. You cared a great deal about him."

"There is nothing natural about it, Papa. I feel as if this bond has gone beyond the grave and it will never fade. It frightens me." She shook her head. "I never should have allowed closeness in the first place, not with him. And now I should accept his death and go on. Isn't that how it's done?"

"Not always. Though I think acceptance will come in time." His voice faded. "A bond like that—with a person you love—isn't easily broken. To this day I feel tied to your mother in inexplicable ways. To this day, Chai is alive to me, a part of me so consuming that I've never been able to find ease with another woman."

"Papa, I don't want to live my life with nothing but a memory."

Her life. Samuel winced at the pressure in his chest, the sensation that his heart was swelling and about to burst. He had to think of Cameo and secure her safety and her future—tonight. His life was slipping away, fading like his voice, the thoughts that came, then disappeared like mist on a warm morning. Breath was coming harder; he could never seem to get enough, and his chest burned and clutched at him from the inside. His left arm hurt and responded more and more slowly to his commands.

He gazed at his daughter with a mixture of pride and fear. Something had changed her. Since she'd regained consciousness, she had acted as if their earlier agreement had never taken place. In their late night conversations, she'd chattered about the daily happenings on the ranch and how she'd given this order, or made that decision. He knew that she was waging a subtle battle for the right to control her own future. She had changed from an impulsive and reckless young girl into a realistic, practical, but still reckless woman. She had a way of staring down obstacles, whether they were problems or men or her own infirmity. Growing up on the frontier had given her strength and resilience, but now she had a certain toughness that almost made him believe she might overcome the handicap of being a woman in a man's world.

She would try. Thank God Zachary would soon return. No one could protect Cameo better than Zach. No one could hurt Cameo more than Zach. Yet, there was no choice but to allow the arrangements to stand. A broken heart would mend, but there was no cure for death.

· If only Zachary had arrived in time.

"Cameo, I'm going to see your mother tonight."

"No, Papa." She shook her head, denying the truth. It was there in his face, a fading, as if life were stealing away from him a bit at a time. She grasped his hand.

"Sloane . . . promise me."

She knew what her father was asking, knew, too, that he needed her promise and understanding if he were to have any peace at all. It defeated her, that silent plea so eloquent in his eyes. "It's all right, Papa. I promise not to fight Sloane. You did the right thing.

"Actually," she admitted as she looked down at her hands, "I'm relieved that I won't be alone. I've never learned how to do it well."

"Good girl," Samuel whispered. His body felt weightless, as if his soul were already departing and only a small part of himself clung to life.

She felt coolness steal into his hand. The gray washed out of his flesh, leaving an absence of color. She straightened in the chair and forced a saucy smile. Her father, she knew, had little tolerance for words of sorrow and tears of grief. "As long as Sloane is honest and competent and willing to respect my position as owner of the ranch, I will be glad to have someone share the responsibilities and problems with me."

"Always . . . have . . . last . . . word . . ." A pain gripped him and squeezed, forcing the breath from his lungs. "Remember . . . diamonds . . . sky . . . reach for . . . them—"

"I will, Papa." His fingers squeezed hers once, then slackened. She stared at his eyes as they closed. A last murmur of air escaped him, like a sigh of relief.

She blinked once. She thought she'd been prepared for this, but she hadn't reckoned on the surge of hostility she felt, the overwhelming anger and the gnawing hunger for revenge. For the first time in her life, Cameo experienced the true meaning of hate. Somehow she would find the perpetrators and see that they were punished. If she didn't take matters into her own hands, no one else would. After all, Sloane would be only a hired hand, regardless of the title her father had bestowed on him. It wasn't his home being threatened. It wasn't his father who had been murdered.

Leaning over, she kissed her father's eyelids and placed his hands on the counterpane in a natural position. "Rest well, Papa," she whispered, "and give Mama my love, and Zach, too." A drop of moisture fell on his cheek, then another, and Cameo realized that she was crying. She studied the bedchamber, full of her father's presence, every item and sensation of scent and touch a jealously hoarded memory. Tears slid unheeded down her face as she wandered around, talking mindlessly, saying what had to be said before she could let him go. Somehow she knew that he would hear.

"You didn't fail me, Papa. I always knew you loved me. I always left a candle burning. Did you know that? When you were home, it was magic, and you were mine—every day throughout the winters. You were happy, following the trail, painting the world, doing what was important to you." She folded his robe, so much like hers, and set it just so on the end of the bed. "I wish—" A sob broke out. "I wish I'd understood that sooner. I'm sorry, Papa . . . so sorry."

She turned to look at him. His smile had softened into a look of peace and contentment. Always, that was how she would remember him, a man who had known what was in her heart even when she hadn't. She swiped at her face with the sleeve of her robe and fumbled in her pocket for a handkerchief to blow her nose. "I love you, Papa," she said in a childlike voice. With a last look, she turned and walked out the door.

She found Sofia puttering in the kitchen. The housekeeper turned around slowly to face Cameo. As if she knew that Samuel had died, she crossed herself and whispered a prayer.

"Will you please ask your sons to prepare Papa?" At Sofia's nod, Cameo gave instructions, her face expressionless, her voice a mere thread of sound. "No viewing, Sofia. Papa would have hated it. We'll have the funeral tomorrow."

"*Sí, Patrona.* But first you must rest." She placed her hand on Cameo's forehead. "You have the fever again. I will bring you tea."

"Thank you, Sofia. I will be in the parlor."

Two men glanced up and broke off their conversation in midsentence as Cameo entered the parlor, her body fighting weakness and rigid with pain. Her mind screamed with it, her heart too shattered for her to believe it would ever be whole again.

Seamus Casey and Kit Carson rose, both with identical expressions of careful scrutiny and guarded emotion.

Her face was pale beneath the flush of recurring fever. She held her arm as if it weighed too much to be at her side unsupported. Her injured shoulder was angled lower than the other in an unconscious cringe.

"Papa is on the trail again," she said simply.

Seamus gave her a puzzled frown, his bushy red brows meeting above his nose. "Are ye daft with the fever, girl?"

She smiled at him fondly. Seamus Casey, owner of several trading posts along the Santa Fe Trail and retired trapper, was not a man for subtleties. If it wasn't straightforward and spelled out letter for letter, he didn't understand it. Cameo thought it was a matter of his constant preoccupation with money and business rather than slow-wittedness.

"He's gone, then," Kit said.

"Yes . . . a little while ago."

Seamus's gaze dropped to his feet, then climbed up to the ceiling. His loud sniff made his bushy red beard vibrate like tiny kinked wires. Shaking his head, he turned his back to Cameo and Kit and stared down into the cold fireplace.

"Damn it all to hell!" Kit swallowed and opened his arms to Cameo.

"My sentiments exactly," she said as she stepped into them, comforting and taking comfort. Her teeth were beginning to chatter from the chill that accompanied her fever.

A sound like a growl came from Seamus. "We'll find the bastards, girl. I promise ye that."

Kit placed the back of his hand on Cameo's cheek. "You're burning up, Cameo. It's time to go to bed."

"No! Please, Kit, I can't. I don't want to be alone."

He nodded and guided her down to the settee and covered her legs with a rag throw.

Within minutes, Cameo was settled with her back supported by the arm of the settee and two pillows. A quilt from her bed covered her from feet to chest. The men had moved their chairs to face her in an intimate little circle.

"Drink," Sofia ordered as she shoved a cup of tea under Cameo's nose.

"Can't you give the poor lass something else for her fever? That brew is enough to make you gag."

"No, *Señor* Casey. The saffron-and-catnip tea is very good for the burning blood. The *Patrón*—" She sniffed, wiped at her puffy eyes, and crossed herself again. "The *Patrón* send to far away for the spices."

Cameo sipped and gagged and sipped again.

"What in the hell is wrong with givin' the girl powdered chili peppers?" He and the housekeeper had been arguing about which herbs to use in Cameo's care since he'd arrived.

Under her breath, Sofia spoke in rapid Spanish as she bustled out of the room.

With a sigh of relief, Cameo finished the tea and set the cup on the high table backing the sofa.

Red-faced, Seamus clumsily refilled the cup from the pot Sofia had left behind. He pressed the cup into her hands. "Drink."

"Much more of this and I'll go as lunatic as the barn cats after they've raided the herb garden," she joked, needing to ease the strained silence.

"You need rest, Cameo," Kit said.

"All I do is rest." She looked from one somber face to the other. "Please, I cannot tolerate this sudden discomfort between us. You've both known me all my life. Can't we be like family, and talk as we used to?"

"I don't know what to say, lass."

Kit's nod echoed Seamus.

Leaning her head back, Cameo stared at the ceiling beams.

"Remember when you used to play Saint Nicholas on Christmas Eve for me, Uncle Seamus?"

"Aye, that I do, lass. . . . You knew?"

"I peeked once—when I was eight, I think." The chills subsided, allowing her body to relax. Her memories were as warm as the tea and, in a different way, just as healing. "I knew that St. Nick didn't have red whiskers, nor did he wear buckskins. I used to lie awake and wait to hear your 'ho-ho's.' " She smiled and patted his hand. "I missed you so when you were in the gold fields in California."

Kit added his reminiscences to hers—of times when they had all been together, helping one another in the bad times, celebrating the good ones, or simply sharing moments. Seamus and Kit didn't seem to notice as Cameo contributed to their recollections less and less—she was content simply to listen to the drone of familiar voices.

The tea was doing its work, and Cameo suspected that Sofia had added something to calm her. She felt numb and floated beyond pain, beyond thought.

"It is done, *Patrona,*" Sofia said from the doorway, her

eyes even more red and puffy, the corner of her apron wrinkled and damp from wiping away tears.

"Thank you, Sofia. I know it was hard for you."

"You are sure—?"

"Yes. I want to remember Papa as he was, alive and talking to me. Please explain to everyone why I didn't want him to be laid out in the parlor."

"*Sí.* They will understand." Sofia's tone suggested that she would pound comprehension into the *vaqueros'* heads with a cast-iron pot if they were slow to grasp Cameo's reasons for defying tradition. In an unprecedented crossing of boundaries, Sofia bent over Cameo and hugged her tightly before leaving the room. Cameo couldn't remember a time when Sofia had been anything but an efficient and disapproving housekeeper. Cameo's independence had always baffled her, and she'd assumed the role of teacher and disciplinarian. There had been times when Cameo had so desperately needed hugs instead of rebukes. . . .

"What was that about?" Kit asked.

"Sofia and her sons have taken care of Papa. We will bury him tomorrow. The weather is too warm and—" Her hands fluttered helplessly as she felt her throat close around a lump of despair. "He wouldn't want . . ."

Kit's hands gathered hers in a firm, calming grip. "No, he wouldn't. He's been waiting a long time to be with Chai again."

"And paint sunsets for real," Cameo said around a watery smile.

"Yes, that, too—a new one every day."

Clearly uncomfortable with sentiment of any kind, Seamus harrumphed loudly. "Do ye have plans, lass? About the ranch and all?"

"Seamus, your brain is as useless as tits on a boar hog," Kit said. "This isn't the time."

"Well, I had to do something before ye both started blubbering out more nonsense. The girl is on her own now. It's time to be practical."

"Uncle Seamus is right, Kit," Cameo said as she reached for more tea. "Papa and I were talking about that very thing just before he died."

Defeated, Kit sat back in his chair.

Seamus shot him a smug look and sat forward, his hands clasped between his outspread knees. "I know that Sam had planned to have young McAllister take care of ye."

"Yes." It was like being shot twice in the heart, hearing her father and Zach mentioned in the same sentence. Lost. Both of them, gone, leaving her to do whatever was necessary, to be practical. Maybe later she would find a reason for doing so. Right now she wished the world would pass her by until she had the strength and purpose to deal with it.

"Would ye like to sell out, lass?"

"Sell?"

"I'll buy the whole caboodle, if ye want. The money would take care of ye for life."

Startled by the suggestion, Cameo stared at Seamus. "You, Uncle Seamus?" How many times had she heard Seamus tell her father that he wouldn't have the headaches of running a ranch?

He confirmed her recollection with a jerk of his head. "Aye, 'tis so, but ye're like my own, darlin'. Ye could travel the world and the valley would always be yer home when you wanted it."

It touched her, a pinprick where there had only been

numbness, to know he cared so much. It made her feel less alone.

"Ye can't stay here alone, lass. 'Tis no life for a young girl."

"Thank you, Uncle Seamus, but I would be alone wherever I went. This is home. I belong here. And, I'll have help."

Shifting his position, Kit draped his arm over the back of his chair. "You should think about it, Cameo. With Zach gone—"

"Papa has already taken care of it, Kit. He hired a manager, who will also act as trustee."

"What's this?" Seamus sat up straight, fidgeted, then stood. "There's none around here to take on such a thing."

"An old friend, Papa said. A man named Sloane."

Kit's head jerked. Abruptly, he stood and walked straight to the decanter of whiskey. "When did this happen?"

"Papa received a message the day we were ambushed."

"Never heard of him," Seamus said. "Kit?"

Hesitation.

"Do ye know him or don't ye?"

"I know him," Kit said carefully. "Comes from the Northwest. Good man."

"Well, why in blazes don't I know him?"

With his back to Seamus and Cameo, Kit busied himself pouring a glass of whiskey, drinking, pouring again. "Probably because you were in the gold fields when we met up with him. We spent a cold winter together up north. He was a real greenhorn then, but he learned fast."

There was something strange about Seamus's agitation and Kit's easy answers contradicted by the way he was belting down her father's imported spirits. Kit could be eloquent when the need arose, yet his answers struck her as being too glib. Cameo frowned and tried to concentrate, but her mind refused to settle on one thought.

"Why would he agree to such an arrangement?" she asked. "What does he have to gain?" She watched Kit lower his head, take a deep breath, turn slowly to face her. His eyes were bright with emotion, his expression blank, as if he had received a shock.

"An easy mind, I expect." Amber liquid swirled in his glass as he gripped it more tightly. "Sam staked his peo . . . his family to a new life. Men like Sloane take honor and gratitude seriously."

"I see. A man of lofty ideals." Cameo sighed. "Zach was that way to a point. Papa had to blackmail him into taking responsibility for the ranch . . . and me."

"McAllister wasn't no fool," Seamus snorted. "He knew what a pain in the ass Sam's 'empire' was."

Kit released a lengthy breath and slapped Seamus on the shoulder. "Then you should be glad you won't be saddled with it."

Seamus snorted. "That I am," he said gruffly as he looked at Cameo. "Don't get me wrong, darlin'. I just wanted to take care of ye—"

"I know, Uncle Seamus," Cameo said, her throat tight, her smile watery and tender. "Thank you. It's good to know you and Kit are close, that I'm not really alone."

Seamus cleared his throat as he sat back and folded his hands over his middle.

It was over. Samuel Fielding was finally with his wife. Cameo stood ramrod-straight by the open grave, denying illness and pain and weakness. The *vaqueros* and their families were all there, watching her, wondering what would happen now, wondering if the girl they had respectfully called *Patrona* could, or would, live up to the implications of the title.

She spoke with each of them in turn, met each pair of eyes in turn, and breathed a tiny, silent sigh of relief at their words of encouragement and faith.

It had begun. A different life. A woman grown overnight from the ashes of youth.

She was alone, now—truly, completely alone. She had to go on, to survive, and to win. Without fully realizing it, she took another step toward making the changes in herself that normally would have been more gradual. Except that nothing in her life had been normal. It couldn't be. Not in this part of the country. Not in these times.

Fight or die. She'd heard a frontier woman say that once, and it was true. *Out here you can't languish or take the time to feel sorry for yourself. Shed a tear, three at most, then get on with it.* It had been good advice, words to live by—literally.

The gauntlet of men and women passed her and climbed into wagons and onto horses and burros for the ride back to their homes. Kit and Seamus lingered by the open grave, their heads bent, before picking up shovels and bending to the task of burying all that was left of their friend.

Unable to stand any longer, Cameo walked to the buggy, the rough places in her emotions glazed by fever, her thoughts as watery as her strength. She had passed the first test. Only one thing came through, the one thing that had always sustained her when she had no one to rely on but herself. She had to concentrate on doing what was necessary rather than what she wanted to do.

She wanted to be a child again, free to cry, scream, and

find safety in the protection of someone older and wiser than herself.

Cameo had shed more than her allotted three tears during the long night as Kit and Seamus hovered over her, indulging her insistence on remaining in the parlor. If she'd had one more dream of Zach at that point, she would have cried until next week. That tough-as-jerky frontier woman would surely have come back to haunt her.

The woman had been Zach's mother.

Get on with it.

"You need a long nap, girl." The buggy dipped with Seamus's weight. Leather creaked as he took up the reins. "You need some more of that witch's brew for your fever, too," he said.

Glancing up, she saw Kit mounting his horse. Her gaze swept the plateau, and caught on the fresh mound of earth, the simple headstone that matched her mother's. They'd found it in an unused corner of the loft, gathering dust and cobwebs, and Jorge had stayed up all night working on the inscription. How long, she wondered, had it been there? Since her father had discovered that he was dying? Or since he'd ordered the one for her mother from St. Louis so many years ago?

The *vaqueros* and their families were gone, nearly home by now. Home. Somehow, the word and the concept had lost its meaning. . . . Her eyes drifted shut, closing out reality; her head fell back against the seat. She focused on the discomfort in her shoulder and chest, allowing it to take over the agony in her soul—another necessity. Physical pain was so much easier to bear, for it always ended. Other forms of suffering were not so easily eliminated. Even when it was necessary.

* * *

Seamus fussed with the pillows and pulled the counterpane on Cameo's bed up to her chin. The saffron-and-
catnip tea was made more vile by the laudanum Sofia had
added, but Cameo obediently drank it all and sank back,
exhausted. The fever sapped her strength—the one thing
she needed most. She was impatient to get well, to heal.
She desperately needed rest. . . .

"I'm sorry I have to leave so soon, Cameo," Kit said as
he picked up his saddlebags.

She cocked her head and smiled faintly. "War waits for
no man, or woman, Kit. The Union needs you far more
than I do."

Seamus snorted. "War. There's no profit in it—especially when both sides will lose in the end."

"You go, too, Uncle Seamus. Please."

"I can't leave you alone, lass."

Cameo shook her head. "My new manager will be here
any day now."

Kit stepped in before Seamus could protest. "She's right,
Seamus. The *vaqueros* will look after her."

"You just want me ear to chew while you ride back to
Fort Craig," Seamus said. "I have better things to do."

Cameo offered the one inducement that would sway
Seamus. "Yes, you do, Uncle Seamus. You have a business
to run. And so do I. The sooner I begin, the better."

"You sure, lass?"

"Yes." She watched Kit, his expression of relief as he
realized that Seamus was giving in. All day, Kit had
seemed anxious to leave the valley and take Seamus with
him. Odd, but she could have sworn that Kit had come
prepared to stay much longer—had, in fact, shown no impatience about leaving.

Before she could elaborate on her impressions, Kit was

walking out the door, and dragging Seamus with him. "Cameo doesn't need interference from us when Sloane arrives. A man like him doesn't cotton to watchdogs unless they're his. . . . Cameo, stay put and rest."

Seamus turned to Cameo. "If that sonofabitch Sloane gives ye any trouble, girl, you send for me, you hear?"

Kit rolled his eyes, then winked at Cameo.

She smiled, feeling warm and less alone. Seamus's burly arms were big enough to provide support and protection. It comforted her to know that she had someone to go to— if it became necessary. She was determined to make sure it didn't. "I promise I'll cry 'Uncle' at the top of my lungs. Now, both of you go, or you'll be riding in the dark."

Within minutes, she heard hoofbeats fading out of the valley as they rode away. The laudanum had slowed her blood, made her legs feel like lead, her head like air. Her hand slipped off the edge of the bed; her eyes drifted shut as she prayed for a silent sleep, free of shadowy recollections.

12
False as Truth

It was worse than any nightmare.

Cameo stood on the porch later that day, forcing herself to stand straight and tall, to appear in control, though her limbs were trembling and her wits refused to move faster than a crawl. A chill shivered over her, caused not by fever but by the terror reflected on every one of the sixty faces of men, women, and children gathered in front of the house.

"All of it, *Patrona*. While we are at the *Patrón's* burial, our gardens disappear—the vegetables and herbs and flowers—gone," Victor, her foreman, said.

A shepherd nodded and crossed himself. "Our little church is robbed of everything. Where our Holy Mother stood—nothing, and the priest, he is late for two months now. Our homes, too, *Patrona*. Our crucifixes and rosaries —all of it—poof."

"It is an evil omen," another shouted.

They looked to Cameo for answers she couldn't give. No vegetables and herbs meant restricted diets through the winter. A sanctuary without icons meant hopelessness, vulnerability to evil, excessive superstition.

Even now, her people were wondering what transgres-

sion they had committed to deserve abandonment by God.
She was afraid of the conclusions they might draw. The
ranch had been plagued by mysterious incidents. The owners had been attacked with murderous intent. Evil did indeed seem to be lurking in every shadow.

She pulled the first explanation she could think of from
her medicine-fogged mind and held up her hand, hoping
that in their agitation they wouldn't see the tremble in her
fingers. "We are in the middle of a war and this is a rich
valley. The enemy—"

"The valley is cursed," the *curandera* shouted and
pointed a fat finger at Cameo. "You are cursed."

A cold sweat broke out on her brow and quickly spread.
As casually as she could, she took two steps sideways and
propped her good shoulder against the post supporting the
porch roof. It was insane. What could she possibly tell
them that they would comprehend, when even she didn't
understand? Unable to look at the panic on their faces a
moment longer, she looked over their heads.

Dear heaven, what else could happen?

A shadow moved next to a tree beyond the crowd. She
bent slightly forward and squinted. It shifted again, just
enough to catch the light filtering through the leaves and
take on detail and dimension. Her heart began to pound
and she felt an odd sense of expectation as her gaze collided with the figure of a man leaning indolently against
the thick trunk. The form and stature seemed so familiar,
and for one quick breath of a moment, she felt as if her
memories had been altered. Memories drawn for her by
Pigeon of a battlefield and death and a cold, open pit.

But, no, it couldn't be. This man was too different, too
menacing. He was tall with strong shoulders, lean to the
point of gauntness, yet attractively broad. His clean-shaven

face was thin with creases on either side of his mouth. His hat was pulled forward, shading his eyes, eyes that somehow seemed to be touching her, thoroughly, intimately. Rough, serviceable clothing and well-worn boots proclaimed him accustomed to labor on the range, yet his skin was lighter than—*No! I can't think of Zach.*

He tipped his hat back to meet her dazed stare.

His eyes . . . oh, God, his eyes. They were silver-blue —twilight eyes. Like Zach's. Breath escaped her in a rush. Her knees threatened to give way. Her body vibrated in shocked awareness as she looked him up and down—once, twice, three times. In some indefinable way, he reminded her of Zach, yet it was blatantly obvious that he wasn't Zach.

One by one, the *vaqueros* turned to see what had captured their *Patrona's* attention. Whispers erupted in the crowd, followed by suspicious glares and darting glances at Cameo.

She licked her lips and gathered her voice to speak with authority, rather than emotion. "Who are you?" she asked, fighting her reaction and attributing it to having a stranger appear in the midst of so much trouble, a dangerous-looking stranger with his hard face and eerie calm.

With studied nonchalance, he straightened away from the tree and briefly raised his hat, a token gesture of respect. "Sloane, Miss Fielding. Your new manager."

"I see," she said and slumped against the porch rail. *Sloane. Just Sloane.* With sudden force, hatred was born and grew to maturity. Because his eyes were like Zach's. Because his stature was tall and proud and lazy all at the same time. Because mockery tipped a corner of his mouth and defined the slight cleft in his chin. He looked sinister and strong without a trace of the dreams she had glimpsed in Zach's eyes. Most of all, she hated him because Zach was dead and Sloane was taking his place.

The mockery grew and his eyes narrowed on her. All she could do was stare at him, struck dumb by the animosity she felt for him. Silence descended on the knot of people as he bent to pick up his saddlebags, then sauntered forward with a pronounced limp, apparently unconcerned by the anxiety that hung over the valley like gunsmoke.

The *vaqueros* parted for him, allowing him to saunter through. He never missed a step as he began issuing orders to each man he passed, ignoring her as if she were of no consequence. His voice was a low, drawling rasp, lazy and calm, restoring order and instilling confidence at the same time. The people of the valley were soothed by the establishment of routine and discipline, the image he presented of power and control.

With a visible effort she straightened, resentment building until she wanted to scream at him. Zach would have worked with her, listened to her, cared about her ideas for the ranch. Sloane struck her as a man who would listen politely, then do what he thought best regardless of her wishes, expecting her to be rarely seen and never heard.

Cameo had a childish urge to throw a rock at him. With every step he took, she felt her control slipping further away. The *vaqueros* had dispersed, each to perform his task, as if nothing had happened to turn all of their lives topsy-turvy.

"Mr. Sloane," she called out before she knew what she was doing. He stopped at the bottom of the porch steps and looked up at her.

"Ma'am?"

"My father is dead."

A shadow seemed to pass over his face as he replied heavily, "Yes, ma'am, I know."

"I own the ranch now."

He raised his brows and stared at her indulgently. "Yes, ma'am, I know—"

"You won't be needed, after all." *Forgive me, Papa,* she prayed. Never had she broken a promise before. Before Sloane.

"Sorry, ma'am. Your daddy had me sign a contract, and I have a copy of his will." His grin was engaging. At least, she thought, it would have been engaging on anyone but him. "He warned me that you'd be contrary."

"I am not contrary, Mr. Sloane. This is my land, my life. I will not have a stranger interfering in the management of either."

"With all due respect, Miss Fielding, you weren't *managing* for shit a few minutes ago." He took his time climbing the steps, his gaze never leaving her.

Humiliation brought a scalding flush to her face. She wanted to cringe away from that penetrating stare. Instead, she unwrapped her fingers from the white-knuckled grip she'd kept on the post that had been her only support and faced him defiantly. It was difficult to adopt a proper attitude of authority when she had to tilt her head so far up to maintain eye contact. And those eyes! They fascinated, captured, held her with an awareness that staggered her. And they brought Zach's loss closer somehow, sharpening her grief, strengthening her resentment.

He appeared to be waiting for her to argue with him, defend herself, offer excuses. She refused to accommodate him and maintained the silent, glaring showdown, jade-green against silver-blue, measuring, challenging.

His sigh was long-suffering as his expression sobered to

brooding intensity, his gaze once again wandering over her as if he were conducting an examination of her person. As if it mattered to him whether she was well or not.

Ha!

"Which room is mine?" he asked shortly.

"The fourth cottage of the employee quarters is empty," she said through clenched teeth, amazed at his gall.

Sloane walked past her; his arm, brushing hers, produced instant warmth and shocking feelings of intimacy. He glanced back at her once, then continued into the house, forcing her to follow him.

"Sorry, ma'am. My job is to protect you. I can't do that from a distance." He opened one door after another, inspecting each of the five bedchambers in turn. "This one is yours?"

"Yes."

He nodded. "Smells like mustard and sour milk," he commented as he proceeded down the hall to open the next door.

Cameo hunched her shoulders, suddenly conscious of the mustard plaster on her chest and the milk poultice on her shoulder.

"Is your wound infected?" The inquiry was tossed out so offhandedly that it struck her as being more a social obligation than genuine concern. He paused, his hand on the doorknob of what was once Zach's room, and waited.

"Yes," she said. His regard unnerved her. His hand on the doorknob nettled her. He turned it, pushed open the door, and walked in.

"This'll do," he said as he threw his gear on the bed. With his hands on his hips, he surveyed the furnishings, his attention snagging on the small table by the door, the new doily lying on the polished wood. He nodded toward the new doily. "Nice. You do that?"

"Yes." His choice of bedrooms added insult to injury. She couldn't bear it—the casual way he had moved into her life, replacing Zach, taking everything that she would have gladly given to the man she loved. "This room will not do, Mr. Sloane."

"No? Why not? It doesn't look like anyone else belongs in here." His eyes gleamed, watching her . . . always watching her.

"It's not proper."

A smile brought out faint indentations in his hard face. "Maybe not, but it's necessary."

Her gaze jerked up to his and she shivered. For just a moment, as she caught the glitter of silver-blue eyes, she again imagined that she was seeing Zach. *Stop it,* she told herself. *Just stop it! Zach is gone.* That was the truth, absolute, final. The tricks Sloane played on her mind and her emotions were just that—tricks and lies. Yet, knowing the truth, she still stared at him, unable to withdraw, fascinated in spite of herself.

Cameo shook her head and mentally listed the visible differences between her memories of Zach and the reality of Sloane, convincing herself that she was feverish and her wits were muddled. Zach's eyes had always looked at her with humor or admiration or passion—even anger—not with this blank, hard expression that made her feel as if she'd just slammed into a wall.

Zach is gone.

Sloane's mocking drawl was faintly ominous, chilling her to the bone, and had nothing in common with Zach's softly spoken bass, smooth and warm as a lover's caress. Sloane's short hair was a deep, rich chestnut with streaks of gray on each side, not black and long and tied with a strip of Indian beadwork. He was younger than she'd expected, yet older than Zach had been. Zach had still had a look of youth about his strong features and a relaxed way of giving himself over to the pleasure of the moment. Sloane looked as if he'd never had a gentle moment in his life, as if he'd fought his way out of hell. . . .

Or the grave.

Again she shook her head and tore her gaze away from his. Her voice was smooth, clear, and layered with ice. "Sofia will have dinner ready in two hours. I will see you then."

As she abruptly turned on her heel and stalked into the hall, the man called Sloane winced at the message behind her words. She was the boss and he the hired hand. And the hired hand had been dismissed. He couldn't help smiling. The sass was still there, and the strength. Cameo looked like hell and probably felt even worse, yet she was gritty as desert sand, contrary, and every bit as predictable.

It had thrown him at first, seeing her so weak and obviously sick. Her actions had reassured him. His smile broadened as he remembered her ploy to banish him from the valley. He'd have been disappointed if she hadn't tried it. He'd have been alarmed if she'd accepted her fate without taking at least one shot at him from the hip.

The news he'd received of the attack on the Fieldings had filled him with a fear so strong that it had been the only thing that kept him upright in the saddle on his uninterrupted journey back to the Empress Valley. A cold sweat had broken out on his forehead when he saw her so weak and pale, the lively sparkle gone from her eyes, her rich voice so thin and shallow. It had been all he could do to keep from giving himself away just to have the right to hold her and reassure himself that they were both alive.

At least she hadn't put Zach and Sloane together yet. He should be relieved. But if she'd recognized him, there would be no further need for deception. The hardest part was remembering to roughen his voice, and his throat ached with the effort. The effort didn't seem worth the deception. He was tempted to tell her the truth and be done with it. Sooner or later she'd figure it out anyway.

And when she did, she'd likely shoot him with the rifle he'd given her. Cameo was not a woman to appreciate the elaborate and often pointless games politicians were hellbent on inventing. He didn't blame her for that either. Acting on a stage was one thing, but knowing that he was falsifying the truth at the expense of an innocent victim sat in his belly like rotten eggs. Disgusted at his lack of concentration on the job at hand, he stomped out of the house and slammed the door behind him.

Dinner with Sloane was a terrible mistake, Cameo thought as she sat at the head of the table, a tactic that was supposed to make the pecking order clear to Sloane. But his head was as thick as the adobe walls of the ranch house. Her first error had been in having him sit at the foot of the table—the woman's place. The implications of that had amused her, but he had a way of taking over, making any place he occupied seem to be wholly his—a position of command.

He'd actually chuckled as he took his seat without either waiting for her to sit or offering to hold her chair. Zach had always observed social protocol and made her feel feminine and cosseted in little ways, like holding the door for her and giving her a leg up when she mounted her horse. Once he'd even lifted her clear of a puddle as if she'd been wearing the finest of kid slippers rather than her work boots.

Silence ruled their repast. Other sounds were magnified: the clatter of cast iron and pottery in the kitchen, the creak of the water pump filling the dry sink, the distant howl of a coyote, Sloane cutting into his meat with the grate of a sharp knife on porcelain. Sloane hadn't even spoken to ask for the saltcellar, but had leaned over the table to reach it himself, slanting his brow at her in mockery.

Thoughts of Zach intensified with every breach of respect and propriety Sloane committed. She had the feeling that Zach was somehow *there,* pointing out the disparities between himself and Sloane and reminding her of all the reasons why she had fallen in love with Zach.

She remembered other meals shared at this table, the food consumed yet not tasted for the awareness that had consumed her; the conversations filled with humor and friendly arguments rather than with antagonism and freezing politeness. With Zach, not Sloane.

Every word, every movement had produced an anticipation of the slightest touch, the rush of excitement when it came, her naughty imaginings when Zach's hand lingered or he smiled in his special sidelong way, as if he were sharing a secret. . . .

Dear heaven, she was not only remembering, but *feeling* it all over again. With Sloane, not Zach. How could it be? She was angry at herself and at the cocksure man across from her. Yet despite her antipathy, the boorish clod was drawing involuntary responses from her, resurrecting memories that brought only anguish.

Questions plagued Cameo as she tried to appear unruffled. How could she respond to one man while still haunted by another? Why did her body confuse the two when her rational mind knew them as different? She refused to consider that it was actually Sloane evoking familiar longings and naughty thoughts. He was arrogant and presumptuous—not at all the kind of man she considered suitable, not the kind of man she could like, not one for whom she could feel anything but annoyance and outrage.

The answers were equally plaguing as they drifted just beyond her grasp, then darted closer, within reach if she had the courage to capture them, accept them. She feared the situation as she'd never feared anything, sensing that the truth would be worse than the lie. She'd never been frightened by a man before, yet Sloane terrified her.

Sofia bustled in and set cups of coffee, first in front of Sloane, then Cameo. "You wish something else, *señor?*"

"No, *gracias,* Sofia. That will be all."

Cameo's mouth tightened at his audacity, and Sofia's obvious desertion to the enemy camp. Since when was a hired hand consulted rather than the *Patrona?* And since when did said hired hand dismiss the household staff? More disturbing was Sofia's obedience. Panic fluttered in Cameo's chest. Since when had she been supplanted as mistress of the house? She felt cut off, or cut away, from all that had been familiar and constant in her life. She felt as if she were the usurper and Sloane the one who belonged.

"I'm not finished yet, Sofia," Cameo said as the housekeeper reached for her plate, still half-full of food.

Sofia left with a nod to Sloane.

China clinked and silverware pinged as Sloane added a dollop of brandy to his coffee and stirred. He lifted his cup, drank, and closed his eyes as if the spirits and warmth soothed him.

His silence was driving her mad. Folding her napkin, she

placed it beside her plate. "Were you wounded in the war, Mr. Sloane?" she asked.

He leaned back in his chair, stretching out his legs. His foot brushed hers, and she jerked her feet back as far as they would go.

He stilled in the act of lifting his cup to his mouth. His gaze caught hers, then slid away. "Wounded?"

Damnation! It was like pulling a chicken's teeth to pry civilized conversation from him. "Your limp," she explained with exaggerated patience, "and the scar on your head. Is that why you're not serving in the army?"

"Yes."

Yes. Cameo closed her eyes and heaped silent invectives upon his head. "I see. How fortunate that you are exempt from duty when most able-bodied men are—"

"The key is able-bodied, Miss Fielding. I am not," he said shortly, leaving her no recourse but to abandon the subject.

"You said 'duty' as if it were a curse. I take it you've lost someone to the war."

Her hands clenched in her lap. "No." *No one who was mine to lose—except, perhaps, myself.*

"No one?" he asked with a hint of disbelief, watching her intently as if her reply mattered to him.

She didn't give a hang about what mattered to Sloane, and she certainly wasn't about to speak of Zach to him. Zach was a private memory, a man who had become hers more completely in death than he ever would have been had he lived.

"No one," she said and almost gagged on the lie.

He lowered his cup and stared at her, his brow creased slightly. His face was rigid, his expression carefully blank. Before she could wonder at that, he slid his gaze away.

Bare hints of emotion played about his eyes and mouth, emotions she couldn't identify as he ran his hand down his face as if wiping it free of expression.

Bemused, Cameo wondered at the quicksilver changes in his manner. Had it been her imagination or had the cocky Sloane—just for an instant—the look of a man who had been attacked from behind?

"You don't consider your father a casualty of war?" he asked with an attitude of remote interest.

"I didn't lose Papa to the war, Mr. Sloane." She had the urge to confide in Sloane, to tell him that her father had never really been hers to lose. She'd always felt as if those precious few moments she'd had of his life were borrowed. It had been the same with Zach—borrowed. It occurred to her that whenever she'd tried to harvest a dream, the time had always been wrong. Out of season.

"I would have thought so—indirectly."

"The war didn't kill Papa; men did," she said shortly, hoping her tone would convey her wish to end the subject. Picking up her fork, she scooted her food around on her plate and gave the patterns she drew in the mess of potatoes and gravy her utmost attention: a *Z*, then an *S* followed by a question mark. She gazed down at her plate and blinked. "We must find some vegetables soon, before winter comes again—" She swallowed. "Or we'll all have scurvy."

"That's a good reason for you to clean your plate," Sloane said. "You'll never heal if you don't eat."

Distracted by the almost tender quality in his voice, she glanced up at him. His features, too, had softened into what appeared to be genuine concern. She didn't want his concern, his pity, or anything else he had to offer—unless, of course, he offered his resignation. "I've long since out-grown the need for a nanny, Mr. Sloane."

"That may be true, but you sure as shit need a keeper, *Miss* Fielding. Someone who will tie you in your bed and keep you there until you're well."

Her fork clattered to the table and splattered food in her face. She wiped her cheek. "Now let's get one thing straight—"

"Straight? Lady, you can't even walk a straight line. You've been shot and your wound is infected." His voice remained level, tightly controlled. "You're so tired your eyes are twice as big as they should be, your skin is blotched with fever—"

"I have a mirror—"

He nodded. "Then you know that you look like a de-mented hag."

"Thank you," she said, her voice sharp and cold as an icicle.

He continued as if he hadn't heard her, as if the issue had been festering inside him and required purging. "You've been pushing yourself, and throwing what little weight you have around. The *vaqueros* think you're five bullets short of a loaded gun, and I'm beginning to think they're right. Just who in the hell are you trying to im-press?"

His anger stunned her, held her still and staring wide-eyed at him. Anger as if he had a personal interest in her health, in her. It was strange, that feeling of not being alone. Vulnerability brought a lump to her throat, thicken-ing her voice as she gave in to the need for understanding. "I'm trying to impress myself, Sloane. Only myself."

"Cameo—" His voice was as husky as hers, a whisper

that seemed ripped from him, leaving only rawness and pain in its place.

She closed her eyes against the poignancy of it, the memories it brought so vividly to life. *All I can offer is hours—not enough for either of us.* There had been that same wrenching quality to Zach's voice when he'd said that, the same need and regret. The same suffering.

Again the coyote howled, a long, plaintive cry that filled the night. She opened her eyes, meeting his, entranced by their glitter, *feeling* the mournful song of a solitary creature wandering through the night. She wanted to howl, too —for the emptiness of a coyote's cry echoing like memories that wouldn't die, memories that followed her relentlessly into the present.

She blinked, but still he held her gaze, his eyes gray with turbulence, glittering with an emotion she was afraid to acknowledge. Her breasts swelled and became taut. Her blood simmered with a different kind of fever. What strange power did this stranger have to command her memories, her body, her behavior? Never had she thought to feel this way again; she had feared never feeling this way again. Yet it seemed like the worst sort of betrayal, not only to herself but to Zach.

She shook her head, unsure of what exactly she was denying.

Sloane drew a breath, then released it and shifted in his chair as he again wiped his hand over his face, his fingers lingering at his chin as if he sensed something unfamiliar. "You were right," he said, his voice strained and heavy with frustration. "It's time to get things straight, Miss Fielding."

The spell was broken. Cameo pulled herself up in her chair, faced him squarely, nodded. "Yes, it is," she said

smoothly, determined to take control and keep it. She gave
him an aloof stare, her cold smile—one that she had often
seen the headmistress at the Academy for Young Ladies
wear when she was about to dispense reprimands and punishment. "I won't waste words with you—"

"God forbid."

Cameo took her time to dab her mouth with her
napkin, then folded the linen just so and set it next to her
plate. "I don't like this arrangement, Mr. Sloane. You're a
stranger—" The flicker in his eyes interrupted her and ruffled her composure. If she didn't know better, she'd have
thought her statement had hurt him in some way. "And
you presume too much. The only thing that keeps me from
fighting you tooth and nail is a promise I made to my
father. The only thing that will keep me from opposing
you in the future depends entirely on you."

Silence. Awful, intimidating silence.

"The fact is that I own this ranch and Fielding Freight.
You are welcome to manage both as long as you take your
orders from me." She smiled in satisfaction and congratu-
lated herself on how well she had done.

"Is that the best you can do?" he asked.

"I beg your pardon?"

"You should." He sat forward. "I'm not here for the hell
of it, *Patrona,* but because an old and valued friend asked
me for help."

"Ah, yes, I'd almost forgotten about your lofty ideals.
Nevertheless—"

"Nevertheless be damned, lady. You're not stupid. You
know you can't handle your father's empire. The teamsters
won't listen to you because you're a woman. The *vaqueros*
respect your position, but you're a woman, the weaker sex,
best suited to bedrooms and kitchens." He resumed his

former relaxed position and continued talking as if he were commenting on the weather. "You need me and you know it."

"Why do I need you, Sloane? Because you have a . . . an appendage that I don't?"

A lazy smile spread across his face. "Jealous?"

"From what I've seen, Mr. Sloane, there is *very little* to be jealous about."

His skin appeared to pale and his mouth tightened. "A woman of experience, I take it."

Cameo drew herself even taller in her seat, and primly folded her hands on top of the table, forgetting that her plate was still there. "Enough experience to know that men don't possess a second brain . . . *there,*" she said as she tried to ignore the squish of cold potatoes and gravy under her hands.

He laughed. *Laughed!* Uncaring of what she did in her utter humiliation, she lowered her hands to her lap and wiped them on her skirt, then stared down at the stained fabric in horror.

His chuckle infuriated her. "You're a bastard, Mr. Sloane."

"Remember it."

"What?" Usually that kind of insult sparked anger in a man, but Sloane actually looked pleased.

"It takes a bastard to handle the kind of problems you're having, Miss Fielding. Being anything less makes his life worth less than a bucket of warm spit."

"I see," she said and began to rise.

"Sit down. We're not finished, yet."

She glared at him. "You will take orders from me, not the other way around."

"I will take orders from you, Miss Fielding, as long as

they make sense and won't get you into trouble. *Then* you will do as *I* say." Without giving her a chance to reply, he stood abruptly, his chair sliding back so fast it overturned behind him. He stepped over it and stalked out of the house.

Outraged, Cameo followed him, determined to shoot down his insufferable insolence if it killed her. Her eyes bored holes in his back. "Mr. Sloane, we are not finished with this—"

The door slammed so hard behind him that it rebounded and swung open. Apparently they were finished, she thought indignantly—but only until she caught up with him. In the doorway she stopped short as he took the porch steps two at a time, stumbled, and muttered a curse. He rubbed his thigh, and his limp was more pronounced as he walked across the yard to the stable. Though his gait was uneven, there was a smooth rhythm, a glide that held her transfixed. A glide as if he were stroking the ground . . .

Her hand flew to her throat as she experienced a recognition so strong she reeled with it. Shock warred with emotion; anger struggled with hope. Her body shook. Her heart danced in skippy little beats. At her side, her fist clenched as her other hand moved down to her stomach. "No," she whispered, and shut the door gently, her fingers numb on the knob. She backed away through the entrance, then turned and walked into the parlor, carefully, as if she were picking her way through a nest of vipers.

Her sewing basket lay on the floor next to an old rocking chair. She focused on it, knowing that if she reached it, the world would right itself.

No. It can't be. Shivering, she raised her hand to touch

her forehead. Perhaps it was the fever. Perhaps she was delirious.

She sat down heavily and reached for her basket. Embroidery silks sifted through her fingers, becoming snarled and knotted in her hands. She stared at the colors: bright and soft, light and dark, hopelessly tangled together.

It's impossible.

The night was silent, moonless. Then hoofbeats pounded in the yard, away from the ranch. *He's gone. You can find out—*

No!

All became quiet again. Cameo stared at the doorway into the hall, picturing the front door, the porch, the man walking—limping—away from her.

Limping. He was limping. Shot in the leg. Shot in the leg . . . Oh, dear God . . . limping away—

How cruelly ironic that her suspicions would be aroused most strongly, not in hearing him speak or by studying his expressions, but in watching him walk away.

He was gone, the hoofbeats long since faded into the darkness. She could find out for sure . . . if she wanted to. She could—

No!

It became harder to breathe as she stared at the doorway, remembering how he'd walked away. Slowly she took air into her lungs, released it, and inhaled again, then concentrated her attention on the tangle of thread in her hand. Resolutely she began to pick out one thread from the other, separating the colors, laying each freed strand just so in her lap.

Her gaze returned to the hallway, her thoughts fixed on the room next to hers. "It isn't. It can't be," she said aloud and bent her head. The threads were frayed from her picking, their luster gone. "He's different," she chanted as she fussed with the strands of silk until one by one, they pulled apart into little pieces—useless. "He's hard, and cruel, and he doesn't care."

He has dark copper hair . . . twilight eyes.

Again she touched her forehead. Abruptly she rose from the chair and walked out of the room. Tea. She needed some tea for her fever.

The door next to hers stopped her, held her attention. Tears fell and she swiped them away. The kitchen was just down the hall, close, so close. It was the fever—

No! It was that walk . . . those eyes . . .

She grasped the doorknob, held fast, turned it. *I can't do this. I don't want to know.* The crystal knob turned; the door squeaked as it swung on its hinges. *I have to know.*

Enough!

Her step was firm as she walked into Zach's room, not caring that every step shot pain through her shoulder and her breath labored with the exertion. She stood in the middle of the bedchamber Sloane had so deliberately taken over. Zach's room. It would always be his no matter who occupied it.

She felt his presence—saw it—everywhere she looked. Sloane's presence . . . and Zach's: in the shirts hanging within the open wardrobe, the rifle—a Henry Repeater— propped against the wall by the bed and the box of shells on the bedside table, the straight razor, shaving mug, and brush on the dresser. They were all different from those she remembered Zach having. But like Sloane, Zach had always left the wardrobe door open, always placed his weapons just so by the bed, and always kept his shaving gear next to the bowl and pitcher on the bureau.

She had asked him why he'd needed them when he wore

a beard. He'd handed them to her reverently, shown her
his father's name engraved on the handles. And Pigeon
had given them to her father. She'd put them away—had it
only been yesterday?

It was all different, yet it was the same. Like him.

Dammit, Zach, quit haunting me!

Pausing uncertainly, she was reluctant to look further,
afraid of what she might find, afraid she'd find nothing,
though she had to know either way.

Prayers tumbled through her mind. *Please let it be—
Please make it stop hurting. Please . . . what?*

Almost, Cameo turned to leave. How could she do this?
Why? How could it be? And if it wasn't—if he wasn't—it
would be like losing Zach all over again. If she was right,
she would still lose. She'd lose her ability to trust.

As she looked around the room, the truth seemed so
obvious, yet still in the back of her mind, she was loathe to
take her suspicions further. She needed to trust—her father, Zach, her memories of them.

Saddlebags lying in a chair caught her eye. Watching
them as if they harbored a snake about to strike, Cameo
walked across the room and opened them, then snatched
her hand back. *Stop this. Why are you afraid of the truth?*

Determined, she searched inside the saddlebags, her
movements unhurried and careful not to disturb the order
of his possessions. She found a book of Shakespeare's son-
nets, several kerchiefs, more bullets, a packet of jerky, another packet with a single half-eaten stale piece of corn
bread. *Nothing. You see? He's a drifter . . . like
Zach . . .*

He reads Shakespeare.

Softness brushed the back of her hand and she leaned
over to look more closely. It was fine linen. Softness edged

with a rougher texture. She gripped it, lifted it from the bags as if it were heavy.

Please have mercy . . .

She stared down at her hands, absorbing the shock of what she'd found, and the reality. Fear became betrayal. Doubts were replaced by fury. She shook with it, unaware that tears fell onto the scrap of fine-linen-and-crocheted-lace doily. The doily that had been missing from the bedside table in this room for six months.

Zach.

She should have known right away. How could she have been so blind, even for a few hours? Though the doily had obviously been washed many times, it was stained with blotches of faded brownish red. Blood stains. He'd come close to death. So close. She'd heard the tale over and over again in her dreams. Shot in the leg and the head. Hit his head on a rock. Blood and a mass grave. How much had been truth?

He limps.

He's alive!

The thought blurred the edges of her anger—until she also remembered that Zach and her father had let her suffer and mourn and live in a world dulled and made empty by Zach's "death." For all Zach's show of respecting her intelligence and her father's talk of trusting her abilities, neither man had trusted her enough to confide in her.

Oh, Papa, why? Did you think me such a fool?

She crumpled the doily in her hands. Damn all men to perdition. While they were off fighting wars and engaging in masculine pursuits, what did they think their women were doing? Embroidering doilies? Who did they think kept the homes and farms and ranches going? The good fairy? With an inelegant snort, Cameo stuffed the doily back into his saddlebags and marched to her room, ignoring the pain of betrayal, the elation of knowing that the truth she'd hated since Pigeon had arrived with news of Zach's death was a lie.

I don't understand.

A vase sat on the table next to the door. The same vase she had filled with wildflowers and a single satin rose to put in Zach's room. With a swing of her hand, she knocked it to the floor, and then she stared at it in disbelief. She was nineteen—too old to throw tantrums.

Damn you, Zach.

Cocking her head, she listened to heavy footsteps climb the front steps and walk across the porch. The front door creaked on its hinges as it was pushed open and she made a note to have Jorge oil it. The steps turned into the dining room. China clattered. She smiled grimly. He was taking the remaining dishes into the kitchen—something Zach would have done, but not Sloane. He came closer, paused outside her door, walked on. Minutes passed and she heard the bed ropes groan under his weight. Zach she knew, had slept on the floor during his previous stay. Her mind worked of its own volition.

Betrayed. By the two men she loved most in the world. Deceived. By those who should have trusted her. Games. Always games. Was there not a man anywhere who knew the meaning and value of honesty?

Why, Zach?

She curled up on the bed, holding her middle. Games with her life, her heart. Forgetting her shoulder, she flipped onto her back and winced. She realized that she hadn't lit a candle. Her hands began to shake. Beads of moisture broke out on her forehead. The world was such a dark place.

Fumbling for matches, she found the box and shook it open. Little sticks of wood and phosphor fell to the floor. The bed in the next room creaked. Footsteps approached the wall between the two rooms.

"Ca—Miss Fielding, are you all right?" a muffled voice asked.

She swallowed hard. "Yes, I'm fine, thank you," she replied politely as she picked up a match, struck it, held it to the wick until the flame flared and caught. So polite. So normal.

It infuriated her, that politeness and normalcy. *Yes, thank you for lying to me. Thank you for putting me through hell. Thank you for teaching me about lost hope.*

Oh, God, thank you for saving him.

She raised her hand, held it over the flame of the candle, and felt the heat as she hovered between resolution and fear. Her shoulder ached from the strain of keeping her arm raised, and she let her hand drop over the wick, extinguishing the light. They wanted to keep her in the dark. So be it.

Suddenly she knew what she would do. If she were to survive in a world of men, then she would have to learn to think like men. If Zach wanted to play games, far be it from her to spoil his fun. For the time being, she'd play it his way. And as soon as she figured out the game, she would invent some rules of her own. Perhaps it would all work to her advantage.

Too drained to undress and change the poultice on her shoulder, Cameo pulled a quilt over herself and focused on the discomfort of it, wanting to feel nothing but anger. It was the only emotion that didn't hurt beyond bearing. She would not spend her gentler feelings on a man whose truths were as false as his lies.

For the rest of the night she lay rigid in her bed, staring at the ceiling, looking for shadows and the light that created them.

Thank you, God . . .

She was fine, thank you.

So don't ask a question unless you really want the answer. Zach fell back on his bed and wished he'd had the sense to follow his father's oft-repeated advice. Tonight Cameo had not only shortened his pride by several inches but pounded it on a wet rock and hung it out to dry.

He'd spent the last three hours riding hell-bent for leather, risking his horse and his hide. Pegasus was a better night horse than most, but you just didn't take any kind of terrain at full gallop after dark unless you were either running for your life or hoping to end up in a dark hole. He'd already been there and he hadn't liked it.

He'd wanted her to need him.

No matter how fast he'd ridden, he hadn't been able to escape the memory of dinner with Cameo. Worse, he hadn't been able to escape the things she had said. Like that smart remark about men's appendages. *From what I've seen there's very little to be jealous about.*

Just how much had she seen and where? Whose *appendage* had she been referring to? Had she been so bent on gathering rosebuds that she hadn't cared who the gardener was? Or had she been referring to the time she had spied on his bath? That possibility offered little comfort as it implied that he was less than impressive. Now that he thought about it, she'd made light of the matter later that night and her only comment had been on the color of his body hair.

The remaining possibility had him gritting his teeth.

Had Cameo met someone else, loved someone else? If so, she hadn't wasted any time replacing him in her affections. He'd been away for only six months, and he knew that news of his death hadn't reached her until last month. Didn't she believe in a respectable period of mourning?

She'd said that she hadn't lost someone in the war. He'd been wondering how to broach the subject and discover how she'd taken the news of his "death." After months of thinking of nothing but Cameo, he'd needed to know if it had been the same for her. Finally he'd been given the chance. Her answer had felt like a knife in the back.

No. No one.

What in Sam Hill did that mean? he wondered. That she considered Zachary McAllister nobody? The man she'd tried to seduce, the man she'd allowed to touch and taste her? Was her memory and affection for him so insignificant that she didn't consider his death a loss? If she were to be believed, then he was the only one who had lost someone. Someone that he might never have had. Someone as false as the truths he had been telling her about Sloane.

Forget me. Forget my name. Who would have guessed that he'd be so persuasive? Who would have thought that a woman as perverse as Cameo would actually listen? She sure as shit hadn't listened to him when he said no to her advances. She'd kept him so hard that he'd been afraid his *appendage* would become as petrified as the trees in Arizona.

With an abrupt movement, he flipped onto his side and concentrated on relaxing. All he could think about was Cameo in the next room, the nights he had lain here listening to her movements and imagining what part of her body she was uncovering.

Just whose appendage had she seen? With a snarl, Zach

sat up and pulled off his shirt. At least she hadn't been impressed. She'd seemed to be fascinated with his once upon a time.

He kicked off his pants and stretched out once more. A moment later, he sat up and stared at himself. Maybe she had been talking about him.

Well, hell.

13

Weeds Among Roses

*D*amn! Damn! Damn! Cameo cursed into her pillow as she beat it with her fist. Pain surrounded her, overwhelmed her to the point where nothing else existed. It radiated up her shoulder to her neck and down to her fingers. Her flesh was swollen and hot, and ominous red streaks were creeping ever farther from the wound. Yesterday, before the funeral, the *curandera* had insisted that her wound must be opened and allowed to drain, but Cameo had ordered her out of her room at gunpoint when the evil old witch had refused to clean her knife.

The concept might have been rather unorthodox, but it had made sense. Infection allowed to run from the body was less likely to fester within. After a long night of agony, Cameo was willing to try anything as long as it didn't involve a dirty knife.

Cameo bit her lip, swallowed down her sobs, and forced her body upright on the edge of her bed. With a shaking hand, she reached for the bottle of laudanum and measured out as much as she dared. She had to work quickly, before the opiate began to dull her mind. It didn't occur to her to ask for help. The *curandera* frightened her more than the prospect of the death she would suffer if she failed.

Call Zach.

She shook her head, refusing to display her weakness to him. It seemed important to know that she could rely upon her own strength to survive.

She rose and walked to the bureau, checked the stack of clean bandages, the lantern, the open bottle of whiskey, the basin full of warm water . . . the knife. Removing the glass chimney from the lantern, she turned up the wick, passed the blade of her knife through the flame, then carefully set it across the lip of the basin. Her gaze slid to the window and she focused on the darkness outside, willing it to blanket her thoughts, smother the fear that tasted like copper in her mouth.

It couldn't possibly be worse than the consequences she would suffer if she didn't do something. Resolutely she untied her loose gown and let it slip to the floor, then pulled the poultice away from her shoulder. The red streaks had spread even more. Panic flared, choking her. *It can't be any worse. It can't be any . . .* She pulled in a deep breath, held it, fixed her gaze on the mirror and the patch of swollen flesh that throbbed with death.

For good measure, she passed the knife through the flame again, watching through the mirror to accustom herself to the reflected image. A thick strip of leather lay next to the bandages. She clenched it between her teeth and bit down hard as she washed the wound with a cloth soaked in whiskey. The knife moved slowly as she lifted it to her shoulder.

Think of nothing. Think of darkness, of silence, and how much you hate them both.

The cords in her neck stood out. Leather was a welcome

taste in her mouth. A strange fascination occupied her as she watched her image push the newly sharpened blade into flesh and draw a line of red across her shoulder. She didn't feel anything but the pain she had lived with for days. The woman in the mirror felt it, though. She could tell by the tears streaming down her face, the muffled scream that came from her throat and broke into pieces when it hit the rawhide obstacle, the chest that heaved with short, shallow breaths.

Cameo felt detached from it all as she watched the woman in the silvered glass: warm, wet cloths on the open gash; rinse and wring; wash again; press a thick bandage against the shoulder and change it when it became soaked with blood. It wasn't her. *She* felt nothing. Only that other woman suffered and cried with it. She heard nothing. The darkness and silence had come at her beckoning. Silent screams. Silent sobs. The horror of what she'd done to herself wasn't real, but an illusion. It hadn't happened.

Her body swayed. Her tongue became thick, unmanageable, her mouth dry. The laudanum, she thought dimly. How well she had timed it. She had managed to save that other woman—the one in the mirror whose skin was as white as the bandages being wrapped awkwardly around her shoulder. She wouldn't think about failure—that what she'd done might not be enough.

Light dimmed; the image became misty, insubstantial. Securing the bandage by pulling it tightly and tucking the end into a thick fold, she stumbled to the bed. Her knees gave way and she fell to the floor. Burning agony lanced through her shoulder, down her arm, into her chest, up her neck. How far away the bed seemed. Too far. Too high for her to reach. She was cold, yet hot. With all the strength left to her, she reached for the counterpane, grasped a corner and pulled. It billowed over her head, settled darkness around her.

Finally . . . finally, her pain was silent as the night.

Zach's eyes abruptly opened; he listened intently, but the silence was complete, the night undisturbed. He closed his eyes and opened them again. A scraping sound. A rustle. It was only Cameo turning in her sleep.

Except that Cameo always turned more than once—her shoulder, he reckoned. She'd land on her bad side and have to shift again. This was only his second night here, yet already he knew her habits. Earlier he'd heard her muffled sobs, her restlessness. Finally, when she'd grown quiet, he'd allowed himself to relax and find his rest. He glanced out of his window, waiting for the next sound. Nothing. Light spilled out into the yard—light from her room, unusually bright. She always slept with a light.

Something was wrong.

He shot into a sitting position, twisting his body at the same time and planting his feet into his pants arranged on the floor. On one foot and then the other, he hopped to the door as he pulled his pants up and buttoned them just enough to keep them from falling around his knees. Grabbing his gun, he ran to her room.

Her door was locked. "Cameo?" he called. Apprehension knotted his insides. Nothing stirred. He balled his fists and pounded. Silence. After tucking his gun into the waist of his pants, he backed up to the far wall and leaped forward, ramming his side into the door. The wood creaked and shuddered and held. Sam might have built his walls out of paper, but the doors might as well be steel.

Cursing, he stepped back and kicked with his uninjured leg—once, twice, three times. The solid wood splintered and swung at an odd angle on its hinges. The strain of bearing all his weight buckled his bad leg. He lurched backward into the wall. Wincing, he rubbed his thigh, then his bare foot.

The odor of soap, whiskey, and sickness permeated the air and rushed out to meet him. He scanned Cameo's room before entering. A bundle of bedclothes was rumpled on the floor. The bed was empty. His gaze swept over the bureau and stopped. Stained linen littered its surface and draped over the edge of a basin filled with reddish water. The lantern was uncovered and its wick turned all the way up. Cameo's knife lay on the floor with a blood-encrusted blade.

Dread constricted his chest and made his blood race as he identified the nightgown on the floor by the bureau.

He saw her then, her feet sticking out beneath the fallen quilt. The answers came to him with a chilling certainty as he reached her side in two strides and fell to his knees. He pulled the quilt away from her, gently turned her, and stared in horror at the blood that soaked her bandage and pooled beneath her. Her naked body was smeared with it, a sharp contrast to the paleness of her skin. He felt her pulse, checked her breathing, then sagged in relief when he found both.

Staggering under her weight, he lifted her and laid her on the bed. Her head tossed, and her mouth moved with a thready whisper. "See, Papa, I can take care of myself."

Zach groaned and pressed the heels of his hands against his eyes.

"I did it, Papa. Everything will be fine now."

He had to do something, yet he felt helpless as a babe. Rapidly he considered and rejected possibilities. The open window beckoned him. Cloud Walker. He and several other watchers were out there, lying in wait for those who would inevitably return to the ranch and wreak more havoc. Cloud Walker would know what to do.

Zach ran to the window, put his fingers to his mouth and blew. Nothing came of his effort but a hollow rush of air. He wiped his mouth, tried again, and again. More hot air. He pulled his Colt from his waistband and emptied the gun into the sky.

Minutes passed as Zach searched the room for clean bandages, and finding none, rushed to the linen press built into the end of the hall. Quilts, sheets, and woolen blankets tumbled onto his head as he pulled out a handful of napkins and a tablecloth and raced back to find Cloud Walker climbing in through the window.

"Do something—fast," Zach snarled.

Cloud Walker ran a practiced eye over Cameo. "Dear, sweet Jesus. What happened?"

"What in the hell do you think? Damned fool woman tried to be her own doctor—cut herself from here to Sunday."

"Good job," Cloud Walker commented as he bent over Cameo and cut away the soaked bandage. "Looks like she has poisoning."

Good job? Zach lunged for his cousin. "Get away from her. You don't know any more about it than she did. She's bleeding to death."

Cloud Walker grasped both of Zach's arms and pushed him out of the way. "Nope. It's slowing down, and the bleeding will wash out the poison. It's my guess that she'll be all right. Would have died in another few days otherwise."

"Your guess? What do you mean, she would have died?"

"Blood poisoning, Zach. The accepted treatment is amputation, and you can't take off a shoulder."

"She didn't say anything," Zach said in a choked voice. "I heard her crying—thought it was because of Sam." He stared down at Cameo, then with a growl, rammed his fist into the wall. "Why didn't she tell anyone?"

Cameo's head tossed on the pillow, and she mumbled, "No one to tell, Papa. The witch's knife was dirty."

Zach felt it then, her words like the brutal stroke of the same knife that she had used on herself. She had no one to tell because he had become no one, because she knew him as dead.

Another man appeared in the window. "Everyone on the ranch is awake and gathering out front. Why didn't you use our signal, Zach?"

"I wanted to get your attention fast," Zach said flatly.

"Couldn't get a whistle out, huh?"

The basin was shoved into Zach's hands as Cloud Walker moved around the room, gathering the bottle of whiskey, the cloth Zach had dumped in the chair, the scissors sticking up from Cameo's sewing basket. "I need clean water—hot—and sheets. I can't use this lace shit for bandages. While you're at it, tell the *vaqueros* you were shooting at gnats and send them back to bed." Zach walked toward the door and paused in the threshold to glance back at Cameo.

"I've seen this done before, cousin," Cloud Walker said without looking up from his task of dousing Cameo's shoulder with whiskey. "It usually works if it's not left too long."

"Makes sense," Cameo said. "I didn't do it. She did—the girl in the mirror. I saw—"

"What do you mean, it usually works?"

"Get out of here, Zach."

"Zach. The happy warrior . . . plays in the many games of life." Her eyes opened, stared at Cloud Walker. She smiled. "Oh, it's you—my guardian angel. I never told, not even Zach."

"I know. Go to sleep, Cameo," Cloud Walker ordered softly as he brushed her hair away from her forehead.

"All be as before, Love—only sleep." Cameo sighed; her eyes drifted shut.

Zach's vision blurred as he recognized the bits of prose she recited from Browning and Wordsworth—from the book he had left her. Without a word, he walked out of the room. *All be as before* . . . It was too late for that. Too much had been lost or altered. By him.

Everything had changed. Cameo sensed it before she opened her eyes and wakefulness took hold. The smells of milk poultices and mustard plasters were gone, replaced by fresh air laced with a spicy steam. Her skin felt cool, though dry and pulling over her bones. The pain had changed, too, from overwhelming torture to something between a heavy ache and a burning. Breath no longer hurt her lungs, though her chest felt tight and strained. Memory of what she'd done filled her mind with stark clarity.

He had been there—the man she'd seen only in times of trouble, her guardian angel since he'd saved her from snakebite so long ago. He had pulled her and her father from the icy creek, and taken care of them after the attack. Somehow she knew all those images were his. Cloud Walker had been his name. Walker McCloud, the prairie farmer who hadn't looked or acted like a farmer. Another deception. The thought rang loudly in her head like a warning.

She opened her eyes and looked first at the mirror. The glass was clear, free of images. The bureau was clean and neat, her brush and comb and hand mirror lying just so on its polished surface. Light and fresh air poured in from the open window. A bird sang in the tree nearest the house. She frowned at the hole punched in her wall. A snore came from across the room.

She turned her head and found Zach sprawled in a chair at the end of her bed, his bare feet propped on the brass footboard, his chin resting on his chest. Another soft snore, a twitch of his right foot. He had big feet, she thought inconsequentially. Strong feet, calloused—one was bruised, the toe swollen.

She was alive. She had to be because she knew that Zach was alive, and bruises and callouses and snores were real. Another snore began and was cut short. Zach's head snapped up; his eyes opened, already fixed on her. *Who are you?* she asked silently. *Zach or Sloane? Will I ever know?*

He stood and walked to the side of the bed, favoring his leg and bruised foot with an odd lopsided gait. His hand touched her brow, her cheek, then fell away.

"May I have some water, please?" she asked.

His chest heaved with released breath as he poured from an earthenware pitcher on the bedside table and held a glass to her lips. "Sip," he said roughly.

"How long?"

After setting the glass down, he ran his hand around the back of his neck. "A day and a night." Abruptly he turned on his heel to pace the room. "You could have killed yourself."

"No. I was very careful."

He stood wide-legged, clenched his fists at his sides, and stared up at the ceiling. "You were crazy to try it alone."

His eyes narrowed as he glanced at her over his shoulder. "Or were you fool enough to think that you could keep it a secret?" He swung around to face her. "I hope you impressed yourself, lady, because you sure as hell didn't impress me."

Warily she watched him stalk toward her, every movement speaking of controlled fury. "Why didn't you send for the *curandera?*"

"She wouldn't clean her knife."

"Why didn't you tell me that you were in trouble?" The question seemed torn from him.

"I am not accustomed to running for help every time I am in trouble, Mr. Sloane. And, I'm not accustomed to having to explain myself to the hired help."

"People just don't go around cutting on themselves," he roared.

"They do if there is no one else to whom they can run."

A red flush climbed up Zach's face even as he appeared to blanch beneath it. He took another step forward, stopped, then reached her in one long stride, and leaned over her with his fists propped on either side of her head. "Well, things are going to change. One way or another, I will know every one of your movements, every ache, every pain, every hiccup. You can either tell me yourself or I'll have Sofia and Jorge watch you and report to me on the hour."

"They won't do it." She felt his warmth surround her and thought of how easy it would be to reach up and pull him down to hold her, soothe her fears, share his strength.

"They'll do it. You're a smart girl, Cameo, but you're also willful and so damn convinced that you're alone. Those people care about you, and they'll do what they have to do to protect you."

Pressure built behind her eyes—such a foolish weakness to want to cry over his anger. The only anger she had faced in her life had always been inspired by caring and love. She recognized it now. He cared, but he didn't love. If he did, he wouldn't present himself to her as a shadow of the truth.

"Do you understand me, Cameo?"

"We speak the same language," she said flatly.

"Good. Until you're completely well, you won't go any farther than the porch . . . and I will decide when you're well."

"Fine."

His eyes widened. "What, no sass, Miss Fielding? No orders? No tantrums?"

"I never throw tantrums, Mr. Sloane."

"No? Then what do you call doctoring yourself when there's help in the next room?"

Cameo looked him up and down, as if he were a tree she had to cut down. "It worked, didn't it? I have a vague recollection of hearing your 'doctor' say I'd done a good job."

"You could have bled to death," he mumbled.

"If it pleases you to think so . . . now, if you will please excuse me, I would like to go to the water closet."

Pushing away from the bed, he hooked his thumbs in his belt. "Use the chamber pot."

"My father went to a great deal of trouble and expense to import indoor facilities. If we still have chamber pots, I wouldn't know where they are, nor would I use—" Her mouth snapped shut as he bent over and retrieved a gaily decorated porcelain basin with an elaborately curved handle. His smile was fiendish as he dangled the convenience from one finger.

"Is there anything else, *Patrona*?" Without waiting for her to reply, he set the pot on her stomach and sauntered out the door.

A moment later, she heard his footsteps fade. Chamber pot indeed! She flipped the porcelain bowl off her stomach and sat up. Dizziness rushed through her as she stood and groped for something to hold on to. Her body shook as she leaned her head against the wall and gulped in draughts of air. Nominal strength returned to her limbs, giving her confidence that she could make it down the hall.

She made it to the doorway and beyond, then was brought up short by the tall, lean figure standing outside her room. With raised brows, he offered his arm and bowed slightly. The wretch. He'd known all along that she would defy his last, humiliating order. She could brazen it out or retire to her chamber. Either choice meant defeat.

Holding her head high, Cameo slipped her hand through the crook in his arm and walked beside him to the water closet. From the corner of her eye, she saw his head turn toward her and felt his gaze gently touch her. A haughty smile curved up the corners of her mouth. Even in defeat, there could be found a measure of victory.

Victories were useless when they were empty, providing neither satisfaction nor gain on vital territory. The territory she was fighting for, Cameo discovered, was her heart, a torn battlefield she could not defend. Still, she tried. Like now, as she listened to Zach's footsteps, moving across the porch, down the hall, into the kitchen, then toward the parlor, toward her. Every day, he came to her, manager to owner, yet he treated her as if she were the owner of the ranch in name only. It had been only a week since she'd awakened to find Zach at her bedside, but it was beginning to feel like a year.

Though his tersely delivered reports set her teeth on edge, she hadn't questioned his judgment or countermanded any of his decisions. She spent the days rocking in her chair and knitting herself new woolen stockings for the coming winter as she played the part of blissfully ignorant female to the hilt. He seemed to be at ease with the arrangement. She wanted to have done with the farce.

"I'm moving the cattle to winter pasture." Zach strolled into the parlor, a mug of coffee in one hand, his hat in the other.

"Fine."

"Ash is frisky. He's been trying to get at Diamond."

"No. I won't put him to her this season. Giving birth to Twilight was too hard on her. I'll think about letting him mount one of the other mares." She bit the inside of her lip, too late. It was the first time she had taken a stand on anything, yet the Andalusians were her pride, the only part of the Fielding properties that was wholly hers. She would not jeopardize the project for the sake of pride.

"He doesn't seem to be interested in another mare." He turned his back to her. "He wants Diamond."

"He'll get over it. Stallions are not faithful by nature."

Zach slapped his hat against his thigh. "Another train of freight wagons will be heading for San Francisco in a few days."

"Mmm." She rocked faster. How she hated the game of tag their gazes always seemed to be playing.

"We're hauling more gold."

"Not surprising." Cameo said. "Is there any missing?"

"Not yet."

"Maybe they've stopped."

"Maybe they're just being more careful."

"Maybe. Either way, it's not your job to worry about the missing gold." An impatient sigh escaped her. Again, she had blundered into speaking her mind, breaking the vow of silence she'd imposed upon it.

He turned on her. "They murdered Sam."

Once begun, she couldn't seem to stop. "Yes. For that I'll find a way to make them pay, but I will not continue to risk everything Papa built for a few bars of gold." *And I don't want you killed, too,* she added silently. Such a bitter truth. Deceiver Zach might be, but he was still the man she loved. She could not mourn him twice.

His shadow loomed over her. She met his gaze and clenched her jaw against displaying her reaction to his nearness, the turbulent anger in his eyes. "You're in my light, Sloane." The name stuck in her throat every time.

"You'll make them pay?" he asked softly.

"Who else? It was my father, my land—"

"Your shoulder, your life." He slammed his hands down on the arms of the rocker and brought it to a halt on the backward swing, holding it so that she looked up at him from an almost prone position. Her head spun and her breath jerked. It had been like this in her dreams: Zach above her, gazing down at her with love and promise. Except all she saw now were impatience and anger.

"You try one more fool stunt, and I promise you won't see the light of day until the war is over."

His threat tore the dream away from her and brought her back to her senses. "I'm not going to try anything except to find an expert to discover who is responsible. The army can take over from there." She almost smiled at how easy it was to lie to a liar.

"You expect me to believe that? Since when do you ask

for help from anyone?" he asked, a bitter slant to his mouth.

She did smile then. "You misunderstand me. I'm going to hire help, not ask for it." She rocked so violently her teeth rattled as he suddenly released the rocker and stomped across the room. She stiffened her legs as her feet hit the floor to stop the motion.

"No strangers, Cameo."

"Why ever not? You're a stranger." She stared at the knitting in her lap and frowned at a dropped stitch. "Since the government won't do anything, it's quite obvious that I must."

"The government is doing something."

"Of course they are," she said in a patronizing tone.

"They've sent someone—an agent. I met him yesterday."

Her gaze jerked up to his. At his hunted expression, she tilted her head, narrowed her eyes. "They sent someone? A spy?"

He nodded curtly.

"Why didn't you tell me?"

"Because spies work in secret," he said, irony heavy in his voice. "The fewer people that know, the safer everyone is."

It had the sound of a warning, frightening her. "Spy" was such a sinister word. More lies and deceit. Sanctioned criminal activity—for the good of the nation, of course. But, what kind of man took on such a task? She'd read about them, the legends that, to the enemy, could so easily turn into nightmares, the heroes that were content to live anonymously in the shadows, a lie even unto themselves.

A thought formed and scattered before she could grasp it, a thought that bordered on suspicion.

She wasn't ready to face another problem yet, not when there were so many others that consumed her mind and depleted her energy. Immediate problems that affected people she knew. "We must find vegetables for the winter."

"I bought a farm."

"You what?"

"The Hindeman place. Jack died at Glorieta." He slanted her a glance. "Mary is going to open a boarding-house in Denver with the money I paid her."

"Just whose money did you use for your noble gesture?"

He slammed his mug down on the mantel and glared at her. "You've turned into a selfish bitch, *Patrona.*"

"If being concerned for my own people first is the definition of that word, then yes, I am a bitch. If expecting to be consulted before you make large expenditures means that I am selfish, then so be it," she said, her temper seething.

"Fine. I'll pay for the farm and you can buy its produce from me."

Again, she sighed, this time with exaggerated patience. "The Hindemans grew wheat. We have plenty of flour, and corn meal, for that matter."

"The Hindemans," he said, his voice gritty with disgust, "also have one of the biggest and best gardens in the area. They supplied Fort Union with preserved vegetables in winter and fresh in summer." He picked up his cup and frowned at finding it empty. "Mary's cellar is well stocked with jars of squash, peppers, pickles, peas, snap beans, stewed tomatoes, corn, and next month her peaches and late vegetables will be ready for harvest."

"Well, why didn't you say so?"

"You're the one who has lived here all your life. I expected you to be able to figure it out." With that, he stalked out the door.

Cameo picked up her knitting, her fingers working quickly between the four needles to pick up the lost stitch. She wished she could pick up the threads of her life as easily. Her fingers began to tremble and more stitches slipped away. Runners spread through the stocking. She sniffed, swiped at her eyes, sniffed again, and rubbed at the soreness in her shoulder. Then she set her chin at a defiant angle and began methodically ripping out her work.

Today victory belonged to Zach. She knew that Zach had expected her to rebel at his orders and find ways around them. Until today she'd succeeded in disappointing him, and she knew that her docility had been getting under his skin like a bad rash.

Unfortunately she, too, chafed at the role she had chosen to play, and her antagonism grew in direct proportion to the effort she had to make not to give her discovery of his identity away. As a result, she'd spent the days sitting in her chair by the window, soothed into frequent naps by the creak of old wood and the knowledge that he was nearby.

In truth, she had no choice but to give in to the demands of her healing body. Her lung fever seemed to be better, though the infection in her shoulder had been annoyingly slow to improve. Weakness was her worst affliction. Her body betrayed her time and again, responding to the mere sight of Zach, yet miserably slow to obey her own commands.

The only consolation she found in such infirmity was that Zach evidently thought that a feeble body meant a feeble mind. Every night, he sneaked out of the house, no doubt believing that she was none the wiser. No matter how hard she'd tried, she could not find rest while he was gone, and fell asleep only when she heard him climb into his window at the crack of dawn.

She didn't know how much longer she could stand living this way, living a lie, living on the lust for revenge. Lust, she'd discovered, had many forms and she was experiencing them all, not the least of which was for Zach himself.

Her skin prickled. Something seemed to change the peace of the room, though all was quiet. Awareness mixed with excitement crackled in the air. It was always there when he was near, a third presence lurking in the room, waiting to be welcomed. Resigned, she allowed herself to admire the sensual glide of his booted feet, his hips, the counter movement of his wide chest and broad shoulders as he drew near and set a cup of chamomile tea on the table next to her.

"Thank you." Instead of leaving again, he pulled a chair up in front of her and sat down, watching . . . always watching her. "How are you feeling?"

She shrugged. For a brief moment his gaze touched her intimately, devouring her, with a need so stark it plundered her emotions.

"Are you sleeping well?"

"Fine. Why?"

He cleared his throat, stared down at his knees, then hers, a bare inch away. "I'll have to be riding out late at night for a while. I don't want you to . . ." He cleared his throat again.

"Be disturbed?"

"Yes."

"I won't be. Are you going to meet the sp . . . the agent from the government?"

He changed the subject without answering. "About the farm—Mary had two other offers, and I had to move fast.

One was from the army. They were going to post some of their negro recruits there to keep the farm going."

Startled, she looked up. "They would send soldiers to run a farm?"

He sagged back and stared at her, then stood and walked away, his limp barely discernible. Pausing in the doorway, he reached for the hat he'd left on a peg and held it up in salute. "Negro soldiers, Miss Fielding. You'd better learn that emancipation is just a word with only as much meaning as people choose to give it." With that, he left her staring at an empty doorway.

And that said it all, Cameo thought as she remembered her father saying something similar about freedom. What good was freedom, she wondered, if trust was lost? Like her trust for Zach, and the lies that multiplied like weeds. His lies and hers—she could hardly tell them apart anymore. She bit her lip. Roses, she was learning, did not fare well in a garden of weeds.

14

A Moment's Ornament

Two days later Cameo came to the conclusion that if she were to survive in a world ruled by men, then she must learn to be as sneaky as they were. The decision was easily made after another restless night waiting for Zach to return from his nocturnal wanderings. It was better than suffering the dreams that came with sleep, dreams that whispered to her of longing and hope. She had discovered that whispers were more difficult to ignore than shouts.

The moon arced across the sky as she waited and listened and plotted. Soon she would hear the stirring that would surely come from the bedchamber next to hers. Tonight she would ease her curiosity and learn the depth of Zach's deception.

Her thoughts took a diabolical turn. She'd heard his restless tossing in the night and knew that he'd been swimming regularly in the pond fed by melting snow running down the mountains—a very cold pond—when the water in the tank was sun-warmed and more convenient for outdoor bathing. According to the talk she'd overheard from the men on the ranch, cold baths were particularly beneficial in shrinking male ardor. A wicked smile played about her mouth. Oh, yes, Zach still wanted her—even if only as a moment's ornament.

She had learned early that time was better measured in moments than in years.

The sound came from his room: a creak of bed ropes, a rustle of clothing, and the scrape of a window opening. She rose from her bed, fully clothed, gathered her pistol and knife, and tiptoed down the hall to watch from the small gun hole set in the front door.

Shadows broke from the stable—a man leading a horse, walking away from the ranch buildings. When he was far enough down the trail, she ran to the stable and into Diamond's stall. The Andalusian was the best night horse she had. Unfortunately, she was also taller than the mustangs used for working cattle. Favoring her arm, Cameo slipped the bridle over Diamond's head, then struggled with the heavy saddle, managing to drag it to where Diamond stood. It slipped her one-armed grasp as she tried to lift it to no avail. By standing on an overturned pail, she managed to sling it over Diamond's back only to have it slide off the other side.

Obviously plans of the moment were frivolous when such lofty heights must be attained. Cameo cursed under her breath and grabbed Diamond's mane as the horse sidestepped restlessly. It was either fall flat on her face or hoist herself onto the mare's back. Seeming to divine her purpose, Diamond sidled closer to her mistress. Cameo swung a leg up and over, using Diamond's mane for purchase, but she overshot the mark. Pain lanced down her arm as she frantically tried to regain her balance and failed. She squeezed her knees into the horse's barrel, held tightly, and slid down the other side to land on a prickly cushion of straw. With great care she lifted one side of her seat, then the other, checking beneath her, and breathed a sigh of relief. Thankfully, Diamond had not left a calling card buried in the hay to further cushion her fall.

Using her good arm, Cameo levered herself off the ground and dusted off the seat of the old pants she'd pulled from the depths of her wardrobe as she walked around Diamond and stepped up on the pail. She stared longingly at the saddle lying in a corner of the stall. "What do you think, Diamond? Is it worth it?" Diamond turned her head and nudged Cameo. "Of course it is," Cameo said firmly as she pressed her knees firmly into the horse's sides and paraphrased, "Faint hearts never won proud warriors."

Within minutes she was on the trail that led to the small settlement that her father had built to house a general store, a saloon, a way station, and Fielding Freight. She hung well back, keeping her eyes on Zach's distant figure.

Sure enough, she saw him disappear around the side of the freight office. The urge to quicken Diamond's pace was strong, but she fought it, knowing that riding bareback with only one good arm was dangerous enough without committing the folly of undue speed.

Her earlier suspicions had returned with a bit of memory here, a piece of logic there—fragments of truth she could no longer ignore. It kept her going forward when fatigue coaxed her to go back, and it occupied her mind while she kept her gaze on the dim shadow of the buildings.

The government has sent someone—an agent. Disguises. *Spies work in secret.* Lies. *The fewer who know, the safer everyone is.* It explained so much: his altered appearance, his two colors of hair, the way he seemed to melt into his surroundings like a shadow. She had read the stories written far and wide about the hero with a thousand faces.

The shadow warrior. It made a bizarre kind of sense.

Never had she so wanted to be wrong, yet she couldn't dismiss it out of hand. She blinked back the cursed tears that had been so close to the surface the two weeks. Not Zach. Oh, please, don't let it be Zach, she prayed. The entire Rebel army was after the man in the stories, and if they caught him, he would hang. Southern sympathizers in the territories had even put a price on his head, though his true identity was not known. *For both our sakes, forget me, forget my name. . . .*

As if she could forget, she thought bitterly.

Diamond stopped at the side of the freight office that faced the open plains. Pegasus stood quietly at the hitching rail; his ears pricked at their arrival. Cameo glanced around quickly to make sure that she was unobserved, then swung her leg over Diamond's neck and slid down from her perch.

There was no light in the building, no light anywhere. Walking softly, she crept up to the barred rear window and stood to its side. She sensed his presence before she saw him, a shadow moving stealthily around the room, testing the weight of various crates and barrels, avoiding obstacles as if he had the light of high noon to see by. She peered into the corners of the room, searching, and wanted badly to discover that her suspicions were mere musings, that in this instance he had been honest and there truly was an agent.

But he was alone in the building. No meeting had taken place.

A loud bang echoed from the saloon, followed by footsteps. Zach tensed and walked softly toward the window. Cameo flattened her back against the rough siding and bit her lip to keep from crying out. Waiting, barely breathing, she listened to the crunch of boots over coarse dirt, the sound magnified on the prairie and scattered in all directions. A creak. Silence. Her mouth dried. Where was the intruder? Where was Zach?

For long minutes she stood there, barely breathing, her muscles aching from tension, her gaze darting around her.

More creaks. More steps. Another loud bang. Cameo breathed deeply at the realization that it had simply been one of the teamsters making a trip to the necessary. Cautiously she peered around the edge of the window, squinting as she searched for Zach's form.

Evidently he'd divined the source of the noise sooner than she had, for he was bent over a barrel, a crowbar in his hands. His movements were fluid, soundless, as he pried open the lid and set the heavy metal bar down, each furtive action evidence of split-second forethought.

Carefully he lifted out pieces of china from the top of their container, then slid his hand down inside, searching the contents by touch without dislodging them. She barely heard the rustle of straw packing as she stared, fascinated by the ease and patience with which he conducted his search. Such large hands to work so gently among delicate things. Everything he did was smooth and practiced, dramatic in its subtlety. Heat flowed through her body as she watched him bend over and run his hand around the inside walls of the crate, then pause.

A dull gleam startled her as Zach's hand emerged from the barrel, an oblong shape grasped between his fingers. He set it down and struck a match, shielding its flare within the cup of his palm. Again color flashed briefly, then faded back into the shadows as the flame died.

Her stomach rolled and knotted. Gold bars were packed with the china destined for the luxury-hungry nouveau riche in California. Stolen gold bars that had been shipped in their own crates from Denver City. She sagged back against the plank siding and stared into the darkness, stunned by the implications.

No wonder they hadn't been able to find the missing ingots. They had been checking the shipments as they arrived, finding them intact. The gold was being removed from the strongboxes—one or two from each—after that, and then repacked in barrels of china and crystal, perhaps even furniture, and likely received by a Confederate agent in California. Who would have thought to search the shipments a second time? Who, that is, but Zach?

Or had her father also made the discovery, and been murdered for it?

Dazed, she stared at the rough wooden wall of the adjacent building. Someone in Denver City had supplied one of her employees with keys to the strongboxes. Someone who worked for her was shifting the gold to other, more innocuous containers and delivering it to the enemy. Someone close.

She hadn't considered the possibility that their enemy might be someone who actually knew her and had probably spoken to her father every day, a man—or men—who had been paid by him, trusted by him. The world seemed to grow smaller and darker, a stifling world closing in on her. She couldn't catch her breath. Her heart beat a heavy dirgelike rhythm. The murdered cows, the ambush, the loss of their much needed vegetables, the health and well-being of innocent families threatened by someone they all trusted.

Sound penetrated her distress: rustling and grunts and shuffling in the dirt. Animal sounds. Had someone discovered the horses? Disregarding caution, she pushed away from the building and pulled her gun from its holster as she ran around the side of the freight office.

Where she had left two horses, two distinct shapes in the darkness, there was only one, rising and undulating like a two-storied structure split between floors. The horses had discovered each other. She stopped a safe distance from their heaving bodies. Too late, she remembered that Pegasus had not been gelded. With a final heave, Pegasus took his pleasure, lurched from Diamond's back and took his place at the rail he'd pulled from its supports in his frenzy to get at Diamond.

It was the last straw. Blind, unreasoning anger consumed Cameo as she stormed over to the horses, her gun dangling from her hand. "You randy beast," she raged, then lowered her voice to a whisper. "Five years of careful breeding will be wasted by your lust. I want thoroughbreds, not bastard half-breeds." Thunking Pegasus on the forehead, she ranted on, giving him all the fury she'd had to contain over the last few weeks. "You're just like your misbegotten master, taking without a by-your-leave—"

Pegasus raised his lips in a parody of a smile and snorted. Diamond answered with a soft whuffle.

"Harlot!" Cameo said. "This is not a breeding pasture, but an . . . an *alley!* I'd shoot that rutting ass now but—"

"It would wake the teamsters," a raspy whisper interrupted.

Cameo nodded. "It would wake the . . ." Her mouth fell open and then clamped shut. The rest of her tirade was lost in dawning horror. She whirled around, her eyes wide. "Oh, it's you."

"Fortunately." Zach stood loosely, his right knee bent,

his hands on his hips. She'd learned to distrust that easy manner of his.

"We've got to get out of here," she said breathlessly as she untied Diamond's reins and led her to the porch steps where she could mount more easily.

Nothing betrayed Zach's mood to her—an ominous sign. With undue haste she awkwardly pulled herself onto her mount. "I'm going now." Without waiting for his reply, she turned Diamond toward the trail that would take her back to the valley. At Zach's curt nod, she nudged Diamond's sides with her heels and rode away.

Of course, she thought with resignation, he would never let her off so easily. Pegasus drew up beside them, Zach a tall shadow on his back, staring straight ahead, his mouth set in a tight line.

This was not the time for meekness.

With that in mind, Cameo attacked. "Do you know what that rutting beast of yours did?"

"I can guess."

"He raped Diamond."

"He scented Diamond," Zach corrected. "She's an invitation for any stallion who can get to her."

"Invitation! She was tied to the rail."

Zach shrugged. "She's bigger than Pegasus by a hand. She could have thrown him off if she was disinclined to accommodate him." He grabbed the reins from Cameo's hand and pulled Diamond to a stop. "And what are you doing out here, *Patrona?* Taking the air?" His voice was low, dangerous, tightly controlled. Escape seemed to be a wise course to follow—with all haste.

"I'm snipe hunting," she snapped and grabbed back the reins, kicking Diamond into a run, wanting to get as far away from Zach and the settlement as she could. The place was no longer familiar to her, no longer a pleasant sight full of happy memories. Betrayal tightened her throat and pounded in her head as she pointed Diamond toward home and wondered if traitors nested there, too.

Heedless to the need for caution, she leaned low over Diamond's neck and kicked her into a faster pace. Her hair streamed out behind her, as wild and tangled as her thoughts. Nothing was safe. No one could be trusted. Except Zach. The irony of it made her laugh. Zach the shadow, the liar, the man who had betrayed her heart, was also the only man she could trust. Now she understood why a wanderer like Zach had taken on the guardianship of a ranch, a freight business, and a moonstruck girl who didn't have the sense to know that stars were not diamonds in the sky. Government business. An assignment to be carried out by order of the Secretary of War.

Such a bitter truth in the midst of all the deception. A truth she wished to be a lie. She urged Diamond to more and more speed and closed her eyes, blinding herself to danger, willing her mind to become equally blind.

She didn't hear the hoofbeats or the shout ordering her to stop. A vise gripped her around the waist. She felt weightless, suspended, then a jolt. She cried out as her shoulder slammed against something hard, solid—a man's chest, and beneath her a man's lap. She knew that lap, recognized the familiar soap-and-leather-and-man scent. There was no mistaking her peculiar mixture of feelings— safety and apprehension, anticipation and dread.

Her stomach lurched and seemed to go on without her as he reined in his mount. His body was rigid with anger, his arms holding her far too tightly. She squirmed in an effort to loosen the constriction of his arms.

He tightened his grip and swung her around as if she

were a rag doll to sit sideways across his thighs. Warily she raised her eyes to his face. Why didn't he yell at her and get it over with? Then she could yell back at him and release some of the rage and heartache she felt over the treachery of men. But all he gave her was a hard glare and a silence that devastated her. He looked as her father had when she'd committed a foolish act that worried him.

Pressure built behind her eyes—that wretched weepiness that had sorely afflicted her lately. Her chin quivered. She bit her lower lip to contain the sob rising in her throat.

Cupping her chin between thumb and forefinger, Zach lifted her face. "Are you going to be sick?"

She shook her head, gulped a draught of air. "I'm going to cry."

He looked away, his mouth grim. "I'd rather you'd be sick," he muttered, but his arms wrapped around her protectively.

That simple act undid her. Protection. Safety. The feeling that all was right as long as she was in his arms. A sob slipped past her control, then another.

"It won't work, Cameo," he warned and lightly spurred Pegasus into a slow walk. "Here." He shoved a handkerchief at her and stared ahead resolutely. "It damn well won't work."

She buried her face in his shoulder and cried out a year's worth of anguish.

"Oh, hell." Zach pulled on the reins, took the bandanna from her, wiped her face, held her, and stroked her hair. "This isn't going to make a difference."

"N-n-n-o."

"You haven't got the sense God gave a rock. I'm going to tie you to your bed, or lock you in your precious water closet."

"I don't want to come out—ever. I don't want to see any more. Why did I have to know the truth?"

"Because you think it's the only goddamn virtue that counts."

"It isn't. I hate it. I don't want to know anything—"

Careful of her shoulder, he pried her away from his shoulder. "That's enough, *Patrona,*" he said harshly. "It's too late for you to be playing the timid little girl. . . . Now squeeze out that last tear so we can go home."

The utter lack of sympathy and understanding in his tone silenced her sobs. "I wish I were timid and stupid and blind."

"So do I," he said. "Then you'd lose the ranch and I could get on with my life."

Stunned at the sharply delivered cruelty, she raised her head, hiccuped, and swiped at the tears on her face with a corner of her shirt. His gaze was turned away from her, fixed on some unseen point on the horizon. That hurt most of all. "Then, leave now."

He fixed his hat low over his brow and shook his head. "I will when you turn timid, stupid, and blind and lose the ranch."

Cameo saw a small twitch of his mouth and peered under his hat. His eyes had just a hint of a twinkle. Relief swamped her. He was still the same Zach—the one who had always found a way to scare the fear out of her, the one who cared enough to make the effort. Somehow it righted her world, made it familiar again. She sighed and confessed, "I'm really a coward."

"Spineless," he agreed.

She glanced down, hiding the beginnings of a watery smile, and plucked at her trousers. "I think I've just thrown my first *real* tantrum."

He nodded. "You did a hell of a job . . . now will you turn around so we can get home?" Without waiting for her to comply, he reached around her to cup the underside of her knee and swing her leg over the neck of his horse.

"I'll ride my . . ." she looked around. "Where's Diamond?"

"Home by now, and a hell of a lot safer than if you were riding her."

"We were fine. I didn't ask you to rescue me."

"I rescued the horse. I'd just as soon let you walk home."

"I knew what I was doing."

"If you believe that, then you are stupid."

Cameo tossed her head, her hair whipping him in the face as she glared up at him over her shoulder. "That," she said with raised brows, "makes us quite a pair."

His arms tensed on either side of her as he picked up the reins and clicked his tongue for Pegasus to move on. "Yes, Cameo, that makes us quite a pair."

It was a rough ride home. The roughest he'd ever had, Zach thought as he blew another strand of Cameo's hair away from his mouth. And long. Funny, but he didn't remember the ranch being so far away from the settlement. Every dip seemed like a ditch, every rock like a boulder with Cameo's body fitted to his like an iron maiden, pressing into him, rubbing and torturing him.

Visions of strangling Cameo were giving way to more carnal images. Her bottom had slid backward, pressing into him with a soft warmth and a suggestive sway as she gave over her body to the movement of the horse. The rub of her soft seat on him was like the friction of a match on stone, and she radiated enough heat to rival a bonfire. Only one thing could feel better than this. The one thing he couldn't have as long as he was Sloane. Beads of perspiration formed on his brow. His forearms grazed the sides of her breasts as he directed Pegasus over the pitted terrain. Dammit! He was supposed to be rigid with anger, not desire.

He focused on the reasons for that anger, hoping it would keep him from flipping her around and doing what he knew was next to impossible to do on a saddle. Talk about stupid.

She thinks you're Sloane, he told himself. And never mind her little declaration that she hadn't lost anyone in the war. More than once in the last few nights, he'd heard her cry out in her sleep—for Zach. He should be satisfied by that, but it only made him feel lower than the devil's cellar.

He didn't know who he hated more: Zach or Sloane.

As for Cameo, he still didn't know how he felt about her little adventure into spying. He was supposed to be angry, but relief was stronger. Relief that she hadn't been caught by anyone but him. She had no business courting danger as if it were a reluctant lover. If anyone had seen her tonight, her life wouldn't have been worth the powder to blow it to hell. He grimaced as she shifted and snuggled deeper against his groin.

Damn. Why didn't she concentrate on courting him, as she had six months ago? This time he wouldn't be reluctant. This time he'd gladly let her draw blood with her thorns for the pleasure of plucking the rose. Except she would be courting Sloane rather than Zach, and that would bring another kind of agony.

Hell.

Her head fell back against his chest and rolled to the

side, her hair whipping around his face and blowing into his mouth. Her body became boneless, conforming to his like a down quilt. He gritted his teeth as he shifted farther back in the saddle. The rim dug into him and he slid forward again. Damn contrary woman was sound asleep while he literally—and painfully—grew too big for his britches.

Again she slid backward, pushing into him until he wasn't sure where he ended and she began. If he thought that Cameo knew what she was doing, he'd teach her how to play with fire. The soft lap of water caught his attention, and he glanced to his left, surprised to see the pond yawning black against the yellowing grass. If he jumped in the frigid water now, it would surely evaporate into steam. . . .

The ranch buildings took form in the darkness, looming close and welcoming. Zach sighed in relief and spurred Pegasus into a trot. Let the movement jar Cameo awake. It was little enough revenge for the torment she was inflicting on him.

Zach reined in at the hitching post in front of the house and bent to her ear. "Cameo, wake up."

She stirred immediately and looked around. "Oh. We're home."

"Hold on." Standing in the stirrups, Zach swung his leg over Pegasus's rump and dismounted, grimacing as his feet hit the ground. It felt as if a cannonball had lodged in his groin. With a grim set to his mouth, he grasped her waist and lifted her out of the saddle. He stared down at her as her body slid slowly, provocatively down the length of his. Her nipples pressed into his chest as she stared back, her half-closed eyes sultry, her mouth parted. She looked as ready as he was, and twice as willing. . . .

Before the significance of that hit him, she pried his fingers from her waist and stepped back. Her expression was satisfied and taunting all at once as she climbed up the steps with a jaunty sway to her hips. At the door she turned her head and tossed him a glance over her shoulder. "I may have been hasty in my judgment of a man's appendage. I'll think on the matter."

With slow, lazy deliberation, he tipped back his hat and flashed her a devilish grin. "Don't light the fuse on a cannon, *Patrona,* unless you can handle the recoil."

She tilted her head. "It's simple enough to jump out of the way, Sloane." She disappeared through the door, then peeked out again. "I'm sure Diamond is in her stall. Take care of her, please."

He stared at the closed door, his eyes narrowed as he wondered whether she had just issued an invitation or a warning. One thing was sure, though. By the time he finished with the horses, it would be time to start another day, and he'd been up since dawn.

Well, hell.

15

Bottom of the Night

No! No more! Cameo cried out in her dream, praying that it was a dream, yet knowing that if she opened her eyes it would be all too real. She lay in her bed, unable to stop listening, unable to deny the screams and crashes of destruction coming from the yard.

Men's voice shouted orders and warnings. Another shrill scream vibrated through the air. Sounds of hooves pounding, wood splintering and giving way, thrashing bodies of horses and men followed in rapid succession until she couldn't distinguish one from the other. A door slammed and the slap of bare feet pounded down the hall, and she knew it was Zach running to the door without waiting to put on his boots.

No dream, then, she knew, for only in passion and love did Zach inhabit her fantasies.

Moisture beaded on her brow as she kicked off the covers and bolted from the bed. Without pausing to don a robe and slippers, Cameo followed the noise and ran across the broad porch only to stop short at the sight in the yard. She focused on the stable with its heavy doors hanging askew on broken hinges, unable to comprehend the scene of violence and madness and a world run amok. She tore her gaze away from the smashed door and forced herself to accept what she saw.

Her prize Andalusians had gone mad. Streaks of silver whirled and leaped and bucked in demented frenzy as they collided and attacked and blurred into a haze of sweat-foamed coats and bloodied flesh. Their hooves pounded into the ground and against wooden rails and splintered the bones of the men in their paths. Ash, her favored stallion, pitched and spun like a dervish. Mares and colts ran in terror, their eyes rolling back in their heads. Unable to get close enough to control the animals, the *vaqueros* stood well away, holding wounded arms and legs and heads, their eyes wide with fear, their lips moving in silent prayers.

Only Zach dared proximity with the crazed horses—moving first to one downed animal, then to another. Seeing that Ash was dangerously close to a jagged protrusion of what was once a stout fence post, he ran toward the horse and waved his arms, trying to prevent Ash from being impaled on the point.

His limp became more pronounced with every step he took.

Cameo found her voice. "No . . . don't . . . go back—"

He turned his head as he ran. "Get in the house, now!" The hem of her gown caught on her toe as she stumbled off the step and landed facedown in the dirt. Pain ripped through her shoulder, paralyzing her. Gasping to catch her breath, she lay there, hearing nothing but her own whimper and the sound of hoofbeats that grew louder and louder.

"Cameo, roll! Move!"

She looked up at Zach's shout, watched in fascinated horror as Ash swerved from the broken fence and stampeded toward her. No time. She couldn't pull herself up with her bad arm, couldn't find the strength to lever herself out of the way.

"Dammit, Cameo. Get the hell out of there." Zach shouted as drew his gun from his holster and ran toward her, his leg dragging badly.

Her voice was an unintelligible croak as she shook her head. "Stay away. You'll be killed."

Zach stopped between her and the horse, his legs planted wide apart, his body tight. She raised her head, watched from between Zach's legs as the stallion bore down on them. Ash bared his teeth and his eyes glowed with unholy light as his shriek filled the night like a trumpet of doom. The stallion skidded to a halt and raised his forelegs high, pawing the air above Zach's head.

Cameo belly-crawled the few feet to where Zach stood, and reached out, ignoring the pain in her shoulder. Her vision blurred, softening the edges of panic and reality. Motion became slow and graceful, a macabre dance in the bottom of the night. Dimly she watched as Zach bent his knees in a crouch, raised his gun, and fired point-blank into Ash's chest.

The crack of gunfire echoed and bounced off the walls of her mind, but found no place to lodge within her singular thoughts. Ash's eyes rolled back as he shrieked once and then was silent, his heart pierced by a bullet. His great body seemed suspended for a moment as his blood streamed to the ground. Then his hooves descended— slowly it seemed—aimed for Zach's head.

With sheer force of will, Cameo twisted her body, brought her legs around, and kicked at the backs of Zach's legs. Only one thing was clear. Zach could not die, not again. She wouldn't allow it.

His legs buckled from her blow, bringing him to his knees. It wasn't enough. Still, Ash's hooves descended toward Zach.

Cameo moaned as she pulled herself to her knees and reached out with both arms. With all her strength, she wrapped her arms around Zach's legs and used her body to tip him over, away from the stallion crashing onto the ground.

Dust rose from the impact, choking her. Breath whooshed from her lungs as Zach's body landed on top of her. She felt something tear, heard the sound of ripping flesh from inside herself. Stunning pain raced up her neck, down her arm; a sticky warmth spread over the top of her gown. She lay there, aware of nothing but the agony and the relief of feeling Zach's body pressed into hers, warm and alive.

The weight eased as he propped himself up on his elbows, and stared down at her. She would have lifted her hand and touched his face, but movement was beyond her. Welcome and reassuring, his breath touched her, hard, fast gulps of air. Pain was nothing. Fear dissolved. Strength melted away from her. The night seemed to become deeper, darker. The noises around them seemed to become distant and hollow.

"I'd . . . like . . . to . . . tan . . . your . . . hide," he muttered between breaths.

"Not now. I think I'm going to faint."

His expression changed to something softer, gentler. His hand brushed back her hair, cupped her cheek. "Don't," he ordered. "Don't you dare." Straddling her, he ran his hands over her, checking for broken bones.

"That's nice," she murmured. The pain had diminished to a burning ache. Zach's touch warmed and soothed her.

"Your wound has opened," he said grimly.

"Your fault." Her tongue felt like a dry ball of wool in her mouth. "You're heavy."

Another cry rent the air. Cameo turned her head toward the sound and saw Diamond fall to her knees and lunge back up again. "Save my horses . . . please."

Zach cursed and barked orders at the *vaqueros,* breaking them out of their prayers, drowning out their panic. The men moved all at once, coiling lassos, snapping whips, firing their guns into the air.

For the first time, Cameo noticed other figures among her *vaqueros.* They worked as silently as phantoms and began herding the horses toward the corral. Cameo sighed. They were here, her gentle guardians—the Others, who were always nearby and seemed to belong nowhere else. Everything would be all right now.

The world came back into focus, a merging of lines and shapes she could recognize as Zach rose to his feet, then bent to lift her in his arms. He cursed as he staggered under her weight.

"No, the horses."

"Screw the horses," he snarled and carried her into the house.

Zach's stomach felt like a tangled bale of wire as he laid Cameo on her bed and stared down at the blood soaking through her nightgown. The wound Cloud Walker had left open to drain had surely ripped all the way open. Now the healing process would have to begin all over again. And this time Cloud Walker was at the mesa, too far away to hear a whistle or a gunshot.

He was on his own.

"Stay put," he ordered and turned toward the door. Damn her. She had no regard for her own safety or his sanity.

He grabbed some sheets from the linen press and returned to her room. She was watching the door, calm, with a little smile on her paste-pale face. "You don't even have the sense to be scared," he said. He'd feel a lot better if she was was tied up in knots as he was.

"Of you?"

He snorted. "We might have to cauterize," he said brutally.

"It'll heal. Cloud Walker can—"

"He's not here."

"Oh." She swallowed. "What does that mean?"

"It means that I have to sew you up."

"I'm sure it's not serious enough for that," she said hastily. "It doesn't hurt—"

"It damn well does hurt," he shouted.

"All right, it hurts a little," she agreed, her tone reasonable, as if she thought him as demented as the horses and needing to be humored. "Actually, it's not pain—just burning, and my nightgown is sticking. I think the bleeding has stopped."

He glared at her.

"You're limping," she continued. "Did I hurt you?"

Refusing to dignify that with an answer, Zach tossed the sheets on the bed and leaned over her. He grasped the neckline of her gown and with one, swift motion, tore it down the middle.

That got her attention, he noted with satisfaction. Her eyes widened and she bunched the edges of fabric together in her hand. He smiled as he opened up her fingers one by one and moved her hand away. With slow deliberation, he held her gaze as he inched one side of the gown away, exposing her shoulder and the rise of a breast.

She sucked in her breath as the cloth tugged at her skin and the wound that had broken open again. Sweat beaded his upper lip as he slid his gaze to her shoulder, expecting the worst, and finding relief. The bleeding had slowed to a trickle and the wound had opened only partway.

"You're lucky," he said, his voice thick. "That fool stunt you pulled could have gotten us both killed."

"I beg your pardon?"

"You should, lady. If you'd stayed in the house where you belong, none of this would have happened." It felt good to cut loose and tear into her now that he knew she'd be all right.

"You'd be nothing but mush in the dirt if I'd stayed in the house," she said, her voice coated with frost.

"I was fine until you ran out there screaming like a banshee and spooking everything that moved."

"You had no business in the middle of those horses. At least the *vaqueros* had the sense to stay clear."

"Sense? *Sense?*" Zach sloshed water on a piece of cloth and cleaned her shoulder. "You wouldn't know sense if it walked up and handed you a calling card . . . hold still." Squinting, he poked thread at the eye of a needle and missed.

With a sound of disgust, she snatched them out of his hands and licked the end of the thread before sliding it through the tiny eye and knotting the ends. "I had enough sense to save your stubborn hide."

"And look where it got you."

"You weren't supposed to fall on me."

"It beat the hell out of rocks and dirt," he said as he

fixed his gaze on her shoulder and the rise of her breast bared by the tear in her gown. Beneath the fine cloth, her nipples puckered and hardened as he watched. A pink flush spread over her skin and he followed it up to her face, seeing no evidence of embarrassment in her expression.

With a muttered curse he grabbed a sheet and whipped it open over his lap. Her breasts weren't the only things that were swelling and getting hard. His mouth curled in mockery as he shredded the linen into strips and quickly grabbed another sheet to cover his arousal. He wanted to cover himself with his hands, cross his legs—anything to keep her from seeing exactly where his thoughts were coming from. But it was too late. Her eyes were wandering over the lower part of his body and she had a knowing-as—Eve smirk on her face.

Why couldn't she howl and complain so he could keep his mind on patching her up?

"It's only one little shoulder," she said, eyeing the mound of bandages, then the growing mound in his pants. "What else are you planning to bandage?"

"One shoulder, one woman, one smart-mouth," he growled as he glared at the threaded needle she dangled in front of him. Christ, his hands weren't even steady enough to do that simple chore. How in the hell was he supposed to sew Cameo up without botching it? He glanced away from Cameo, afraid she might see his hesitation, the damned weakness that always sneaked up on him when she was hurt or upset.

It stuck in his craw how one mule-headed, crazy woman could reduce him to a lily-livered fool.

"Um, do you know what you're doing?"

"You'd better hope so," he said as his gaze caught on a dark bottle on her dresser. The laudanum. She'd need that while he sewed her up. Hell, he needed it, too—to make her insensible and hopefully silent. The sheet and pile of bandages fell into a heap on the floor and tangled in his feet as he rose. With barely controlled violence, he kicked them out of the way and reached for the laudanum. Sitting back down on the side of the bed, he pulled the cork and held the bottle out to her. "Drink up."

"No, thank you," she said. "I don't need it."

"Yes, you do." He poured some into a spoon and shoved it at her. "Swallow this, then keep your mouth shut and don't move." His eyes narrowed as her hand crept toward the blanket, not quite reaching it. "I said, hold still." With a flick of his wrist, he flipped the blanket over her. "Is there anything else, your highness?"

"I don't see why you're so angry. I'm the one who's hurt, not you."

Exactly, Zach thought. "No thanks to you. Hang on. This will hurt." He pulled the edges of her wound together and stuck the needle through, talking to keep himself from thinking about what he was doing. "If you want to get rid of me that bad, there are better ways to do it."

He stitched and winced, stitched and winced—a dozen times in all—examined his handiwork, and knotted the thread. Alarmed by her silence, he glanced up to see if she was still conscious. She was. Her lip bled where she had bitten it and moisture welled in her eyes. When he put aside the needle and thread and began to bandage her, she tilted her head to the side with a look of perplexity and something else—something innocent and honest. He didn't like that look. As she took a deep breath and opened her mouth to speak, he almost cringed.

"I wanted to keep you with me," she said, her voice soft,

trembly, her expression sober and full of wonder, as if she'd just made an important discovery.

Zach felt as if he'd just been cut in two, each part left too far from the other for them to merge. Sweet Jesus, but the words sounded good. He just wasn't crazy about the man they'd been aimed at.

Sloane, not Zach.

Something seemed to be lodged in his throat as he stared down at Cameo, the slow, steady burn in her eyes, the feelings she couldn't hide—or didn't want to hide. . . .

Feelings for a man who didn't exist.

Rage erupted, overwhelming what little reason he had left. She was giving herself to him with silent eloquence. And he could see, too, that she was resigned rather than accepting. That was a twist of the knife he could have done without.

"I won't always be around," he said, a savage twist to his mouth.

"It doesn't seem to matter."

"You don't know me."

"That doesn't seem to matter either."

Another brutal turn of the blade, leaving him defenseless against her simple honesty. He sprang up from the bed. He had to stop this before she made a final slash upward with that dull-edged blade she called a tongue.

"This is crazy."

"Necessary."

"What?"

"Crazy or not, it's necessary. As you said: you won't always be around."

Raking his fingers through his hair, he glared at her. *Necessary.* The same word with the same meaning that she'd tossed out at Zach six months ago in Spirit Canyon.

If he could be Zach again, he'd think it was necessary, too. But he was Sloane, a bastardization of a man he didn't know anymore, a man who had died, and been forgotten with the changing of the seasons. Maybe to Cameo's way of thinking that had been necessary, too.

He really hated that word.

Without further comment he snuffed out the lantern and stormed out of Cameo's bedroom to seek whatever peace he could find. And in the bottom of the night he lay on his bed, his hands behind his head, listening to Cameo's movements as he had before, in another life, another time, another dream.

16
The Loudest Lie

She stood in the doorway, a wraith silhouetted by darkness in her white gown. Long, heavy braids fell over her shoulders, and were tied at the ends with satin bows—a child's coif, giving the illusion of youthful innocence and trust. Her hands were clasped at her waist, as if she needed to hold fast against their trembling. Only her eyes belied the image of uncertainty.

He knew why she had come.

He should have given her more laudanum and then taken a swig of it himself.

Zach lay still, waiting for the next thrust of her honesty, wishing that he could meet it and end the torment his own lies had brought upon him.

Cameo stepped into the room and paused again, like a child afraid to voice her need. He knew that, too. Her plain speaking two hours ago left no doubt as to its nature. Since he'd stomped out of her room as if he'd been shot in the butt, he'd been trying to figure out what to do about it.

Two hours wasn't nearly enough time. All he could do now was come up with ten good reasons why she had to get the hell out of his room. Judging from the set of her chin, he might need more than ten.

"I don't want to be alone anymore."

He closed his eyes and swallowed. Reasons and excuses deserted him in the face of a truth he understood all too well. He didn't want to be alone, either. Giving in to it, he sat up and held the covers up in invitation.

A small whimper escaped her as she came to him. She climbed up on his bed and scooted over to him, then sat, all vulnerability and awkward silence, with the pillow behind her back and her hands folded on top of the quilt he pulled over her. She didn't move. He was afraid to move, to touch her and discover once and for all that she wanted Sloane and Zach had simply been a passing season in her life.

He heard her take a deep breath and waited for the truth to do him in.

"How is your leg?" she asked as her hand slipped beneath the covers and inched along the length of his thigh, kneading gently with clammy fingers.

His hand clamped down on hers through the blanket and squeezed. "It's fine. Just fine."

Her busy fingers stilled, and her hand appeared in her lap again.

Staring straight ahead, Zach sat stiff as a board and thought of how unnatural it was for a man to be in bed with a woman and not know what to do with her.

"Dammit, do something," she said as fiercely as she had that long ago day when they'd met and held their guns on one another.

Startled, he looked at her, a mistake, he knew, as he saw the unwavering determination in her expression.

"I can't do this anymore. It's awful—not knowing what

to do or how . . ." Her voice faltered as she stared straight ahead. "I'm a woman, Sloane. I want to feel like one, but you'll have to help me . . . just this once. Then I'll know how to do my part."

That stumbling little speech so bravely delivered defeated him. He'd rejected her twice and been diminished each time. Zach or Sloane—it didn't seem to matter just then. He existed. Cameo knew him to be real. He needed to feel real.

"Cameo," he said softly, "you make it sound like we're going to plant a field."

She smiled and tilted her head. "Plant a field. No. Just one flower—a rose."

The way she said it told a story of love and loss and acceptance, their story before it had ever begun. He knew then that Sloane was an understudy in her dreams, that Zach belonged where Sloane did not. It didn't matter. Later, it might. Later, he would call himself a fool for giving in to the lies they both were living in that moment. But not now.

"A wild rose," he dared to say as he raised his arm and curved it around her, careful to angle it downward toward her waist to avoid pressure on her shoulder. Her sigh was a gentle breeze on his bare chest as she cuddled up against him, nothing more than that—a simple gesture of trust.

Idly he stroked her braids, blindly exploring the shape and texture of the coiled skeins of hair. He reached over with his other hand and rubbed a satin bow between his fingers, feeling the silken slide, the feminine delicacy of the ribbons. With a tug, he untied the bow holding the strands together.

One by one he probed each curve of the braid with his finger, then combed through it, smoothing the plaits as they fell free. Her sigh shuddered; her body grew pliant and molded to his side.

The first braid was free and he combed his hand through the crimped fall of hair from her scalp to the ends over and over again, lingering on her head, massaging away her tension. Nothing could make him hurry through the fantasy come to life—Cameo in his arms, nothing between them but a thin layer of finest lawn and the hope that with her he would find himself.

The remaining braid lay between his shoulder and her head. He pushed away the covers and gently shifted her to lie across his lap, her head cradled on his chest. Her eyes closed, not in sleep, but in the contentment he saw on her face. With the same leisurely care, he untied the ribbon and worked his fingers through the plaits, then fanned her hair across his chest. As if divining his thoughts, Cameo rolled her head from side to side, the strands sliding over his skin, clothing him like silk blowing in a gentle breeze.

He bent to touch her brow with his mouth, then, with his finger crooked under her chin, tipped up her head and kissed her eyelids.

Her arm lifted, wrapped around his neck, and drew him nearer as her lips parted and her tongue traced the outline of his lips. Blood heated in his veins and pooled in his groin until he swelled and hardened and pressed into the softness of her bottom. Her hand fluttered to the neckline of her gown. He pushed it away to work the buttons free, slow . . . so painfully slow.

Anticipation was a luxury he would not deny himself or her. Baring one breast, he stared at her nearly translucent skin, the web of tiny blue veins beneath the flesh, the velvet texture of the rose-hued center. Such torture not to touch, not to taste. His hand brushed her gown away completely so that it formed a wide vee that narrowed just below her navel. Such teasing glimpses of what was veiled by purest white.

Her eyes opened, then became liquid green as she watched his gaze slide over her. A flush darkened her nipples and tinted her skin with heat. He knew then that heaven could blaze with fire.

Like a rose, she bloomed under his palm, her nipple the puckered heart of the flower, a miracle that could nurture the passion of a man and feed his longing for other miracles.

At her moan he lowered his head, took her into his mouth, slid his tongue around her, drew in her sweetness, warmed himself with her response. He spent forever tasting her, inhaling the warm fragrance of her skin, then trailed downward with his tongue, between her breasts, down her stomach. Unfastening the rest of her buttons, he cleared away the gown inch by inch and spread the white fabric out around her, a pristine frame outlining pale golden flesh. He found the soft hair between her thighs, a dark intriguing mist heavy with the fragrance of desire.

Heat wrapped them in a cocoon and slid between them where even air could not find a place to drift. He was burning with it, and Cameo had become a bright flame restlessly twisting and writhing beneath his hands and his mouth.

Carefully he lifted her off his lap and laid her back on the mattress. She never stopped watching him, inflaming him with the fever in her eyes. Her hands moved toward him. He caught them and placed them on the pillow on either side of her head.

"Be still, Cameo," he whispered. "Let me—"

Her legs lifted to wind around him. He pinned them

down with his weight. Only her eyes moved now, over his face, his chest, his belly; and her tongue darted over her lips to spread a shine of promise.

He rolled a little to the side, keeping his leg firm over both of hers as his hand wandered down her body, skimmed the slopes of her breasts . . . down her flat, tight stomach . . . ruffled over dusky curls into wet, hot tightness. . . .

She arched her body. He subdued her with his weight, enjoying her torment, provoking his own as his fingers stroked and probed deeper . . . deeper . . . then withdrew. Frustration sharpened her little cry and her eyes began to drift shut.

"Cameo," he whispered—a command and something else. He needed her to see him, to know him. He needed to see and know all of her responses to him. He needed to build a memory in case the dream failed him.

She opened her eyes, questioning yet submissive and held his gaze as he rose over her, paused, advanced, paused again. It was pain to linger, ecstasy to stretch the moment even as he stretched her to accept him.

It was the worst form of agony to hear her startled cry and watch her bite her lip to stop a whimper of pain. It was the ultimate victory to feel her arch again, meeting him, and forcing him to penetrate deeply. Her sigh was a poignant declaration of relief as the stiffness left her body and she once more molded herself to him and rotated her hips.

And still she held his gaze as their bodies thrust and plunged and arched. Through it all they became more and more a part of each other, a single being merging, moving together, urgently, desperately, mindlessly.

Zach felt the beginnings of completion inside her—tiny

quivers and moist warmth; he saw it in the way her fists clenched and unclenched on the pillow, and he heard it in her voice as she cried out again. Her breath caught and held. He stiffened and held—a timeless moment of absolute surrender, absolute joining . . . a cry . . . a groan . . . and their hands became one, reaching for a diamond in the sky. Close. So close. His muscles tightened and strained. He reared his head back and pushed, defying the limits of pleasure. Now . . . *now* . . . an end and perhaps a beginning—

"Zach!" It was like a knife cutting them apart, severing the moment before it could end and shredding the truth into rags. He jerked away from her and felt as if he'd left most of himself behind. He was empty where a moment before he had known an indescribable fullness of life. But that moment was gone, as if it had never existed. Their bodies were no longer joined, no longer driving everything from their lives except each other. Emotion died. His body cooled and changed and died a little, too.

Cameo's eyes widened. Her head shook in negation. "No. Not yet. Please, it can't be over yet."

"Zach?" he asked carefully as he forced his expression into one of guarded blankness. "Anybody I should know about?" he asked as he pulled the edges of her nightgown around her body.

Cameo swallowed and looked away, regret obvious in her eyes as she lay still for his ministrations.

"Cameo. Look at me." Zach levered himself to a safe distance away from her, yet held her prisoner with an unrelenting and brutal stare. He wanted to shake her, make her see *him,* not Sloane. It didn't make sense for him to be so hurt when he *was* Zachary, but hell, nothing made sense anymore.

Especially not the regret he saw in her expression when she had come to him.

He had regrets, too. He shouldn't have lost control, shouldn't have brought deceit to lie between them.

"He's gone," she whispered.

Hearing the utter despair in her answer, Zach sighed in defeat. *So the lies continue,* he thought bitterly. He'd always been able to lose himself in the role he was playing. Now he felt as if the part had swallowed him whole. "I thought you hadn't lost anyone in the war," he said.

"The war was simply a circumstance. Zach was lost long before that."

Lost. How could any truth he might utter compare with that, Zach wondered? *Lost.* He'd been lost before he was born. It was the legacy of his people.

Shaking his head, he leaned back against the pillows and focused on the darkness beyond the footboard of the bed. What a fine mess. What irony. How in the hell was he to know that he'd become a victim of his own deceptions? How could he have known that he'd fall in love with Cameo? And what of Cameo? Had she been giving herself to a ghost?

"You loved him," he said flatly.

"Yes."

"And what was this," he snarled as he spread his arm and gestured over the bed. "What did it signify?"

Cameo shifted and tried to sit up. He turned his head and his arm shot out to pull her back to his side, as if by holding her physically he could keep from losing her.

Not answering, Cameo glanced at him from the corner of her eye. If she had truly wanted revenge, she had it in his changing expressions: stricken, shattered, vulnerable, and then nothing but that hated blankness that concealed secrets and lies.

How easy it had been to respond to the truth of his passion without remembering how many times in the past he'd refused to accept it as more than a moment's pleasure or perhaps a lady's favor to carry into battle. She'd thought that she could deny the memories and turn to him and find the completion that had been so close. Except that truth had stolen between them and demanded a hearing.

She sighed and eased out of Zach's hold.

He let her go, a gesture that told its own story of reckoning. A soft light filtered into the room, fading the darkness. She walked to the window and drew open the curtains. Dawn painted the sky with subtle shades of pink and lavender and gold, making her think of gentle beginnings and tender promises. If only she could believe in them and forget that her life had been nothing but a series of endings.

"Cameo." His voice was gruff with emotion. She stiffened and with precise, careful movements walked over to his saddlebags draped over the chair.

"Come back here," he ordered seductively, angering her that he could use such a ploy when things had gone so horribly wrong. She reached inside the leather pouch, her hand unerringly finding the doily exactly where she had left it. She felt his gaze on her, a probing stare that itched between her shoulder blades. He said nothing.

Two steps took her to the side of the bed and she looked down at him with unflinching regard. His hand reached out and captured her wrist, drawing her near, urging her to sit beside him. With two fingers, she held up the scrap of linen and lace and dropped it onto his face. He released her wrist and sighed, a sound that struck her as being relief and resignation all at once, his exhalation dislodging the doily from one eye.

"Why, Zach?" she asked, her voice slashing like a whip. Anger had her in thrall now—all the fury and frustration and despair she had struggled against for six long months. She had to have the answers. So much depended on them: her future; her heart; her dreams.

"Orders," he said, as if the words left a bitter taste in his mouth, then he shrugged. "They made sense at the time."

"I see. You were ordered to die and let Zachary *Sloane* McAllister rest in peace. It was very convincing, for a while."

"Yes," he said, his mouth a bitter downward twist. "It fooled me, too." He swiped at the doily and crushed it in his hand.

"Why did I have to be fooled?"

"You most of all, Cameo." He took on the patient aspect of a saint and hesitated, as if he were searching for a way to soften the truth.

"Because you don't know shit about lying, Cameo. You would have betrayed me without meaning to."

The reasons struck her as being paltry and inadequate. "Of course," she said mockingly. "And I've betrayed you every day since you arrived."

"You've known since then?" Again he grasped her wrist as she backed away from him.

She nodded, a hard, violent jerk of her head. "I've known a lot of things, Zach."

His sudden stillness was like withdrawal, a marshalling of defenses. "Such as?" he asked in a deadly tone.

It pleased her to see his watchfulness, evidence that for once, he was taking her seriously. "You're a spy. Papa knew. So did Kit Carson. I asked Kit why you were at

Glorieta and he patted my hand as if I were a child asking about grown-up things." She paused to take a breath and then continued, her voice breaking like a flawed dream that had been struck just so. "I thought you were different, Zach. You and Papa. But you weren't. Everything I believed in was a lie. I mourned you for months. Every night my bed felt like a grave and I dreamed of you coming to me—"

Zach opened his mouth to speak, but Cameo shook her head, stopping him. She wanted to say it all before she fell apart. She couldn't stand that. All she'd done for months was fall apart in one way or another. Her voice was tired and dispassionate, tight and controlled. "I deserved honesty. You know I would have cut out my tongue rather than give you away."

"I know," Zach said softly.

"Were you going to tell me, Zach? *Ever?*"

Zach swung his legs over the side of the bed and stood facing her, his hands dragging at the sheet and wrapping it around his hips. "Cameo—"

A quick twist freed her from his grip and she gave him her back as she walked to the door.

"Cameo, would you believe that I love you?" he asked quietly.

She faced him slowly, with defiance and board hard resolution. "Believe *you?* Who are *you?* The man I fell in love with or the man who lied to me? How many men are *you?* Two or a hundred? Tell me *who* to believe, Zach."

Silence filled the air, swallowing the life, the warmth. He looked around the room, breathing in the lovers' scent that was fading as quickly as the night and spoke a truth he could no longer hide. "One man or a hundred—I love you, Cameo."

Cameo seemed to sag as her step faltered. The silence stretched, then finally broke as she straightened her shoulders and spoke without turning back to him. "I only asked for one man, Zach. Just one . . ." And then she was gone.

Staring down at the doily crumpled in his hand, Zach heard the tiny click of the latch, a sound more final than the scrape of shovels filling in a grave. The lies had run ahead of him, then turned on him like traitors to a lost cause. His fault. He hadn't trusted Cameo. Her guileless approach to life had blinded him to her strength and courage. He'd lied to himself by thinking it would all work out and she would understand when he finally did tell her the truth.

Too late, he realized that delayed truth was often worse than a lie. Too late, he discovered that the lies he'd told himself were the loudest of them all.

17

A Trick of Life

*L*oco weed or larkspur. Cameo's mind spun in circles as she tried to convince herself that it had been an accident and three of her horses hadn't died because of evil intent. It would be so much easier to accept a freak accident or one of those nasty little tricks that life played on the unwary.

"Patrona?" Jorge shifted on his feet and stared at her from clouded eyes. "I look at the pasture. No loco weed or larkspur. The feed, it has the weed, but I did not put it there when I feed the horses."

"I know, Jorge. It wasn't your fault, and I doubt there was anything you could have done to prevent it." She smiled at him—all the reassurance she could give in the face of what had happened. Poor Jorge had been on the verge of tears since he'd come into the office. He loved her thoroughbreds as much as she did and took such pride in them.

"I should have watched—"

"How, Jorge? Can you stay awake twenty-four hours a day, every day?"

"No, but—"

"If you had seen whoever did this, could you have stopped them?"

Jorge stared down at his gnarled joints and shrugged. "I have a loud voice."

"Which might very well have gotten you killed," Cameo said wearily. "I don't want to lose you, too, Jorge."

"I am old, *niña,*" he said slipping back into what he had called her when she was a little girl. "The horses—"

"Can be replaced, Jorge. You can't." She watched his head jerk up and smiled. "I don't want to hear any more of this. What we must do now is find out how they got in without anyone knowing about it and take measures to see that it doesn't happen again."

"Sí, Patrona." He bowed his head again and shuffled a step backward. "I must tell you . . ."

His reluctance to finish his sentence made Cameo feel as if spiders were walking over her. "More, Jorge?" *Please say no. Oh, please, God—not more.*

"The *vaqueros*—everyone but my sons who tend the sheep—are *vamos.*"

"Gone? Everyone?" Panic seized her at the way he avoided her gaze. "Sofia, too?" She remembered Sofia's hug the night her father had died, remembered her yearning when she'd watched Sofia cuddle her sons and soothe their hurts. She'd wanted Sofia to be her mother, then. Only Jorge had been there, really been there, as he was now, soothing hurts, loving her, though he, too, had sons of his own.

"Sí. They say the valley is cursed, that you are forsaken by God and they will not stay. They go last night."

"Maybe they're right, Jorge," she whispered. "Why haven't you gone, too?"

"I am too old to worry over curses. My sons—they respect their *padre.*"

"Thank you, Jorge."

"*Sí.*" He shook his bowed head and shuffled out of the office.

Sunlight poured into the window and shattered into prisms of color as it struck her father's crystal whiskey decanters. She felt shattered, betrayed. Zach's deceptions were bad enough, but at least he had a reasonable excuse. The ranch families were another story. Her family. The only constant she had ever known. *Cursed and forsaken.* Perhaps she was. A single sob escaped her before she bit her lip, stifling the anguish she wanted to cry out to the world. How could they be so taken in by the vile acts of greedy and treasonous men?

What in heaven's name would they do? Where could they go without being separated and scattered to the four winds? They had all been on the ranch since before she'd been born—many of them having been born here themselves.

All she had left was Jorge. And Zach.

Except that Zach was a man of moments, as intangible as mountain mist. And she was a woman for years. He had said so. God knew that Zach understood the way of things far better than she. But what good were years if they were to be spent alone?

Cameo propped her feet on the desk and stared at the amber liquid in the decanters and hesitated only a minute. Her body ached in odd places. Her shoulder was sore to the point of annoyance and her emotions were a mess. What the heck. A drink or three was just what she needed to chase maudlin thoughts away. She leaned forward and grasped the bottle of brandy, poured a healthy draught, then sat back holding the glass up to the light as she thought of the night past, their confrontation, the frustration of unfulfilled need.

She cocked her head as she heard the door slam and Zach's voice calling for Jorge. The need became sharper. It really didn't matter who he was supposed to be or what she was supposed to feel. The man she loved was here, calm and strong, solid and alive, making her feel alive.

Zach was all that she remembered, yet he was different —two halves of the same reality. The man who had left her six months ago had been like the wind and rain and lightning, moving on to touch other places, other lives. The man who had stood beneath the shadows of the tree in her yard had seemed like the mountains, solid and enduring.

It was a convenient illusion, she knew. An illusion she desperately needed in the midst of so much painful reality. She closed her eyes as she tipped the glass to her lips and emptied it. The brandy hit her empty stomach and churned uncomfortably before it raced through her veins. With every swallow, she became more calm, more disgusted with herself. She poured another cautiously measured draught and wondered how long the spirits would take to do their work. She could stand a few hours of insensibility.

She heard the low drone of voices and knew that Jorge was telling Zach about the defection of her people. No doubt he wished for a similar escape from an impulsive and stubborn woman who couldn't seem to accept the ways of men, their inconstancies and the restlessness that forever drove them to search for more than they had.

Lately she'd been restless, too. And reckless. Last night had proved that. How could she have known that some moments in life were complete in themselves? How could she have possibly known that physical intimacy could spawn such a sense of belonging and rightness? Now she wanted completion. She wanted to explore intimacy in all its forms. With Zach—only Zach. Since she had nothing more to lose, maybe she would give it a try. Nothing to lose but her soul.

She snapped her fingers in a careless gesture. At least it would be through her own decisions and actions rather than things over which she had no control. She would be her own victim rather than someone else's.

She poured another drink, filling the glass this time.

As always, she felt his presence before he materialized in the doorway, dressed as Sloane, maintaining the lie. Fine. She knew the rules of the game now.

"Sloane." She nodded her head imperiously, playing for all she was worth the *Patrona* meeting with her foreman to issue orders for the day. Her stare was direct, challenging him to deny the charade, telling him that she wouldn't even if he did.

He sauntered farther into the office and stopped a wary distance away from the desk, his hat shielding his eyes as if he was loath to face her. She held up her glass, a silent invitation for him to join her.

"You heard?" she asked.

He took a step closer and nodded. "What are you doing?"

"I'm figuring things out."

"What things?"

"Oh, the differences between wildflowers and roses." She peered at him, expecting blurs and finding brightness and clear focus. He appeared larger than life, every line and curve of him defined sharply, every shadow and texture of him in brilliant contrast. She remembered those textures, as they had stroked her inside and out. She took another drink from the glass.

"Cameo," he said in a warning tone. "The ranch—"

She reached for the decanter, missed, and groped until she found it two inches to the left of where she'd perceived it to be. "Yes—the ranch. I've figured that out, too." Liquid sloshed over her finger as she poured. Returning her gaze to Zach, she noted with satisfaction the way he tipped his hat to the back of his head and stared at her as she licked the drop off her finger. She smiled brilliantly at the two of him that suddenly seemed to be standing in front of the desk. "Don't you want to hear my hyp—hypo—theory?"

"Oh, by all means," he said and stuck his hands into his back pockets. His pants drew tight, outlining him clearly.

Her gaze centered on him below his belt—both of them. "One is quite enough, thank you," she said, and wondered at his look of confusion. "Anyway, I know what they're doing now."

"Who?"

"The prep—perpretr—the culprits, of course. It's all very shimple—simple—really."

"Really?"

She nodded and concentrated on forming her words correctly. "Firsh our cows, then the ambush, then the . . . the . . ." She waved her arm, an impatient gesture at her sudden inability to articulate clearly. "Other stuff. My horshes . . . dead . . . my people are gone." She squinted at her glass. "The only thing I don' undershtand is why the Rebs would risk their smuggling operation. If the ransh fails—" A frown of concentration puckered her brow as she tried to remember her line of thought. Suddenly she smiled in triumph. "So would Fielding Freight."

Zach sighed patiently. "The destruction is select and not enough to ruin you."

"I thought of that," she said matter-of-factly. "Everything is designed to . . . to . . ."

"Frighten and intimidate and threaten, not wreak total destruction?" he supplied when she gave him a blank stare. "Cameo, whoever your enemy is, he intends to break your spirit rather than your pocketbook."

"Doesn't he want my pocketbook?"

Zach watched her eyes cross and wondered how she could think so clearly while drowning in her cups. "Possibly," he answered. The idea made his blood run cold. With Sam dead, Cameo's culprits should have eased up on their attacks. Everyone had assumed that the main problem was Sam's investigation of the stolen gold shipments. Zach had to face the possibility that the smuggling was simply the means to another end, an end that had nothing to do with the war and was more personal in nature. It had bothered him that the Rebs hadn't simply stolen an entire gold shipment and been done with it.

If he was right, and the criminals were just that, then Cameo was in far more danger than he and Sam had originally thought.

And now there was no one at the ranch to look after her and the stock except for the handful of his men he'd installed in the employee quarters. Not enough men. He had to get Cameo out of there—fast—and keep her hidden until he brought in more people to work the ranch.

Her eyes narrowed, then crossed again. "Well I shur—cher—certainly think you should find out what they want."

"I will . . . as soon as I take care of you."

She shook her head vigorously. "You find out. I'll take

care of me." The look she gave him was one of firm determination, and her tone had the ring of absolute authority.

He might have been impressed if her eyes weren't crossing. Zach suppressed laughter and hooked his thumbs in his belt to keep from rubbing them together in glee. He'd wondered how he was to carry out his plan without binding and gagging her and dumping her into a sack. Cameo was playing right into his hands. Another swallow or two should do it.

"Did you hear me, Shloane?"

"I heard." Her use of the name still made him wince, yet he couldn't deny the necessity of it. Cameo, he knew, was an expert on necessity.

Planting her palms flat on the desk, she took a deep breath, and pushed herself upward. "Then do something!"

He sauntered forward and picked up the decanter.

"What are you doing?" Her body swayed as she peered at him owlishly.

"Pouring you another drink."

"Oh. Thank you." She tossed down the brandy with all the irreverence of a teetotaler. It was enough. She tilted her head as if the world had changed angles and it was the only way she could see straight. Her elbow gave way, dipping one side of her body almost level with the desk. A brilliant smile lit her face as she gazed up at him from her skewed position. "I have an idea. We could . . . we could . . . botheration—why won't you stand still?" Her eyes fluttered closed, then opened wide as she began to slither off the desk like so much water being poured onto the floor.

Moving fast, Zach reached across the wide desk and caught her under her arms, holding her up so she wouldn't jar her shoulder. "Damn it, Cameo, hold still or you'll hurt—"

Still smiling, she let all her limbs flop at once and hung in his arms, a dead weight that almost jerked him off his feet. "I don't hurt. Nothing hurts. Ishn't it wonderful?" She peered up at him.

"Wonderful," he said under his breath as he propped one knee on the desk to keep his balance. He listed to one side with her weight and dragged his other knee up.

"What are you doing?"

"Damned if I know." With a careful shift, he adjusted his hold on her, bringing her closer to him and groaned at the way her surprisingly alert breasts pressed into his chest. The rest of her drooped in his arms like a sack of beans.

"Thish is nishe," she purred and favored him with an expression that was seductive in a garbled sort of way. Her eyelids lowered to half-mast as her dreamy smile was interrupted by a series of hiccups.

What, he wondered, was he supposed to do now? He couldn't haul her across the desk and risk hurting her, and he couldn't crawl forward on his knees without losing his balance and tipping over the side. The only thing that would work would be to lower them both down and make love to her as she was so obviously inviting. Except that he wanted to make love to Cameo, not a sack of beans that had been pickled in brandy.

A chuckle alerted him to another presence. Cameo slipped a notch in his grasp as he glanced over his shoulder to find Jorge in the doorway. "Don't just stand there, Jorge. Grab her from behind."

Still chuckling, Jorge took his time to cross the room

and walk around the desk. He shook his head and rubbed his chin. "She is heavy, *señor,* and I am but an old man."

"You won't get any older if you don't get her into that chair—*pronto.*"

With visible effort, Jorge straightened his face and wrapped his arms around Cameo's waist. "I have her." He glanced over his shoulder at the chair, then looked at Cameo. "But how do I put her down?"

Easing himself off the desktop, Zach winced at the spasm in his bad leg. "Just sit, old man."

Jorge sat, Cameo draped over him in a boneless heap obscuring all of the little man but his battered hat.

Zach snorted at the absurd picture and limped around the desk to lift Cameo long enough for Jorge to slide out from beneath her. As soon as he arranged her in the chair, she began to slide downward.

"Goddamn woman is nothing but trouble. Can't even pass out without raising a ruckus," he muttered as he pulled her up and draped one of her legs over the arm of the chair to hold her in place. "Come on, Jorge, we have work to do."

"But—the *Patrona.*"

At the door, they both turned to make sure Cameo was still in the chair. Zach tipped his hat all the way back on his head and propped his hands on his hips. What a sight she made, sprawled inelegantly in the chair, her head leaning so far to the side that her cheek touched her shoulder, her body giving little jerks as she hiccuped in her sleep. Zach looked at Jorge. Jorge looked back and broke into a smile. Zach's mouth twitched. A rumble of laughter began in his chest. "Shit, I wish I could paint."

"*Sí, señor* Zach—it would be a good thing to show her when she is too much the *Patrona.*"

Zach's grin faded; he drew his hat low over his forehead. "Zach?" he said quietly, dangerously.

"You can change the outside, *señor,* but the inside remains the same, *sí?*"

"Men have been killed for knowing less, old man."

Unimpressed by the threat, Jorge stared at him, unblinking. "What do I know, *señor?* The truth? I leave men to find that for themselves."

Surprisingly, Zach felt no sense of danger in Jorge's knowledge, only relief that a burden was shared. The old *vaquero* was at the top of his list of suspects, yet he knew in his gut that it merely a formality that would never become proven fact.

"I am not the evil one that harms the *niña, señor,"* he said softly.

Zach let out his breath in a whoosh. "Then you'll know where to find a spare mattress and blankets for the *niña.* And we'll need the wagon." Narrowing his eyes, Zach watched Jorge shuffle off toward the rear of the house. His mouth twisted wryly. His career had better end soon or he was done for. Taking a man's word for anything was the same as a self-imposed death sentence.

"Damn!" With a last glance at the *niña,* he turned on his heel and strode out of the house, praying for all he was worth that his belief in Jorge wouldn't turn out to be one of life's nastier tricks.

"The wagon is not good, *señor?*"

"Not for where we're going," Zach said as he glared at the featherbed and mound of blankets and peacefully sleeping woman in the wagon bed. For a while at least, he'd have to suffer the slowness of the wagon. In her present state, Cameo would slide off a horse like water slides off oilskin.

If he had his way, she'd stay in her present state for the better part of the day. He had a canteen full of watered-down whiskey to guarantee it. He could use a few hours of peace and quiet.

"You go to the place of lost souls?"

No longer surprised by the extent of Jorge's knowledge, Zach rubbed the back of his neck. "The what?" he asked with half hearted menace in his tone.

Jorge spread his hands wide. "I do not know this place, *señor*. I have never seen those who ride like ghosts through the valley. When I was young I have never been to this place of spirits where *Indios* who are not *Indios* live. You *comprende?*"

Zach frowned. "I *comprende*. What else don't you know, old man?"

"I know nothing, *Señor Sloane*." Jorge gave Zach a toothless grin and held out a quilt.

"What in the hell is that?"

"The *niña's* blanket."

"We have plenty." Dismissing the subject, Zach checked the horses tied to the back of the wagon, then walked around to climb up on the seat.

"No, *señor,* she must have this one."

There was something in Jorge's voice that hinted at an intriguing revelation. Zach looked at the quilt more closely and recognized it as the one that was always folded at the foot of Cameo's bed. It was faded and worn and had lost its plumpness. Suspicion and disbelief made his eyes widen. "Don't tell me she can't sleep without it."

"She can sleep." Jorge opened a fold of the quilt and pointed to one of the embroidered squares. "You see, her *madre* make this for her. It is a story and with this the *niña* is not alone."

Zach leaned over to study the designs, heavily embroidered in each exposed square, each different and full of exotic structures, figures garbed in foreign clothing, and a line of Chinese characters. "A chronicle of Chai's life," he guessed.

"*Sí,* a story. For the *niña,* so she will know her *madre* and always have her near. The *niña* has ordered the silk thread to make another—like this—for her little ones, with more stories here"—he pointed to several rows of blank squares—"so they will know their *madre,* too."

Zach swallowed and stared down at Cameo, swaddled in a blanket like an infant. Her body jerked and a hiccup squeaked past her lips. In a few hours she'd probably be raising holy hell over being kidnapped. But in that moment all he could see was a little girl huddled beneath a faded embroidered quilt—

"You must not laugh at her, *señor.* She thinks this is a weakness, and does not understand that it gives her strength. With this, she knows she has never been alone."

"We all have weaknesses, Jorge," Zach said as he remembered the chronicle of his own distant past that his people had faithfully preserved and carried with them whenever they had to move on to yet another hiding place. Mementos of centuries of running. Reminders of who they were and that, yes, they belonged to each other if not to a place. "Put it over her, Jorge," he said softly.

Nodding, Jorge spread the quilt over Cameo and smoothed it out when her hiccup wrinkled a corner.

Zach smacked the reins over the horses' rumps and drove the wagon away from the house, lulled by the sound of wheels turning on a rutted road and Cameo's squeaks harmonizing with those of the wagon springs.

Life had played the ultimate trick on him. The hero with a thousand faces had, with the telling of a story, become what he thought he would never be—one man who knew where he belonged. Except that he didn't belong to himself. There were still trails he was bound to follow, and a role he had to play out to the end. For now, all he could do was stare straight ahead and see where the road led him.

The hell of it was that he didn't care as long as he wasn't alone.

__18__

A Rose Without Thorns

Being alone had its advantages, Zach decided as the wagon hit another bump in the narrow track. If he were alone, he'd be on the back of a horse instead of having his backside beat to a pulp by the increasingly rough ground they were covering, inch by painfully slow inch. If he were alone, he could hear the birds as they flew overhead on their way south for the winter instead of the caterwauling that passed for Cameo's singing. Every time they hit a bump her pitch went up another notch and every animal for ten miles skittered for cover.

Trees stripped by autumn stood over the trail like ancient spirits whose skeletal arms would close in on unwelcome travelers. Dry leaves covered the ground, and in the distance the land climbed in a treacherous series of terraced plateaus and mesas of red sandstone, their heights already dusted with snow. Spruce, pine, and juniper grew amid aspen, and here and there hardy stalks of wildflowers clung to life. He loved this country—its savage beauty and mystical atmosphere, a place untouched by human progress. It was the only place he knew where a man could strip down to the soul and have a conversation with himself. Usually.

Cameo's voice dipped with the wagon, then soared and echoed off canyon walls.

"Aren't you thirsty?" Zach asked as he glanced at her over his shoulder.

Her head bobbed up from the pile of blankets and she held aloft the canteen he'd filled with watered whiskey. "I jus' took a drink," she said brightly and launched into her version of "The Battle Hymn of the Republic."

A rebel yell had more melody. Zach rolled his eyes and prayed that she would pass out again—soon. He'd never heard such a gawdawful voice in all his life.

For the tenth time in the last mile, he checked the position of the sun and then their surroundings. He'd have made better time crawling on his belly with the wagon tied to his back. The track they were on wasn't meant for wagons and by the time it became necessary to switch to horseback, it would be too late to go on. As far as he could see, the only good thing about the wagon was that it gave him a chance to prop up his leg and rest it for a while.

"Uh-oh." Cameo said suddenly.

Zach didn't like the sound of that any more than he liked her singing. He hauled back on the reins and turned around to find her sitting up amid a tangle of bedclothes, her bottom lip caught between her teeth.

"I need a water closet."

"Third tree to the left."

"But—"

"That's as good as it gets, Rosebud."

"I don'—"

"Float, walk, or I'll carry you. Whatever it takes to get the job done in a hurry, dammit."

"Well, ya don' need t'be so cranky." With a tilted flounce she wriggled out from under the covers and made it as far as the edge of the wagon bed before her arms buckled and landed her flat on her belly, her head hanging over the edge of the wagon. Her legs worked without taking her anywhere, and her bottom stuck up in the air as she tried to find leverage. Another inch and she'd land headfirst in the dirt.

"Oh, what a pretty rock!" Her bottom hiked farther into the air. "I can't . . . reash . . . it."

"Cameo—don't move." Zach leaped over the seat and grabbed her ankles.

"I want th' rock, and I haf to—"

"I'll get you the damned rock . . . just hold still." Planting his palm flat on her backside, he pushed it down and worked his way up her body until he could drag her back into a sitting position. "Stay put," he ordered and climbed out of the wagon. He sighed in resignation as he watched her sway. "I'm going to have to carry you, aren't I?"

"Yes, please."

"Put your arms around my neck. Okay, I'm going to lift you now . . . Cameo, I can't breathe."

Her arms loosened and she peered at him nose to nose. "You be nishe, or I'll fire you."

"You can't fire me," he said with a grunt. "Now move your head so I can see where I'm going."

She moved her head and bobbed it around like a bird. "Third tree on th' lef'," she reminded him.

"I see it," he said as he set her on her feet and propped her against the tree in question. "Call me when you're finished." He managed to escape all of two steps before he heard a tiny little voice calling his name.

"What now?"

"Can't do thish."

"Cameo," he said with forced patience, "you've been doing this all your life."

"Can't fin' th' tape to my—"

"Oh, hell!" He spun around and slid his hands under her skirt, careful not to raise it, and groped for the tie on her pantalets. The ribbon gave at his tug, and one by one, he lifted her feet free of the garment and tossed it aside. "There. You're on your own."

"Zach?"

"What!" he shouted, feeling on the edge of panic.

"Why is ever'thin' movin'?"

His face burned. From the way she was tilting, she'd fall before she'd manage to get the job done. He swiped his hand around the back of his neck. Nothing in his life had prepared him for this. "Lean your back against the tree."

"Where is't?"

"You're hanging on to it."

"Oh . . . oh." Cameo flinched as she leaned back and struck her shoulder on the rough bark. "Th' damned tree hurt me," she said indignantly.

"Oh, hell!" Grimly, he strode toward her and grabbed her hand. "I'll hold you. The rest is up to you." Seeing her sudden frown, he sighed with impatience. "I won't look." To prove his point, he angled his body sideways and directed his gaze at the sky, but not before he caught her wide-eyed, solemn look.

"I trus' ya, Zach."

It was hard to keep his promise then and not look at her. He wanted a full view of the innocent sincerity he heard in her voice. He needed to believe it, but the rustle of her skirts and the tug on his hand as she bent her knees kept him focused on the horizon. He could almost feel it—the trust she'd spoken of—and something else: intimacy of a kind he'd never experienced before. The kind of intimacy that came from comfort with each other, as if they'd been nurturing a mutual dependence for a long time and knew that there were no secrets between them.

Except that, too, was a lie brought on by circumstance and half a bottle of whiskey. With a muttered curse, he promised Samuel Fielding a load of buckshot when they met in the hereafter.

"I wan' to lay down now . . . oh!"

Her abrupt tug on his hand nearly jerked him off his feet. He swung around just in time to keep her from crashing her shoulder into the tree.

"Oh, for—" Thinking of a thousand things he'd rather be doing, Zach lifted her before she could fall and break her neck. Intimacy and trust notwithstanding, he was in no mood to be touched by the profundity of this particular experience. It was damned hard on a man's morale to grope under a lady's skirts and fuss with her underpinnings while trying to preserve her modesty at the same time. Especially when the lady was draping herself all over him. It just wasn't natural.

"Why's your face red?" she asked, squinting up at him. "Wha's wrong?"

It was the hair that pulled his trigger. "Wrong? *Wrong?*" he shouted. "I'm the best goddamn spy in the Union Army, not a wet nurse. I'm supposed to be on a dangerous mission and I wind up escorting you to the damn water closet." He swung her up in his arms and headed for the wagon, his voice lowering to a grumble. "I get you drunk so I can have some peace and you howl like a banshee.

And then you expect me to be a goddamn gentleman while I'm untying your pantalets!"

"I don' 'spect that." Her arms tightened around his neck and she nipped at his ear. "Oh! Look, Zach—a stream. I want t' bathe."

"Where is a good war when you need one?" Zach muttered in exasperation. Her breath was warm on his ear, taunting him with the real reason for his frustration. The rush of the water seemed unnaturally loud all of a sudden. His pants were beginning to feel tight. Cameo's tongue licking at his earlobe heated his blood. He lifted his head and concentrated on the temperature of the autumn air. Warm enough, he decided.

"You want a bath, Rosebud?" He veered off his course and walked right into the water, clothes, Cameo, and all. "Your wish is my command."

Her eyes widened as she gasped at the chill of the water. Then, as she became accustomed to it, she closed her eyes and sighed. "Feels good." Opening her eyes, she gazed at him. "Ya shouldna left our clothes on. They're all wet."

Zach bent over to sit her in the stream. "We have clean clothes in the wagon," he said as he avoided looking at the way her dress had plastered to her, outlining every curve and feature of her body.

"An' soap?"

"I'll get it. Don't drown while I'm gone." Worried about just that, Zach loped to the wagon, rummaged in his saddlebags for soap, snagged some quilts off the top of the pile, and ran back. He skidded to a stop five feet from the water. Somehow Cameo had managed to unfasten her dress and pull it off her shoulders. From her perplexed expression, he reckoned she hadn't figured out how to get it the rest of the way off while she was sitting down.

His step faltered as he walked forward. Her bared
breasts were bobbing on top of the water, pale and soft and
inviting more than a quick look. The bandage on her
shoulder seemed stark against her skin. Her hand raised
out of the water and she wagged her finger at him. "No,
no, no," she said in a singsong voice. "You can't take a
bath unless you're naked."

"I'm not the one who wanted a bath," he growled. In
spite of the cold, soaked fabric of his pants, he was steadily
growing more aroused.

"My dress won' come off."

"Tough."

"But—"

"Shit."

"Soap," she corrected. "Please."

He tossed it to her and watched her reach in the wrong
direction. The bar splashed into the water behind her. She
twisted and lost her balance. Her arms waved and her legs
thrashed as she chased the slippery soap and giggled.

Her dress tangled up in her legs, restricting her movements. Muttering under his breath, Zach shrugged out of
his shirt, kicked off his pants, and charged into the stream.

"I got it," Cameo said triumphantly as she struggled to
gain her feet.

Zach caught her just as she was about to go down. His
arm around her waist, he lifted her and the weight of the
soaked dress pulled it farther down around her hips. She
kicked her legs and it fell free. Her body stilled as he held
her suspended there, her flesh meeting his.

A slow, sultry smile curved her lips as she gazed up at
him and whispered huskily, "Hello."

He snorted and set her on her feet in the thigh-high
water, his hand at her elbow to keep her steady. "Try to

keep your shoulder dry," he said gruffly and lowered his eyes to the water between them. All he could see were her legs, shapely and curved in all the right places with a trace of plumpness in her thighs—

"So tha's what it looks like when it grows."

His gaze jerked up to find hers fastened on his groin. Heat climbed his cheeks at her rapt scrutiny of his swollen privates. He grabbed the soap away from her. "Turn around. I'll scrub your back." Relief did not come with her obedience. Her bottom curved enticingly above the water, the muscles flexing with her efforts to keep her balance. Working quickly, he rubbed the soap over her back, thinking it would be safer than allowing his hands to touch more intimate territory.

He was wrong. The backs of his fingers made contact and lingered of their own accord. She sighed and leaned back against him, her bottom cushioning him like a pillow. It seemed the most natural thing in the world for him to slide his hands around to her front, spread the rich lather over her neck, slowly, and slower still, then her good shoulder, her breasts, her belly.

She rotated her hips, pushed against him a little more, surrounding him with heat. It would be so easy to turn her around and lift her a little—

If he weren't freezing to death. He stared down at his chest, then at hers and saw the goose bumps rising on their flesh. Cameo seemed perfectly happy and at ease, but she had enough alcohol in her to keep her blood running. He, on the other hand was losing feeling in his feet and the swelling of his privates was rapidly diminishing.

Still, he didn't want to lose this—a moment without lies or memories between them, poignant in its simplicity. His arms folded around her and he buried his face in her hair.

It felt like death—the sudden draining of warmth, the weariness and melancholy of knowing there were things that would have to be left undone. He wanted her, the right way, with honesty and a completion that was death of another kind.

Gradually he released her and turned away from her to splash water over himself to wash away the soap. "Rinse, Cameo. It's too cold to stay here any longer." He left the stream and picked up one of the quilts and held it open for her.

Silently, as if she knew it was the wrong time to talk, she stepped into the warm shelter he offered and stood passively while he folded the quilt around her and tucked the ends into her clenched hands. Her docility struck him the same way a green sunset would have. Out of place. Unsettling. Unnatural.

And, he thought as he wrapped a second blanket around his hips and walked back to the wagon, it had taken only enough whiskey to fell three men, a ride bumpy enough to shake her teeth loose, and a dunking in icy water to rid the rose of her thorns.

He glanced back to make sure she was all right and saw her standing there, looking as small and vulnerable as a child, her body shivering as she huddled within a quilt embroidered with exotic characters and symbols.

He missed the thorns.

19

Caught in the Truth

Focus returned to Cameo as she watched Zach build a fire and arrange the feather mattress and other supplies as close as possible to the blaze. He had dressed at the wagon, his back turned to her after he tossed a bundle of clothes toward her with a terse order to put them on. She'd ignored him.

The age-softened fabric of her mother's quilt comforted her as she pulled it more closely around her. She wasn't ready to trade its warmth for the chill of the air. Feeling had returned as suddenly as sharpened sight, acutely tormenting her with a vivid memory of every touch they had shared in the stream. It felt odd—that heightened awareness coupled with the light-headedness and fuzzy thoughts induced by one too many sips from the canteen.

As she turned her head, the world around her blurred past, then stopped. It was all so different from the valley and mountains of home. Wispy white clouds seemed low enough to touch; the air had a crystal shine. Gold poured through breaks in the clouds, drenching the trees and rocks with a rich patina, casting magical shadows in crevices and folds. The flow of the stream sounded like easy, seductive laughter. Gilded ripples undulated in the current, then stroked and embraced the rocks and branches in their path with soft foam and dancing bubbles. Trees surrounded them like benevolent shadows, guarding them, keeping the outside world at bay. Mesas and plateaus rose in the distance, barriers insuring their privacy. She felt as if she and Zach had stepped into a little pocket of the world and it had closed around them. She felt safe.

Zach didn't look as if he felt particularly safe. He kept glancing her way as he worked, then quickly moved his gaze away as if the sight of her disturbed him. She could imagine him watching an enemy in just such a way, his expression tense and alert. Embarrassment flitted in and out of her awareness without a pause as she remembered what she had subjected him to. The memory of Zach's discomfort at having to perform the most intimate services for her made her giggle.

He glanced up and spoke sharply. "Get over here."

The ends of the quilt trailed behind her as she stumbled toward the bed he'd made near the fire. Again she giggled as she sat with a thump on the mattress. "I'll bet no one has ever camped with a featherbed before."

He snorted and handed her a tin mug. "Here's some coffee. Drink it all."

She drank and shuddered. "This's thick enough to use for topsoil."

"I need you sober for the rest of the trip."

"Why? You got me drunk in the firs' place."

"It was expedient at the time."

Expedient. A sobering, official word that made her feel less than human. She held the cup with both hands and turned her face toward the fire, soaking in the warmth. A few minutes ago she'd been amused by the way he avoided looking directly at her, but now it annoyed her. He was cold and distant, as she imagined he would be when carrying out an assignment. This time she was his assignment and he was looking for *expedient* ways to deal with her.

"I will not be expedient." She enunciated the words slowly, careful not to slur them.

"You're not."

"What d'ya do with your other 'signments?"

"Take them prisoner when I can." He shrugged.

She shook her head. "I wouldn' let ya do that t' me."

His mouth twitched. "Seems like I already have."

"Only because I'm letting ya' think so."

"Whatever you say, Rosebud." He knelt on the feather-bed next to her and tugged the quilt off her shoulder. "You got the bandage wet."

"What'd ya 'spect? I took a bath."

Reaching into his saddlebags, he pulled out a length of clean linen and began folding it into a square. He frowned as his gaze searched the campsite. Careful not to touch her, he grabbed the pillow behind her, removed the slip-case, and ripped it down the seam.

Cameo watched as he replaced the bandage on her shoulder and fashioned a sling for her arm. "I don' need that."

"Just for tonight," he said. "Tomorrow, we're switching to horseback and you'll have to use that arm."

"Where we goin'?"

"Get dressed."

"Can't." She held up her arm, tightly bound in the sling.

Zach glared at the sling as if it had been her notion rather than his. With fast, jerky movements, he swaddled her more securely in the quilt and wrapped another over her shoulders, then stalked off into the trees, muttering something about contrary women.

Sighing, Cameo lowered her head and picked through the clothing he'd thrown at her earlier: a leather riding skirt and jacket; flannel shirtwaist and camisole, and two pair of pantalets. He'd thought of everything. Later, when her mind was less inclined to wander, she'd worry about how long he'd been planning to spirit her away—literally. The fact that she'd taken the first drink had no bearing whatsoever—

Something rolled out of the pocket in her skirt and settled in a dip of the mattress. She reached for it and cradled it in her hand. It was a rock. Her rock—the one she'd admired in the road. Her gaze lifted to the direction in which Zach had disappeared and returned to the rock in her hand. The late afternoon sun struck its rough surface and gleamed brightly on the crystal pinks and grays. . . .

He'd remembered her rock. He'd held her hand while she answered the call of nature, catered to her every whim, and made camp when there were at least two hours of daylight left. He'd all but disabled her with the sling he'd suddenly decided she needed, wrapped her like a mummy, and put as much distance between them as possible without actually leaving her. His face had been flushed, as if he'd just been caught in a lie.

The sudden clarity of her thoughts hit her like the shock of cold water. *Expedient.* All his actions had been so for one reason only: to keep himself from touching her again as he had in the stream. Zach hadn't been caught in a lie at all. He'd been caught by the truth.

She picked up her coffee mug and scooted over to the edge of the mattress to reach for the coffee pot, too lost in thought to remember how hot metal could be.

"What in the hell are you doing?" Zach appeared from the trees and rushed over to move the pot from her reach. "It's hot."

"Mmm." Lost in her struggle for sobriety, she held out her cup. "More, please."

"Yes, your highness." The sarcasm in his voice was thicker than the coffee he poured for her.

Before she could draw her hand back, he wrapped his fingers around the tin mug and poured cold water into it from his canteen. Cameo angled her head and stared at him as she drank. So many thoughtful gestures. And a concern for her welfare that went beyond the natural inclinations of most men, as if he were looking out for his own welfare.

"Thank you for my rock," she said quietly.

He grunted as he stirred the beans he'd put on to cook, checked the level of liquid in the coffee pot, opened a cloth wrapped package of jerky and another of dried fruit, and folded the clothing she'd scattered over the bed.

"Sit down, Zach."

"Too busy." His hands were everywhere, repeating the same tasks over again.

"Tell me what to do," she said and bit the inside of her cheek to keep from laughing. "I'll help."

"You can't," he said, looking hunted.

"Why?"

"Because . . ." His gaze struck and bounced off every point of their campsite, then his hand raked through his hair. "Because, dammit, there's nothing to do."

"Then sit here." She patted the mattress when he moved to the other side of the fire. "I'm cold."

He glared at her.

"Please?"

With the dragging steps of a doomed man, he shuffled back to her and sat as close to the edge of the mattress as he could. As if he anticipated her next request, he muttered, "It's warmer here."

She scooted forward to sit next to him and snuggled into his side. He sat like a statue, his profile chiseled in sharp relief, the chin he'd once hidden with a beard jutting out with belligerence, his hard jaw bunching over and over again.

"What are you up to?"

"Isn't it obvious?" Her hand rested on his thigh and stroked in a circular motion. His muscles jerked as if he'd been stabbed.

"Stop that!"

"What?" She played with the buckle of his belt, unfastened it, and deliberately brushed the side of her hand over the growing bulge just below. Memories of the night before stole into her mind, and brought a deep throaty sigh.

"You sound like a cat getting her belly rubbed." He latched on to her hand and held it fast.

"Not yet, but I will." Sliding her arm out of the sling, she stroked his other thigh.

"The hell you will." He slapped her hand away.

"Want to bet?" Rising to her knees on the mattress, she faced him as she eased her hand from his hold, and ran her fingers through his hair, enjoying the texture and thickness of it, and massaging his scalp in long, soothing strokes.

He pulled in a deep draught of air and let it out slowly. "Cameo, you're drunk."

"No. I'm . . ." She frowned in concentration and realized that it was becoming easier to speak, easier to think coherently. "I don't know what, exactly."

"Angry," he said. "You're angry, remember?"

"Mmm . . . furious, but it's not important." She sat back on her heels. "I don't *care,* Zach. I don't want to care. For now, it's all gone."

Zach didn't seem to be listening. He jerked away from her and angled forward to stare at his hands hanging loosely between his outspread knees. "If you want revenge, you had it last night."

She began unfastening the buttons on his shirt. "When Papa had to punish me, he always said it hurt him more than it hurt me. Now I know what he meant."

"This isn't the same as a trip to the woodshed, Cameo. This can hurt a hell of a lot worse." He flexed his legs, began to rise.

"There's nowhere for you to go this time, Zach," she said quietly and skimmed her fingers over his chest.

He sagged back down. "Nothing's changed, Cameo."

"You begin to understand," she said smugly. "Tomorrow you'll do your duty and I'll fight for what's mine."

"I don't understand shit."

Cameo hid her smile and thought that he looked like a reluctant virgin bewildered by the mechanics of love. Were all men so blind? she wondered. How could he fail to see what had become so clear to her? "Look around you, Zach. Names and identities don't matter here. Nothing does except survival. It's so primitive that . . ." She bit her lip as she searched for the right words to make him understand.

"That it strips you down to the soul," he said under his breath.

"Yes," she whispered, "it takes everything away but what we feel." Gazing up at him, Cameo saw that he knew —had always known—what she meant. He was no stranger here. Oddly, she didn't feel as if she were a stranger either, though she had never been here before. She felt his chest rise and fall, his body relax.

"Is this what you call survival, Cameo?"

"Yes," she said and lowered her head to watch the hair on his chest spring back up as she stroked and lightly raked him with her nails. Subtle shadows drifted over his bronzed flesh as his muscles flexed and swelled with her touch.

Relief was eloquent in his sigh as she pulled away and sat beside him, her arms wrapped around her legs, her chin resting on her upraised knees. Somehow she knew that it wasn't fair to tease his body and expect him to listen— really listen—to what she had to say. It was important that he understand the decision she had made.

In a subdued voice, Cameo tried to form her thoughts into words. "Death keeps happening around me, Zach, to everyone and everything I love. Every time it does, some-thing inside me dies, too. I have so little left to feel for that I'm afraid I'll stop feeling altogether."

He turned his head and looked at her through narrowed eyes. "That's desperation."

"Of course it is," she said as she angled her head to look at him. "All I do is mourn. It's all I've ever done. For the mother I never knew . . ." Her voice trailed off as she smoothed a corner of the quilt. "For Papa, who could barely sit still in the winter and left before the spring flow-ers were out. For all that's been lost, and all I've never known." Shaking her head, Cameo swallowed and closed her eyes. "I've mourned for you."

"Cameo—"

"No!" She shook her head, again, opened her eyes to look directly at him. "I'm not listening to you anymore, Zach. You think you know so much about what's right for me—you and Papa, always deciding, always doing what you want with my life as if you knew what I wanted. Papa didn't know. You don't know, and neither of you bothered to ask."

He opened his mouth and shut it again when Cameo glared at him and poked her finger at his chest.

"You listen to me, Zachary Sloane McAllister. Someday you're going to take a trail away from the valley and I'll be saying good-bye. And when that happens, I don't want to spend my nights dreaming about a shadow touching me and making me want something I've never had. I want to know that there is more to life than grief." She stared at the sky, sunset colors fading into silver twilight, turning the trees into shadows.

"Lust," he said.

"Love," she said and pushed at him with both hands. Caught by surprise, he fell back like a tree that had just been chopped down. To keep him where she wanted him, she followed, landing on top of him and wincing at the sudden jolt. His arms wrapped around her as he tried to catch her and take the shock of her descent.

The time for talking was over, Cameo decided. The spirits she had consumed had dissolved her inhibitions, quenched the fires of anger, bringing heat of another kind. Doing what was proper had never meant less. Zach was necessary to her. Loving him was all that mattered.

"Cameo, you can't do this."

"Give me one good reason why not." Her brows rose as she stared at him nose to nose, eye to eye. She smiled wickedly. "No answer?"

"I'm thinking," he said in a low growl and shuddered as her nails raked lightly over his chest, back and forth and in circles through the mat of copper hair that narrowed into a light trail down his tight, flat belly. His chest rose and fell. "A woman isn't supposed to do the seducing."

"Just where is it written that seduction is man's work?" she murmured against his navel, tasting the salt and soap flavor of him. His stomach muscles quivered, then his body tightened, hardened, and warmed at her touch.

She rested her cheek on his chest, feeling the difference between his heated flesh and the rapidly cooling air on her other cheek. "Don't move." With a warning point of her finger, she sat up, and glanced around. From the knees down he was off the mattress, his booted feet dangerously close to the fire. She pointed toward the opposite edge of the mattress and ordered, "Scoot up."

He scooted.

Nodding in satisfaction, Cameo bent over to remove his boots, still wet from their dunking in the stream. "Foolish man," she muttered as she pulled and tugged and wrestled with the clinging leather.

Zach didn't move a muscle to help, but passively reclined on the mattress, staring at the sky, and hoping that she'd fall over with exhaustion before she managed to reduce his convictions to cow pies. A moment ago he'd wondered at her logic. Now everything she'd said made perfect sense. She wanted to know there was more to life than grief. He wanted to be a part of something more than the trail dust on his clothes. Deep inside, he recognized the irony of Cameo offering moments while he longed for years.

If Cameo weren't reaching for the down quilt that had fallen off her shoulders, and pulling it up over both of them like a tent he might be able to think straight, latch onto those deeper instincts and make sense of them.

But the quilt billowed over her head, then settled over

them, an intimate cocoon of warmth and silence. Protests disappeared with the outside world as he watched her slowly unwrap the other quilt from around her body, somehow managing to withhold sight of intimate places until the last fold was released.

Cameo saw his frown of concentration, the struggle he waged with himself for control. She wasn't about to give him time to think. Her fingers opened the buttons on his pants and explored what she had only felt last night. It fascinated her to feel him grow in her hand. From the way he was shuddering, she knew him to be vulnerable even as she knew the power and strength this one part of his body could wield. Skimming his length, she cupped the heaviness between his legs and stroked and cupped again. He grimaced, as if he were in pain, and groaned with pleasure.

The quilt followed her as she slid down his body to watch the changes her ministrations brought, conforming to her and leaving Zach open to the air. He rolled his eyes at the mound she made, like a mole in a burrow. Amusement faded as her hands explored and cupped and kneaded. His body was taking those caresses seriously, and he realized that nothing was going to stop her. She wasn't going to pass out, run out, or give up. He was being seduced by a woman with half a notch on her bedpost.

That woman had the future of his family in her hands. He didn't know whether to laugh or run like hell.

"Damn quilt," he heard her mumble. Then her bottom took the high point as she crawled back up to the head of their bed and groped around in the dirt. Two curses later, she left the mattress altogether, muttering under her breath about men who use all the firewood.

Fascinated, he watched as she flounced—naked—over to a small tree and with one arm wrestled a sturdy branch.

It finally gave with a snap, the momentum nearly dropping her on her backside.

She waved the branch at him. "You could have helped."

He was too busy watching her breasts bob up and down as she pounded the wood into the ground to reply. The quilt billowed over him once more and caught on the stick, forming an arch above his head. Her hands appeared at his feet, took hold of his pants legs and yanked. The fabric chafed the small of his back then caught. In the interest of preserving his skin, he lifted his hips. The pants slid off and he heard them plop down somewhere on the other side of the campsite.

"There!" she said as she burrowed under the quilt and shimmied upward to glare at him and point at his shirt. "Take it off."

He told himself that he was obeying solely to save his only remaining piece of clothing from being tossed out of reach. He knew he did it out of curiosity for what Cameo was going to do next.

Once he was as bare as she was, Cameo didn't waste any time taking up where she left off. Belatedly, Zach realized that he'd had the perfect moment to escape her clutches, and he'd just lain there and stared at her while he grew a tent pole of his own. Now all he could do was clench his teeth at the insistent pressure of her hands on him, urging him—and succeeding—to grow some more.

"Oh, my," she said as she lifted her gaze to his face and tilted her head. "How does it fit?"

He raised his head, looked down at himself and stared as if he had just grown a new limb. He wanted to cover himself with his hands, but she was arranging them on her breasts. He cleared his throat. "It just does," he croaked.

"Mmm, I know," she said with a purr and sat astride him. "Is there more than what I felt last night, Zach?"

"I sure as hell hope so, Rosebud." With a low growl, he reached up, cupped the back of her head, urged her down.

She resisted, a smile on her face that teased him without mercy. But then her expression became solemn, troubled. "It was you last night, Zach. It's always been you—in my dreams, in my heart." Her gaze dropped to her hands. "Let me touch you, Zach. Show me what it's like to hold my dreams."

Zach tried to swallow a lump in his throat that just didn't want to go down. This was it—his last chance to talk some sense into her. He had to try, though his heart and various other parts weren't in it. "Dammit! I'm trying to be noble—"

Cameo interrupted him with a kiss, then spoke against his lips. "To hell with being noble."

"And fair." he said, his mouth taking nips between words.

"That, too," she said and nipped back. "It doesn't belong between a man and a woman who have to live on moments."

"Tomorrow—"

"Surviving today is all that matters." Propping her elbow on his chest, she rested her chin on her hand and smiled. "Don't argue with me anymore. You can't possibly win."

One bushy copper brow arched. "No?"

She outlined his mouth with the tip of her fingers. "No. I'm reasonably sure I can prove that you won't survive the night without me." With that, she trailed her hand downward again and lightly raked him with her nails.

Beads of sweat broke out on his forehead. She snatched

her hand away when he groaned, afraid she might have
hurt him.

"You're right, Rosebud," he said, his voice low and
strained. "I'll never survive the night without you."

Cameo watched him as his eyes darkened to the color of
smoke and his hands found her breasts. Her breath caught
at the sensations he evoked—startling as he rolled her nipples between his fingers, shivery as he lightly grazed the
sides of her breasts, tingling as he kneaded gently.

"Yes, just like that, Zach . . . soft, then . . . oh, my
. . . hard."

"I know what to do, sweetheart."

He was setting fires on her body, inside her, around her.
But it wasn't what she wanted. The problem was that she
wasn't entirely sure of how to get what she wanted. She sat
up, her legs on either side of him, her lower body pressing
against his, feeling the burning heat and hardness of him
that demanded and seemed to command. She ran her
tongue around her suddenly dry lips. "What do you know
how to do, Zach?" she whispered, hoping that he would
take it as a teasing question rather than a quest for much
needed information.

"Come here."

There was a wealth of arrogance in his simple order, an
arrogance she was determined to match, if not in actual
knowledge, then in the certainty that what she had done so
far had worked. With a small shake of her head, her hair
brushed his chest. He reached for the heavy strands, sifted
them through his fingers, watched them fall over him once
more.

So he liked the touch of her hair, Cameo noted. Slowly
she drew back and tossed her head. Her hair fell down her
back—out of his reach. She felt it, too, the brush of each

strand, like the touch of cool breath on overheated skin.
She savored it—the pleasure she could give herself while
giving him pleasure at the same time by rotating her hips
over him. It made her feel less vulnerable, less dependent
on male whims, more in control.

Instinctively, she spread her hands over her waist, ran
them up her sides, cupped her breasts, held them up and
out for him, telling him without words that she offered
herself to him, but she would also take in equal measure.

His expression was intense as he watched her movements. And he waited, as if he knew that she was discover-
ing herself. She closed her eyes at the frustration of not
knowing how to tell him that she needed him to discover
her—Cameo, a woman who could match him in all the
important ways.

As she bent over him, her hair fell over her shoulders,
enclosing their faces in an even smaller world. She tasted
salt and soap beneath his ear, traced the hard line of his
jaw with her tongue, laved his lower lip, then bit it gently.
Then she lifted a little to rub her breasts against his chest
and sighed at the feel of his wiry chest hair on sensitive
skin. Memories of the night before tutored her, resurrected
sensations, goaded her to seek more.

Breathing was all but impossible and seemed unneces-
sary as she moved her hips over him one minute and
dipped her head to lick his nipples the next. She slid down
his body again, liking the friction of skin on skin, the soft
textures against hard, the unyielding stroke of his bones,
the response of his firm muscles as she tasted and
kissed . . .

Suddenly she was jerked upward by his hands under her
arms.

"No, Cameo," he rasped, his face tight and strained.

"Why? Isn't it done?"

He didn't know how to answer that. *Yes, it's done, but no, I don't want you to do it?* He couldn't even explain to himself the sudden reluctance he felt at such a symbolic act of complete giving, complete acceptance. It was a vague discomfort in his mind that had nothing to do with physical sensibilities and everything to do with the emotional honesty he wasn't free to give her.

At his silence, Cameo wriggled her body with restless anger, fighting his grip.

"Cameo," he said softly, "not now, sweetheart. I'm not ready for that, yet."

She stilled, raised her head, and gazed at him with surprise and bemusement that changed to defiance and warning when his grip tightened, pulling her up as he tried to take the initiative.

She shook her head and her hair fell around them again, a fragrant curtain that trapped and beguiled him. Never had he felt so helpless in a woman's arms. "Cameo, you don't know what you're doing to me."

"Am I doing it right?"

Breath caught in his chest at the way her hands circled his nipples, the way her hips fit over his, hot and moist. Her gaze was troubled and a little scared. That look touched him and drove out the uneasiness he felt at not being in control. Though Cameo was orchestrating their lovemaking, it was obvious she wasn't in control either. Instinct was. Now that was something he understood. He'd been living on instinct for years.

He smiled, slow and lazy, his eyelids lowered. "You're doing just fine, Rosebud."

Her sigh was jerky and punctuated by a little whimper as she leaned over, offering her breasts to him, crying out as he took them in his hands. Small shivers rushed through her as he stroked her nipples with his thumbs. "More, Zach, like last night."

"Come closer," he whispered.

She stretched out on top of him, propped her upper body up with her elbows, and gasped as he took her into his mouth. So sweet, that pierce of pleasure that struck all the way into her belly. Set free from her restrictions, his hands were rampant on her with feather touches that teased and tormented and promised sharper sensations.

He tasted her with his tongue, drew on her as if she provided the sweetest wine. The air under the quilt was close and warm, filling her with the heady musk of desire. His hands circled the sides of her breasts as his mouth tugged her nipples—one, then the other.

Cameo reasoned that what felt good to her might also feel good to him. With slow deliberation, she pulled away from his mouth and closed her eyes as he held fast until she was out of reach. She moved down his body in a sinuous slide and laved his chest with her tongue as she went, then caught his male nipples between her lips. Her teeth nipped him gently and he shuddered.

"Cameo," he said through clenched teeth. "If you don't quit fooling around, I'm going to jump the gun and embarrass myself."

She sat up, her legs on either side of him, her femininity folding around him, surrounding him with heat and promise. And agony. He waited. Nothing happened.

Cameo stared down at him, a frown puckering her brow, and watched his mouth flatten into a straight line, his eyes grow cold and distant. "Did you plan to light fires and keep them smoldering until there was nothing left of me but a pile of ash?"

At first she heard only the anger, the brutality of his accusation. But then she saw the way he didn't quite meet her eyes, the flush staining his cheeks, and sensed the rejection he felt at her abrupt withdrawal. Once he had turned away from her, and it had been a chafing hurt she hadn't been able to shake. It hadn't occurred to her that men might feel the same way. She shrugged.

"I don't . . . um . . . I'm not sure . . ."

The frustration and vulnerability in her expression stopped his anger cold. The glaze of moisture in her eyes brought a new suspicion to mind. Relief washed over him. For those few seconds he'd felt unmanned, stripped of dignity and his faith that Cameo was not as capricious and wayward as a wildflower, scattering seeds without caring enough to nurture them. "You don't know how . . . ?" he asked gently.

Pride stiffened Cameo's spine at the twitch of his mouth, then just as quickly melted under his tender regard. She blinked and raised up to leave him.

"You were right. I guess this is man's work."

He grasped her around the waist, stopping her, and held her immobile above him. "You started this, sweetheart. It's up to you to finish it."

"But—" She bit her lip against the quiver she heard in her voice, the tears threatening to complete her humiliation.

"Cameo," he said with forced patience. "Look down."

Obediently, she dropped her gaze, and her eyes widened in comprehension as she saw him rising to meet her—like a challenge. "Oh. You mean I can—"

He did grin, then. "Standing at attention and awaiting further orders, ma'am."

Intrigued by the implications of his quip, she watched

raptly as he slowly relaxed his hold and allowed her to descend.

"Zach. Let go." He was nudging her, probing, teasing. With a quick descent that caught him by surprise, she sank onto him a little more. Her eyes widened at the feel of him —there, yet not quite, a promise of fullness, this time without pain.

"Easy, slow down." His mouth slanted at one corner. "Be gentle with me."

"I want—"

"In a minute, Rosebud—" He groaned as she opened over him, took him in, held him, then took him in a little farther until he was lost in the sweet, wet tightness of her.

"We fit, Zach," she whispered. "Is it always like this?"

"No." He felt himself reaching deeper and needed to move, to take over, but her wonder held him in check.

"It's different from last night . . . better."

"Glad to hear it." Hoping she would take the hint, he rotated his hips.

"Should I move?"

"Good idea." He groaned as she rose up and lowered herself again.

"It's like—" Repeating her motion, she leaned over him, moved her hips back and forth, up and down, and then in a slow, tormenting circle.

"Cameo." Blood boiled in his veins. His vision blurred. All of his weight seemed to settle in his groin.

"What?"

He cupped the back of her head with his hands, brought her face down to his as he arched, filling her. "Shut up," he ordered, his voice a guttural whisper against her lips.

"Good idea," she said and allowed him to take her mouth as fiercely as she was taking his body.

She moved her legs, accepted him over and over again as he entered her, withdrew, entered again. Inspiration guided her imagination as she sank down and felt him filling her, then rose again, slowly, concentrating on the strange sensation of suddenly becoming more.

He stroked her in places she didn't know she had. Following him down, she held him tightly within her, unwilling to release him even for a second.

He waited for her next move, and the stillness dissatisfied her. Urgency prompted her to rock. Greed for new sensations drove her to ride. He matched her, rising to meet her, relaxing when she did, then moving in another direction, exciting new places inside her, bringing her to an urgency that robbed her of mind and body. Everything was feeling, emotion, a part of herself that didn't seem to be attached to bones and skin and muscle.

She heard the sounds—pants and whimpers and soft whispers. She felt the heat—burning, consuming.

Twilight dimmed to darkness. She didn't notice. The campfire crackled and cast dancing shadows over their makeshift tent. The only shadow she saw was Zach, his eyes blazing, his hands pulling her down, his mouth seeking hers, his body thrusting upward, driving her to reach for more and more of him as she thrust against him.

Lost. She was lost, no longer herself, but a part of him as surely as he was a part of her. His heart pounded and became hers, as she stopped breathing, stopped living. He breathed life into her mouth, drew life into his, and poured life into her with a sweet rush of warmth and release.

She strained, tightened around him, quickened with a throbbing deep inside that was another kind of heartbeat. And she knew that she had died, for a moment, just a moment, and would never be the same again.

As her cries filled their cocoon, Zach gave her the control he never relinquished easily, until he thought he would die from her demands. It seemed forever, yet he knew it was only moments that they shared all they had to give, took all that they needed. He knew when her heart skipped a beat and stopped for one shattering moment.

His body stiffened, strained, reached. She tightened around him in little spasms that possessed him, renewing completion over and over again, drawing his life into hers. And when he heard Cameo's breathless cry, felt her body shudder, as if she, too, had released a part of herself into his keeping, he knew that she had caught him in a truth he could never deny. The rose had grown new thorns—soft ones that didn't draw blood but imbedded themselves in a man and became a part of him.

Her head drooped; her lips nuzzled in the crook of his shoulder. Her sigh was thready. A minute passed in silence and closeness and tender caresses. Then she raised her head to meet his gaze with a clear, direct stare. "Zach?"

"Hmmm?"

Her hand pressed against his lips as if she were stifling future argument. "Now I know why so many women are willing to say good-bye more than once."

Pain, sudden and sharp, lanced through his chest. He swallowed and looked away. She had just handed him a victory of sorts. But it was defeat, too. If the future held nothing more for him than one long endless trail, Cameo would be there, in his thoughts, his memories, his dreams.

The soul of the rose was in his blood to stay.

20
Borrowed Lives

The rose looked wilted and more than a little green around the petals, Zach noted as he loaded all but the most necessary supplies on the wagon and pulled it into a heavy stand of brush. She sat on the mattress, her hair over one shoulder as she brushed it with slow, careful strokes. Every move she made was wary, as if the next might be the one to crack her head open or turn her stomach inside out. If he was lucky, her discomfort would keep her quiet for the rest of their journey.

Unable to face her just yet, Zach glanced at her from the corner of his eye as he saddled the horses. This wasn't like any other "morning after" he'd ever experienced. But then, this was the first time he had more to worry about than paying for services rendered and vacating the premises so some other randy buck could take his place. He was uncomfortably aware that at the moment he didn't have the wherewithal to give Cameo what he owed her, what she deserved. The hell of it was that she wasn't asking for anything, and she damn sure didn't look as if she expected even so much as the small talk customary after a night of love.

Last night had given a whole new meaning to making love. Screwing had never meant less. He'd always thought that passion was a law unto itself, an act independent of heart and brain. Last night, he'd been as untried as any virgin in the act of love. All of a sudden his heart and his brain were irrevocably connected to his groin, and all three were connected to the sight of Cameo, her scent, the sound of her voice, the memories of her touch.

She was sitting there as calm and quiet as someone who had experienced nothing more than a good night's sleep. Where were the smiles, the intimate glances, the subtle quest for promises women inevitably expected? Didn't she even feel a little bit shy after the way she'd shed her inhibitions along with her clothes? Couldn't she at least moan over her hangover?

And what was that slop she'd spouted about good-byes? It was damn unsettling to think that a roll in the feathers had made her change her mind about good-byes. It made him feel like something she could borrow whenever her cupboard was bare.

Didn't she know that she had brought him to his knees last night? How could she be so calm, as if everything had been settled and her life was a straight, clean trail from here on out?

Maybe to her it was settled.

If he told her otherwise, she probably wouldn't believe him. *You'll do your duty and I'll fight for what's mine.* He hadn't liked her summation of the situation when she said it and he liked it even less now. Everything contributed to his foul mood: Cameo's hangover, which she was trying so hard to hide; the weather that had turned on them while they'd been sleeping under the blankets; the good-bye that was coming when they reached their destination.

Nothing had been solved last night.

"You ready?" Zach asked tersely as he finished saddling the horses.

"Almost. How long have we been traveling?" she asked, her face expressionless as her gaze wandered from the position of the rising sun to the trail to the surrounding countryside, obviously searching for familiar landmarks.

"You don't know?"

She pressed her fingers against her temple. "No. My memory seems a little fuzzy in places."

"Two days," he said, not wanting her to know how little ground they'd covered. He turned his face away from her so she wouldn't see the bitter twist of his mouth. The Hero with a Thousand Faces had suddenly lost his ability to lie without its sticking out all over him like a flaming case of hives.

Suspicion came to his rescue. This country was savage for anyone who didn't know the secret trails and twisting canyons. "Do I have to tie you up to keep you from escaping?"

Reproach was tangible in her sad smile. "I have more sense than to strand myself in strange territory without food or water."

"You could take our provisions," he goaded her.

"No, I couldn't," she replied, her meaning clear. She couldn't leave him stranded either. Dumping the few drops of whiskey from her canteen, she refilled it from the stream and watched him load the bedding onto the wagon and cover it with branches and leaves.

"Then I guess I won't have to tie you up."

"Where are we going?"

"You'll know when we get there."

"How much farther?"

"A ways." He held out the reins of her horse, a silent order to mount up and shut up. Her questions were making him nervous. Her acceptance was driving him crazy. Her calmness made him wonder if last night had happened at all. Not once had she mentioned it. Not once had she acted like a woman who had spent the night making love and impulsive declarations.

Cameo mounted and waited with studied patience for him to follow suit.

"You feel all right?" he asked. A green cast had come over her face when she'd swung up into the saddle.

"I'm fine." She swallowed, and took a deep, slow breath.

"No . . . uh . . . feebles?" Her wince as Diamond shifted told its own story.

"None whatsoever."

Nodding, he mounted Pegasus, snatched her reins out of her hand, and took a southwest direction away from their campsite. Cameo didn't protest his high-handed treatment, but held on to the saddle horn and focused on their surroundings.

Trees coated by morning frost seemed almost transparent, like ghosts in a living world, each trapped in its own loneliness. Wind swept through the skeletal branches, keening mournfully. The pewter sky offered no hope of sunlight, and the mesas and plateaus layered in the distance rose at forbidding angles. What had seemed so magical to her yesterday now appeared harsh and brutal, like reality.

Reality was Zach, his form fading in and out of the morning mist, the embodiment of the shadow warrior, his back straight, uncompromising, his silence more eloquent than words of farewell. Reality was the way he had left her before dawn to break camp and sort through clothing and provisions. He hadn't looked at her, or spoken, except to deliver curt instructions to her and soothing whispers to his horse.

But, then, he knew his horse better than he knew her. She closed her eyes and swallowed down another wave of nausea. Her head felt like a lead cannonball, and a war was being fought in her stomach. Every once in a while the taste of brandy came back to haunt her. She was in no condition to reason with herself, much less confront Zach with her confusion over his behavior. The best she could do was remain calm and as still as possible.

Her stomach rolling with each step Diamond took over rocky ground, Cameo set her mind on anything but the pounding in her head. What she wouldn't give for a few hours more at their camp—a few more hours to calm her body and observe Zach's behavior toward her.

Before she'd had to move unduly, she'd been fascinated by his reactions. She'd awakened to the barest hint of a new day, the sky a light gray that made it seem as if it were still twilight. For a few disoriented minutes, she'd thought that time had stood still. It had pleased her, that continued sense of being alone in the world—no war, no problems, no inhibitions. There had been only Zach, holding her close, his hand possessive on her hip.

Only her first clear-eyed look at Zach had produced an odd reaction from him. His face had turned red and his gaze hadn't quite met hers, as if he were embarrassed. Hadn't he ever been ravished before? And that was what had happened. Her memory was as clear as her intentions had been last night. The way he was acting, one would think that it had been the other way around and he was feeling guilt or regret.

Neither prospect pleased her. For her, the night before

had been rich with happiness and sharing. One look at Zach had cast shadows over it all and made her feel as if the memories were hers alone. Now she felt as if she were riding through a land that seemed frozen by time with only a shadow for company.

The trail disappeared, and the ground became increasingly more difficult to navigate. Deep ravines opened out of solid ground, entrances to box canyons beckoned like doors to nowhere, and towering mesas rose abruptly from the earth to disappear into the clouds. Trees and brush grew in thick clumps next to bare stretches of stone made slick by the frost. Loose rocks littered the ground, threatening the horses' hooves with every step they took.

Diamond's jerky motions and abrupt stops and starts kept Cameo's stomach in a constant state of conflict with her will. All her blood seemed to be pounding in her head. Releasing breath through her teeth, she grabbed a handful of Diamond's mane and pulled back. Obediently, Diamond stopped.

Zach reined in Pegasus and turned in his saddle to give Cameo an impatient glare.

"I lied," she stated bluntly. "I am not all right."

"The feebles," Zach muttered.

"Among other things, yes."

"Your shoulder?" he asked with just enough concern to annoy her.

"My shoulder is fine. It's my thighs, and my"—she searched for a word and blurted the only one she knew—"my privates."

His brows descended. "We're riding on," he said.

"*I've* been riding all night," she said tartly. "For that, I at least deserve some coffee and a biscuit."

"*Riding,*" he snarled, "was your idea, not mine." With

short, jerky motions, he rummaged in his saddlebags, then tossed a cloth-wrapped packet of biscuits at her. "Eat slowly or you'll lose it."

Cameo reached out and caught the packet, then dropped it into the pocket of her coat. "Thank you so much," she said sweetly. Leaning over Diamond's neck, she took hold of the reins. Zach had been leading her long enough. "I'm ready whenever you are."

The bid for independence cost her. Unable to spare even the smallest concentration on anything but the ground in front of her, Cameo had to ignore her discomfort and the hunger that had begun to nag in earnest. It could have been minutes or hours that the biscuits lay ignored in her pocket as she struggled to keep Zach in sight. They were riding higher and higher into the low-lying clouds. Diamond was as surefooted as a goat, but she had to pick her way carefully over the unfamiliar ground. Pegasus moved right along as if he knew every pockmark in the trail.

Her stomach rumbled, the sound seeming to echo off the rock walls surrounding them. She might have been embarrassed by it if Zach wasn't ignoring her, his head cocked as if he were seeing something besides a sheer cliff face.

A long, thin shadow played on the rock, wavering in the heavy mist, then becoming solid and deep. Too deep to be a shadow. Zach rode straight toward it, his image less substantial than the utterly black slash in the rock. Pegasus's head and flanks vanished into that darkness; then he stopped at Zach's command.

Cameo blinked at the apparition of a man sitting on a horse that appeared to be half-imbedded in the cliff. She looked up and squinted, trying to see through the cloud that sat around the cliff like a threadbare collar.

"Give me your reins," Zach ordered in a hushed voice, his body turned toward her, his arm outstretched.

She gazed at him, a question in her eyes.

"It's like Spirit Canyon, only steeper and darker," he explained quietly. "We don't speak in there. Sound shoots out of the opening like a bullet."

We? That raised questions she had been trying to avoid. There was no sign of habitation, no sign of anyone's having passed this way before. An ethereal atmosphere surrounded them, a feeling of forgotten lives and unknown places. With every step they traveled, she was being taken farther from home, farther from the problems that needed solving. The ranch was abandoned, easy prey for her enemy.

Impatient, Zach rode back to her and snatched the reins from her hands.

The slash in the rock face became darker and lengthened as the sun sank a little lower in the sky. She reached over, tried to jerk the reins from his hand. "No. We have to go back."

"It's a little late for this," he said in an undertone.

"It's late for a lot of things, Zach," she said, pointedly referring to his attitude rather than to her protest.

"Then there's no point in discussing it." With that he jerked on Diamond's reins and led the way into the shadow.

She pulled on Diamond's mane. "You're planning to leave me, aren't you?"

He crossed his arms over his saddle horn and stared at the ground.

"I won't be left behind. The ranch is all but abandoned—"

"You just now remembering to worry about it?"

No. I just needed to be lost for a while. She shook her head. "I worried," she said quietly. "But I wasn't thinking. I have to go back."

"You're still not thinking," he said. "This isn't a democracy, Cameo. You'll do as I say, go where I take you, and stay till I say you can leave."

"Go where? Stay where and with whom?"

"You won't be alone." He straightened and tugged on Diamond's reins.

"Another secret, Zach?"

He turned on her, his expression angry and tight. "Not for long. Now keep quiet and hold on. It's rough going." Giving her no chance to answer and no choice but to comply, he nudged Pegasus forward and lead her into the void.

They rode slowly through a tunnel that spiraled upward, their only light a distant pinprick in the roof. She heard a rustle as they moved through some sort of covering on the ground—rushes, she supposed, that muffled the ring of hoofbeats on stone.

Shivers crawled up her spine at the darkness, and she focused on that tiny point of light. The rock walls seemed to be closing in on her, squeezing out the air, and she felt as if the weight of the mountain were crushing her. The light grew larger, yet still it was far away, sometimes disappearing altogether as the tunnel wound around and around.

After a final bend the light widened—not in the roof at all but the end of the tunnel above a sharp incline. She had the sensation of falling backward as Diamond scrambled to take the rise. Even the watery light of the day seemed bright and spotted her vision for a few moments. Focus returned and she saw that they were still in a tunnel, but without a roof. The sheer walls on either side widened steadily. She leaned over to keep her balance and the better to see what lay ahead.

She grasped Diamond's mane at the sensation of pitching forward as the trail abruptly leveled and the walls fell away. Trees and brush, natural mufflers for sound, surrounded them. She kicked Diamond and urged her to catch up with Zach.

He didn't spare her a look as she pulled up alongside him and yanked her reins from his hold. "Where are we?" she asked again.

"Quiet," he muttered.

"Tell me," she whispered.

Silence.

"How long are we staying?"

Nothing.

Clearly he had no intention of telling her anything. She had other ideas. Fear was trying to get a stranglehold on her. Only when she'd gone to the Academy for Young Ladies in Santa Fe had she been away from home alone, and then she'd known where she was and why. She'd also known when she'd return to the valley. It hadn't been so different from living at the ranch since her father had been a frequent visitor during the winter months. But this was a strange world—isolated, lost.

"Stop," she ordered and dragged back on the reins. Surprisingly, Zach complied. In her present uncharitable state of mind she wouldn't have put it past him to keep on going without her. His long-suffering expression did nothing to improve her temper, but he didn't give her a chance to display it.

"We're on a mesa," he said in a whispered monotone. "It's an abandoned Indian village. I was born here, as was my mother. You are going to stay here with my people until I say otherwise." His brow rose a fraction of an inch. "Any more questions?"

"A hundred," she snapped.

"Pick one."

With that implied ultimatum, she couldn't think straight enough to choose, and so chose unwisely. "Why are we whispering?"

His mouth slanted in mockery. "Because we like our privacy." As if they hadn't just had such an odd confrontation, he spurred Pegasus and continued on his way.

Cameo bristled over every hard-won fact, but again her anger was interrupted. Blurred shapes rose ahead—buildings made of native sandstone that blended in with the landscape, their contours and colors barely discernible from the rock around them. Timber and brush grew everywhere, untamed and free of cultivation.

Cameo saw no movement and heard nothing but the sigh of spirits in the wind, which gave her a sense of age and peace and ancient legends. More dwellings stood farther back, yet appeared to be less desolate, in better repair. There the vegetation had a more restrained look. It was an Indian village as she had never seen before. *Indian.* She frowned at that. No Indians she had ever seen even remotely resembled Zach or his mother. Spring McAllister had been fair of skin and dark of hair, with a streak of blond winging back from her temple, like the slashes of silver in Zach's hair . . .

Like the streak she had seen in Cloud Walker's hair—

Sound diverted her attention—a muted sweetness in the breeze, a harmonious sound of reverence. She cocked her head to listen and picked out a melody. It was an old hymn, one her father had often hummed as he painted, a hymn from the land of his mother. And it was being sung by children, their voices a mere whisper inside the largest structure.

Shapes seemed to materialize from nowhere, moving with serenity and purpose. Their voices, too, were no more than undertones as they greeted one another and stopped to converse. Glancing around her, she realized that they had been there all along, unnoticed because they seemed to be a part of the mesa, like the trees and rocks. All around her she imagined past lives walking silently, invisibly alongside the flesh-and-blood people, the evidence of their passing in the deep furrows where many feet had trodden and she imagined the chant of ancient voices harmonizing with those of the children.

As her gaze skimmed over the inhabitants, she felt a sense of wrong about it all. Clearly this place had been built by a band of natives. These people didn't seem to fit. It struck her that they walked and spoke like visitors who were careful not to disturb their hosts.

Her head turned one way, then the other, as she studied the people and their activities. One man was bent over a chair he was building. Other pieces of furniture littered the area around his dwelling. Near another house a woman placed pans of dough into an outdoor oven, a rack of freshly baked goods behind her. Cameo's mouth watered at the yeasty fragrance of bread and the spicy scent of apple pie. Another woman approached, a basket of eggs hooked over her arm.

Cameo focused on a man who had left his loom and the blanket he was weaving to approach Zach, his hand raised in greeting, his smile showing pleasure. Her thoughts were fragmented, bits and pieces of information and impressions that didn't fit together. . . .

Visitors. Yeast. Furniture and modern looms. Streaks of

light hair and blue eyes and fair features. She knew then what was wrong. She'd expected these people to be Indians, but all of them were dressed in white man's clothing and were conducting their lives in the white man's ways. She heard the children again, reciting the alphabet, their speech English with a western drawl. Automatically her gaze traveled from Zach to the others and back again. . . .

The Others. Cloud Walker. Her guardians. Of course.

As if he heard her thoughts, Zach turned around to watch her, betraying nothing in his expression. The man beside him spoke and Zach nodded. Before she could hold on to the saddle horn for balance, they were moving forward to the outer boundaries of the settlement.

The man who had been speaking to Zach tipped his hat and spoke softly as she rode by him. "Welcome, Cameo." She was too stunned to answer.

Zach stopped in front of a dwelling on the fringe of the community. Another man appeared and began to unpack their supplies before taking their horses away. Zach helped her dismount. Her legs wobbled and her head throbbed in confusion as she wordlessly followed him into the house of stone. A hundred questions hovered on the tip of her tongue, yet she said nothing as she studied her surroundings.

The doorway of the dwelling was strange, a T-shape rather than a rectangle. The rooms were small and opened into one another like a maze. Instead of a fireplace, the main room had a fire pit hollowed from a dirt floor that was packed hard from the weight of many feet. Long narrow windows were sparse, but they had been brightened by gaily colored gingham curtains. The musty smell she'd expected was absent. Instead she discovered all the odors she associated with home: beeswax and soap, lantern oil and herbs.

With quick, economical movements, Zach made coffee over the fire pit, which had already been lit. The fragrance hit her like a blow. Her stomach rumbled.

"Eat your biscuits," he ordered in a low rasp.

Cameo barely heard him as she stood in the center of the room, staring at first one object and then another. An old rocking chair occupied one corner and a table took up a large portion of the center. A doorway suggested another room beyond. Shelves were built on one wall and held all manner of foodstuffs: flour, sugar, salt, coffee, beans, and salt pork.

The same woman she had seen tending her oven entered silently and placed a loaf of bread, a pie, and a bowl of eggs on the table, then left with nothing more than a smile.

Cameo shook her head and immediately regretted it. Her body swayed with fatigue and hunger and the throbbing above her eyes. Stumbling, she made her way to the rocker and dropped into it like a sack of flour. "I have to know, Zach: am I awake?"

"Near as I can tell . . . here, eat first, yell later."

She took a deep breath as she accepted the mug of coffee and slice of bread he gave her. The coffee was laced with sugar and whiskey, and every sip soothed the spasms in her stomach. The bread eased her hunger but not her impatience. She gazed up at him. "Indians, Zach?"

"I didn't say that."

Another evasion from the truth. Another tightening of the rack stretching her control to the limit. "I—"

"Shh." He held his finger to his lips.

"Privacy be damned! Besides, if children can sing, I can speak in a normal tone of voice," she whispered.

He exhaled slowly. "You might as well say it all while you have your dander up."

She didn't need a second invitation and cut loose with the temper she'd been controlling all day. "You've lied to me, gotten me drunk, kidnapped me, dragged me across the most savage country I've ever seen, and now you're proposing to leave me here without a single clue as to who my *hosts* are, much less why any of us are here in the first place." Her voice ended on a squeak as she ran out of air.

"I'm not *proposing* shit, Rosebud. I'm doing it." He raked his hand through his hair, tumbling his hat off his head in the process. "You're staying here because it's safe and the ranch isn't. Your shoulder needs healing. This is the only way I can keep you from getting your sweet little ass in more trouble than you can handle. I have a job to do and you're a distraction I can't afford, and you didn't seem to mind being kidnapped yesterday." He came toward her with the coffee pot. "More?" he asked as if nothing had passed between them but social pleasantries.

"Straight," she said darkly, "and you didn't seem to mind being distracted by my *sweet little ass* yesterday." Gulping the coffee, she burned her tongue, cursed, and glared at him. It had all come to this one issue—last night —the only issue over which she felt she had any control. The only issue she gave three hoots in Hades about at this point.

"Was that expedient, too, Zach? Is that why you were so easily persuaded against honor and nobility?" She swallowed against the aching tightness in her throat and blamed it on the need to yell in a whisper. "How felicitous my ardor must have been for you. How convenient for you to accept passion instead of questions and arguments concerning your plans for me. How blissfully ignorant I allowed myself to be."

Zach slammed the pot on the grate and stood silently staring at the embers glowing in the pit.

The silence stretched long and tough as a rawhide whip between them and cut into her just as deeply. "You could at least tell me that I'm wrong," she said in a small voice, feeling even smaller. Hadn't she sworn to herself that there would be no recriminations, no demands beyond the moment?

Still he didn't speak. Still he stood with the glow of the fire bathing his face in unholy light. Then his shoulders heaved.

"You're wrong," he said flatly and strode out the door.

All she could do was stare at the fire pit—where he'd been—and then at the doorway. His shadow loomed there for a moment before he walked back in with the supplies they'd brought. He stood there watching her as she automatically set the rocker in motion, her eyes blinking furiously.

He moved into the room so slowly that she didn't realize he was walking toward her until she saw his face, its lines drawn and tense, his body straight, his eyes blank and gray as the sky. Pausing in front of her, he stared down at her, his gaze slow and lingering. With movements so careful it seemed that he was in pain, he bent over, slid his arms under her knees, around her shoulders, and lifted her.

Weariness rushed over her. Closing her eyes, she laid her head on his shoulder and allowed him to carry her where he might, for the moment, not caring about anything. She'd been running in too many circles lately.

Softness yielded beneath her as he lowered her onto a feather mattress as soft as any she had at home and covered her with a blanket. She felt his breath on her cheek, smelled the masculine blend of leather and horse and warmth that was uniquely his.

"You're wrong, Rosebud," he said again.

Opening her eyes, she held him with her gaze. "It wasn't about promises, Zach."

His mouth twitched, but not in amusement, as he turned his back on her and walked to the door.

"You said I was a woman for years, Zach," she said as if he were still beside her. He stopped but didn't face her. "Didn't you know that years are built on moments?"

Again his shoulders heaved as his voice rasped with words left unused for too long. "The people here—my people—have been borrowing time for centuries," he said. "Even our lives are borrowed. The only thing I know is that you can't build on something you don't own."

21

Lost Souls Found

The Place of Lost Souls—November 1862

We are outcasts, driven from our land of Wales by a war between brothers. Our leader is strong and brave, but we are frightened and follow without choice or hope. The sea upon which we sail will consume our energies, then spit us out to fall over the edge of the world, if we do not starve to death first. . . .

Our journey is at an end. I do not know how long our pitiful little fleet has traveled, but with our feet seeking purchase in this strange new land, it no longer seems to matter. We have found the soil to be as rich and welcoming as the natives. . . .

It is again time for us to steal away like thieves, though we never take more than is offered and always repay with our skills and knowledge. What a bitter irony that it is our own kind that sends us into flight with their diseases and greed and prejudice. . . .

This is our final resting place—a mesa with its history carved and painted on the walls of the ruins in strange characters and faded scenes. It is fitting, this

*place with no name and no people, for we will die here,
nameless and lost as the spirits we hear keening in the
wind. Centuries of wandering and seeking with no
clear trail to mark our passing. We hear that we have
become a legend. We will die so, like shadows drifting
beneath the clouds.*

The book had no title and the authors no credit. Fitting,
Cameo supposed, for the scribes who had recorded the
history of a nation of lost souls. Over and over again in the
last three weeks she had read entries from the journal she'd
found buried in a chest at the foot of her bed.

At first her questions about the journal had gone unan-
swered and avoided. The Others were friendly, welcoming,
and stubbornly silent on their history. *We are beginning
again,* she'd been told. *We have hope. Our past must be
forgotten or we will be driven over the edge of the world.*
And so the journal—Zach's property handed down from
one generation to another, she'd learned—had been buried
deep in a chest and would be destroyed when the Others
left the mesa. Their children did not even know of their
history and would never know any heritage but the one
fabricated by two enterprising wanderers named Jacob
McAllister and Samuel Fielding.

Her lower lip caught between her teeth, Cameo turned
to the last passage entered over thirty years ago.

*We have been discovered by those of white skin, one who
comes from the old land of Wales and another who seems to
have sprung from the forest itself. Our fears have not come
to pass. Jacob has taken my daughter, Spring, to wife, and
Samuel, the one who knows the old language, has conceived
a plan rooted in insanity. Yet is it more insane than a flight
over uncharted waters? Hope breeds eternal among my peo-*

ple. Perhaps that is why we still thrive and learn and keep the old ways. For such a practical race, we are childishly eager to embrace a dream . . .

"Oh, Papa, what a legacy you've given me," she whispered to the empty room, knowing that a part of her father lingered on the mesa with the people of his blood. People who had understood what it was like to be a tree forever cut away from its roots. She, too, felt a kinship with the Others, for while she had roots, she'd grown in barren soil.

Cameo had been accepted into their ranks as if she'd always been a part of their odd society. In a way, she supposed that she did belong—at least with one fourth of her heritage, since her father's mother was from Wales. She even knew a little of their language—English accented by lilting Welsh.

They never spoke the old language anymore, they'd explained. They had explained a great deal in the last five weeks, and Cameo had been shocked, educated, troubled, and healed until her head reeled and her patience literally hung over the edge of a precipice.

Something had to be done.

"How many times are you going to read that book?" A tall man sauntered into the dwelling where Zach had left her sleeping five weeks ago. This man had awakened her the next morning with breakfast and a twinkle in his blue eyes that belied the Indian garb he wore.

She traced the lines on the page with her finger. "It fascinates me, Walker. Not many people come face to face with a legend."

"Legend, Cameo," Cloud Walker said in a warning tone. "Some secrets are better left unspoken."

"Do you really believe that?"

"In this case, yes." He paced to the fire pit to pour

himself a mug of coffee. At first the Others had insisted on taking care of all Cameo's needs, but it hadn't taken her long to assume her own housekeeping chores. If she hadn't, she would have gone mad with boredom.

"But it's such a rich legacy," she argued, not for the first time.

"Cameo, every year another adventurer in the outside world takes on the quest of finding the lost tribe of Wales. If discovered, we'd be conversation pieces at best and recruits for a traveling circus at worst. What else would a blue-eyed, hairy Indian be good for? Certainly after several hundred years of living among the Indians we wouldn't be civilized." He stared broodingly at the steam rising from his cup, then sighed. "We're lucky that it was Sam and Jacob who found us, and luckier still that Jacob married Spring. In one way or another, they both felt tied to us and were honorable enough to take our best interests to heart."

After adding sugar and fresh cream to his coffee, he sat cross-legged at her feet as he did every evening, to talk, and to watch her while the villagers were occupied with their families. "We have to get out of here before we're found. Time is our enemy. So is science. With every season that passes, more settlers are moving west. Already man has won small skirmishes with gravity with the hot-air balloons the army is using for reconnaissance. The country is getting smaller, and by the time the war is over, there won't be anywhere to hide."

"Except in plain sight," Cameo said wryly. "I understand what you're doing. It makes sense for you to rejoin your own race, but with Papa gone, I don't know how to carry on."

"It will work out, Cameo." Cloud Walker had said that before, too, but Cameo was tired of listening.

"For such a practical race, we are childishly eager to embrace a dream," she quoted.

"Not childishly, Cameo. Desperately," he said soberly. "And it's worked so far. Our young men and women have been educated at the best universities. The children have been raised just like the ones below. The families that have already left are doing well, and they seem to have little trouble fitting in as new immigrants."

"What about the large group that left two weeks ago?"

"Believe me, they're doing better than most."

"Where did they go?"

He shrugged in answer.

Cameo sighed in frustration. "The ranch and freight business are prosperous, but not enough for me to continue with Papa's plans. You have thirty people ready for university now, and there are still businesses to finance for others. Where did Papa find the money to do it all?"

Cloud Walker smiled, his eyes hooded, reminding Cameo that he and Zach were indeed cousins. The ability to dissemble appeared to be a family trait.

"Surely Papa gave you some idea of where the money came from."

"He and Jacob never said anything except that our benefactor was an old man with gold teeth." Rising, he carried his mug to the basin of dishwater and rinsed it out. "As for education and businesses—I think that those of us who are already established should take on that responsibility now. We've accepted enough charity."

"Does it bother you so much?"

Rocking on his heels, Cloud Walker stared up at the wooden beams in the ceiling. "We're a brutally practical people, Cameo. We took the only choice open to us in order to survive."

"But you'll feel better when you can do it on your own," she finished for him.

"Wouldn't you?" He winced as if he knew what door he'd opened with the question.

"Of course," she said tartly. "Why do you think I've tried to escape twice? I don't like other people managing my life either."

"Try it again and I'll put bars on the windows and doors," he grumbled.

Careful not to betray her smugness, she favored him with a look of serene acceptance. "I've learned my lesson."

"Damn good thing. Zach would feed my carcass to the buzzards if you got away."

She snorted inelegantly. "Are you speaking of the coward who slithered out of here in the middle of the night without a word? The only thing missing was a dollar on the bedside table."

"Only a dollar?" Cloud Walker edged his way toward the door with a devilish grin on his handsome face. "Hmm. So that's why he wanted to borrow some money. Unfortunately . . ." He gestured toward his breechclout. "I don't have any pockets."

Cameo sent him on his way with a flush and a reluctant smile. It was a measure of the affinity she'd discovered with Cloud Walker, alias Walker McCloud, M.D., that such teasing could be taken with goodwill. It was a measure of her state of mind that Cloud Walker's joke revived the melancholy that hovered over her like a dismal winter cloud.

You can't build on something you don't own. Zach had told her so much with those words. Hopeless words that left little room for change or doubt, as if he had lost so much of his soul on the legend that there was nothing left of the man. Yet she knew better. The disguises and names were the legend—borrowed lives to suit his purposes—but the soul was his.

And as soon as she put escape plan number three into action, she would find a way to prove it to him.

Cameo strolled through the village, smiling at those she passed and waving to others bent over their tasks. They were accustomed to her daily walks and confident that she was resigned to her captivity. They expected her to explore the mesa and to return each afternoon with a basket full of roots to make paints and dyes. They had no idea that her only talent in the arts lay in whitewashing the broad side of a barn.

She hadn't lied to Cloud Walker; she had learned her lesson. This time she was going to escape in broad daylight when her benevolent jailers least expected it. At night the people on the mesa were more aware of unnatural sounds in the peace that fell over the community. At night she had a guard whose sole responsibility was to watch her dwelling. At night the darkness in the tunnel had paralyzed her the one time she had made it that far.

As far as everyone knew, she'd been "good" for the week since her last escape attempt. But they didn't know that she'd found a way to the tunnel without using the only visible trail. They had no idea that her friendship with Chauncey, an old widower who rode his horse everywhere he went on the mesa, was more than a result of her outgoing nature.

Reaching the edge of the mesa, she knelt in a stand of bushes and began to dig—just in case anyone had followed her progress. The hour passed slowly as she randomly pulled up roots and tossed them into her basket. When she judged the sun to have moved sufficiently, she sorted through her cache and pulled out an old single-shot pistol she'd found among the treasures in the chest, her knife, and a small kit of ammunition. Nervously she glanced about her, searching for Chauncey and, more importantly, his horse. Without the mare, her plans would come to naught.

She began to dig, ignoring roots and feeling for the supplies she had buried in an oilskin. In the pack she'd stashed jerky and dried fruit, four precious cans of milk, and an empty wineskin to hold water. Right on schedule, her transport arrived.

"Ho, Miss Cameo."

"Ho, Chauncey," she called out and waved to the man, who was already weaving toward his favorite drinking spot. From the looks of him, it would only be a matter of minutes before he fell into his usual Saturday drunken stupor. Even a model community of upstanding citizens had their town drunk.

"You goin' t' shtart paintin' yer pixure soon?"

"Soon, Chauncey," she said lightly as she watched him collapse in the shade of the tree and guzzle down half the contents of a bottle of Lightning.

It took an hour of belches and hiccups for Chauncey to launch his sheets into the wind.

Stealthily Cameo made her way to his horse, untied it from a tree limb, and led it toward an overgrown path to the entrance corridor. "Thank you, Chauncey," she whispered.

"Welcome, ma'am."

She stopped in her tracks and held her breath. If caught this time, she would not escape the mesa until Zach decreed it. Knowing him, that would be when the war ended or women won the vote, whichever came first. *Please go back to sleep, Chauncey, so I can go home.*

Chauncey whuffled and snored.

Cameo gathered her courage to face the tunnel alone.

Home. Home. Home. The steady gait of her horse seemed to echo her single thought as she guided the mare through the rough country. She used her memory of oddly shaped trees and rock formations for landmarks and the sun for a compass. All was silent except for the occasional snap of tree limbs made glassy and brittle by the cold as she brushed against them in the dense landscape.

She had a few problems. A lot of the trees had odd shapes, and all the rock formations were unusual. The sun hung like a dim lantern behind an opaque gray curtain of clouds, sometimes becoming lost in the heavy folds. A fragile thread separated her from failure. If she continued forward, she put distance between herself and defeat. If she turned back, she had a chance of returning to the safety of the mesa without becoming lost.

How soon before the Others finished their midday meal and discovered that she wasn't at the far end of the mesa gathering roots and picnicking by herself? She'd made little headway and could still see the outline of the mesa in the all-too-near distance. It wouldn't take Cloud Walker long to track her if she didn't make some fast time.

For the last mile or so she'd been riding right down the middle of a shallow creek, which was thinly crusted with ice and closely hugged by trees. It ended just ahead at another cliff face with a thin trickling waterfall. She veered out of the water and frowned in concentration as she studied her surroundings. A trail lay ahead, and to its right a group of boulders were stacked where they had fallen after breaking away from an overhang high above. An intriguing crevice cut into the pile.

Dismounting, she led her horse to the formation. Picking up a dead pine branch, she brushed over the crevice, then probed inside. The branch was easily six feet long, yet it didn't connect with a back wall of the recess. Better yet, the opening was wide and couldn't be seen from the trail. Longingly she glanced back at the blurred outline of the mesa, then resolutely brushed away her tracks leading from the creek with the dried needles still clinging to the end of the tree limb. Failure was not in her plans, regardless of how foolish they seemed to her now.

She wanted to go home.

With thorough sweeps she brushed the walls of her hideaway to send any tiny livestock and reptiles skittering for a new place to winter. Then she urged Chauncey's placid mare into the space as she swept away traces of their presence behind her.

Inside, she discovered light pouring in from above where no boulders sealed her off from the sky. She was inside a ring of rock and could easily climb up, propping her back on one wall and her legs against the other, to watch the trail as she rested and ate—

At first she thought it was the wind singing through the canyons, so subtle and light was the sound. But as she listened, she realized it was a baritone humming a melody she didn't recognize. The voice was raspy, in perfect tune, and as familiar as her dreams. She scooted down as far as she could and still see and watched in horror as a shadow materialized around the bend of the trail.

He rode slouched in the saddle, relaxed and smiling, a cigar tucked into a corner of his mouth. Lines of strain had been erased from his face as if he hadn't a care in the world. The melody he hummed was light and quick, a sound of pleasure and celebration.

Her heart stalled in her chest as he slowed Pegasus and twisted in the saddle. Her back scraped against the rock supporting her as she slipped down a little farther. He didn't miss a note and his attention was directed to his saddlebags rather than on the trail or above it. He pulled out a bundle and untied the packet with his teeth to reveal meat sandwiched between two thick slices of bread. "That Mellie sure can cook. Too bad you can't appreciate her talents," he said to Pegasus.

They passed by, Zach munching with relish and Pegasus snorting and tossing his head as if he were anxious to end the journey. "Hold your water, old son. We'll face the music soon enough. As long as Cameo doesn't do the singing, we'll come through. . . ." His voice faded with the turn of a bend.

Cameo stuck out her tongue. Let him eat fresh bread and meat. She had the luxury of canned milk. And who was Mellie? How many *talents* did she have?

It set her teeth on edge. Here she was admittedly frightened, steeped in self-pity, and doubting her own ability to survive in this savage wilderness, and Zach was riding along as if it were a Sunday afternoon in the park. She was chewing—and chewing—on jerky and he had just partaken of a feast. For that and for leaving her in the middle of the night among strangers, she'd like to hang him by his . . . his appendage!

Cameo pulled herself higher and glared at the trail. It seemed to her that she was more acquainted with his backside than with his front.

What in blazes was he so happy about? Didn't he know that once he arrived at the mesa, he would have to face the full power of her ire? She'd concocted a dozen imaginative and diabolical ways to make him pay for his precipitous desertion of her, from putting ants in his bedroll to tying him to a chair and making him listen to her sing for a week.

Except that she wasn't at the mesa.

Panic gripped her, the urge to put as much distance between herself and the search party he would no doubt organize. She winced as she slid down the rock and landed on the ground, bottom first. The mare stepped aside and grunted but otherwise continued to munch from her feed bag. Belatedly it occurred to Cameo that she'd been stupidly careless. She'd been so preoccupied with Zach that she hadn't spared a thought to the danger of the horse giving her away. Thank heavens the mare was as concerned with her feed as Chauncey was with his bottle.

On her hands and knees, Cameo crawled to the opening and peered out. Zach had completely disappeared, but she could hear the echo of hoofbeats. Apparently he'd spurred Pegasus into a livelier pace. She cursed him for knowing the trail so well that he could move quickly. He would reach the tunnel in a fourth of the time it had taken her to get this far away from it.

Cameo bit her lip in indecision. Should she remain in her hiding place or ride as fast as possible for the ranch? Zach's tracks would at least lead her in the right direction.

What had happened to ease the air of tension that had surrounded him when he'd left? She quelled her next thought, refusing to dwell on the fear it bred. What if he'd solved the mystery of the missing gold? What if he'd come to take her home, tie up loose ends, and leave again? Oddly enough, she'd rather blame his relaxed manner on the mysterious Mellie and her "cooking."

Cameo shook her head, removed the feed bag, and pulled the mare out of the ring of boulders. There was no time to waste, and she could as easily think on the long ride back to the valley. Pointing her horse in the direction she thought home might be, she nudged its barrel and clicked her tongue.

Twenty feet down the trail, her eyes blinked furiously. Tears chilled as they ran down her cheeks. No! She would not do it. Home was freedom. Papa had always said that freedom was a prize reserved for those with enough imagination to want it, enough strength to hold on to it, and enough balls to go after it in the first place. Her trembling chin lifted a notch. She had balls—where they counted the most. A giggle fought its way out of her misery.

The mare moved on as Cameo struggled against the insistent tug of her bond to Zach, drawing her thoughts back the way she had come. *Puppet strings,* she told herself. *I am not a wooden doll to be yanked to and fro.* The ranch seemed too far away; the mesa was all too close. She bit her lip to stifle a howl of anguish. Never before had she lost sight of her goals, the certainty of what she wanted—needed—from life. Zach had turned her convictions into lies; he'd jerked her world out from under her and left her to dangle in his wake. Zach—a wanderer with no thought to the future beyond his next disguise, his next deception.

Still she felt the need to follow him, a drag from strings hopelessly tangled. She swiped away tears with the back of her hand. How could she dance at his direction, inhabit scenes of his choosing? She kicked the mare forward.

Soon Zach would be searching for her under every pebble in the territory, thus delaying his own return to the ranch. What a sad state she was in to acknowledge that the ranch needed him more than it had ever needed her. He had it all—the fate of the ranch and the direction of her future, and like a puppet master, he held her soul.

"Damn and blast!" she said, and wheeled the mare around. Self-pity gave way to self-disgust and resignation. How appropriate that she not only couldn't escape but had made a conscious decision to return to a place of lost souls in search of her own.

22

Stripped to the Soul

The village looked as if a giant child had lost a toy and had turned everything upside down looking for it. Pandemonium reigned among the normally tranquil inhabitants as men saddled their mounts and women filled saddlebags with food, canteens with water, and gun belts and rifles with ammunition. Zach stood in the middle of it all, barking orders, his mouth tight, his glare at Cloud Walker angry.

Cameo paused on the fringe of the village and swallowed down laughter. Though her mind was cluttered with emotion and her eyes were swollen from the tears that had dried on her cheeks, her expression was serene.

One by one, people stopped in their tracks as she rode calmly down the narrow road. Silence swept their ranks in a slow, rolling wave, keeping pace with her progress. With nods and crocodile smiles, she greeted each man, woman, and child. Always she kept her gaze focused on the man standing in the middle of the chaos. Naturally, she thought wryly, his back was turned to her.

The progressive wave of sudden silence following in the wake of slow, measured hoofbeats caught Zach's attention before he felt the tingle on the back of his neck, the warmth working its way through his body, a presence that shouldn't be there. His muscles tensed; his shoulders squared.

Cloud Walker glanced up, and his mouth fell open. He blinked, a smile widening across his face. "Well, I'll be damned."

Zach's head jerked up. With forced leisure, he turned around as the hoofbeats grew louder, closer. For some reason he wasn't surprised to see Cameo riding through the village like a queen reviewing her troops. Evidently she considered him the lowest member of the ranks. Her gaze skimmed over him as she rode past, a patronizing smile barely tipping up the corners of her mouth. He stared after her, as mute as the rest of the population, but not nearly as shocked. Cameo did crazy things on purpose, like being mad as hell at him one minute and seducing him the next. Like escaping just for the pleasure of confusing him by her return. Like not stopping until she reached her "prison," then dismounting and walking into the dwelling as if it was home.

Confusion was becoming a familiar feeling to him and he didn't like it one bit. She was as adept as a master spy at changing tactics to fool the enemy. By now he should be used to her erratic methods instead of feeling as if he were chasing his own tail in endless circles around her.

She ought to have the decency at least to look apologetic for scaring the piss out of him. She ought to be worried about his anger and the way his hand itched to connect with her backside. But then she probably knew that the minute it did, he'd be stroking her instead of paddling her. His face burned at the memory of their night on the trail, and how easy he'd been—

"You've got trouble there, Zach," Cloud Walker said with a chuckle that frayed Zach's nerves like a dull knife. "It'll be interesting to see how you handle the problem, or how it handles you."

Disgusted at himself, Zach shoved his reins at Cloud Walker, unbuckled his gun belt, carelessly letting it fall to the ground, and strode away. He considered retrieving his Colt when Cloud Walker's taunt followed him down the lane.

"Won't shoot her, huh? Why, cousin, I do believe you care."

Raising his hand, Zach flipped up his finger in a time-honored message that crudely told Cloud Walker what he could do with himself. That simple childish gesture released enough tension to make it possible for him to ease his gait and enter the house with a semblance of control.

The dimness of the interior made him squint until his eyes adjusted, but he could hear the steady creak of the old rocker, the swish of her feet as they brushed back and forth on the floor. There was something about a woman in a rocker that brought out the protective instincts in a man, gave him visions of gentility and peace and serenity. But Cameo was never serene—not even in her sleep. She sat a rocking chair the way a general rode his war horse into battle.

"I take it the ranch is—"

"Fine," he interrupted, annoyed that the ranch was the first thing on her mind. "We have a full crew, plus extra guards. Your Andalusians are settled down again, though you need another stud to take Ash's place. What was left of the gardens have been plowed under until spring."

"And the gold shipments?"

"Still disappearing."

She seemed to sag a little in the chair, giving him an impression of relief. "I see." The impression didn't last long. She pulled herself upright and smiled. "Well, then, I assume you've come to take me home."

"You're doing fine here," he goaded, ready for a fight any way he could get it.

"Then I'll escape again." Her glance from beneath her lashes held a hint of slyness, a suggestion of teasing. "Wouldn't you?"

He'd had enough of gentility and peace and opened his mouth to tear into her—

"Of course you would," she said. "I'll be ready to leave in the morning."

Her feet thumped on the floor once . . . twice . . . He waited for the third slap of leather against the dirt floor. Wariness kept Zach standing a distance away from Cameo as he watched her. This wasn't right. There was too much gentility and peace; her tone was too amiable. Sure her primary concern would be for the ranch, but she was acting as if he hadn't left her at the mesa without a word, as if she hadn't escaped and returned without a word. The hackles rose on the back of his neck. She was up to something. Too bad he still hadn't figured her out, so he could anticipate—

"I would dearly love to shoot you, Zach, and feed your gizzard to a pack of rats," she said quietly.

He blinked. Had she read his mind and decided to slip in before he had the chance to think it through? "Funny, I was going to say the same thing to you."

"Save it, Zach. You had to know that I'd find a way to go home. I would have made it, too, if you hadn't come riding along with a smug grin on each of your two faces." Her feet thumped—once—on the floor. "And who in the hell is Mellie?" She bit her lip as if she hadn't meant to bring the subject up.

"I'd swear you didn't pick up that language around here, Rosebud."

"I grew up around teamsters, ranch hands, and mountain men," she muttered and left the chair to fuss with the coffee pot, the coals in the fire pit, and a mug that was already clean.

Zach grabbed her arm and whirled her around to face him, so close that their noses touched. "Don't you *ever* do anything that stupid again," he shouted.

She raised her finger to her lips. "Shh. Remember the privacy you value so highly." Smiling sweetly, she kissed the side of his mouth, eased out of his grasp, and returned to the fire. "I hope eggs, potatoes, and bacon are all right for dinner."

He shook his head in an effort to throw off his confusion. It didn't seem to matter what he wanted for dinner since she was already slicing bacon and laying it out in a cast-iron frying pan. It was equally obvious that she didn't give a hoot for his justified anger or his need to vent it. "Don't change the subject."

"I'm starving."

"Cameo," he said, advancing on her with balled fists, "you were lost out there."

"Really?"

"If you saw me, then you were headed in the wrong direction . . . I was coming from the direction of Fort Craig."

A frown crossed her face, quickly hidden by a loose strand of hair as she dipped her head to turn the bacon. "I knew that. I was riding in circles for a while to throw everyone off."

"Which way is the valley from here?" he asked, his jaw tight.

"Oh, dear, we're almost out of bread."

"Cameo—"

"I think there's enough. Would you like gravy, Zach? There are some cans of milk in my saddlebags."

He shoved his hands in his back pockets to keep them from wrapping around her neck. "Damn you," he said savagely. "You would have died. This country doesn't forgive fools."

She rounded on him, her hands on her hips. "Yes, damn me. If this country doesn't forgive fools, then it's already too late for me. And *if* I would have gone on, and *if* I would have died, then at least I would have died *free.*" Thick pieces of bacon spattered grease as she speared them with a fork and flung them onto a platter.

"What in the hell does that mean? I don't see any chains around your ankles."

Her face paled, and she swiftly turned away to slice potatoes, every cut a precise, even stroke. "No chains," she murmured, her voice becoming thicker with each word, "just strings."

"Strings? What strings?" Zach knew he shouldn't have asked—knew, too, that if she told him his anger would disappear, and life would become even more complicated than it already was. A sense of melancholy filled the air as if the cloud that ringed the mesa had condensed into this one room.

She shook her head once, then dropped the potato slices into the frying pan. "You choose the direction; I follow, no matter where I want to go."

His gut twisted to hear the defeat and failure in her voice. Neither suited Cameo. And it brought his anger to a boil that she held him responsible. "Don't blame me because you got scared and decided to be sensible for once," he lashed out.

"Fear is a powerful jailer, Zach. Especially the fear that I might miss one moment of being with you. Fear that one lost moment might have been the last." She turned the potatoes in the pan, then cracked eggs into a bowl and beat them with a fork. "My dreams are gone, Zach. Freedom— I used to be able to see it."

"Why in the hell do you think Sam worked up his crazy scheme? Why do you think I went along with it?" He reached for her, pulled his hand back. "We did it so you'd eventually have the freedom to come and go as you please."

"Yes, all of you, arranging my life, trying to pull the strings as if I would fall in a mindless heap without you." She scraped at the potatoes with a spatula, turning them so savagely that some flipped out and hit him in the chest. "You confine me to the house, then cart me up here. Papa tells me how capable I am, then sets Walker and his friends to keep an eye on me. Even Uncle Seamus tried to buy the ranch so I can travel the world and come home for visits."

The sadness in her voice felt like a shroud around him, weighing him down. "What do you want, Cameo?"

She straightened her shoulders, stood taller, and drew a deep breath, her manner letting him know that defeat would pass and she would find victory another time, in some other way. She didn't know that her proud spirit had already won.

"Tell me," he whispered.

Another breath, a release, a bend of her head to stare at the potatoes browning and spitting grease. "I want the valley thriving and peaceful, my horses breeding beauty and speed and stamina, a garden to plant in the spring and harvest in the fall, a husband to chase the loneliness away from dark nights, children to conceive and carry and birth and raise." She turned the potatoes again, wiped her hands on a scrap of linen, and beat the eggs again. "I want to cook and pick up after my family, embroider doilies, and make story quilts for my children.

"Instead, I turned my back on home and followed a man who can't possibly give me enough moments to fill a single year."

He listened and saw in his mind the shadow of his own longings, dreams that had faded to mere illusions.

"What do you want, Zach?"

The question stopped him stone-cold, rooting him to the spot. No one had ever asked him before. His life had been manipulated for so long that he'd forgotten what it was like to determine its own course. If Cameo felt like a puppet, then he felt like a beast of burden being jerked up one mountain after another without ever being allowed to go downhill.

Without pressing for an answer, Cameo walked outside, then returned with four cans of milk balanced in her arms. "Dinner will be ready by the time you wash up."

Nothing irritated him more than her obvious acceptance that he wasn't going to answer her. She had a right to an answer. It didn't help to know that he didn't have any to give her.

"Dammit, Cameo, you'll have your freedom—soon!" It was a shout and a snarl, the rage and frustration of impotence. He unsheathed his knife, pried open a can for her, and stalked out of the house.

And, fading with every step he took, he heard her say, "That's what I fear the most."

He wanted to promise her all of it and more, but he couldn't—not with any kind of honor. *Honor.* A strange word for a man who employed it only when convenient in his vocation, a man who snatched moments with the desperation of knowing each one might be his last.

Conscious thought deserted him as he crossed the settlement in long, rapid strides and knelt at a pool that bubbled up from an underground spring. His eyes squeezed shut when he couldn't see his reflection in the foaming water. Even here, where he was known, he couldn't seem to find himself.

The odor of bacon and seasoned potatoes tantalized him as he returned from washing up. He stood in the doorway, watching Cameo turn the crispy potatoes into a bowl, then pour a mixture of canned milk and water into the pan with one hand and the eggs into another pan with the other. He hadn't known that she could cook, though he should have guessed. Cameo was, in spite of her survival skills, an entirely feminine woman. She always wore feminine clothing, ribbons and lace and toilet water. The pleasure she took in her needlework and the way she'd pause over a table to wipe away a water ring or a streak of dust showed her enjoyment of the household arts.

Those traits made him more uncomfortable than having her point a gun at his head.

"Sit down, Zach. It'll be ready in a minute."

Her smile increased his discomfiture. This was too domestic a scene, too settled. It felt too right at a time when he couldn't accept it and produced an anguish that couldn't be eased. Not yet. *Oh, God, Cameo, you have it all mixed up. I'm not the one holding the strings.*

He took off his hat, sat at the table, and stared down at the china plates, the silver, the tablecloth. Until now, he'd always taken the civilized trappings Sam and his father had brought to the mesa for granted. He glanced around at the stone walls cut and laid by ancient hands, the dirt floor, the primitive fire pit, and found the incongruities blatantly in keeping with Cameo's manner and the conflicts they shared.

She served him, piling his plate with food, spreading gravy over his bread the way he liked it. Damn her. He'd willingly walk into her woman's trap if he was free to do so. Instead, she beckoned and he had to resist, had to ignore the pleasure for fear he wouldn't be able to walk away when the time came. He stared at the food, inhaled it, yet was afraid to touch it. This wasn't the time for his dreams to become more than idle illusions.

"I'm sorry, Zach," Cameo said softly. "I know you're angry, and I understand why. I just . . ." Her voice trailed off and she shook her head as if nothing she could say would make him understand.

Her implied acceptance of her loneliness in all things yoked him with guilt. He picked up his fork and dug into the eggs. "So you're through shoveling self-pity in here until it's hip deep," he said flatly as he speared a slice of bacon, his force breaking it apart to fly off his plate in all directions.

Cameo flinched, then recovered from the verbal blow. "I'm—"

"Don't," he snarled. "Just. Don't. You're not sorry for what you did, so don't lie about it."

"No, I'm not. I'm sorry for worrying you."

Worrying him? He slammed down his fork, clamped his mouth shut and held his breath to slow its angry cadence. Worry was a meager word to describe how he'd felt over her escape. "You can stop now," he said. "All this docility,

the civilized and homey atmosphere. You think I haven't
known what I was riding away from a thousand times
before?" The way she kept right on eating as if they were
having a discussion of the weather irritated him. He
sighed, a harsh tearing in his throat that roughened the
edges of his words. "I don't make promises, Cameo."

"I heard you the first three times, Zach," she said as she
buttered a slice of bread and slathered it with honey. "I'm
not asking for promises. This isn't a trap set to capture
you, but merely a sample of what I'm offering."

A poleax had nothing on Cameo. "Didn't anyone ever
tell you that a woman isn't supposed to admit to using her
wiles to trap a man?"

She smiled. "Why pretend otherwise when you know
what I'm doing?" Setting down her fork, she stared blindly
at her plate, her eyes blinking suspiciously fast.

He lowered his head onto his hand, raked his fingers
through his hair, and rubbed the back of his neck. This
wasn't going well. He had learned how to arm himself
against female trickery, but how in the hell did he resist
the artless honesty of a sincere woman?

"I'm not asking for promises either, Zach," she repeated.

"No," he said. *But you're making them, Rosebud, and
that's the worst trap of all.*

She went on as if he hadn't spoken. "I'm trying to adjust, Zach. The world is upside down. I'm turned inside
out. Nothing that was important to me seems to matter
anymore. The only thing I understand is that I love you."
Her voice faded into a wisp, then she looked up and pinned
him with wide bright eyes.

Leaning forward, he lowered his gaze to the table and
began to shove bits of bacon around on the tablecloth. "I

have a handful of close friends, Cameo—people I really care about. That's too many in my line of work." He paused, swallowed, and spoke in a monotone that chilled even himself. "There was a boy at Glorieta—Calvin Boyd —no older than you, and just as real. He died in the battle." Visions of that day held him with the memory of brutal lessons. At Glorieta, he'd faced his own mortality, a chimera as insubstantial as frosty breath, come and gone on a sigh. "I was so damn mad when he was killed that I stopped thinking. Did you know that I shot myself by accident?"

He moved the bacon pieces around faster, leaving stains on the white linen, and smiled with self-deprecation. "You'd have thought I was his father or something the way I spouted wisdom and philosophy to him. He argued with me and I thought for a while that he might be right."

Cameo said nothing, did nothing but sit straight in her chair, unmoving, listening.

"He married a girl, a camp follower, just before we left for Glorieta. I didn't approve, and he said—" A lump rose in his throat, strangling him with the grief he'd been able to hide from as long as he hadn't thought about it or spoken of it. "He said that he wondered what it would have been like if his pa hadn't whistled and his mama hadn't sung in the mornings. He was looking to have that kind of contentment, even if it only lasted a day."

Cameo's smile was soft, wistful. "Was he happy?"

Silver clattered; china rattled as he raised his fist and smashed it onto the table. "He whistled all the way to his death through freezing winds and neck-deep snow." He looked up at Cameo, met her gaze, and knew that he was showing her more than he'd ever shown anyone. "Yes, he was happy, but his widow isn't. She's sixteen, alone, and pregnant."

Solemnly she watched him, her eyes bright with moisture. "Did his wife sing in the morning?"

Zach had to drag in breath, hold steady against the tightness it brought to his chest, the pain. "She cried because Calvin had given her the only pleasure she'd ever known and wasn't likely to have again. She's sixteen, Cameo. Sixteen! And the worst of it is that she was right."

"Maybe, maybe not. But, Zach, at least she knew it was possible. At least she knows what to look for in the years to come and she won't settle for anything less." Rising from the table, she stacked dishes and cutlery and carried them to the basin.

"She has nothing but a memory and a baby to feed when the time comes." He turned in his chair, and gave her a hard look. "When do you suppose she'll have time to look?"

Cameo left the dishes stacked in the dry basin and leaned back against the sideboard. "She has a lifetime to find more. And if she doesn't, then she'll always know that for a day she had the best of her dreams." She pushed away and walked toward him. "You haven't learned very much from your own people." She knelt in front of him and reached up to cup his face in her hands. "I've learned, Zach."

Her fingers over his lips stopped him from interrupting. The soft, sure timbre of her voice kept him from getting up, leaving the house, ending the farce. He couldn't afford to ask for more until he had the freedom to stay. Nothing could make him ride away again if he let himself believe in more.

"Zach, your people know the difference between today

and tomorrow. One is real—now. The other is simply something we wait for until the day we die."

The words sank into him and twisted his insides into a knot. "You really believe that?" he asked hoarsely.

She rose to her feet. "I'm trying to," she said honestly. "I've said good-bye too many times not to recognize the truth of it."

"Let me know when you do believe it."

"You know, Zach, maybe I'm closer to believing it than you are. At least I'm willing to take the risk." With that, she walked toward the bedroom.

"And if you lose?"

She paused in the threshold, but didn't turn around. "Papa used to say that the only failure is in not trying."

He watched her disappear into the bedroom and listened to the rustle of clothing being removed, her humming as she poured water from the pitcher on the nightstand, the creak of boards supporting the mattress.

To follow her was crazy, Zach knew, so he remained at the table thinking that it was funny how Cameo had learned her lessons so well and so quickly. Funny how he was the one believing that every dream had to be perfect or it wasn't worth having. A small framed portrait caught his eye. His mother. A better mountain man than most men.

Spring McAllister had been like Cameo—resilient, practical, honest. She'd taken what life threw at her and had made the best of it. Not once had he heard her complain or cry about what might have been. Spring. Renewal. A promise that nothing really ends. He wished he could accept that, but he kept remembering Cameo's losses and the love she showed him with every gesture, every word.

How many frontier women have you known whose spirits starved to death on wishes and prayers? How many times has loneliness eaten away a mind? He knew Cameo wasn't like that, would never be like that. It wasn't Cameo who kept him from making promises, but himself. A vow to her meant a vow to himself. Cameo's dreams changed and grew and multiplied. After he left again, Cameo might find another dream, more moments without him. And it would be his dream, the only one he'd ever had, that would be lost.

No, Cameo would be all right. And if he didn't return to the valley, someone else would ride in. She wouldn't be alone for long. She'd have a lifetime to find more.

Jealousy was a welcome presence in his thoughts, an intruder whose shadow blocked out other questions, worse torments. He fed it with resentment. To hear her talk, Cameo was "offering" him the chance to become a memory, a yardstick by which she could measure other men. Men with promises. Men with freedom.

Coward. He bent forward, propped his arms on his thighs, and ran his hands over his face. No wonder so many men in the world made it their lifework to avoid getting tangled with any one woman. There was safety in numbers.

He didn't know how long he'd sat there in the same position bucking the demons that rode his thoughts. The glow from the fire pit dimmed and shrank. The candle Cameo had left burning had guttered, its light dying in a pool of its own fuel. Yet still he stared at the doorway as if all the answers would come out of the darkness.

"Zach." It was a whisper, an ancient chant that beckoned with the promise of a ritual dance and timeless joy. She stood in shadow, a flowing gown falling from her shoulders, hiding the fullness of her breasts, the dip of her waist, the curve of her hips. Her hair fell over her shoulders and down her back, shadows upon shadows.

"I didn't know you were still here," she said.

"What are you doing up?"

"There's no moon tonight and the candle burned out."

"Don't tell me you're still afraid of the dark?" He said it purposely to an end he didn't know. Her hands twisted together as she sidled into the room, appearing small and fragile and too young for him to be thinking of loving her through the night.

"I . . ." She paused, then straightened and walked proudly into the main room. "Not afraid, exactly. I just don't like it. It's so empty and always feels so heavy." She opened a drawer in the sideboard and plucked out a fresh taper. Her hands worried the candle, up and down, back and forth. "It's silly, I know, but . . ."

Her breasts swayed as she shrugged, and her gown followed the curves of her body as she rushed back to the bedroom in fits and starts.

"Will you get the hell back to bed?" he growled. She was doing it again, calling to his body, seducing his mind until he couldn't separate right from wrong, today from tomorrow, wishes from promises.

She halted, her back to him, only her arms moving as she twisted her hands around the candle. It snapped and dropped to the floor. Strands of hair fell around her face as she lowered her head. "Will you come with me?"

It was a child's voice he heard, a woman's body he saw outlined by the dim light from the fire pit, a human yearning he recognized in her stillness. A yearning that matched his own. Right then he wanted to tell her that they shared the same dream, that he loved her, and he would be back.

But the words wouldn't come. He kept them locked in his mind for fear he would be exposed as a liar.

Abruptly, Zach rose, skidding his chair backward with the force until it crashed into the wall. He reached out, grasped Cameo's wrist, and dragged her to him with a hard pull. His arms tightened around her, holding her so close he could feel her breath on his chin, smell the freshly laundered scent of her nightgown, feel the imprint of her body burning through the layers of his clothing.

"You want another 'moment,' Rosebud? Well, this is as good as any." He leaned over her, bending her back over his arm until her hair brushed the table, and crushed his mouth over hers. His tongue speared into her as harshly as his words. The kiss was hard, hot, and brutally ended. "Moments don't last long," he said, his voice sounding inhuman to his own ears. "Sometimes you have to settle for a quick 'moment' over a table, or in the front yard—"

Somehow she managed to free her hands from between their bodies and clutched his shoulders. The same fever seemed to consume them both. Her eyes were bright and wild beneath lowered lids. Again he took her mouth as he jammed his hips against hers.

She met him, every thrust of his tongue, each drive of his hips pushing her against the table and onto it. Her hands tore open the buttons of his shirt, plucked at his belt buckle, ripped open his pants. Her finger closed around him, kneading him, encouraging his urgency.

He shoved her gown up over her waist. Her legs opened and wrapped around his hips as he plunged into her. Silently they fought for control in a battle that could have no winners. She pulled him closer. Her hands scratched one moment and gripped his buttocks the next, pulling him closer and urging him to move harder, faster. Fiery need that drove him further and further over the edge until he couldn't hang on anymore.

Her voice reached him through harsh gasps. "You can't intimidate me anymore with your anger. I'm angry, too." She arched upward to meet his thrust with equal force. Her breath shuddered. "Angry that we're both reduced to this."

Her release was violent, spasms that drew him into a bottomless whirlpool of hot, liquid sensation. She cried out and gripped him tighter, as if she were trying to absorb him. And he knew that in that moment they were both stripped to the soul.

"Damn you, Cameo."

Her hands gentled on him as her shudders subsided into tiny quivers. "The table was your idea, not mine."

Air seemed to rush into his ears, a roar that drowned out everything. He pushed himself up, closed his eyes, threw his head back, his teeth bared in a soundless howl of madness. Once, Cameo had rejected his angry assault. Now she had matched it, shared it, accepted it. *Reduced to this.* This wasn't anger or desperation, but hopelessness.

The cool touch of her fingers shocked him and jerked his gaze to hers. So tenderly she caressed his face, his lips. He couldn't stop himself from kissing those fingertips, drawing one into his mouth for a taste . . . just a taste. He drew back, severing the connection of their bodies, surprised to feel her close around him, trying to hold him within her.

"Cameo—" It stuck in his throat—whatever he'd wanted to say. He didn't know. What could he say?

Levering herself up on her elbows, she gazed at him, her brows arched. "Now that we've gotten that settled, could we please go to bed?"

We? He could have sworn that they'd just fought a battle on that table. He was damn sure that he was being eaten alive by guilt and contempt for his actions.

She pushed him away and sat up, then lowered her feet to the floor. "Zach," she said with a tone of uncertainty and shyness.

Shyness?

"I'm not quite sure what happened just now. Maybe later you could explain it to me?"

His mouth twisted in self-mockery. Maybe later he could explain it to himself.

Pushing herself up, she lowered her feet to the ground and stood beside him. Instead of settling her gown down around her ankles, she tugged it off over her head and cursed when the snug, buttoned neckline caught on her chin. With a yank, she popped the buttons and swept the cloth away from her face. The gown landed in a far corner of the room.

"Maybe later it won't matter at all," she said. "Come with me, Zach. I've missed you, and it's terribly dark when you're alone."

It was a whisper, an ancient chant that beckoned with the promise of a ritual dance and timeless joy, new and filled with different meanings each time it was performed. She called again as she backed up a step. It might have been her voice, or the spirits singing in the trees. The moon rose over the mesa and cast a magical glow into the air. He followed her, chasing mythical tomorrows a moment at a time.

23

A Man Named Sloane

It might never have happened, that night of desperation and anger and primitive passion. Cameo might never have been at the mesa, walked in the footsteps of an ancient race, or lived among a mythical people. She remembered it all so clearly, yet it didn't seem a part of the world she knew.

She no longer felt a part of the world she knew.

The journey back from the mesa a week before had retreated into a dim corner of her memory, a time so fraught with confusion and conflict that it seemed more a part of a book she had read than an actual happening.

Zach had greeted her the morning following her escape and the subsequent confrontation with tight-lipped reticence and none of the tenderness he'd shown her through the night once they retired to her bed. Only that night had brightness and clarity in her memories.

Like when he'd kissed her everywhere and whispered lines from Byron and Shelley and Shakespeare against her flesh. She'd cried out when he'd touched her back and she'd reared away from him like a spooked horse. A splinter from the table had lodged in her skin. She remembered vividly how he'd worked it free, his hands trembling so much he'd almost given up and called Cloud Walker. Only her protest had stopped him. She hadn't wanted intrusion of any kind into the world they'd created in that room— nothing to mar the feeling that for one night Zach was wholly hers and she was wholly his. She belonged with Zach, no reservations, no arguments from him, no thoughts of tomorrow.

Tomorrow had arrived all too soon, the beginning of an end she'd known would come. Zach had saddled Diamond and announced that they would be leaving for home within the hour. How strange it had been to think of the stone dwelling as home rather than the ranch. She had slowed Diamond's pace as much as she dared, and looked back at the mesa often until it disappeared from view. She needed to talk then, to dissolve the loneliness and silence that wrapped around her like morning mist. Zach had obviously preferred the silence, but she had pressed on, determined that nothing would end between them until it became necessary.

Her first comment had been spontaneous upon seeing yet more structures built into shallow caves and depressions at the base of the mesa, their lines fluid, conforming with the rock and sandstone curves of the mesa itself.

"It's a city, Zach, bigger than above."

He grunted.

"Where did they go?"

He shrugged.

"Don't you know anything about them? Don't you wonder?"

"We used to, but all the theories were exhausted."

Encouraged, she asked, "What theories?"

Again he shrugged. "That they were wanderers and simply moved on. That they died out, trapped by the isolation and defeated by the hardships."

"Walker said that your people had settled here expecting to die out."

"We didn't."

"No, you flourished instead."

He'd squeezed his eyes shut when she said that, then opened them again to stare at the horizon ahead. Always ahead, never at her, as if he had already left her behind. His voice had startled her after long minutes of silence.

"We thought we'd found a home, and set down roots. Most things flourish when they have roots. The mesa seemed to be waiting for us. It had a feeling of permanence and continuity, even though the people who built the city had disappeared." He sighed. "We sensed that wherever they went, the old ones were still together. My ancestors thought that a good omen."

"It must have been," she whispered.

"Bullshit!" He pulled Pegasus up short, turned in the saddle, and stared back the way they had come. "The spirits of the old ones might be together. I've felt it, too, as if they were singing in the wind." His gaze caught her and pierced her with an emotion she couldn't name.

"But we won't be together. My people are scattering to build lives that have no relation to what we once had." He pointed to a tree, its branches naked in the winter cold, most of its leaves having long since blown away. "We're like that, now, the last of our families waiting to be absorbed into civilization. Come spring, we'll all be gone."

She stared at the ground, the few remaining leaves soggy and falling apart, being absorbed into the soil, and she felt as if the moments remaining to her and Zach were like that, too—scattering, diminishing, blowing away.

But not without a fight. She'd taken advantage of their proximity, the pause in their journey. "Was it so wrong, Zach—what happened last night? I don't know about such things."

He nudged Pegasus, altered his grip on the reins, his expression set and blank.

Reaching over, she grabbed his reins and tugged enough to keep his horse from moving. "Tell me, Zach. I thought it was always supposed to be the same."

"This isn't a fit subject for discussion."

"If it's fit to do, then it's fit to talk about," she said. "It has been my experience that men are allowed to discuss anything they want in the crudest possible terms."

"Not with . . ." He shook his head and avoided her gaze. "Not when it's . . . dammit, Cameo, I can't talk about this."

Instinct warned her that arguing would be futile and a more direct approach was called for. "All right, Zach. But I can, and I expect you to listen." She tugged on Pegasus's reins, drawing horse and rider closer. Pegasus butted his nose against Diamond's and sidled even closer, trapping Cameo's leg against Zach's. "If what we did on that table was somehow wrong, then I don't care. It was good. It felt right to know that we could share everything, even our frustration."

"It was in anger."

"No, I don't think so. A bit . . . um . . . urgent, perhaps, but definitely not angry."

"I hurt you." Again his tone was flat and dull.

"Really? I didn't notice. Did I fight you? Did I scream? Did I pull my knife and stab you in your sleep afterward?"

He looked away, his mouth straight and tight.

She loosed her hold on his reins and backed Diamond

up. "Even when I'm angry, I love you, Zach. Even then, I want to show it, and be a part of you." Smiling sadly at the warning that darkened his eyes to smoke, she whispered, "It's the only way you'll allow me to love you, and you didn't hurt me. You wouldn't have."

After that, he spurred Pegasus to a pace faster than was wise through the trees. She followed at a distance, barely keeping his form in sight, a shadow once more.

It had been like that all the way home—not for the two and a half days she expected, but nearly half that, and she realized that he'd stretched the truth about the distance. Of course the wagon and her inebriation had slowed them considerably on their journey to the mesa.

When they reached the ranch, she saw people milling about, their expressions serene, their voices still lowered in whispers. They'd smiled and waved as she and Zach rode through the valley, and she recognized, with a jolt, that they were the families who had left the mesa shortly after her arrival there. She turned to Zach with a smile and a whisper of her own. "You've made sure that some of your people will be together, Zach. Thank you."

"The name is Sloane—remember it."

At that moment, it had truly felt like home.

"Miss Cameo." A young woman timidly walked into the office, interrupting Cameo's thoughts.

"Breakfast will be ready in a few minutes, ma'am."

"Yes, thank you. Please send someone to tell Sloane that I wish him to join me." Every morning, Cameo awakened after Zach left her, and every morning, after the early chores were done, she asked him to join her for breakfast. Every morning, she ate alone.

The girl nodded, and with her hand under her distended

belly, as if to support the added weight, she backed out of the room.

Cameo opened her mouth to say more, then shut it again. She was at a loss as to how to deal with her new cook and housekeeper. The girl had been waiting on the front steps as she and Zach rode up to the house a week ago. She'd been stiff and formal and terrified.

Zach had swung down from his horse and walked straight to her, wrapping one arm around her, looking down on her golden-brown head with fondness, then at Cameo in challenge. For one stomach-churning moment, Cameo had stared at them, a united front against her, it seemed, her gaze taking in the girl's trembling chin and very pregnant body. For one horrible, frightening moment, she'd thought the worst and had her first taste of jealousy.

"Cameo Fielding, this is Melanie Boyd—"

"Mellie," the girl had whispered shyly and added, "Please, sir."

Instinct had saved Cameo from making a fool of herself. Instinct and the thin, gold band on the girl's finger. "Calvin's wife?" she asked, praying that it was true as she dismounted.

"Yes, ma'am." Mellie had actually curtsied.

As the days had passed, Mellie had shunned any type of personal conversation and refused Cameo's attempts to help with the household duties. The girl was completely alone in the world except for Calvin's parents, who had been too poor to feed one, let alone two extra mouths. Somehow she had made her way to the valley and Zach. Cameo sighed at the fear and sorrow that seemed to be Mellie's only expression. Mellie was so young—too young to be a widow. Yet in Mellie's eyes she'd recognized an age and weariness to match her own, an age far beyond her years.

It was a good feeling, having a woman so close to her own age in the house. She would have liked to confide in someone, share her confusion, and see her problems through the eyes of another, but Mellie held herself unapproachable and comported herself with the utmost formality. That and Zach's prevailing attitude made Cameo feel more alone than ever. Even the valley failed to comfort her. She was beginning to think that everyone had a place to belong but herself.

She shut the ledger she'd been trying to work on with a snap and gave in to her thoughts of Zach.

It might never had happened—that last night on the mesa seemed to be fading further and further back in her memory. That night she'd felt as if they'd both been stripped to the soul. She'd been so sure that Zach would again tell her that he loved her. She was ready to hear the words and accept them as truth. But he said nothing.

She knew now that he wouldn't, and it was becoming more and more difficult to hold on to the certainty she felt that night. With every step they'd taken toward the valley, she felt as if Zach was once again clothing himself in pride and secrets, anger and resolve, until all she saw was Sloane rather than Zach—the shadow rather than the man.

Nothing had changed since their return to the valley. Zach maintained his persona of "Sloane," and maintained, too, the distance between them during the day. At night she refused to acknowledge any man but Zach. Silently she went to him when darkness fell, willing to give him the very essence of herself. Silently he accepted, a phantom lover, holding her through the darkness and changing before her eyes in the first light of dawn. At night they wordlessly communicated, with their bodies, sometimes with a leisurely gentleness, often desperately, insatiably, but always purposefully and openly, taking whatever they could, giving all that they dared. Only in the dark of night could she see the stars, reach for them, touch them as they faded in the passing hours, knowing it would never be enough.

He hadn't put so much as a sock in the bureau, but kept all his clothes in his saddlebags, emphasizing the fact that he was not there to stay. Her acceptance made her feel as if she was losing a little bit more of him with the passing of each night.

It was killing her by inches.

The front door slammed and booted feet stomped down the hall. She looked up, hoping that Zach might have decided to join her after all.

But it was Sloane, a silhouette in the doorway, standing stiffly, as he always did, as if he were steeling himself to face her. Her welcoming smile froze, as she felt the color drain from her face. His expression was grim, his eyes dark as storm clouds.

"What's happened?" she asked.

"Ambush."

"Where? Who?"

"One of our wagon trains from Denver City. Close enough for us to find it," he said as if it were an effort to speak through his outrage.

"Our men . . . ?"

"Dead."

She closed her eyes and swallowed. She'd known most of the teamsters all her life. More of her family—gone.

"All they took was the gold."

"Of course," she said bitterly. "What else is worth fourteen lives?"

Zach slapped his hat against his thigh as he strode to the gun cabinet. "It won't buy any more lives," he said. "Have Mellie pack enough food for three days." With exacting thoroughness, he checked a shotgun, then a Henry and ammunition.

"How many men are you taking?"

He didn't answer.

"Zach? How many men?" Dread wound around her heart, squeezing, crushing.

"Don't call me that."

The silence lengthened as he worked, giving her the answer. Dimly she heard a commotion outside but ignored the whoosh and roar in the air, the sound of running feet, the clang of the warning bell attached to the porch of the house. . . .

Zach tensed, raised his head from his task, listened, and sniffed like an animal scenting danger. Dropping the box of bullets he'd been checking, he ran toward the front door just as Cameo heard the combined shouts of several men.

"Fire in the barn!"

She bolted out of her chair, picked up her skirts, and ran after Zach.

Smoke poured out of the loft. Flames reached up from the roof. Waves of heat shimmered across the yard. Women and children formed a bucket brigade. Men ran spooked horses into a far corral. Chickens squawked and thrashed against the wire fence in panic. Milch cows bleated from within the barn. . . .

Jorge. Dear God, Jorge worked in the barn. Without further thought, Cameo ran toward the open doors of the burning building.

A figure staggered out, carrying a limp body, both covered in smoke and coughing. "You're all right?" she called as she ran up to them.

Zach nodded and laid Jorge down under a tree. He stood half-bent, his hands on his knees, pulling in great draughts of air.

With dawning horror, she heard coughing and shouts from inside the building. Cameo ran toward the sound. Heavy bodies broke through the smoke, rushing toward her as men stampeded the cows down the aisle and into the open. All she heard was the roar of flames and the hacking gags of the men. "Get out!" she shouted, then cried out in pain as Zach caught her long braid and jerked her back. A terrified cat streaked through the doors, tangled in her feet, and toppled her to the ground. Her eyes watered from the smoke. Her lungs burned.

His hands gripped her under her arms and dragged her the rest of the way out of the barn. "Don't," she croaked. "The rest of the men . . . the animals—"

"Shut up."

She looked up at Zach, his face streaked black, his eyes glittering dangerously as he dragged her across the yard. She dug in her heels and squirmed when she heard a man's desperate call for help. "Let me go. I have to—"

He dropped her next to Jorge and turned back to the fire. Two men stumbled out, half walking, half crawling, and signaled that all were safe. Zach faced her again, looming over her. "Don't you move a goddamn inch!"

She blinked and stared at him as he dipped his kerchief into a bucket of water and wrapped it around his nose and mouth on his way back into the barn. She crawled over to Jorge. "Are you all right, Jorge?" Was that flat monotone her voice, she wondered?

"*Sí, niña.* The *Patrón* take me out in time."

Patrón. That said it all, she thought as she wearily pulled herself to her feet, using the tree for support, and leaned against it until she saw Zach follow the last of the animals out. Hours passed and twice she tried to help. Twice Zach set her out of the way as if she were nothing more than a rag doll that kept flopping about—always in the way. Finally she sagged against the tree and just watched as the barn burned in spite of the fight everyone waged against it. The roof collapsed and still they poured buckets of water onto the blaze. Walls crumbled into ash and still they tried.

The light turned a rich gold as the setting sun fired the sky. She stared at the winter-gray clouds rolling in, their rippled undersides glowing with pink and orange and yellow, like embers dying. Then with utter finality, the sky dimmed to a twilight silver that wiped away all color and turned the earth to shadow.

She gazed at the pile of rubble, its embers doused with water until only ash and twisted metal remained. She couldn't stand it anymore. "Stop it," she shouted as she ran into the middle of the fray. "Just. Stop. It's over. Can't you see?" As she turned in a circle to look at every man, woman, and child, she swiped at her eyes, swallowed a sob, refusing to give in to yet more grief. Another splash of water on the flames. She whirled to the little girl who had wielded the bucket. "Why do you keep fighting? Why . . . ?"

The child walked over to her and took her hand. "It's our home, too, Miss Cameo."

The people walked away, silent and weary, except for the promises they delivered as they passed by her.

"We'll start cutting trees for a new barn, ma'am."

"You'll have a new barn in no time."

"Take a week."

"Maybe less."

When the last person had disappeared down the path to the cabins, Zach sauntered her way as he unwrapped the kerchief from around his face, holding her gaze with an enigmatic one of his own. "Your animals are safe," he said. "The men, too."

Her fists clenched as she straightened away from the tree. "Nothing on this ranch is worth one person's life," she said, her voice hard, controlled. "Who sent them in there . . . or do all men measure themselves by senseless acts of heroism?" Two weeks of frustration fed her anger. Two disasters in the space of a day fed her frustration.

"I could ask you the same thing." He tossed the kerchief onto the smoldering ashes. "You were hell-bent on scorching your bloomers."

He'd been spoiling for a fight for two weeks, she knew. But she was too tired and heartsick to accommodate him. "When are you leaving?" she asked to change the subject.

"It'll have to wait."

"Why?" She raised her arm, waved it in a wide arc. "Because of this? You heard the others. We'll have a new barn raised within a week. I can hammer and saw with the best of them. You're free to play soldier all you want." The shrewish note in her voice stopped her from saying more. As they'd done virtually everything else in the last weeks, they climbed the steps and entered the house in silence.

Cameo stopped in the hallway and laid her hand on his arm as he opened his bedroom door. "Zach . . ."

"Sloane," he said in a low, menacing voice. Raking his hand through his soot-blackened hair, he glanced down at her. "I need a bath. You take the water closet. I'll use the cistern outside." Swallowing hard, she nodded and forced a smile. "Keep my side of the bed warm," she said, striving for lightness and failing miserably.

His eyes darkened, grew hard, and glittered like rough-edged stone. His jaw bunched as he threw off her hand. "Dammit, just once," he snarled, "would you stop trying to be the man around here?" Shoving the door open so forcefully it banged against the wall, he limped into his room.

The words sank into her like a dull blade, twisting and tearing. Blindly she walked to her own room, one hand on the wall, the other pressed to her chest, her fingers clenched around the fabric of her dress as if she could confine the pain and keep it from digging deeper.

It's over. Why do you keep trying?

The night air was close, heavy, a dark blanket that muffled and strangled Zach as he struggled for sleep, for peace. His thoughts battered from within, bringing the restlessness and aches that were magnified by the gloom and silence around him. Over and over, he saw Cameo in the midst of the crowd, her question desperate, as if she were begging for an answer to refute her own statement.

It's over.

Kicking off his covers, Zach stifled a moan at the spasms that wracked his leg. He punched his pillow, tossed from one side to the other, and flattened himself on his stomach with the pillow over his head, then stuffed it under his knee as he flipped onto his back. As he had done often in the last few hours, he opened his eyes to stare at the ceiling and listen for sounds from the next bedroom. Cameo was a noisy sleeper, good for dozens of tosses and turns and usually a whimper or two—when she was alone. She'd slept like a baby when she was with him.

So when was the last time you had a good night's sleep?

He folded his hands behind his head. He'd slept soundly after his people arrived and he hadn't had to keep an eye out twenty-four hours a day. While Cameo was still at the mesa he'd rested better than he had since he met her.

You're ruined, McAllister.

Not ruined, just worn out, he argued with himself. Every night Cameo had come into his room, and every night he'd sworn he would send her away, or at the most hold her for a while then carry her back to her bed. But it never worked out that way. He'd hold her, make love to her, and take advantage of every moment they had together.

During the day he kept himself awake with constant activity and kept himself sane by widening the distance between them. Here, in her home, companionship would only reinforce the illusion of permanence and the hope that it might become more. Yet every time she called him Sloane, he felt less like a man and more like a shadow. Cameo made it easy for him by reinforcing his false identity, by looking through him and speaking to him as if he didn't really exist.

It's bungling the mission.

There was no argument for that. All day his guts had been knotting up with guilt. Thirteen men massacred. Animals slaughtered. All of it had happened less than an hour's ride away from the freight office. He hadn't corrected Cameo on the number of dead. Only thirteen bodies found, and he knew who was missing. If he'd had his mind on his job, he might have been more watchful and suspicious of the new man Sam had hired just before he'd been killed.

She's going to get you killed and lose the valley to boot.

He couldn't argue with that either. Distraction was his

worst enemy. Caring about anything was a sure way to commit suicide. For everyone's sake, he'd learned long ago that he couldn't lose what he didn't have, and it was best to keep it that way. Now, he knew exactly how much he had to lose.

She's got you by the balls.

Who'd have thought that he'd fall in love with a girl-woman with more sass than sense? A girl whose artlessness bewitched him? A scamp whose impulses enraged and frustrated him? A woman whose wisdom and honesty compelled him and whose face and body appeared to him to be more beautiful and more seductive than those of any other woman on earth? In his mind he knew it wasn't true, of course. His heart just wasn't in a listening mood.

By the balls.

The absolute silence distracted him. Maybe Cameo had been awakened by the darkness. Maybe she, too, was lying in bed, hurting because of how he'd treated her and what he'd said to her. Maybe—hell. He'd stood in that hallway and heard the catch in her breath, seen the pain flicker and die in her eyes, and then he'd seen nothing but a stunned dullness where mischief and intelligence and defiance usually burned. He twisted and looked out his window. No subtle glow came from her window. Maybe she was enjoying a peaceful sleep. Maybe there was enough moonlight to keep her demons at bay.

Maybe you should pull your brain out of your crotch and figure a way to keep any more men from dying.

Telling himself that he was looking for excuses to check on Cameo, he ignored his sudden uneasiness and went back to studying the ceiling.

Why hadn't he paid attention to that new man? Sure, it was possible that the man was from one of the Mason–

Dixon border states whose loyalty was with the Union. Sure, it was possible that he had come west to escape fighting friends and neighbors and family in a war he didn't believe could be won. Sam had bought the man's story. John Childress had been a good worker, quiet, refined, sharp. Too quiet to mix well with rowdy teamsters. Too refined to come from a little farm in Missouri. Sharp enough to keep his mouth shut and his ears open. Zach's mouth twisted into a sneer. How had he missed it?

Again the silence interrupted his concentration. Again he glanced out the window. No light. No creaking of Cameo's bed . . .

No moon.

With a twist, he sat up, his feet landing precisely in the legs of his pants. In one motion, he bent, pulled his pants up and stood. He grabbed his gun with one hand and his shirt with the other as he raced across the room, fighting his way through sleeve and neck holes. He felt the bite of panic and calmed it, heard the slap of his feet on the floorboards, and slowed down to a silent stalk toward Cameo's room, his gun cocked and ready. At her door, he bent down and peered through the keyhole, looking for surprises.

Her bed was still made with only a slight rumple on one side. The candle on the nightstand was new, its wick still white and untouched. He straightened and opened the door.

The room was empty.

24
Necessities of Life

Cameo looked back at the clustered buildings of the ranch, dark squares in a night overcast by clouds and the pall of smoke hovering over the valley. She wrapped her blanket-wool coat more closely around herself and rode on toward Spirit Canyon.

She didn't know how long she'd sat on her bed, staring at nothing, hearing only the echo of Zach's voice, then old Jorge's and the little girl's.

"Would you stop trying to be the man around here?"

"The Patrón . . ."

"It's our home, too . . ."

The walls had closed in on her, driving her out to seek shelter from the demons that had taken over her home. Demons that haunted her with memories and wreaked havoc on innocent people as they traded lives for bars of gold. She hadn't bothered to wash the smoke off or change her clothes, but had donned her coat and sneaked away from the house, not mounting Diamond until she was well away. It would have been more than she could bear to be followed and guarded and watched, her every move reported to Zach.

The darkness was thick and oppressive, yet she didn't notice. She didn't want to notice anything. She didn't want to think, for she knew her thoughts would lead to Zach.

The *Patrón*. The man who made her feel as if she still hadn't grown into her womanhood. The man who seemed to belong at the ranch more than she ever had. It had always been that way—the *vaqueros* and their families more a part of things, each of them having a purpose, a function, and someone to share their burdens, their joys.

It's our home, too. The families from the mesa had fitted right in as if they'd always been in the valley. They were happy, always talking as they went about their work, always smiling and helping one another, always going home to full houses. A legal deed to property made a poor companion.

"So you're through shoveling self-pity in here until it's hip deep." She raised her head and glanced around as if the words had just been spoken from over her shoulder. Ruefully she smiled to herself. If she didn't stop wallowing in her own misery, she wouldn't have the energy to live her life the way she wanted to; she wouldn't have the will to change its course.

Diamond stopped and raised her nose to the air. Distant voices seemed to be mere echoes. The rustling sounds were simply movements in the wind. . . .

Except there was no wind.

Cameo scanned the darkness as her hand instinctively stroked Diamond's neck, soothing her. Lights flickered through a thick growth of trees—a rectangle of gold standing out before narrowing to the barest sliver of a glow. In that brief moment she recognized the old abandoned trapper's cabin butted up against the mountainside. Burdened

mules and men on horseback slowly climbed the track up
the slope.

Dismounting, she walked Diamond closer to the cabin
and hid behind a large spruce a few yards away. Upon
reaching the cabin, the men began unloading crates and
carrying them inside. As the door opened again and light
poured outside, she read the lettering on a crate: Fielding.

Panic caught her in a paralyzing grip as she realized
what she had stumbled into. Thieves and smugglers and
murderers—at least ten of them. Here. She had to move, to
get home, to tell Zach.

"Don't move, missy." A man stepped out from the other
side of the tree and spat tobacco juice out of the side of his
mouth as he leveled a rifle at her.

There was no hope of mounting Diamond and riding
away. The man was too close, his aim too sure. Instinctively she slapped Diamond's rump, then dived toward the
man, all in one continuous motion. Startled by her action,
he stumbled backward, his rifle discharging as he fell.

Crates fell to the ground. Mules brayed. Men surrounded her before she could get to her feet, silhouettes
standing around her like a ring of stones. She could feel
their gazes—malevolent, dispassionate. A single shape
pushed through the circle, spared her a glance, and walked
away with a barked order.

"Bring her inside."

Shivers ran up her spine at the sound of his voice. The
familiarity of his form robbed her of strength and sapped
her will. She knew she should fight, but nothing wanted to
work—neither her mind nor her body. She hung limply as
another man dragged her to her feet and hoisted her over
his shoulder. Snow crunched beneath her captor's weight;
a door creaked open, then slammed shut. She watched the

dirt floor of the cabin blur past and saw a hand pull the ring of a trapdoor and a ladder reaching down a dark hole. A light flared at the bottom, illuminating the face of the man climbing down ahead of them with macabre light. Closing her eyes, she prayed that she was trapped in a nightmare as she bumped against cold, damp stone on the way down.

Unceremoniously, she was dumped into a chair, and her arms were jerked behind her back. She felt a man's breath on her neck and the abrasive texture of hemp around one of her wrists. Her other arm fell limply to her side.

"Please, ma'am, hold still," the man who was tying her whispered. "I don't want to hurt you." The diction was cultured, with a gentle southern drawl.

Her lips curled in amusement. She was being tied to a chair in a den of cutthroats and a Southern "gentleman" was worried about hurting her.

"She carries a knife on the back of her belt."

Strong hands lifted her jacket and found the sheath. With the slipping of the knife out of its leather carrier, Cameo felt the last of her hope fade.

"Open your eyes, girl."

She shook her head, refusing to see, preferring—for once —darkness over light. Her hair was grabbed roughly, her head pulled back. She wondered when it would hurt. Still she refused to look at him, her soul retreating deeper into itself before he could strip it of her last illusion.

"I'm not your lily-livered old man, Cameo. You'll do as I say."

Involuntarily, her eyes opened and stared at the round cheeks, always rosy, and the gray-peppered red beard and moustache, the familiar brown eyes that had twinkled with merriment on many a Christmas Eve. The twinkle was still there, but the smile was the smirk of a man who had filled a child's toy with gunpowder.

Santa Claus did not exist after all.

She shrank inside herself, tucked away where nothing could touch her in any real way. This was worse than the betrayal she'd felt over her father's manipulation, far more devastating than Zach's lying to her and allowing her to grieve for him. Her father's actions had sprung from love and good intentions. Zach had acted out of duty and his own brand of honor. In the face of Seamus Casey she only saw a happy memory of childish faith transformed into self-serving treachery.

"You too, Uncle Seamus?" she whispered, her voice seeming to come from somewhere above her, as if she were outside looking in on a strange tableau.

His hand lifted to her face, stroked her cheek with a feather touch. "You should have sold me the valley, darlin'. I really wanted to keep you out of this."

Unblinking, she stared at him, seeing a stranger, knowing that it had always been so. "Why?"

He shook his head. "Your Uncle Seamus has no quarrel with you, darlin'. I'm sorry you were hurt in the ambush. My men were told to leave you alone."

"You don't think Papa's death hurt me? You honestly believe I could leave my home without feeling pain?" She marveled at the calmness, the clear thoughts that echoed so vividly in her head. It couldn't possibly be her voice, her thoughts. She was too numb with shock, too cold and empty.

Seamus snorted. "Sam was no more a father than I'm a priest. And from what I hear, he was already a dead man. As for the ranch—I'm doing you a favor, darlin'. That place will make an old woman out of you. It's nothing but hard, dirty work and loneliness." He shook his head, his eyes sober. "You're too young and pretty for that kind of life."

"I'm sure the South will be grateful that you're giving them such a burden," she said. "But I fail to see how they will occupy a valley in the middle of enemy territory."

"I don't give a damn about the South or the ranch or this piddlin' amount of gold," he said evenly.

She sensed a sudden movement from behind her and remembered the man who had tied her. "I see."

Seamus pulled a chair from a corner of the room, reversed it, and straddled the seat, his arms hooked over the back. "I wish you did, darlin'. It would have saved me a hell of a lot of groveling to the tight-assed Rebs." He flicked a narrow-eyed look at the man behind her. "Still, they've been useful. I don't begrudge them the gold."

"You want the ranch?"

"I want what your pa cheated me out of."

Cameo stared at him, not understanding. "Papa gave you your land, staked you to the trading post—"

Seamus snorted. "So I could work the rest of my life while he and Jacob lived high on the hog and doled out charity to their friends. You think I should be grateful?" Leaning forward, he rested his chin on a balled fist and spoke as if he were telling her a bedtime story.

"I was wintering in a dugout up in the Wind River country when St. Vrain and Bent divided up that land grant the Spanish gave them. Sam and Jacob got the biggest parcels, and I got nothing. Somewhere on your land is a mother lode that made them rich. They had their fun, and now it's my turn."

She had to laugh—it was so absurd. It was too much to absorb, much less believe. Of course she'd known that her father had found gold, but so had many others from Colorado to California, but she'd never heard of a mother lode. Her laughter became wild, uncontrolled, and between gasps she choked out, "You murdered Papa, butchered livestock, and chased twenty families from their homes for something that doesn't exist."

Her head jerked as he slapped her across the face, and her ears rang. Again he slapped her, then sat back, calm once more.

"You have a choice, darlin'. You can sign over the deed to me for a fair price, take yourself off to Europe"—he sighed heavily, as if the words hurt as they came out—"or you can choose how you'll die."

His voice had the fatal ring of truth, chilling her as lies never had. "I see."

"This time, I think you do see," Seamus said as he rose and swung the chair back into the corner. "I have work to do. John here will keep you company till I'm finished." His bulk disappeared little by little up the ladder, a malevolent Santa Claus leaving through a chimney after reclaiming all the gifts of love and laughter and magic he had ever given her.

Feeling returned to Cameo in a rush—pain in her jaw from the blows Seamus had dealt her, a burning ache in her shoulders from their unnatural position, cold and damp sinking in her bones from the rock walls . . .

Rock? She blinked her eyes and tried to clear her mind as she focused on the details of her surroundings. The chamber was deep in the ground, high-ceilinged, with a pile of rubble along one wall. Sharp spikes of stone grew down from the ceiling and up from the floor, some dripping moisture, some ribboned in subtle colors, yet others throwing off sparkles from the light. Several tunnels branched off, like wide mouths waiting to swallow anything that dared to venture into the darkness.

"A cavern?" she whispered.

"Yes, ma'am." A man stepped out from behind her. "These mountains are riddled with them."

"John Childress," she said with dull acceptance, unsurprised by yet another betrayal.

"I'm sorry, Miss Cameo."

She noted how he couldn't quite meet her eyes; his mouth was grimly set, and an indecipherable emotion glittered in his eyes. "Of course, you're sorry," she said flatly. "Everyone is sorry—Seamus, you, me . . ." Her voice cracked and broke. Breathing deeply, she tried to keep feeling at bay. This was not the time to cry or submit to panic.

"What is your stake in all this?" she asked. It was so much easier to talk about inconsequentials than to grieve for yet another loss.

He shrugged as he sat in the same chair Seamus had occupied. "My duty to the South is over. After the war, my plantation will need rebuilding. My share of the gold will come in handy."

"You're doing this for money?"

A faraway look softened John's blue eyes as he stared at the opposite wall. "It's a beautiful place, Miss Cameo, with oaks lining the drive and a little lake surrounded by weeping willows." His mouth curved downward, and his voice grew distant and hard. "The Union Army burned the fields and the house." He looked at her, his expression etched with sorrow. "The South won't win this war, but I will. When it's over, I'll have enough money to reclaim my property and build again, maybe raise horses." Tipping his chair back on two legs, he angled his hat forward and leaned his head against the wall. Evidently he was through talking.

What more was there to say? Oddly enough, she understood his motives and could almost sympathize with his plight. The land was a powerful keeper—possessor rather than possessed, promising security and sustenance, permanence and growth—all the things that people had never offered or promised her. People came and went, but the land remained.

Why then did she feel more tied to a man than to her home? The question shocked her. She lowered her head and closed her eyes against the questions that were replacing the certainties in her life.

Awareness flooded her senses—the copper taste of fear in her dry mouth, the energy that suddenly bubbled in her blood, the warmth that raced through her. Her hands were shaking. A stitch in her chest drew tight, and no matter how deeply she pulled in air, it never seemed to get into her lungs. A void edged her vision, expanding until light became an ever-shrinking circle. Her heartbeat thundered in her ears, louder . . . louder . . .

"You have some thinking to do, Miss Cameo."

"How long?" she asked thickly.

"They won't be finished for another three hours or so." Three hours or so. Three hours to decide the course of her entire life.

With that thought came sudden calm, a clear mind. She lifted her head, inhaled deeply, then held her breath. The darkness retreated; the thunderous beat faded.

What was there to decide? Life or death? Seamus hadn't given her a third choice. Reduced to that, what decision was there to make? It would be so easy to sign over the valley. No more fighting. No more dreading the day Zach would leave. She could go with him, ride the trails as his mother had done. He would be her home.

It's our home, too. The image of a little girl, soot-smudged and bedraggled, haunted her, telling her that her choice wasn't that simple. The little girl had said "home" as if it were a brand-new concept, something safe and magical all at once. There were nearly thirty families depending on the valley for more than a livelihood. Nearly thirty families belonging in the only place they could stay together. It was a legacy she couldn't deny.

Seamus would let the ranch go to seed. He'd rape the land in his search for gold. The families would scatter. Zach would have no place to return to when the snows fell.

Sell the valley or be killed.

Either way she would be giving up. Either way she would die.

The rope chafed her wrists, and she realized that she'd been unconsciously twisting her hands, struggling against hopelessness. She relaxed her fingers, seeking ease. The rope slipped down and rubbed against her palms. She sagged back, relieving the tension in her shoulders, the stiffness of her muscles. Her gaze swept the cavern.

Crates and barrels were stacked against the wall nearest her. A natural shelf on her other side held jars of preserved fruits, jerky, and vegetables, interspersed with lanterns, candles, and jugs of whiskey. Propped against John's chair was a shotgun. She cocked her head and listened. Boots thudded overhead as men walked in and out of the cabin. Water dripped from a crevice. John snored in easy rhythm.

Cameo smiled. Seamus had given her only two choices. A Southern "gentleman" had given her the third.

With patience and careful manipulation, Cameo worked the rope lower on one side and higher on the other, grimacing as the hemp bit into her flesh. Pain shot up her arm as she bent and twisted her thumb in unnatural angles. Water continued to drip in the crevice, and she marked time by it, counting each splat, keeping her mind free from the panic that hovered on the edge of her mind.

Her hand cramped and seized. She forced herself to stop, to relax and ride with the discomfort, to keep counting the drips. The rope slipped a little more. She turned her hands flat against each other, then folded her thumbs and little fingers into her palms. She sawed them up and down, urging the rope to give a fiber at a time. The bonds caught and held at the widest part of her hands. With a sob of frustration, she eased one hand up and slipped the thumb of the other over the rope. Cursing her short fingernails, she stabbed at the knots over and over again. And still she counted the drops of water falling into a puddle across from her.

The rope fell open and slithered to the ground. It was all she could do not to move suddenly. She wanted to laugh. She wanted to kiss John for his misplaced chivalry. There were times when a man's low opinion of a woman's ability and strength was indeed a blessing.

It took minutes for her to block out the sound of water and concentrate on the cadence of John's snores, the footfalls overhead, the memory of her capture. She closed her eyes and summoned the details of which way the cabin faced and where she was.

This particular mountain slope, she knew, was opposite the one wall of Spirit Canyon. With luck, she could find her way through the maze into the painted cavern of the canyon. Or she could lose herself in the passages honeycombed throughout the mountain until the men gave up searching or left. Being lost by her own inclination was far more preferable than being at the mercy of another. Focusing on the tunnel that opened in the direction she thought Spirit Canyon to be, she measured the size of the entrance and judged it to be large enough for her to stand upright.

Slowly she flexed her hands and brought them forward as she watched her jailer. Carefully she slid forward in the chair and used the back for support as she stood up on legs that felt like air. Silently she reached for an earthenware whiskey jug, hooked her finger in its handle, and lifted it off the shelf. The weight threatened her balance as it yanked her arm down. She bent her knees and caught the bottom of the jug with her other hand. Cautiously she straightened and tiptoed toward John.

Fear jumped into her throat as she reached for the shotgun and drew it away from its perch. . . .

John snorted, sniffed, and wiped his sleeve across his nose. Forsaking caution, Cameo let the gun drop and lifted the jug over his head. With all the force she could muster, she brought it down. Shards of pottery flew everywhere. The fumes of Taos Lightning made her eyes water as the liquid streamed down John's body. He jerked and opened his eyes, staring up at her with a dazed expression. The jug hadn't been heavy enough.

She bent over and grabbed the shotgun, swung it around, and slammed the stock against his head. Cameo watched in horrified fascination as blood gushed from his nose and he toppled sideways onto the floor—chair and all —with a clatter.

Panic grew and became a stone in her throat, cutting off her breath. She stood frozen in the middle of the cavern, listening to the sounds above her and around her. Men shuffled across the floor, boxes crashed onto the wooden planks overhead, and water dripped into a puddle.

Her tension eased. She grabbed her knife from John's belt and searched the room for a way to fashion a sling for the shotgun. Her gaze fell on John's belt and she smiled. Working quickly, she unbuckled it and slid the leather free of the loops in his pants. Her smile grew as she unfastened the buttons of his fly. When he awoke and tried to stand, his trousers would fall around his knees and trip him. Next she pulled matches, candles—easier to carry than a lantern —jerky, two jars of peaches, and two boxes of shotgun shells from the shelf, and divided up her meager supplies into the deep pockets of her coat and skirt. A Colt was hidden behind the ammunition and she took that, too, checked its load, and added two more boxes of bullets to her cache.

At the entrance to the tunnel, she shivered as dank chill met her skin. Absolute darkness cut off her sight. She flattened herself against the wall and waited for her vision to adjust. If only she could use a candle. But it would be like a beacon. Able to discern solid shadows from empty space, she inched her way forward using her hand to feel her way.

The sound of moisture dripping from the rock echoed eerily around her. Afraid she might trip if she walked normally, she slid one foot forward, then the other, as her hand groped over cold, damp rock. Right foot, left foot, over and over again. The utter blackness closed in on her, smothering and oppressive. The world ceased to exist. Nothing seemed real except the cold, unwelcoming emptiness, the fear of stepping into nothing, the knowledge that she could forever be lost in *nothing*. Time lost all meaning as she shuffled over the stone floor, scraped her hands on sharp outcroppings, and bumped into spears growing from the ceiling. Her hand met empty air as she tripped over a large rock, and she almost fell into a cavern opening off the tunnel.

She heard footsteps and shouts. Desperately she followed the cavity, found a wall, and tripped over a boulder. On hands and knees, she crawled around the obstruction and wedged herself into the seam between it and the wall. She let out her breath, drew in another, and gagged at the overwhelming odor of bat *guano*.

Shuddering with revulsion, Cameo groped behind her for her knife, unsheathed it, and clamped the leather case between her teeth to keep them from chattering. She held the knife, ready to fend off the night creatures if any became curious about the intruder in their midst.

Again she counted drips of water and listened to an occasional flutter of wings overhead. Booted feet rang over stone, nearer, then farther, then nearer again, each sound echoing from every direction. Try as she might, she couldn't trace the progress of her pursuers. If only they would speak—call out to one another—so she could figure out where they were and what they were doing—

"Jesus!" a man gasped as the pungent odor hit him in the entrance to the chamber.

Cameo pressed back against the stone wall as the man gagged and coughed. Panic-stricken, she felt for her weapons and wondered which she should use if he discovered her.

"Ain't nobody could hide in here, boss," the man said. "Smell's enough to gag a maggot."

Footsteps approached. With grim determination, she eased the shotgun from her makeshift sling, wrapped her kerchief around it to muffle the click as she broke it open, then slipped a shell into each of the two chambers. She lifted the shotgun to her shoulder and listened to Seamus gag and cough.

"There's no woman alive could stand this," Seamus said. "Split up the men. She can't be far. Poor mite is afraid of the dark."

"What should I tell 'em to do with her?"

Cameo heard a heavy sigh echo off the rock like a mourning wind.

"Shoot her and leave her here. No one will ever find her."

Her fingers ached as she eased her grip on the shotgun. Experimentally, she slid the pistol from the front of her belt for easy access. Slowly breathing through her mouth to lessen the stench, she crouched there, waiting for a target. With icy certainty she knew she could and would shoot to kill if it became necessary. She thought of how blithely she had thrown that word at Zach, not realizing back then that "necessary" was another word for survival and it was the only choice that remained.

Madness stalked her, fitting precisely into her footprints, and followed her through corridors as twisted and dark as loneliness, its presence a void that threatened to overtake her. Everything was black—the stone heart of the mountain and the air that had the scent of age and touched her with cold, like breath from the dead.

Cameo thought only of the space she occupied with each step, in each moment as she felt her way through the tunnels, and when—as now—she drew too close to despair, she forced herself to take one more step before sitting against a dripping wall. And then she forced herself to wait for the count of ten before she pulled out one of her precious candles and a bit of food. For a while she savored the sweet flavor of a peach slice, a sip of the thick nectar, and the texture of dried jerky as the candle burned into nothing.

How long had she been curled up in that chamber filled with bats that had been her refuge and the beginning of madness? How long since her life had been reduced to her essential self, stripped to the most basic instincts? The memory of that interminable time would not fade or soften. The attendant reactions clung to her like her straggling hair, the stains on her clothing that were set in by the cold sweat of panic and stark terror, the bruises on her body from countless missteps and sudden stumbles. The farther she walked, the stronger her fear became that she was going in circles and would once again find herself trapped in the chamber. No matter how far she staggered through the corridors, she could not escape the memory of that time spent with creatures that thrived on darkness.

Her teeth had chattered as she'd lain on the floor of the cavern, her face pressed into the space between boulder and wall, drawing air from the tunnel. The ammonialike fumes of *guano* had burned her eyes and chafed her throat. Her stomach had threatened to heave as she listened to men's voices cursing her, the scrape of boot heels, the passing flare of torches as the searchers combed the tunnels. She didn't know how long she'd sat with the shotgun pointing toward the cavern entrance before she realized that the sounds had stopped. Dimly she remembered hearing Seamus order the men back to the surface with the prediction that she would either die there or seek them out when the need for food and light became too great to deny.

Afraid to venture out until she was sure they were gone for good, she'd remained still until her hands cramped from her hold on the shotgun and the searing fumes in the chamber had become the only reality of her existence. Still, she'd been afraid to leave the refuge for fear that the men would return for another look.

"We can't waste any more time on the girl. She's as good as dead anyway."

No! She would not believe it, would not succumb to the fear and the weight of a mountain bearing down on her. She had escaped her guard and the cabin, she told herself. She was close to Spirit Canyon. She had to be.

She'd felt an overwhelming need to get out of that cavern and to escape the stench that made her feel as if she were being poisoned.

Taking a deep draught of air, she'd held her breath as she inched her way back to a sitting position. Every joint in her body ached and protested movement; her bones were as brittle as ice as she groped for a handhold on the boulder and pulled herself to her feet. Needles of pain in her feet and legs and arms had brought a cry to her lips. Dizziness had swirled in her head like a heavy cloud waiting to carry her away.

Stiffly she'd secured the shotgun over her shoulder, reseated the pistol in her waistband, and sheathed her knife before slipping it into her right-hand pocket. Disoriented, she'd stared down at her kerchief, which she had arranged on the ground to show her which way to go.

Thank you, Papa, for teaching me so well. With the silent prayer still in her mind, she had found the courage to leave her hiding place.

The pattern had begun—blind gropings through the maze, desperate decisions as to which turn to take, grim refusals to think of the consequences if she made the wrong choice. And when the darkness began to steal into her mind, she'd stop and bathe herself in sweet light.

Right foot. Left foot. On and on she went through the tunnel, finding an odd companionship in fantasies of her own choosing, dreams of a future that would never be.

They stood on the hill where she and her father had shared so many afternoons. Papa and Mama were gentle spirits in the clouds, watching as she and Zach tended the graves, played with their children, and watched God paint sunset after sunset.

She and Zach would share a meal by candlelight at the little table in the master bedroom, feeding one another morsels of food, sharing the same glass of wine, reaching across the table to taste the other with a lingering brush of the tongue, and trailing fingertips over intimate flesh. Sometimes Zach would sweep the table bare and lay her upon its smooth surface. Sometimes she sat on his lap, facing him, rocking on him, lifting herself up and down on his length, holding him within herself and bringing him pleasure. Sometimes they would stroll arm in arm to the bed, recline upon cool sheets and embracing feathers, urgency dictating the casting off of clothing, the seeking of mouths and hands and bodies, until finally they lay spent in each other's arms, diamond dust floating around them in a magical dance.

She and Zach sat in the parlor, cradled in matching wingback chairs, she embroidering new doilies, he reading aloud from his book of poetry, their hair silvered by time, their faces lined with experience and knowledge and happiness. . . .

Madness! Cameo knew it to be so, yet it was a dementia that kept her going, and when she slept, it followed her into her dreams, a light in the darkness that otherwise whispered of defeat.

How long had she been wandering since Seamus gave up the chase? Perhaps hours. Perhaps days. Her mouth was dry, her tongue swollen from thirst, yet she forced herself to go on—just one more bend, just one more step, just one more prayer for deliverance, a prayer filled with dreams of what she would find when she finally stepped into the light.

A bath, hot water laced with sweet-smelling salts in an imported tub. A pretty dress with bright colors and gay ribbons. Clean hair whipped around her face by fresh breezes. A soothing balm for her scrapes and bruises. Hot tea and fresh bread and newly laid eggs.

Zach, waiting for her, his arms open, his smile intimate, his socks and underwear neatly folded in the bureau, his shirts hanging in the armoire—all silent promises of forever.

Somewhere in her musings, her dreams changed into nightmares and the fear that Seamus had been right; she would never leave the mountain, never escape the darkness. It weakened her resolve to keep moving and strengthened her desire to lie down and sleep so deeply she would escape the nightmares and the sweet visions that were merely delusions of Zach and diamond dreams scattered across the sky. Every time she made a blind turn, she wondered if this would be her tomb and her good-bye to Zach would be spoken in the lonely silence of eternity.

It would be the final irony that she would be the one to leave first.

Finally she became aware of the short pants in her breathing, the cold sweat that bathed her, the suffocating panic that built in her throat and chest with every step she took deeper and deeper into the mountain. It happened more frequently now. It was harder to fight.

I will not die. I will not give up, she chanted over and over again as she forced herself to keep moving, forced herself to picture each face of the people in the valley—the little girl, Jorge, Mellie, Zach. They had to be warned. She had to fight back. She had to be waiting for Zach when the snows fell every year.

Ahead, the tunnel branched right and left. The decision was too much for her, too difficult, the consequences of another mistake too overwhelming. Again she'd have to backtrack. Again she'd battle the hope that had become a nemesis as she wandered through the perpetual night beneath the earth.

With trembling fingers she fumbled in her pockets for a candle and the precious matches. She removed one from the packet and struck it against a dry stretch of rock. The light flared, blinding her. Heat touched her flesh before she struggled to unite flame with wick in the glare of the match. She drooped against the wall, blinking and staring at the two tunnels until the blindness passed.

Gradually her heartbeat slowed and her breathing gentled. Hot wax dripped down the candle, burning her fingers again. She retrieved her kerchief from another pocket and wrapped it around the base of the candle, then sighed with relief. With light came sanity and clear thought. Did she imagine that the air flowing from the right seemed to be fresher, less musty?

A shadow appeared on the wall opposite her, elongated and distorted by the texture of rock, undulating like lazy waves in the capricious dance of candle flame. Her breath caught as she stared at the image of a man projected from the tunnel on the left, unmoving, waiting. The shadow thinned as its owner turned sideways, presenting a smaller target. Her gaze darted from side to side and back, finding no avenue of escape, no place to hide.

Her mind worked apart from her terror. Surely he was as blinded by the light as she had been. Surely he was waiting for her to panic and try to flee. Surely there was only one man.

Please, God, let it be so.

She held the candle high, her arm outstretched so the light would reach him more fully. And she waited, counting to a hundred as she used her free hand to pull the Colt from her waistband, her fingers caressing the wooden grip as if it were the flesh of a lover. . . .

Fifty-three, fifty-four.

With her eyes closed, she lifted the sling over her shoulder and let it fall again, making sure that it would not catch if she needed quick access to the shotgun.

Eighty-eight, eighty-nine.

Her hand groped in her pocket for the comforting feel of worn leather, drew her knife from its sheath, and slid it into her waistband. She sensed movement and opened her eyes to see the shadow moving closer, stalking her. She couldn't wait any longer, couldn't risk her opportunity for surprise. Surely he wouldn't expect her to fight back, much less attack first.

Ninety . . . a hundred.

Closing her eyes again, she held the candle close, inched her hand up its length, pinched out the flame with her fingers, pulled back the hammer of the pistol, and waited for another count of five. She felt the presence of evil growing within herself and named it necessary.

It was necessary to escape the man who stood between her and light. It was necessary to survive.

And she would kill him to do it.

25
Dreams by the Ounce

He was there, in front of her, a dense shade of black, like the rock surrounding her. She felt a rush of air as something hit her wrist. A lightning shock vibrated up her arm, then pain—in her wrist, her elbow, her shoulder. Her ears rang with the explosion of the gun, the ricochet of a bullet as it struck stone, the ring of metal as the gun fell from her lifeless fingers. A cascade of dust and shattered rock fell over her head, and she wondered if the mountain was going to bury her after all.

She couldn't make her fingers work, couldn't move her arm. He was too close for her to use the shotgun, too fast for her to free it from the sling and aim. Left-handed, she gripped the hilt of her knife, pulled it from her belt, and held it poised in front of her as she charged her assailant, thrusting her arm forward to meet him with sharpened steel—

Her feet tangled with his outthrust leg. She lunged forward, refusing to fall. Hands deflected her blow, grasped her arms, twisted her around, bound her arms to her sides, and held her fast against a hard body. The shotgun pressed into her back, the edge of the stock digging and hurting.

"Cameo—"

The shout was lost in her determination to fight, to win her freedom and escape. The arms squeezing her ribs were the embodiment of the tunnels, unyielding stone crushing her. The breath thundering in her ear was as heavy and threatening as the darkness. Lowering her head, she took a deep breath and used all the force she could muster to rear back and crack the back of her head against his chin and nose.

The blow glanced off him as he jerked his head back. His hold tightened.

"Stop it!"

She refused to listen, refused to give in. Twisting in his grasp, Cameo lifted her feet off the ground, swung them out, then kicked back, catching his knees. Her hand reached back and found his crotch, her fingernails digging deep and twisting. His groan of pain gave her a curious pleasure. She twisted harder.

His hold loosened, then tightened even more as he extended one arm around her and the other released her to press her wrist bones together, numbing her hand, forcing her to let him go.

"Rosebud!"

The name reached her through clouds of rage, the drive of instinct. She stiffened, her feet still suspended in air. "Say that again," she whispered, afraid to believe, afraid to hope.

"Stop fighting, Rosebud."

The whispered order touched her ear, a warm breath, a sigh, the barest touch of lips, caressing her. She clenched her fingers, felt the knife hilt still clutched in her hand. *Never give up your weapon, Cameo,* her father had taught her. Her feet touched the floor as she sagged in his arms.

"No. I won't drop it." Rationally, she knew it was Zach, knew she was safe, yet she was still reduced to the essential law of survival. And he was a man, stronger than she, capable of bending her to his will. Never again, she knew, could she allow that to happen, no matter who the man was or what he meant to her. As long as she had the knife, she could maintain some control, protect herself. The danger and horror were still too recent, too real.

"Let me go."

His grip loosened. "Light a candle, Cameo, and look at me," he said through harsh, uneven breaths, his voice strained.

The arms fell away from her and she heard him step back—out of range, she guessed. Clumsily she pulled a candle from her pocket and lit it while still holding the knife. She had to squint in the sudden brightness, but held her knife pointed at the shadow crouching half-in, half-out of the light.

Features materialized from the blur, all planes and angles carved by a primitive hand, features that hadn't seen a razor in days. The eyes were as light as twilight mist, and his mouth was twisted. She sheathed her knife and stuck it in her belt.

In her heart she wanted to go to him, to take shelter in him and for just a while allow herself to be helpless. But her body wouldn't comply; her instincts held her rooted to the stone floor of the tunnel, as if Zach, too, presented a threat to her survival. It was important that she hang on to herself, important that she walk out of the tunnels under her own power. It was important that she finish this journey without giving up.

"You're all right?" he asked as his arm reached for her.

She stepped back. "Don't touch me."

"Are . . . you . . . all . . . right?" he asked again, this time pain evident in his voice, the way he bent over, his hand cupping himself.

"Yes." It seemed to be what he needed to hear. "But you're not," she added, realizing that she had hurt him.

"Damned right I'm not . . . excuse me."

She tilted her head to watch as he limped around the bend with a funny, slumped-over gait. A moment later she heard him stop, his pants multiplied by echoes on the stone walls.

"Aargh!"

The howl of pain rebounded over and over again, though he gave only the one shout. Something rustled as if he might be unfastening buttons, loosening his clothes. Moments passed and for each one, he cut loose with a string of curses.

With the candle burning, Cameo waited, listening to his sounds of distress, watching the movements of his shadow on the wall, yet not feeling as if they had anything to do with her. She worked her fingers to restore feeling, rubbed her wrist where he had struck it, stared at his shadow.

The shadow straightened up, went through the motions of fitting buttons into their holes, heaved with a sigh, lengthened as it approached her, bowlegged as if its owner had been in the saddle for a solid month.

Again he reached for her. Again she stepped back. His expression became bleak, haunted by a different pain.

"I'm ready to go." she said.

His gaze remained on her, steady and searching as he picked up the Colt and reloaded the empty chamber. Watching the gun, she leaned toward him, as if the weapon were a lifeline dragging her in its wake.

Thoughtfully he glanced from the Colt to Cameo, tested

its weight, then held it by the barrel as he offered it to her. She snatched it from his hand and tucked it into her belt alongside the knife.

Without comment, Zach took her hand in his and turned back the way he had come.

Zach's anger at Cameo for taking off in the middle of the night had long since dissipated. He wanted to wrap his arms around her and never let go. He wanted to take that cold, hard look from her eyes. He wanted to skin alive Seamus and his men one inch of flesh at a time. Impatience and anger and relief churned inside him—to do something. Anything. But Cameo was all rough edges, brittle and ragged, and he had the sense that with one wrong word or touch, he would fracture her control.

From what he'd learned of the events in the trapper's cabin, he knew that Cameo had already lost too much.

He wanted to promise Cameo that she would always be safe and her life would be happy and all that she needed it to be. Except that he'd promised himself that he'd never again lie to her. And so he held his silence and did all that she would allow; he led her to freedom and lit one candle after another to keep the darkness from touching her.

It seemed unreal, improbable, that he'd found her after all this time. Even more unreal was her silence as they walked through the tunnel, the distance she kept between them. He wished for tears, for questions—anything to convince him that she wasn't still lost in the underground maze of Spirit Mountain.

He wanted to know what the bastards had done to her.

The tunnel widened and wound into a final series of turns. Dawn glistened like diamond dust in the air as he led her into a cave, its three outside entrances concentrating rays that shot onto the floor in widening beams of shimmering light.

Cameo walked past him and flattened her hand on one wall and traced her fingers over faded paintings. A sob escaped her as she leaned her forehead against the stone. "Oh, God," she said. "I was going to take the tunnel on the right."

A chill shivered over his scalp at how close he'd come to losing her. A few minutes and she would have taken the wrong turn and found a sheer drop into the bowels of the earth. A few minutes between life and death. "Cameo," he said, clearing his throat, "are you all right?"

"It was Seamus," she said, ignoring his question.

"I know."

"He must be stopped. He doesn't care about the South or the North. He wants the valley—"

"I know."

Cameo drew the Colt and checked its load. She shifted her knife to its normal place at the back of her belt, then counted the shotgun shells in her pockets. "We must catch them before they get away—"

"It's done, Cameo." Zach watched her from across the cave, afraid to approach her, afraid he would frighten her with the strength of his emotions, the desperation of his need to hold her. But her voice was cracked, thready, as if she would shatter into a thousand splinters if either one of them made a wrong move or said the wrong thing. Her flesh was pale, almost transparent, in the ethereal light of the cave. Stains covered her clothing, and her leather boots were marked by moisture. A large three-cornered tear in her skirt revealed a once-white petticoat smeared with blood and grime.

She gazed up at him out of wide, lifeless eyes, the skin

surrounding them bruised by fatigue. "Done?" she asked. "What is done?"

Zach shoved his hands into his pockets to keep from reaching out to her. "We followed your tracks," he said in a soft, melodious tone meant to smooth the edges and banish her frailty. "Seamus and his men were still at the trapper's cabin. Cloud Walker and some of our men are taking them to Fort Union."

She blinked as her fingers wandered over the images on the wall. "The paint is fading. It never has before. Everything seems to be fading. . . ." Her voice trailed off as she scraped a spot with her fingernail. "It's all chipping away."

With a frown, she glanced around the cave, her search ending at the pile of supplies Zach had stored in a corner in anticipation of a long search and finding her in need of food and warmth and light.

A chill of apprehension crawled up his spine. This wasn't the time. Not now when she had already been betrayed at every turn. Not now when she was already so far away from him that another shock might make her withdraw altogether.

With grim resignation, he watched her walk over to his cache and light the lantern on top of the pile. She carried it back to the wall she'd been studying. A patch of color gleamed in the light as she scraped more paint off the wall.

Her laughter burst in the chamber, a low chuckle, then louder, wilder, punctuated by stifled sobs.

"Cameo, *don't.*" Three steps took him to her, but she backed away, shaking her head, her hands flattening on the rock as she collided with the wall.

It stopped him, seeing her there, trapped in a corner and sidling away from him. Her eyes were wide and bright, and still she shook with laughter until tears flowed down her cheeks. Then she started to speak.

"No wonder I always felt safe here. I came here when everyone else was afraid to even admit that the canyon existed. Papa always seemed to be so close here." She swallowed, then continued, her words rapid, tumbling like water over rocks. "Of course he was close—"

"Cameo, don't."

"Don't? *Don't* what, Zach? Don't laugh?" She stepped away from the wall and began to pace now that he had backed off. "People always laugh at fools, and that's what I've been—a naïve, simple-minded, complacent fool. I didn't recognize my own father's handiwork. I never once questioned anything. And I felt so safe, coming here to dream. I even sat outside on summer days and talked to the Old Man of the Mountains as if he were my father and he had all the time in the world to listen and to just be there."

Her circles grew wider as she paced nearer to the walls, her hand reaching out to skim the paintings, memorizing them before they became nothing but flakes of drab color on the floor. "I should have recognized the brush strokes, the style. God knows I'm familiar enough with it. I've lived every day of my life looking at my father's memories neatly framed and hung on the walls of my home, dreaming of—just once—being able to go with him, being a living part of those memories, and seeing what he saw."

Zach listened and kept himself in check, hoping it was the right thing to do, hoping that her outburst would purge the bitterness he heard in her laughter, the sobs she couldn't swallow down in time.

"The old man with gold teeth. The perfect place to dream." Cameo flung her arm wide. "I've been agonizing over your people, wondering how I could help them. I was going to sell some of the land, Zach. Your people had a right to their dreams, too, and I was going to—" Her laughter pealed out; tears ran down her face. "I was going to give them those dreams."

She kept pacing around the chamber, not once looking at him, as if she were talking to lifeless stone. "You knew. This is the mother lode Seamus would have killed me for. This is where all dreams come true. Dreams by the ounce." Hair whipped around her face as she tossed her head and turned in a circle, her arms wide. "The paintings scared people off, and now that Papa is gone, the paint is fading and chipping away." She was out of control, hysterical, and the tears were blinding her, causing her to stumble as she made yet another circuit around the cave.

"Tell me, Zach, where is the actual mine? Where did Papa dig up his dreams?"

"The tunnel on the right." Zach said dully. "There's a deep shaft going straight down to keep trespassers from going too far. On the other side—"

"You've made your point," Cameo said in a hard voice. "How appropriate that I would have met the same fate as a *trespasser* if you hadn't come along in the nick of time. I *am* a trespasser."

This time, Zach didn't worry about her aversion to being touched, but caught her by the arms and pulled her around to face him. "Stop it!"

"I own a mountain of gold! When were you going to tell me, Zach? *Were* you going to tell me?"

He shook her once, then again, harder.

Wildly, she raised her arms and flailed about. She laughed harder and the tears came faster. "You can have it, Zach. All of it—the whole mountain. I don't want dreams I have to buy by the ounce."

He slapped her face, lightly, in desperation, then again with more force when she didn't seem to feel the first blow.

Suddenly the cave grew silent as Cameo stilled in his hold. She gazed up at him. "Seamus slapped me, too," she said in a whisper, and lowered her head. "No one has ever hit me before, and then in one night—"

His hands lifted and gently cupped her face, his thumbs caressing the twin handprints on her cheeks. Anger flared and burned all the way through him. Anger because the best he could do for Cameo was to hit her.

"It's been five days, Cameo." The words were wrenched from him with the force of all the anguish he'd felt while he searched for her. Five days and nights of desperation and urgency as he traveled through the empty veins of the mountain, tormented by the knowledge that Cameo was afraid of the dark, always knowing that enforced fear could lead to madness. A madness that had stalked him, too, for without Cameo the entire world was a shadow without substance.

"Five days?" Her body began to tremble violently, and she wrapped her arms around her waist.

"Five days, six hours, and thirty-six minutes—give or take a few seconds."

All the rough edges dissolved as she curled her shoulders forward and lowered her head. "So many times I wondered how long . . . and I dreamed . . . nightmares and delusions. It . . . was almost comforting to believe them and not have anyone around to call me a fool." Her knees buckled.

Zach carried her to a worn rock near the hot pool and lowered her to the ground. Retrieving the supplies, he stacked wood, struck a match, and nursed the flames. Smoke curled upward and drifted out of the twin openings far above as he opened a flask and poured brandy into the cap. "Drink this."

A shudder wracked her as she obeyed, then looked at the water. "I dreamed of a bath. I smell."

Relieved at the mundane statement, Zach smiled and unbuttoned her coat and shirtwaist, then freed the buckle of her belt and the laces at the back of her skirt. Like a sleepy child, she obeyed his instructions, her limbs falling limply once a task was completed. "You'll drown if you don't get some starch in your body," he quipped, hoping for a smile, a response, anything.

"You can't drown twice," she said flatly.

No matter how hard he tried to swallow, the emotion in his throat wouldn't go down. He'd seen it over and over again—Cameo drowning in darkness, the rock walls of the mountain closing over her head, holding her apart from the world she loved, hiding her from those who loved her. He'd seen it and banished the nightmare with dreams of his own. Dreams of Cameo, full of sass and sparkle, lightning impulses and crazy notions. Cameo, whose loyalty and capacity for trust awed him. Cameo, whose courage lay not in her impulses but in her ability to do whatever was necessary even when she was scared to death.

That Cameo didn't seem to exist anymore. The woman leaning against the rock had dull, empty eyes. The weariness he saw on her face overwhelmed him. The hopelessness he heard in her voice scared the living hell out of him.

He knelt beside her. "Cameo, what happened?" he asked, hating himself for giving in to the driving need to know.

Her breath shuddered in and out. Her eyes blinked, and

her trembling increased. "It was all a delusion . . . Santa Claus and Uncle Seamus," she babbled, words and thoughts leapfrogging without order. "It was so dark. He said I c-could sign over the valley or die . . . I thought about it . . . ac-actually considered it."

Her breath came in gulping sobs that vibrated through his body as he gathered her close, stroked her hair, pressed his lips to her temple. Her voice was becoming more normal, and he knew that this, too, had to be endured.

"It seemed s-so easy. I could f-follow you, be like your mother . . . or a . . . a wildflower. John Childress . . . he did it to s-save his home in the South. He told me about it . . . the trees on his land . . . as if he was one of them . . . and I kn-knew. I can't be a wildflower. R-roots too deep. Roses can't grow just anywhere."

"Shh."

"I was ready to d-die. But I saw the food and John fell asleep and he was a gentleman and I unbuttoned his pants after I hit him so he would fall down and I slept with bats . . . oh, God, the smell . . . and it was so dark—"

"Shh." He held her with one hand as if that would be enough to hold her together, and unfastened his clothing with the other. The struggle to shuck off his clothes without losing contact with her was a lost cause. His shirt hung off one arm; his denim pants were unbuttoned, but he couldn't pull them off while kneeling. "Cameo, don't move," he said softly.

He might as well have saved his breath. Her eyes were wide and fixed on nothing. Her only movements were the shivers racking her body.

Cameo, where are you?

Quickly he yanked off his boots and stood to throw off his shirt and unbutton the front of the union suit he'd worn for warmth. He stumbled clumsily as he tried to pull off long underwear and pants at the same time and managed to tangle himself up in his own legs. Hopping on one foot, then the other, he finally managed to drag off his trousers. Repeating the process, he bent to pull off his socks.

After so much silence, the sudden activity and movement startled and frightened Cameo. Instinctively she reached for a weapon—only her belt was gone. She looked down to find herself only in camisole and pantalets. The shotgun was just out of reach, leaning against another rock with her knife and pistol on the ground beside it. A flash of red caught Cameo's eye, and she frantically turned her head, searching for danger, finding Zach's familiar form twisting and hopping and contorting between pauses to rub his thigh.

She blinked, once, twice. Her mouth twitched. Something came alive inside her and curled outward. Contrasting with the worn and faded red cloth covering his lower body was a square of flesh, smooth and tight and slightly rounded. She smiled whimsically. "You lost a button," she said, feeling her world begin to stabilize the more he lurched and hopped and cursed. Her scalp tingled with the giggle that escaped her, then pleasant flutters of sensation moved over her skin and deeper sensations of life and normalcy.

Zach's movements stilled abruptly. His gaze shot over his shoulder, his eyes wary. A flush climbed from his neck to his face as Cameo poked a finger at his bare buttock.

She giggled again as her head tilted to the side. "Your trap door is open."

A part of him was relieved to hear the life coming back to her voice. The rest of him had trouble coping with a completely foreign state of embarrassment. He jerked upright and presented his exposed backside to the wall, away from Cameo's engrossed study and that all-too-cavalier finger that was teasing his all-too-sensitive skin. This was asinine. It was unnatural. Insulting. First she'd damn near twisted his balls off, then she touched him with a brazen familiarity that most wives wouldn't dare, and she was still giggling.

The anger he'd been nursing since finding her gone five nights ago was fueled by the way she made him forget everything else with just a look, a touch. An hour ago she'd refused his touch. Ten minutes ago she'd been white and cold with shock. Five minutes ago he'd had to hit her in an effort to calm her hysteria. Yet all of a sudden she had bounced back to her sassy, contrary self. Her smile was whimsical in a face that was rapidly regaining its natural color. Her body was relaxing and the worst of the shivers had stopped.

It irritated the hell out of him that Cameo seemed to be taking care of herself without his help.

"If you keep whittling away at my pride, I won't have any left when I need it the most," he grumbled.

Her smile faded, and her gaze dropped to her lap. Twisting her hands together, she hid the finger that had touched him so brazenly a moment before. _Will you, just once, stop trying to be the man?_ She bit her lip at the humiliation the memory brought and kept her gaze fixed on her lap. "You were wrong, Zach," she said quietly. "I never wanted to be the man. All I wanted was to be a woman."

"What the hell—" Puzzled, he raked his hand through his hair as he tried to figure out what she was talking about. Then his words came back to haunt him—those angry, frustrated words that he'd thrown at her because he hadn't liked the way she humbled him with her willingness to give him everything when he couldn't even give her a promise.

"Is that why you took off?" he asked hoarsely.

Her silence goaded his rage.

"Of all the stupid, thoughtless, crazy, reckless, *stupid*—"

"You already said 'stupid,' " she pointed out calmly as she wrapped her arms around her drawn-up legs. She rested her cheek on her knees and gazed at him like a child.

His mouth hung open. He glared at her. No, dammit! She was always doing that—catching him off guard, making his brains drop into his crotch. Closing his mouth, he took a deep breath and cut loose with all the fury he'd been nursing for five days. "You risked your life, the ranch, everything just because you were in a snit."

"I found the criminals you couldn't find," she said reasonably. For every angry word of his tirade, she felt strength and defiance returning. She was in her cave, in her canyon, safe and warm and bathed in light. Zach was here, with her. Zach, not Sloane.

"Those bastards were going to kill you!"

"They didn't hurt me—not physically."

"Right," he said sarcastically. "I shouldn't have worried. "You have such a talent for *disappearing*. Hell, I could have been relaxing back at the ranch and just waited for you to show up." Needing movement and feeling like a fool arguing with her without a stitch on, he swooped her up in his arms and carried her into the pool.

"I was going to take the tunnel on the right, Zach." She paused a moment as she stared back the way they had come. "What would have happened to me if I—"

"You would have fallen down the mine shaft. You'd still be falling," he said brutally.

Her body convulsed, and her face paled, but she recovered quickly, a tremor in her voice the only evidence of distress. "Why did you come?"

"Who did you expect?" he asked, stung.

"If I expected anyone to find me, it was the Others—my guardians."

"Why?"

She shrugged. "They're always here."

And I'm not. There was nothing he could say to that, nothing he could do to prove it wouldn't continue to be true.

Ribbons of coffee-dark hair streamed out in the water as she laid her head back and sighed. Her hand touched his side and lingered. Lightning shocks jolted through him at her touch. He closed his eyes, concentrating his senses on the pleasure, focusing his mind on controlling his response. A grimace flattened his mouth as he told himself that it was the wrong time and place. She didn't know what she was doing to him.

Anguish pierced her at his grimace. The way his body strained away from her drove the point home. A twist of her body freed her from his hold, and she paddled away from him—out of reach.

"It's over," she whispered, her back to him. *I'm falling, Zach . . . still falling.*

"Yes." His eyes opened at her sudden withdrawal, the pain of having his soul wrenched from him. *Don't touch me.* Circling the pool, he watched her float on her back, her arms spread out in the silky water. *Come back, Rosebud. Let me hold you.*

"I dreamed of a bath." She rolled over and dipped her face in the water to hide the tears.

"Tell me your dreams."

"A bath, clean clothes, food, you, forever." *The necessities of life.*

Forever. A dream he didn't dare consider. A word that made him want to bury his body so deeply in hers that nothing could separate them again. Instead, he climbed out of the pool and wrapped a quilt around his waist. "Food coming up." Forcibly keeping his gaze from straying to her as she followed, he picked up another quilt and draped it over her shoulders. "How did you escape?"

A smile barely curved her lips. "I beat the pants off of my guard." The smile grew as she rubbed her cheek over the tattered quilt with the scenes of her mother's life embroidered in fading colors. And while he unwrapped the bundles of food, she told him in greater detail about her escape. It seemed to calm her and to put a distance between her and what had happened to talk about it, to imagine John Childress losing his pants and tripping over them when he awakened to find her gone.

A bark of laughter filled the cave as he watched her wrestle off her wet pantalets and camisole under the quilt. *Don't hide from me, Cameo.* Disdaining the union suit, Zach tugged on his denims and dug in the pile of supplies for the clean clothes Mellie had gathered for Cameo.

Wet cloth slapped against the rock as she tossed the pantalets aside. "You'll be leaving," she said without a trace of feeling. Before the last word was out, she turned her face away from him.

"As soon as I tie up some loose ends . . ." He couldn't finish, couldn't express the emotions that had been battering him for days, couldn't tell her how each minute that she'd been missing had been like another shovelful of dirt being thrown into his own grave. . . .

It would have been like selling her dreams by the ounce.

26

To Crush the Rose

Aprofound sense of change followed Cameo as she and Zach left Spirit Canyon and drew closer to the valley. She could feel it, and she grieved for all that would never be again. Zach's mission was over. The freight business could be sold to Butterfield or Wells Fargo. With the families from the mesa in place at the ranch, everything was working as it should. There was even a good candidate for foreman. She'd manage the ranch just fine, especially with people working for her who didn't adhere to the code that proclaimed men to be Supreme and classified women as Domestic Comforts.

It was all over. The ranch no longer needed Zach. She knew that she didn't need Zach either. Without him, she would still survive. Living, though, was going to be more difficult.

As they rode into the valley, she waited for the pang of homecoming, the rush of pride and sense of belonging. She felt nothing but a detached interest in what was going on. Everything seemed normal and tranquil. Men were riding in from pastures and performing tasks in the ranch yard. A little girl fed the chickens as she sang a child's song. Smoke

curled up from chimneys and a potpourri of cooking odors
wafted through the air. The sun poked a hole of weak light
through the clouds tenting the sky, too weak for shadows
to play on the ground before twilight put them to rest.

All is as it should be . . . except me.

"No smoke is coming from the chimneys in the house,"
she remarked, shaking off her dismal thoughts.

"Mellie won't be expecting us. Maybe she's staying with
one of the families, with her time so close."

One by one, the people stopped in their tracks as Cameo
and Zach rode by. Silence fell a sound at a time until all
that was left was the sweet voice of the little girl. Smiles
grew from openmouthed stares. Hats were doffed and a
woman who had stepped outside to empty a pail of water
dropped her burden and wiped her eyes with a corner of
her apron.

It was all so familiar, yet it felt so strange.

Diamond stopped when Jorge drew near. Jorge—all that
was left from the past. He stood beside her, staring at her
as if she were an apparition.

"Niña?"

"I'm fine, Jorge." *I'm dying, Jorge.*

"They did not hurt you?"

"No." *I did that all by myself.*

Jorge nodded and bent his head as he pulled a handkerchief from his rear pocket and loudly blew his nose.
"Never will you do that again, *niña,*" he said gruffly. "I
am an old man. It is for the old to go before the young."
Reaching up, he waited for her to slip into his hold.

"I'm not going anywhere." Conscious of his arthritic
joints, she hesitated to allow him to help her down, knowing she was too heavy and his strength waned with the
passing of each day.

"Come down, so I can know you are here." Dignity straightened his body and leveled his stooped shoulders. Pride hardened his jaw.

Beside her on the other side, Zach nudged his leg against hers. Casually he leaned over to take the reins from her hand.

"I'm home, Jorge," she said with a tender smile as she swung her leg over the pommel and slid off the saddle, careful to keep him from bearing too much of her weight.

His hands lingered at her waist. "You are sometimes foolish, *niña.*"

Impulsively she hugged the old man and kissed his cheek. "I won't worry you again. I promise."

He studied her expression with world-weary eyes and nodded. "*Sí.* You are a woman now, I think—not a child to find trouble just to see what it is like." With that, he accepted both sets of reins from Zach in one hand and tipped his hat with the other. "*Muchas gracias, Señor* Sloane."

Strangely reluctant to enter the house, Cameo stood in the yard and glanced around, smiling at the people and waving to the ones too far away to see her expression. One by one, they smiled back, waved, doffed hats, and returned to work. A sudden breeze whooshed through the trees like a collective sigh.

Zach cupped her elbow in his hand. "Let's go in, Cameo."

"Yes, all right." Her gaze swept the valley once more. *Normal. So normal. Why do I feel so misplaced?*

"Why do I have this feeling that you meant what you said to Jorge?" Zach asked as they climbed the steps. At her puzzled frown, he explained, "About not worrying him." He opened the door and stood aside for her to enter first.

She breathed in the scents of lemon oil and beeswax and even after all this time, a lingering trace of her father's cigars. "I did mean it. After the last few months, I'm ready for a long spell of embroidering doilies, gardening, and raising horses." The house was quiet and dark, the air chilled for lack of a fire in the hearth. She turned at the sound of Zach's footsteps and the slam of the door. "Zach—"

"Sloane," he said softly.

Sloane. A sudden thought brought panic into her throat. "Did Seamus recognize you?"

He hung his hat on a peg. "No, it was too dark and he hasn't seen me since I was a boy. The other men only know me as—"

"Sloane. I won't forget again." she said, and walked briskly toward the parlor. "We need a fire, and light. The place seems so abandoned—" She cocked her head as a sound reached her. It came again, weak and muffled from the kitchen.

"Jesus. It's Mellie." Zach pulled his gun. "Stay here, load a rifle, and aim it at the doorway," he whispered as he walked silently toward the back of the house.

Numbly, Cameo obeyed without question.

"Cameo! Help!"

Zach's bark scared her to death. Still gripping the rifle, she followed his voice to the pantry attached to the kitchen and stopped outside the open door. Not knowing what to expect, she shouldered the rifle and peered cautiously around the doorjamb, then realized if there was any kind of threat at all, Zach would never call for her, never endanger anyone but himself.

The trapdoor set in the floor of the pantry had been thrown back and a lantern cast dingy yellow light on the wooden steps leading down into the root cellar. Propping the rifle in the crook of her elbow, she descended the steps, one hand braced along the wall.

Mellie lay on the dirt floor, her skin pale and tinged with yellow from the glow of the lantern. Her legs were drawn up, and her body writhed as she whimpered in pain. "You came," she gasped as she grabbed Zach's hand and held on for dear life. "Nobody . . . could . . . hear . . ."

Zach was kneeling beside her, feeling her forehead and looking utterly helpless. "She's in trouble. What's wrong with her? She doesn't have a fever."

"I . . . fell . . . steps," Mellie said between breaths.

Propping the rifle against the wall, Cameo bent over Mellie and saw the girl's stomach bunched in an unrelenting contraction beneath her soaked Mother Hubbard gown. "Her water has broken and she's bleeding. Carry her up to bed," she ordered as she preceded him up the steps.

While Zach carried Mellie up to the housekeeper's rooms off the kitchen, Cameo ran to the linen press for sheets and towels. Back in the kitchen, she gathered string and a bottle of whiskey.

"Dammit, Cameo, will you hurry up?"

"I need hot water first; then get Cloud Walker," she ordered as she ran into the bedroom with linens piled high in her arms.

Zach started out the door, then stopped. "Shit! Cloud Walker is on his way to Fort Union."

"Get one of the other women, then," she said, distracted by the way Mellie's stomach didn't relax, but seemed to knot in a perpetual clench.

"No time," Mellie moaned. "Please . . . don't leave . . . it's coming . . . oh . . . please . . . help . . ."

"Put the water on and come right back to light a fire and help me—" Cameo glanced over her shoulder and saw Zach run from the room. Mellie's cries of pain didn't give her time to think. With shaking hands, Cameo drew her knife and cut off Mellie's gown, then her pantalets, leaving the camisole intact. "Mellie, I don't know how. We have to find help."

"Don't . . . leave . . . oh, God . . . I'm . . . scared. You . . . can . . . do . . . anything . . . Miss—" Another pain seized her.

"No! I can't," Cameo cried, more afraid than she'd been in the tunnels. "I—"

"Cameo."

Startled, she twisted around. Zach was bent over in front of the fireplace, touching a match to kindling. There was something about the timbre of his tightly controlled voice that soothed her and pulled her thoughts together. His face had taken on a green cast. He avoided looking at Mellie. His hands were shaking as badly as her own.

"Remember Diamond, Rosebud? You saved her when Twilight was born."

"Twilight and Diamond are horses."

"You have to do it." He stared at his hands and clenched them as if he were willing them to become steady. "I know you're worn out, sweetheart. Just one more thing to do and you can rest."

She knew he was right. There wasn't much time, and her exhaustion was nothing compared to Mellie's. Something was wrong and Mellie didn't look as if she had enough strength to last another minute. At least twenty women lived on the far end of the compound, yet they might as well have been as far away as the mesa.

"How long has it been, Mellie?" she asked more calmly than she felt. *Oh, dear God, please don't make me responsible for two lives like this. I couldn't stand to lose them, too. Then don't fail.*

"Morning . . . I was . . . getting potatoes . . . a-and I fell."

Appalled, Cameo struggled with her own fears. Morning. Mellie had lain helpless in the cold, damp cellar since morning. Never once while she herself had been lost and in danger had she been so completely powerless. *You're not helpless now. You saved Diamond. You knew what to do. Can it be so different?* As she covered Mellie's upper body with a sheet and slid another under her, Cameo fervently prayed that it wasn't.

"Let me die," Mellie whispered.

Cameo forgot her own panic and ruthlessly shoved away her doubts. "No! You're not going to die. I have to examine you, Mellie." She washed her hands in the basin of water Zach had placed on the table and slipped them into the birth passage.

"I want to be with Calvin."

"Just try it, Mellie, and see what happens. Calvin would send you right back here to take care of his baby." Biting her lip, Cameo probed and tried to identify which part of the baby she was touching. "I can feel the head. The baby is turned the right way . . . dammit, where's that water?" She was talking to air. Zach had already gone back to the kitchen.

He carried in two buckets of steaming water. "What's it for?"

"I have no idea." As gently as she could, Cameo began

to arrange Mellie's body for delivery. Perspiration beaded on her forehead when she saw Mellie bite her lower lip and draw blood. "Mellie," she said gently. "I'm sorry. It's going to hurt until the baby is born."

Mellie cried harder, her head shaking frantically on the pillow.

Inspiration struck. "Mellie," Cameo shouted above the sobs. "The only way it will stop is for you to help me. Otherwise this is going to take a long time." At first she didn't think she'd gotten through Mellie's hysteria, but then the gulping sobs began to subside until there were only silent tears coursing down her cheeks. Little by little, even those disappeared.

Cameo smiled weakly at Zach in relief. It was one thing to know she was hurting Mellie and quite another to hear and see evidence of it. "Try to get her to relax. She's tight as a spring," she said to Zach.

"How?"

"Think of something. Rub her belly. Recite poetry. Anything."

Clearing his throat, he began with the first thing that came to mind. *"To be, or not to be—"*

Cameo glared at him. "Good choice," she said sarcastically.

He cleared his throat again, and recited a poem by Robert Herrick that she remembered from Zach's book.

> *"Bid me to live and I will live,*
> *Thy Protestant to be:*
> *Or bid me love, and I will give*
> *A loving heart to thee. . . ."*

The melodious tone of his voice reached Cameo first, then the words penetrated through her concentration on Mellie. She didn't dare look at him or acknowledge the foolish hope the borrowed words gave her. It was, after all, simply a poem written by another man.

"Bid that heart stay . . ." He faltered, his expression stricken and guilty as his gaze shot to hers, then dropped to his hand.

With a grim smile, Cameo silently amended the last part of the quotation. *And it will not stay. My heart will weep for thee.*

Again he cleared his throat. *"There was a young man from Nantucket—"*

"Forget the poetry," Cameo snapped.

"My baby won't come." Mellie's voice slurred as if she'd just awakened. Her body had relaxed a little, but still she struggled against the pain.

"Mellie, he's in position now. You have to push."

"I . . . can't. Please . . . let me die."

Cameo took a deep breath, rose from the end of the bed, and bent over Mellie—so close that they were practically nose to nose. "Not one more living being is going to die on this property. You are going to take a deep breath, and then you're going to raise up your shoulders and push."

"No stren . . ."

"Z—Sloane will help you raise up. You will do as you're told when I tell you to do it."

Amazed that she would remember her promise even when all hell was breaking loose, Zach raised his head in time to see her bitter smile come and go. Later, he knew, her faithfulness in keeping a promise was going to haunt him.

"When I say so, you raise her shoulders up," she said to

Zach. Then to Mellie, "And when I say push, you'd damn well better push."

Mellie nodded, her eyes wide and skittish as if she were more intimidated by Cameo than by her labor.

"Do you know what you're doing?" he asked.

"I'm pretending that I'm delivering a foal," she snapped again and bent over the end of the bed between Mellie's outspread knees. "I want children in this house."

From then on, Cameo tossed out orders. Zach and Mellie obeyed. "I can see his head. Push now. For heaven's sake, Mellie, quit using your energy to fight and do something useful like scream."

Mellie obeyed with alacrity. An earsplitting, blood-curdling scream drowned out Zach's curses. His face turned from green to gray. Sweat beaded his forehead and ran down his cheeks. It occurred to him that Cameo could very well be delivering her own child within the next eight months or so, and his color paled from gray to white.

"Whiskey," Cameo ordered.

"Where do you want it?" he asked as he reached for the bottle.

"In your stomach, and hurry."

Zach downed a slug of whiskey, then raised Mellie's shoulders. He glanced at Cameo and couldn't take his eyes off her. She had lifted an arm to wipe moisture from her face. Her bottom lip was caught between her teeth, her brows puckered in concentration.

"I have the head! Just another push or two, Mellie."

"Boy or girl?" Mellie asked between grunts.

"I can't tell from the head. Push, Mellie. The shoulders are the hard part." *I think,* she mumbled to herself.

Tears fell from Cameo's eyes to the bed as she listened to Mellie's weakening cries, watched the girl's body tear with the passage of the baby, and felt the warmth and movement of life in her hands. The baby slid free. Gentleness touched her face—Zach wiping away her tears with the back of his hand. A series of wails filled the air.

"A boy, Mellie," she whispered. "As fine and handsome as his father." Mechanically, she finished up the process of seeing to the afterbirth and cutting the cord, then held the baby out to Zach. "He needs to be washed."

"Me?" Zach stared down at the spindly arms and legs that seemed to be everywhere at once. The baby's head was lopsided from his difficult passage and his red face was skewed in outrage at being held in the open air. "I don't know how—"

"Neither does a mother the first time, but she manages," Cameo said, bending her head to finish taking care of Mellie.

"Zachary Sloane Boyd," Mellie sighed. "That's a nice name."

Zach stiffened.

Cameo lifted her head.

"What?" they said in unison.

"Zachary was Calvin's friend," Mellie whispered, her voice thick with exhaustion. "He died trying to save Calvin."

"How did you know that?" Cameo asked.

"The commander told me in a letter, and Sloane was Calvin's friend, too. He had another man check up on me, and he took me in so I wouldn't have to go back to the sold—" She shook her head. "Calvin would want his boy to be named after his friends."

Cameo snared Zach in her gaze, holding him with tenderness and a certain wry humor. His mouth twitched upward in a parody of a smile. Zachary Sloane. His name given to honor two men when only one existed. Perpetuation of a myth.

Abruptly he turned his back to the women and swallowed. His eyes were fixed on the squirming baby as his hands carefully washed away the signs of his difficult entrance into the world, yet he wasn't aware of anything but his own thoughts. All of the dreams he'd buried beneath a thousand masks broke through, shattering everything that was false, sweeping away the fragments of all the beliefs forced on him by the brutal demands of his job and the shallow concepts of honor in war.

And he couldn't help thinking about Cameo and the possibility that she might be carrying a child. The baby in his arms became more real, the sensation of holding him more poignant. So much energy and life in such a small package. So much perfection in spite of the out-of-proportion body, the misshapen head, the red and wrinkled skin.

Little Zachary chose that moment to draw his legs up and wave his arms. Over and over again the baby tried to aim both of his closed-up fists at his mouth, but managed only to hit himself in the face. Wailing, he turned his face into Zach's hand and began sucking on the side of his thumb. That fast, Zach understood how parents were able to fall in love immediately with such pathetic-looking creatures. He understood the miracle. Understanding brought a yearning and a need so strong that he felt crushed by it.

Cameo, will there be two children in the house come summer?

Never again could he live as a shadow without heart and soul. He stole a quick glance at Cameo. Her head was bent as she bustled around the bed, helping Mellie to roll one way, then another so she could change the linens. Never again could he be satisfied with a lifeless rose preserved between the pages of his memory.

Here was honor—in helping to bring new life into being. Home was the only concept that held any reality for him. Cameo was the only dream worth having. . . .

A stream of warm liquid hit him in the chest. Startled, he looked down at the baby, afraid that in his preoccupation he had dropped him and made the bath water splash. But he still held the baby above the water. And the liquid still streamed upward, soaking into his shirt. Zachary Sloane Boyd's eyes were closed and he was innocently sucking on the side of his godfather's finger. The stream subsided to a trickle, then nothing.

"Who's getting the bath—you or the baby?" Cameo asked as she peered around him to check on the baby.

"He peed on me," Zach said, bemused.

Cameo glanced from the baby to Zach and back to the baby, and laughed, genuine, honest, happy laughter that entranced him. Laughter and the feel of a baby and waves of tenderness rushed through him at the sensation of that tiny mouth reaching out to him for sustenance or comfort.

He was turning into a sentimental ass.

"No doubt we'll all be christened by little Zachary before he's out of diapers," Cameo offered in the way of comfort.

"Get a diaper on him before he shits in my hand," Zach ordered darkly, though he knew he had a silly grin on his face.

Smiling, Cameo took the baby and insured against future accidents before swaddling him like a mummy and laying him in his mother's arms. "Thank you, Mellie."

"For what, Miss Cameo?" Mellie gazed up at her, her expression serene and dreamy as she cuddled her son.

Cameo smoothed a lock of hair from Mellie's forehead. "For sharing your miracle with me. I can't tell you how much it means, how much it helps . . ." Her voice faltered and she shook her head. "How do you feel?"

"I expect I'm fine, ma'am—just tired and sore."

"Do you need anything?"

Sadness crossed her features as Mellie looked down at the baby. "Nothing you can give me."

A lump in her throat, Cameo nodded. "I wish I could bring Calvin back for you. Get some rest. I'll have one of the women sit with you for a while. I'll check on you both later."

"Miss Cameo?"

"Yes?" Laden with soiled linens and a bucket of water, Cameo stopped in the doorway and looked at Mellie over her shoulder.

"Ma'am, this baby does look like his daddy."

"Mmmm."

"Ma'am, you were wrong. Calvin wasn't handsome."

"No?"

"No, ma'am. He was sweet and honest and serious and he always saw the good side of things, but, ma'am, I got to tell you he was homely as homemade soap."

Cameo's gaze shot to Zach, whose mouth twitched as he soberly nodded in affirmation. For some reason, she wanted to laugh again. And she wanted to cry for the girl who had lost so much. "Well, then, Mellie, I think Calvin must have been the most beautiful man in the world."

The minute they'd left Mellie's room, Cameo had become a model of brisk efficiency, her arms always full of one thing or another as she bustled around the kitchen, setting things to rights. Zach had followed her out of Mellie's room carrying nothing but the whiskey bottle he'd hooked between his fingers.

Where did women get their energy? Zach wondered as he leaned his hips back against the sink. As far as he was concerned, childbirth was the hardest work he'd ever done, and he had done damn little except wring his hands. He lifted the bottle and stared at the two fingers of bourbon left in the bottom. Since he had it in his grasp, he thought he might as well relieve it of some of its weight. Popping the cork with his thumb, he raised the bottle to his mouth and took a long, throat-burning pull. It hit his empty stomach and churned, refusing to settle.

"Aren't you tired?" he asked Cameo.

She glanced around the neat kitchen and sighed. "Exhausted."

"Want some?" He held the bottle high and waved it.

Without a word, Cameo walked over to him and took the bottle. As she emptied it, Zach remembered the last time she had imbibed and offered silent thanks that it hadn't been half-full. He couldn't cope if Cameo was in her cups tonight.

She slammed the empty bottle down on the cabinet. "Give me your shirt. I'll soak it till morning."

Halfway to having it unbuttoned, Zach paused, a bemused expression on his face. "My 'christening' shirt. Maybe I ought to frame it."

"Certainly. We can hang it with all of Papa's memories." Blinking her eyes, Cameo turned away from him with a nervous little laugh. "Framing shirts, carrying doilies into battle, pressing flowers into books of poetry. One wonders where you store all the mementos of your life."

"The book is in my mind. I carry the doily in my chest

pocket . . . and the soul of the rose is in my blood." He said it softly as a thought—one he was afraid to voice, afraid it might wither and become dust if not treated with utmost care. But it seemed to grow instead, a living thing winding around them. Promises stuck in his throat, yet he felt driven to tell her—

What? That you'll be back for sure?

To ask her—

What? To believe you when all you've done is deceive her?

To show her—

What? That you're more than a shadow?

He jammed his hands into his pockets. "They're not mementos, Cameo."

She watched his face, foolishly searching for meanings between the words. "Will you ask one of the girls from the compound to sit with Mellie while I sleep for a few hours?" she asked.

"They're symbols of hope," he continued. God only knew when he would have the guts and the stupidity to do this again. "And they're my dreams—"

Her voice was impersonal, seemingly distracted as she peered into the buckets of boiling water on the stove. "There's enough boiling water here for both of us. You can use the tub in the water closet. I'll wash up in my room."

Rubbing the back of his neck, he turned his head to stare out the window. "I want to leave them here—with you."

Her heart began to skip in an erratic rhythm. Breath was suddenly scarce and painful. She didn't understand, yet she knew deep inside herself that he was giving her what she'd never expected to have. It was exactly what she didn't want—declarations with about as much substance as a shadow. "A symbolic gesture?"

"That and more."

"Thank you for trying . . ." She'd started to say his name, but her promise stopped her. Somehow, she couldn't bring herself to call him Sloane either. "I'll always remember that you gave me that. I wish . . ." Her breath shuddered in and out. "I wish it were enough."

"It's something to build on—"

Facing him with her hands clenched at her sides, she spoke in an anguished whisper. "No! I don't want to build on promises that you won't make."

He stared up at the ceiling while Cameo picked up a folded towel and lifted a bucket of hot water off the stove. "There's a big difference between *can't* and *won't*, Cameo."

Her hand lifted to rub her forehead. "Don't forget to ask one of the girls to come in for a few hours," she said and turned away.

"Damn you," he shouted. "Don't leave it like this. Don't say good-bye as if I'm already on my way out the door." Water sloshed from the bucket as he grabbed her arm to stop her. "I *can't* make a promise I might not be able to keep," he said in a strained whisper.

Cameo gently pried her arm from his grasp. "I know." Adjusting her hold on the bucket, she walked toward the door. His voice stopped her, so quiet she barely heard it.

> *"Thou art my life, my love, my heart,*
> *The very eyes of me;*
> *And hast command of every part,*
> *To live and die for thee."*

It almost defeated her—that declaration. She believed him; she accepted the truth Zach had injected into the words of another man. How easy it would be to carry the memory of this moment through the years and build her life around it. Her shoulders heaved with an anguished sigh. "Thank you. I needed to know how you felt. I wish that it could be enough."

Unable to look at the weary slump in her shoulders, the way her head dipped as if she were being slowly crushed, Zach faced the window. "Words are never enough, Rosebud, but it's the best I can do right now." Willing away the sudden pressure behind his eyes, he stared at her reflection in the window as she turned down the hall and disappeared from view.

"I'm sorry I can't promise you a dream, Rosebud. So damn sorry," he whispered to the empty room.

__ 27 __
Finished Business

Irrational fear rooted Cameo to the floor outside her bedroom. It was so cold and empty, as if there had been no life within its walls for a very long time.

She didn't know how long she stood on the threshold staring at the familiar shapes in the moonlight. Everything was the same: her neatly made bed by the window across from the door, the bureau and wardrobe along the adjoining wall. Both the bedside table on the other side of the bed and a smaller table next to the door had fresh candles set in small brass chambersticks. A rocker and a wingback chair were arranged in front of the fireplace to her right. Even the large pieces of furniture didn't crowd the large room.

Inexplicable dread intensified the chill. She even imagined that she heard breathing—

Nonsense. All she needed to do was to light a few candles and build a huge, roaring fire. She cocked her head and heard the kitchen door slam—no doubt Zach going to the compound to find someone to sit with Mellie. Everything was fine. She would wash up, don her nightgown and

robe, then check on Mellie and the baby before she went to
sleep.

She had only to take the first step.

Three steps into the room, she set the bucket down and
picked up the chamberstick as she groped on the table by
the door for matches. The match hissed as she struck it.
Light wavered and held as the wick caught and began to
burn. Phosphor fumes stung her eyes. Her shadow leaped
onto the opposite wall. Defying her uneasiness, she kicked
the door shut—

The candle holder wobbled and then steadied as she
dropped it back on the table.

Another, larger shadow loomed behind her, its arms
reaching for her. . . .

Before she could react, he grabbed her, jerked her up
against him, and wrapped his arm around her neck. The
squeezing pressure on her throat held her immobile as his
fingers bit into her wrist and bent her arm up behind her
back. Her sob of pain was strangled by the tightness of his
hold.

"Be still, girl," he rasped in her ear.

His hold eased enough to allow her to draw in air. He
released her hand and she felt the cold metal of a gun
barrel at her temple. In fascinated horror she watched
their shadows on the wall merge in a macabre embrace
with the gun hovering at the side of her head.

"We have unfinished business, darlin'."

"Uncle Seamus. How . . ." Her voice cracked at the
lack of moisture in her mouth. "How did you escape?"

"You think an old mountain man like me survived the
early days without a few tricks up his sleeve?" Her gaze
moved and snagged on the mirror above the bureau.

Seamus was smiling, and the candle cast an eerie glow on their faces.

"I want you to sign this paper, and then I'll be on my way."

"After you kill me?"

"I'm sorry, darlin'. I really am. But you give me no choice. It's gone too far for me to leave witnesses behind. I'm too close to having what's rightfully—" His bushy brows drew together in a frown. He put his forefinger to his lips. "Shh."

She heard the front door creak as it opened, then a click as it was pushed shut . . . the steps of booted feet . . . the door of the bedroom next to hers opening . . . more steps . . . a rap of knuckles on her door.

Witnesses. Her heart lurched in her chest. Zach. Mellie. The baby.

"Cameo? Are you decent?"

"Answer carefully, darlin'." Seamus eased back the hammer on his gun.

"No, I . . ." Her lips stuck to her teeth from the dryness. She ran her tongue around her lips, tried to swallow again, and tried to think. "I'm going to put out all the lights and go to sleep," she called. "Why . . . why don't you go ahead and see about Diamond's foreleg without me?"

"What?"

The gun leveled a few inches away from her forehead in warning.

"I'll trust your judgment, Mr. Sloane."

There was a pause, then, "Are you sure?"

"Yes! Thank you, Mr. Sloane," she called.

Mr. Sloane? On the other side of the door, Zach's body tensed; his senses became alert. *Put out all the lights? Dia-*

mond's foreleg? She trusted his judgment with her horse?
Instinctively, his hand found his holstered gun and rested
on the grips. Cameo couldn't have made it more clear that
something was wrong. Judging from the number of clues
she'd dropped, he'd better think fast and act even faster.
"Whatever you say, *ma'am.*"

Cameo sagged in defeat at his answer. His voice had
been insolent and mocking as it often was when she issued
orders. Hope faded down the hallway with his retreating
footsteps.

Seamus chuckled. "Sounds like the poor bastard thinks
he's too big for his britches. The world won't miss him."

"You don't have to hurt Sloane and the others, Seamus.
They have nothing to do with—"

Ma'am?

Zach had noticed. Cameo swallowed again, took a deep
breath, and focused her thoughts on possibilities. Zach
would be back. He'd need an advantage.

"You always were a good girl, darlin'," Seamus said ap-
provingly. "I hope Sam had the sense to be proud of you."

In the mirror, Cameo watched as he let back the hammer and seated the pistol in the holster on his belt. It
would be too noisy, she realized. Seamus would kill her
quietly.

Moving her foot slowly upward, she stomped down hard
on his instep, not hurting him through his boots but catching him by surprise. She moved her free arm forward and
back, using all the strength she could muster to jab him in
the diaphragm with her elbow. In one continuous motion
she raised her hand, slammed her palm up into the underside of his chin, then pushed up and dug her fingers into
his eyes.

He grunted from the blow and she felt his breath

whoosh past her ear. The smell of coffee and cigars on his breath seemed unnaturally sharp. She lost her balance and hung in his grasp as he flattened his back against the wall for support, dragging her with him. His arm tightened around her throat. Blackness edged into her vision. Her fingers slipped down his cheeks.

Frantically willing herself to remain conscious, she pushed her fingers upward, digging them harder into his eyes. *Please, Zach, hurry.*

A shadow passed outside her window. Cameo struggled harder.

Sound exploded and glass shattered as Zach burst through the window, disregarding the sharp spikes still sticking to the frame.

Cameo applied more pressure to Seamus's eyes, lowered her head, jerked it up again, jarring his chin, slamming his teeth together, stunning him. Suddenly she was free and she lurched forward, stumbling into the little table by the door. She fell across it, instinctively tightening her grasp on the candle to keep it from toppling over. Her other hand knocked against the bucket, the metal hot from the water it held.

"Cameo, get out of the way," Zach shouted, from where he crouched by the bed, his gun aimed at Seamus.

She sensed Seamus's presence behind her, using her as a shield. His hand caught at her skirt and jerked. Cameo twisted around, raised her knee, and rammed it into Seamus's groin. His hand opened, and she fell backward, landing on her rump, her leg bumping into the bucket of water. Stunned, she sat there, still in the line of fire. She closed her fingers around the handle and balanced the bucket with her other hand as she lifted it. With a barely controlled swing, she threw the water toward Seamus's head.

Seamus screamed and staggered backward, his hands tearing at his face as if he could rip away the scalding water.

"Move, Cameo!" Zach shouted as he ran forward, gripped her arm and pulled her to her feet.

Roaring, Seamus dived toward her and again seized her skirt.

There was a wrench in her arm as Zach tried to jerk her away. She couldn't move. She was caught between Zach and Seamus, each of them pulling her in a different direction. Ruthlessly she bunched folds of her skirt in her hand and yanked. The seam ripped where skirt met waistband. She tripped over the fabric pooled around her feet as Zach jerked her away from Seamus and flung her, belly down, onto the bed.

Never taking his eyes off Seamus, Zach lowered his voice and barked out an order. "Get down!"

Cameo pulled herself up on her hands and knees, dived over the side of the bed, and landed in a heap on the floor. Cautiously she peeked up over the edge of the mattress.

Roaring like a mad bull, Seamus fumbled for his gun and fired blindly as he regained his feet. Zach ducked low, grabbed him around the knees, and brought him down. The floor shook with the impact.

Seamus bellowed and cursed as Zach straddled him and crashed his fist into his face. Seamus bucked hard, throwing Zach off. Rolling out of reach, Zach sprang to his feet with his gun in his hand.

Cameo watched in horror as Seamus raised his gun and aimed.

"Give it up, Casey," Zach ordered in a quiet, deadly voice.

Seamus's gun tracked Zach as he inched to one side, away from the bed.

Tears flowed down Seamus's face. Anguish twisted his expression as he switched his aim to Cameo, her head barely visible above the mattress. "I loved you, darlin'. You should have been mine. I would have been a good father to you." His voice was thick and choked. The gunsight found her forehead. His thumb cocked the hammer. "I'm sorry, darlin'."

Cameo ducked.

"Casey!" Zach shouted.

Seamus started, then swung his gun in an arc toward Zach.

Cameo crawled to the end of the bed and peered around the footboard.

Zach crouched and fired.

His arms flung wide, Seamus Casey fell backward, his eyes fixed on the ceiling in a blind stare as he labored for his last breath and blood pooled on the floor beneath him. He choked once, and then was still.

With a low, keening moan, Cameo squeezed her eyes shut and cradled her head in her arms.

His chest heaving, Zach kept his gun trained on the body lying on the floor as he kicked Seamus's gun away and checked for signs of life. Finding none, he lowered his arm and stared at the body of an old friend. "Damn you, Seamus. Damn you to hell for making me do this." He crouched beside Seamus, his head bowed, his elbows propped on his thighs.

"Cameo."

Her eyes opened and she lifted her head to see Zach walking toward her, his hands held out to her.

Obediently she accepted his help and rose from the floor. Willingly she stood within the shelter of his arms, her cheek resting on his chest. Unblinking, she stared at his shadow on the wall and listened to his heartbeat, the harsh cadence of his breathing.

"It's over, sweetheart," Zach said, his hand smoothing her hair over and over again.

"Yes, I can see that." The shadow blurred, two bodies merged into one, swaying in the flickering light of a single candle. Funny, but she couldn't seem to feel anything, not Zach's embrace, not grief, not the cold air blowing in through the broken window at her back. "Do you have to notify the authorities?"

He sighed heavily. "I am the authority."

"Yes, of course."

"I'll send a couple of men to find Cloud Walker and make a report to the commandant of Fort Union."

The sound of shouts and running feet reached her from the front of the house. A face suddenly appeared in the window, peering in cautiously at first, then more boldly. Cameo recognized him as Simon, the man who would become foreman when Zach left.

"Sloane?"

"It's okay, Simon. Send two men out to find out what happened to Walker—"

"A rider just came in. He's okay."

Zach released a breath. "Get someone to build a coffin and bury"—he swallowed—"Seamus."

After a sweeping glance into the room, Simon nodded and disappeared.

"When are you leaving?" Cameo asked.

"Tomorrow." The word tore out of him.

She nodded gravely. "Tomorrow." She pushed away from him and stepped back. "I think I'll move into Papa's room for a few days until this is cleaned up. I need to wash. There's so much blood."

"Cameo, listen to me," Zach growled.

Shaking her head, Cameo gathered clean clothes from her drawers. "No, Zach. As you said—it's over."

Lanterns glowed brightly from every corner of the water closet. Water lapped at Cameo's shoulders, a warm and soothing blanket of liquid silk as she lay in the tub with her eyes closed and her mind blank.

Zach was taking care of everything just as he'd taken care of her: making sure that there was plenty of light in the small room, heating the water to perfection, helping her undress and step into the tub.

Too weary and heartsick to think beyond the moment, she listened to the commotion in the yard die down as Zach issued orders. He seemed to be everywhere. She recognized his voice coming from the housekeeper's room, a low, steady drone as he explained what had happened, then reassured Mellie that all was well. Another voice joined his—the girl he'd recruited to sit with mother and baby. Shuffling came from her bedroom, and she knew that someone was removing the body and cleaning the floor.

She waited until there was nothing but silence before she stepped out of the tub and dried herself with the towels stacked on an upturned basket Zach had put within her reach.

He'd made sure everything was within reach. Except himself.

Dressed in nightgown and robe, she opened the door.

Zach stood in the hall, propping up the wall, waiting for her with yet another lantern. She hadn't realized they had so many sources of light.

Silently he looked her over once, then turned on his heel to lead her down the hall.

Dazed, Cameo followed the light to the master bedroom. Candles burned everywhere, bathing the room in gold. A fire danced in the hearth. Shadows played on the walls.

She would almost prefer the dark.

Zach helped her out of her robe and folded it neatly on the back of a chair. His mouth twitched when he saw that she had put on her nightgown wrong side out. Then he folded down the covers and led her to the bed, tucked her in, and kissed her forehead.

As if she were a child.

She wondered why he was still standing beside the bed, saying nothing, his gaze tracing her features as her father's had when he was painting her.

"Why are you here?" she asked him.

"Because I don't want to go."

"I'm not sick."

"No."

"You need to sleep if you're leaving in the morning."

"Do you want me to go, Rosebud?"

"No."

His sigh mingled with the hiss of flames, the rustle of branches outside. With one hand, he unbuttoned his shirt and then his pants. The fire burnished his chest to hammered copper and emphasized the contours of hard muscles softened by curls of hair gleaming against his skin.

He sat on the edge of the bed, and she heard his boots fall to the floor. Wool rasped against his legs as he pulled off his socks. He stood to shrug off his shirt and skim out of his pants. Not once did his gaze waver from her face.

Not once did she lower her eyes.

Seconds passed. Her nipples tightened and thrust against the lawn of her gown. A subtle, moist heat flowed from her belly downward. Her body grew languid, submitting to the contours of the bed. She watched his manhood grow and harden.

Zach held up the covers and slid beneath them. His arms reached for her.

She met him halfway.

Their shadows entwined upon the wall in an exotic dance as they melted together and swayed within embrace after embrace. Mouths touched and tongues mingled. Hands caressed, soothed, pleasured. Eyes clung, never closing, never moving away. Scents of burning pine, rose soap, and beeswax blended with the musk of passion. Her gown fell to the floor. The slide of flesh aroused gently, then more urgently.

And the vibrant music of Zach's voice murmured verses from Robert Herrick as his teeth raked her nipples and his lips caressed and his tongue bathed them . . .

> *"Thou power that canst sever*
> *From me this ill,*
> *And quickly still,*
> *Though thou not kill*
> *My fever—"*

. . . as his hands turned her and explored her spine, kneaded the sensitive flesh of her buttocks, skimmed the backs of her legs . . .

> *"Thou sweetly canst convert the same*
> *From a consuming fire*
> *Into a gently licking flame,*
> *And make it thus expire; . . ."*

. . . as he turned her back into himself, his fingers dipping into her, stroking, bathing in her moisture, then his mouth tasting her flesh downward, downward and tasting, too, her desire . . .

> *"Then make me weep*
> *My pains asleep,*
> *And give me such reposes . . ."*

. . . as he covered her, sought entrance, and, finding her waiting with hot, moist anticipation, penetrated and found a home within her depths . . .

> *". . . That I, Poor I,*
> *May think thereby,*
> *I live and die*
> *'Mongst roses."*

. . . as she cried out softly so as not to interrupt the song he spoke into her mouth. She moved with him, arched to meet him, tightened to hold him, then trembled around him . . .

> *"Fall on me like a silent dew,*
> *Or like those maiden showers*
> *Which by the peep of day, do strew*
> *A bapti'm o'er the flowers."*

His thrusts struck her heart with exquisite pain. Over and over again their bodies met; he plunged, she arched, slowly, then faster, harder. Sensation became too great to bear, yet still she listened to the beat of hearts and the quickened breaths accompanying the love he made with his body and the words that she knew came from his heart . . .

> *"Melt, melt my pains,*
> *With thy soft strains,*
> *That having ease me given, . . ."*

His voice deepened. Breath grew shorter still. She swallowed her cry of release, listening, always listening to the promises his soul whispered to hers . . .

> *". . . With full delight*
> *I leave this light,*
> *And take my flight*
> *For heaven."*

She flew with him, soaring above the clouds into the heart of the universe where diamonds glittered in the darkness, beckoning with colors unimagined. Completion brought mingled moans of death, cries of rebirth, sighs of wonder that such beauty existed.

Embers died in the grate. Candles guttered and winked out. Bodies clung and nestled beneath the covers. Eyes closed out the darkness and saw dreams beckoning with promises too fragile to voice.

Gold-and-pink light streamed through a part in the curtains. Fresh logs had been laid in the grate and a fire blazed with warmth and cheer. Cameo fought wakefulness, knowing that dawn had crept in to steal her dreams.

She rolled toward the other side of the bed and opened her eyes to face the emptiness. She'd known when he left the bed, had listened to him silently walk across the room and ease open the door. How long had it been since he had gone into his own room to dress and gather his belongings? How long since she had sensed his presence by the bed, watching her? How long before she would hear him ride out of the valley?

The bed wasn't empty.

Cameo blinked as she propped herself up on her elbow and stared at the items nestled in the indentation where Zach's head had rested on the pillow: a tattered and well-read book; a scrap of muslin, stained by blood and frayed from handling; a pressed rose, thorns and all.

They're my hopes, my dreams. The sum of a man's soul.

With joy and sadness winding around her heart, she slid her hands beneath the small pile and cradled them to her chest.

Footsteps echoed from the back of the house, coming down the hall, toward the front door. A horse whinnied from the hitching rail by the porch. She bolted out of bed, ran to the door, and flung it open.

Zach slowed when he saw her standing on the threshold waiting for him to pass her by. He drew near and stopped in front of her just out of reach.

She stepped forward, his treasures still clutched to her body. "I'll keep them for you."

He searched her expression. "How long?"

She smiled at the irony of Zach asking her the one question she'd vowed never to ask him. Raising her hand, she smoothed the hair above his ears, then cupped the side of his face, her thumb skimming the faint stubble on his cheeks. "I'll keep them until tomorrow." And then she softly closed the door.

Never again would she willingly watch him fade into a shadow as he walked away from her. Never would she say good-bye to him.

Zach swallowed hard and stared at the door. "Thank you, Rosebud," he whispered. "Come heaven or hell, I won't make you wait that long."

Tomorrow—something you wait for until the day you die.

28

Season of Beginnings

Snow came on the heels of Zach's departure, erasing his tracks as if nature conspired with the government in its secrets. The day Zach left, Cameo instructed some of the men to load Seamus in his coffin onto a wagon and drive it to Spirit Canyon. She buried him beneath a clump of mature aspens beside the cave. It was a bittersweet irony that she had, after all, given Seamus what he'd wanted. He would forever lie in the shadow of the mother lode that had driven him to his death, and in the fall the aspen leaves would turn to gold and drift down to carpet his grave. When it became possible, Cameo would order a simple stone marker engraved with only his name. No one—not even Seamus himself—had known when he'd been born.

That had taken care of one day. One day among many to come. Having seen to the last of the immediate necessities, she slept for two days straight before voluntarily taking an active part in the care of her new godson. More days filled.

But every night became an empty, silent space in her life as she lay awake and wondered where Zach was and what he was doing. The ranch seemed to run itself in Simon's capable hands, and Cameo was content to consult him each morning, then allow him to get on with his job. She took care of the bookkeeping, the concerns of the many families in the valley, and began to carry out her plans for breeding her Andalusians. In the spring she would have to find another stallion to take Ash's place.

Diamond was breeding the results of her night spent in an alley.

On Thanksgiving Day Cameo sat in her rocker by the front window and began to knit Zach a pair of heavy winter socks.

At Christmas, life became richer when Mellie dropped the "Miss" and simply addressed her as Cameo. They even shared a few late-night giggles when Mellie showed Cameo the notes Calvin had made on lovemaking. Poignancy followed Mellie's story of her past as a camp follower, her eyes wary, her voice flat, as if she expected their newfound closeness to disappear. Cameo had simply covered Mellie's hand with her own and said, "I wish I had that much courage."

Three months later, the bureau in Zach's room held three pairs of woolen socks. Cameo ran out of yarn and sent to Denver for more.

Fort Leavenworth, Kansas—February 1863

Impatience marked every step Zach took as he paced the office of General Hunter, who was formally his commanding officer. He'd already reported to Kit Carson and been ordered to observe protocol and file an "official" report at headquarters in Kansas. For ten minutes, he'd been left cooling his heels. *You'd think that when a man rises from the dead, he'd at least be given the courtesy of a prompt welcome,* he thought sourly.

Of course, the general knew that he was alive—had known since Zach had regained consciousness long enough to send a dispatch from the mesa. But he'd been deliberately silent since then. The general probably thought that first dispatch, sent a month after the battle of Glorieta, had been a hoax. Only carefully worded messages from Cloud Walker had given headquarters any indication that the problem of the missing gold was being dealt with.

But Zach wasn't in the mood to be reasonable. A trip that should have taken six weeks at the outside had stretched to twice that. He'd ridden Pegasus hard through a blizzard and snowdrifts higher than his head, then walked beside his mount the rest of the way to Fort Leavenworth after one of those drifts had tripped and lamed Pegasus.

He wasn't in much better shape than his horse.

All the while Zach had been conscious of time passing— time that he counted by the term of a pregnancy. *By now, she was probably beginning to show . . . was she waddling like a duck yet?* He didn't know if Cameo was pregnant, but he fantasized about it regularly. *A wife. A child. A family and a place among his people in the valley.* Come hell or high water, he would return—soon!

Out of habit, Zach glanced out the window and gauged the time by the position of the sun though he had a perfectly good pocket watch tucked inside his coat. Zach muttered under his breath. "Three minutes more and the general can screw his protocol."

"Not if my wife has anything to say about it, Colonel McAllister." General Hunter strode into his office and sat behind the desk. "Report," he ordered.

This was more like it. No small talk. No more time wasted. In terse sentences, Zach gave the briefest report of his career.

"Mmm." The general leaned back in his chair. "So the whole thing was done for the sake of simple greed. Too bad we hadn't thought of that. It would have saved months of looking in the wrong places." He watched Zach pace the room over and over again. "How's the leg?"

"Feels like hell . . ." Literally. The muscles burned like fire and his joints were inflamed and aching with strain and fatigue.

"You always limp like that?"

Zach stiffened and altered his gait to conceal the limp as much as possible. "No. A forty-mile walk through the snow is enough to lame any man."

"Your devotion to duty is admirable."

"Duty, hell," Zach said spontaneously. He was too tired and irritable to exercise tact. "I need to get back home."

"I wasn't aware that you had a home, Colonel . . . sit down before I have to order a litter."

Zach sprawled in the nearest chair, his legs stretched out, his hands tight around the arms as if he were ready to spring at the slightest provocation. Dread rolled in his stomach. The general had a dispatch from Washington in his hand—presumably new orders for the Shadow.

"You're being replaced, Colonel McAllister," the general said without preamble.

Zach's mouth dropped open, then snapped shut.

General Hunter smiled. "Now, I know this is a blow . . ." He paused as if he expected a reply.

Zach couldn't reply. Either this was a dirty joke or Secretary Stanton's idea of cruel and unusual punishment because his top agent in the West had kept out of touch for so long. Zach couldn't for one minute believe the general was serious.

General Hunter continued. "Your injuries in the battle of Glorieta Pass would be a detriment to the performance of your duty. Especially"—his eyebrows rose when Zach instinctively opened his mouth to argue—"especially if those duties require you to walk forty miles in the snow. Aside from that, your limp makes you easily identifiable."

Impulsively, Zach started to argue about his "fitness." Common sense stopped him. The limp, no matter how slight it usually was, would be a dead giveaway, impossible to disguise with the rest of his body. "Yes, sir." His hands relaxed on the arms of the chair.

"I'm glad you aren't letting pride stand in the way of sound judgment."

Pride, hell, Zach thought. His pride was centered on being present for the birth of his baby—if there was a baby —and collecting on his dreams. Still, he experienced a sense of betrayal that the government would find him so entirely dispensable. He didn't want to get out of doing his duty. He just wanted to do it in a different, less ephemeral way.

"Am I being dismissed from service, sir?"

"We've discussed that possibility."

Zach frowned. Oddly enough, he felt as if he were an old dog being thrown scraps because he'd outlived the ability to find food on his own.

"But you're too valuable to be put out to pasture."

Zach snorted.

Retrieving a bottle from a drawer in his desk, the general poured whiskey into two glasses and slid one across the desk to Zach. "Now I realize that you have a fondness for travel, Colonel . . ."

"Sir—"

"But we have something else in mind. Did you know that Miss Fielding tried to sell the freight business?" The general waved his hand to silence Zach. "Of course, we put a stop to that—"

Zach shot forward in his seat. "You *what?*"

"Fielding Freight is just what the Army in the West needs."

"Miss Fielding needs that damn business like a boar needs tits, sir."

"With the right man in charge," the general said as if Zach hadn't spoken, "Fielding Freight could be the perfect solution to our supply needs. The Indians are restless, Colonel McAllister, and we have forts spread out to hell and back. Those forts need supplies delivered by a reliable carrier who will deliver off the established routes. A carrier who understands the *Army* way of doing things."

"Cameo Fielding is not the right carrier."

"No, but you would be, and Samuel Fielding's will gives you authority over all his holdings for at least"—the general consulted the papers on the desk in front of him—"six years.

"You will continue operating out of the Sangre de Cristos. This will give us more control over our supply routes and the supplies themselves, not to mention the Santa Fe Trail. It will also give us a permanent agent in the Colorado–New Mexico territories whom we can trust to coordinate the activities of our other agents and the information they gather."

For the second time in ten minutes Zach was speechless. He reached for the glass of whiskey and downed it in one gulp. The aged bourbon was smooth as hot butter, instantly warming the cold he'd thought would never leave him after his trek across the plains.

"I hope you aren't too disappointed at not being able to . . . ah . . . wander anymore."

"I'll learn to live with it, sir." Zach nearly strangled on his reply.

"Tell me," General Hunter said. "Do you and Miss Fielding get along? My intelligence tells me that the two of you are at odds."

"We compromised," he said, suppressing a laugh.

"An armed truce, eh? Good. That will make your job much easier. I hear she's a feisty little thing—acts like she thinks she's a man."

"Feisty," Zach agreed with a straight face. Images drifted through his memory. Cameo sitting in a rocking chair knitting socks. Cameo wearing a dress that looked like spring itself. Cameo deftly slicing potatoes in a primitive hut. Cameo turning her body into his, melting over him, falling on him like a silent dew. Cameo, a wild rose growing in her own directions—

Abruptly, Zach crossed his ankle over the opposite knee and casually folded his hands across his lap.

"I'm sorry to give you such a bitch of an assignment, Colonel McAllister, but you are the best man for the job."

I'm the only man for the job. "I'll manage, sir."

"Knew you would. Now, we've assigned Walker McCloud to you permanently. Unlike you, he was pleased at the idea. Says he's ready to set up his medical practice— at least on a part-time basis. It's my opinion that a man with his training shouldn't be exposed to the kind of danger he's faced in the past. Good doctors are hard to find, and some of the forts in your area have no medical personnel."

"I agree, sir."

"He's your cousin, isn't he?"

"Yes."

His eyes distant, General Hunter smiled sadly. "It'll be good to know that at least one family is kept intact in this war. Gives me hope." Clearing his throat, he stood and held out his hand to Zach. "Get back to that valley, Colonel McAllister. I hear that Miss Fielding is digging in her heels about selling to Butterfield. The girl has no respect for government."

"You should have told her it was necessary, sir."

The general looked startled by such an outrageous suggestion. "The U.S. Government does not confide in civilians, Colonel—particularly female civilians who think they can meddle in the affairs of men."

Biting the inside of his cheek, Zach shook the general's hand and left the office as fast as he could without seeming too eager to follow orders. If the general thought he was actually happy about his new assignment, he'd probably rescind Zach's orders personally and send him back out on the trail again.

With controlled haste, Zach put distance between himself and headquarters until he judged himself out of sight. He stopped Pegasus in front of a shop in the settlement and stared blindly through the window as his chuckle grew into a full-throated laugh.

The Hero with a Thousand Faces had died ten months ago during the battle of Glorieta. Now he could be buried and forgotten.

Lately he'd been a lousy agent anyway.

Slowly Zach's eyes focused on the contents of the shop window and he slid off Pegasus. Acting on impulse alone, he entered the store and pointed to the display. The woman behind the counter frowned and shook her head. The item in question was not for sale, she said. It would take three weeks or more to make one for Zach.

Zach recited poetry to her and left the shop a half hour later, poorer by an outrageous sum of money, yet feeling richer than at any other time in his life.

A man passed him on the boardwalk, stared at Zach's purchases, and snickered. "Kinda young t' be retirin' t' the Boardin' House with th' ladies, ain't ya?"

Zach grinned and continued to tie his acquisition to the back of his saddle. He was himself again, doing what he wanted rather than what he had to do.

In March, Cameo decided that the doily Zach had carried into battle was beyond reclamation and began to embroider an exact duplicate. Carefully folding the old one, she pressed it in his book of poetry with the dried rose.

Little Zachary lay on a blanket on the floor, trying to stuff his foot into his mouth. When he succeeded, he screwed up his face and howled in outrage after biting down too hard. His two top teeth had made an early appearance, and when he smiled, he reminded her of a beaver.

Hoofbeats approached from the mouth of the valley, crunching in the ice-crusted carpet of snow. Anticipation thumped in her chest as her gaze shot to the window. Disappointment nearly crushed her. It was just another army officer coming to make sure she hadn't been successful in her stubborn attempts to sell Fielding Freight.

Out of sheer perversity, she decided not to tell him that she had given up . . . on just about everything.

* * *

Urgency drove Zach to ride day and night back to the valley, but respect for his horse kept him to a saner pace and forced him to stop and rest from time to time. The cold monotonous glare of the snow-covered plains forced him to seek shelter in towns along the way for the sake of his eyesight, though the settlements were few and far between.

He could have sworn that Kansas had grown tenfold, and that half its population had mysteriously disappeared. Every time he did encounter people, he was met with curious stares and, more often, smart remarks on the parcel tied to his saddle.

"Uh-oh, Vern, we got us a peculiar one ridin' into town."

"Looks like, Jasper. He probably wears lace on his under britches."

Zach's initial amusement had long since vanished to be replaced by the urge to dump his purchase into the nearest slop jar—if he could find one big enough.

In spite of his irritation over the time that was passing all too swiftly and the distance between himself and the valley that seemed to stretch rather than diminish, he rode straight for Denver City rather than angling to the southwest and a shorter route to Cameo.

His impulsive purchase in Leavenworth had given birth to a plan, and after all the indignities he'd suffered, he was determined to see it through. Every day he calculated the same figures—months lapsed against months to go if Cameo were pregnant. He'd make it in time to see her waddle like a duck with a belly that cleared the way for her.

If she wasn't pregnant, it wasn't for lack of trying. Over and over again, he remembered that last night, the sharing, the unspoken commitment between them. It had been more than he had ever imagined. It had been right.

He had awakened her with gentle touches of breath on her body. His tongue had caressed her, moving from earlobe to eyelids, from neck to shoulders to breasts, and down . . .

Her hands ruffled through his hair then urged him to raise his head. "Zach, on the way to the mesa . . . you said—"

"Hush, Rosebud." Again his mouth found her, tasted her most private places, drank of her passion.

She wriggled away from him and pushed him down on the bed, reversing their positions. She knelt over him and took him in her hands, kneading him and teasing him with featherlike strokes. "Now Zach? Are you ready now?"

He was ready. The lies were behind them, and in spite of it all, she trusted him, loved him, accepted him for what and who he was.

"Now Zach?" she asked again, her voice breathless, her eyes wide and vulnerable and frightened. Her hands stilled on him as she waited for his answer.

He wondered how she could understand the reluctance he'd felt that afternoon on the trail, the feeling he'd had that to share such an intimacy with so much deception between them would be the final betrayal. Somehow, he knew that she did understand, and that her question asked for surrender rather than an answer.

He reached out to her and touched her cheek. "You're on top, sweetheart. To the victor go the spoils." It had been meant as a quip, but she stared at him with a somber expression and nodded, once, before lowering her head and accepting every part of him. Her hair fanned out over his hips and his belly as she took him into her power and drained him of his soul.

Only with Cameo could he be complete.

Denver City seemed to grow before his eyes like an overfed child. Signs of domesticity and graciousness replaced the raw virility of the boom town he remembered. Uneven wood sidewalks offered respite from unrelenting mud streets, and the citizens were at least making an effort to control the livestock that roamed freely into the buildings. .

Here it was hard to remember that a war was ripping apart the fabric of the nation.

A house caught his eye. He felt another impulse coming on. Mentally recalling how many more settlements he had yet to go through, he cast his fate to the sidewalk philosophers, made his way up the brick path, and knocked on the door.

Two hours later he grimly strode from shop to shop, alternately making purchases and pinning scoffers with his most formidable stare. Only one purchase earned him any expressions of respect and approval.

If Cameo laughed at him, he'd volunteer for the front lines.

Empress Valley—April 1863

Winter had been a cold, barren time when nothing grew but dreams and hope. But now, spring warmth awakened earth and people alike, a season of beginnings, and Cameo faced her need to become a part of it all rather than to dwell in the past.

Dawn light filtered into the master bedroom as she stood in front of the fireplace. The edges of the new doily glowed and curled in the fire, then in a sudden flare the cloth turned to flame. Refusing to cry, Cameo watched a dream crumble into ash.

Over the months, she had carried on as she'd learned to do all her life. She'd realized that she'd lied to both herself and Zach. She had learned more than she wanted to know about loneliness and heartbreak. And she'd discovered that hope could be a slow way of dying.

There had been no word. Even Cloud Walker didn't know where Zach was. It was as if Zach or Sloane had never existed except in her dreams, a shadow that faded with the seasons.

It was time to wake up. She wanted to live. She knew she didn't need Zach. Perhaps, someday, she would stop wanting him.

If only Zach could have promised her a dream.

Sounds of activity began to fill the yard. Shouts of greeting mingled with hoofbeats and roosters crowing and cows lowing in the dairy barn. She no longer ran to the window at the sound of hoofbeats.

She heard men riding out to meet the day's work. Smells of coffee and bacon came from the kitchen. Little Zachary wailed for his breakfast. There was a knock at the door. A moment later, Mellie's footsteps ran down the hall. Without interest, Cameo opened the book lying on top of her bureau. A pressed rose, faded and crumbling around the edges, fell out. She picked it up and rubbed it against her cheek.

Perhaps tomorrow she would find the strength to stop reaching for diamonds in the sky.

"Cameo!" Mellie shrieked from the front door. "Cameo!"

Too alarmed to worry about her appearance, Cameo ran

out of her room and down the hall. Mellie never raised her voice.

Mellie stood on the porch, the baby propped on her hip, her eyes wide and sparkling with excitement. "That's the most beautiful thing I've ever seen," she whispered.

"What, Mellie? I don't see anything."

Mellie stepped aside and pointed downward.

Cameo's gaze followed. Her eyes widened and her mouth fell open. Unaware of her own movement, she dropped to her knees and reached out with a trembling hand. "That" was a large square basket, its twin hinged handles garnished with silk ribbons and ecru lace. An ornate brass plate and latch held it closed. She worked it free and lifted the lid. The inside of the basket was lined with thickly padded and quilted satin brocaded in shades of rich antique gold. An enameled thimble rested in a corner with a fine pair of scissors. Every color imaginable was represented in skeins of embroidery silks and cottons. A packet of precious steel needles peeped out of a side pocket along with an exquisitely carved rosewood crochet hook and a set of knitting needles. Pieces of muslin and linen and lace in various sizes and shapes were neatly folded next to several balls of cotton yarn. Tucked in another pocket were several cloth-wrapped packets of flower and vegetable seeds.

A leather-bound book lay on top. Dazed, Cameo turned the pages. They were all blank except for the first sheet of fine parchment. Her hand covered her mouth to hold back a cry, and her gaze swept the yard, the trail, the horizon. No one was there.

"Who's it from, Cameo?" Mellie asked, her voice tinged with awe.

Slowly Cameo rose to her feet, a whimsical smile on her

face. "I'll let you know, Mellie, as soon as I'm sure." Leaving the basket on the porch, she led the way into the house. Inside the door, she glanced over her shoulder once more, searching, searching, searching . . .

"Don't you want the—"

"No," Cameo said as she shut the door. "Leave it there for now."

"But—"

"It's all right, Mellie," She said as she entered her room and began to close the door. "I'm not sure I understand either."

With a frown Mellie nodded absently as she returned to the kitchen.

Cameo leaned back against the door with her heart turning somersaults in her chest. *Dreams.* The page in the book had said *Dreams.* And it had a hundred empty pages waiting to be filled.

Pushing away from the door, she threw off her robe and struggled to pull her nightgown over her head as she ran to the wardrobe. With the gown still stuck on her head, she groped blindly for the touch of watered silk. It was there— she just knew it. She remembered hanging it in here when she'd moved all of her things into her parents' room.

Buttons flew as she ripped off the nightgown and shoved it into a corner of the wardrobe. A flash of shimmering forest-green caught her eye. Smiling, she reached for the gown that had been waiting for her to grow into it. She had fallen in love with the creation when she first saw it in Santa Fe almost two years ago. A woman's dress, not right for a girl just graduated from the Academy for Young Ladies but perfect for a woman who knew what she wanted.

She took a deep breath and forced herself to slow down as she selected her best underclothes and most elegant petticoats. For a brief moment, she regretted her lack of a corset, then dismissed the feeling as being absurd.

Petticoat tapes became the center of her world as she fumbled to tie them just right. Camisole straps refused to lie the way she wanted them on her shoulders. It required fifteen minutes and the patience of a saint to slip the tiny buttons into their corresponding loops. "Damnation," she muttered under her breath. God knew she wasn't a saint. She lowered her aching arms and stared at herself in the mirror.

The deep-green silk molded her upper body from the widely cut neckline to just below her waist where it flared into yards of skirt. Heavy ivory lace, scalloped around all the edges, yoked the bodice from the deep vee between her breasts to the tips of her shoulders and up to mold around her long neck. Green silk encased her arms tightly to her wrists.

A woman's dress that fitted her to perfection.

She picked up her brush and ruthlessly tugged it through her sleep-tousled hair, sweeping it up on the sides and securing it with carved ivory combs. Her mother's jade earrings complemented the gown and her eyes perfectly. She heard hoofbeats in the yard and ran to the front of the house, abruptly slowed her steps, and sedately opened the door.

The basket was exactly where she'd left it—beautiful, extravagant, symbolic of the dreams she had expressed to Zach. The book still lay open on top of the fabrics and threads. Cameo took courage from the single word written on the title page in a familiar scrawl and raised her eyes. Her breath caught. Her hand pressed against her chest.

Hitched to the rail was the most magnificent horse she'd ever seen. A stallion, big and graceful, power in every curve and line of his body. His subtly mottled coat glistened in the sun like liquid silver. He returned her rapt stare with intelligent, spirited eyes and pawed the ground.

Cameo closed her eyes, then opened them again. The Andalusian was still there. For the first time she noticed an unremarkable mustang tethered to the rail on the opposite side of the porch. Sweeping the yard, her gaze collided with the form of a man leaning indolently against a tree, his arms crossed over his wide chest, his hat tipped down to shade his eyes.

Twilight eyes.

He was tall with shoulders strong and broad enough to carry a lifetime of dreams. Everything about him was fine: the strength that was as much a part of his mind as his body; the humor that deepened the creases on either side of his mouth; the heart and soul that reached out to her with a simple word, a touch, a gift that another man would hide in a wagon of fertilizer so no one else would see. He was a man who seemed to know instinctively how to charm her senses, stir her emotions to life.

"I'm not looking for temporary help," she stated, refusing to be charmed.

"I'm not looking for work."

"If you want a place to spend your nights, go elsewhere."

"I came for more than nights," he said, his voice husky, his gut tied in one hard knot. She was so damn calm, so damn beautiful. He'd come to keep promises. Promises he'd made to himself. Promises he wasn't sure how to make to her so that she'd believe them. He was painfully aware that she didn't need him. Riding in, he'd seen enough proof of that. The ranch was flourishing. The hands and their families loved her and would do anything for her. She had survived. Without him.

He reached down behind him, picked up the last of his gifts and pushed away from the tree. Awkwardly holding his offering in front of him, he left the last of his pride lying in the dust of the yard and stepped all over it to reach Cameo.

His hat still shaded his eyes, yet Cameo had the feeling of being touched very thoroughly—intimately—by them. She squinted at the object, a tangled mess of stripped branches that extended from his hands nearly to the ground and twisted upward as if looking for a place to cling. He walked slowly toward her, looking like a bride carrying a dried bush for a bouquet.

She fought laughter and the impulse to run down the steps and crush the delicate branches between his body and hers. "If you think I'll settle for a season of your time here and there, you can walk west till your hat floats."

He paused and tipped his hat back with his thumb, his expression tense and watchful. "I've been permanently assigned to the territory to keep Fielding Freight operating and—"

"And you'll still have to leave me—"

He shook his head. "Only once in a while, and I'll take you with me." At the bottom of the steps, he stopped. "We'll always come back to the valley." His gaze raked over her, lingered on her waist. She wasn't pregnant. His inspection swept farther down and stared intently at her feet peeking out beneath her hem. She was barefoot. He smiled whimsically at the mixture of relief and disappointment he felt. "Did you know that you don't have any shoes on?"

His intent stare caught her off guard. Nervously she

shifted her feet and blinked. A flush climbed her cheeks. How could she have forgotten her shoes and stockings? "Don't change the subject."

He sighed and carried the bush over to the fence surrounding the house and patch of lawn. "This is home. *You're* home," he said as he began to scoop the newly tilled soil from the ground near the fence with his hands.

Cameo took a deep breath to steady the churning in her blood, the trembling that was an exquisite kind of torture. "What is that?" she whispered as she pointed to the . . . whatever . . . he carried.

Concentrating on his work, he didn't lift his gaze, but kept digging until he had a hole big enough to hold the root ball of the bush. "A bush."

"I can see that, but what kind of bush, and why do you have it?"

Still he didn't look at her. Working quickly, he set the bush into the ground and gently packed soil around the roots.

"Embroidering doilies and gardening and raising horses." He pointed to the basket full of seeds and silks, the magnificent stallion. "I came to promise you a dream, Cameo. This"—he nodded his head toward the bush, rose to his feet, and wiped his hands on the kerchief he pulled from his pocket—"is part of my dream." The smile twisted into a grimace. "The woman who sold it to me told me that wild roses grow almost anywhere."

Wild roses.

"They're like you, Cameo. They don't grow just a few blooms every season, but blossom more every year. The flowers aren't perfect, but they're the sweetest sight this side of heaven." Again he stood before her at the bottom of the steps. Cameo didn't seem to be impressed by his romantic nature, Zach noted wryly. Defiance and wariness sparkled in her eyes. Evidently she was hell-bent on setting ultimatums.

She stood firm, not budging an inch. She stared at him, at his eyes, afraid to believe what he was saying, afraid not to believe him. Her voice wobbled as she asked the final question, the most important one. "Who are you?"

"Just one man, Cameo," he whispered as he lifted his hat. "Zachary McAllister, at your service." His chest rose and fell. "Seems that the man who died at Glorieta borrowed my name. Some people say he was the Shadow in disguise."

The air seemed to be alive, the sun brighter, hotter, its light penetrating the shadows cast by the roof of the porch. Everywhere shoots and buds were poking through the grass with spots of color. It truly was spring, she thought. A season of beginnings.

"Enough, Cameo," Zach said gruffly. "I can make promises till the next ten wars are fought and won, but the only way you'll ever believe them is if I show you." Cocking his head, he smiled up at her. "You're just going to have to put up with a few doubts, Rosebud, until enough time has passed."

Knowing he was right and she was asking the impossible, Cameo tripped over the basket as she ran to him and lurched down the steps. Strong, hard arms caught her, held her off the ground, and wrapped more tightly around her. Looking up at him, she saw the uncertainty he had concealed until now.

"No more shadows, Zach?"

He opened his eyes, stared at her with an intensity that robbed her of breath. "No more shadows—except the one that's attached to the man."

"Zach?" she said softly. "You'll have to move the bush."

His brows descended.

"I want it planted on the hill near the graves of my parents where the roses will overlook the whole valley."

His lips caressed her eyelids and cheeks and hovered teasingly above her mouth. "Later, Rosebud," he said against her lips. "Right now, I want to plant some seeds of my own."

Epilogue
Diamonds in the Sky

Secretly, men rode from the Empress Valley to Spirit Canyon to enter the cave known as the Old Man of the Mountain, the spirit who had blessed a race of lost souls with a future. The people took from him only what they needed, then left him in peace to dream of ancient times.

Every spring, Cameo and Zach spent a week alternately lying in the sun by the pools of the canyon and renewing the mystical paintings on the stone walls of the cave. With the end of the War Between the States, the western territories saw an influx of settlers moving westward, by wagon and horseback and, after the completion of the first nationwide system of tracks, by train. No one seemed to notice that some of the families sprinkled from Taos to Denver City bore resemblances to one another. Among them were doctors, lawyers, bankers, farmers, and merchants.

And a town drunk named Chauncey.

Often they traveled from one area to another to give aid or comfort or simply to visit, renewing bonds forged by six centuries of wandering the land, belonging to nothing but the places where they had made camp for a night or a year, belonging to no one but one another. They were no longer the Others, but were part of a nation founded by wanderers looking for a home.

And in the years to come, two silhouettes could be seen standing at the top of a hill as the sun melted into the horizon, its fiery colors flaring, then dissolving into the silver-gray of twilight. Other, smaller silhouettes would join them, dance around them, and point upward.

"Look, Mama, Papa. Grandpa is painting a sunset."

The man and woman turned to look at the base of the single tree where Samuel and Chai Fielding met every tomorrow together. Memories flowed gently and sweetly between Cameo and Zach. So many dreams realized. So many yet to come.

Just for you Cameo Regine. And if you wish for dreams at twilight, the angels will sprinkle them like diamonds across the sky.

AUTHOR'S NOTE

The legendary "Indians" descended from a Welsh prince and his followers have been a source of fascination since the days of early exploration in the West. Since to this day their actual fate is unknown, I indulged my idealism by embellishing the legend and giving the people in question a fate that appeals to me.

The Civil War battles of Valverde, Apache Canyon, and Glorieta Pass—which was later named the Gettysburg of the West—did in fact take place much as I have depicted them. The incidents concerning the surrender of Fort Fillmore, the exploding mules, General Sibley's retreat to an ambulance wagon to imbibe medicinal whiskey while the battle of Valverde raged, the Rebels' failure to occupy Fort Craig after the same battle are all true with the exception of Zachary McAllister's part in them.

Paddy Graydon's "spy company" did exist and was assigned to Fort Craig. Since no official or organized secret service existed on either side in the conflict between North and South, both sides employed such units to scout, do reconnaissance, and, whenever possible, disrupt and sabotage enemy activities. On the night before Valverde, Paddy Graydon did lead two or three of his men on an ill-fated mission, the two unfortunate mules the only heroes. That same night, two hundred mounts of the CSA cavalry broke loose from their corral and left their owners to muddle through the battle on foot. Kit Carson, who commanded the New Mexico Volunteers, was present at the battle and was later put in command of New Mexico forces for the

Union. The opposing commanders in the battles, General Sibley and Colonel Canby, were indeed brothers-in-law.

History records the story of a young man who, on the eve of the Battle of Glorieta Pass, dreamed of his own death. The young man's vision came to pass. Anyone who has the courage to face battle after such vivid premonitions, I felt, deserved as much of a happy ending as I could give him. I'd like to think that Calvin Boyd (a fictional name) lives on through his descendents.

The Pueblo Indian uprising of 1847 mentioned is recorded as a part of New Mexico history. All other incidents relating to the Civil War are factual with the exception of Zachary's, Cameo's, Samuel's, Seamus's, and the Others' participation.

Colonel Chivington was an elder of the Methodist Church before insisting on a commission as a fighting man. He had a reputation for going by the book though, at times, he indulged in some creative interpretations. He was the same Chivington who later led the infamous Sand Creek Massacre.

Though Mesa Verde is a historic landmark in southwest Colorado and one of the last known sites of the extinct Anasazi culture, I merely used it as a model for the mesa of Zach's people. The history of the Anasazi is still clouded in mystery and I did not wish to tamper with the actual facts. I'd like to think that the spirits of such an enterprising race still sing in the wind. Mesa Verde was not discovered by the white man until 1888 when two ranchers stumbled upon the site while searching for stray livestock.

The Miranda Land Grant was awarded by the Spanish–Mexican government to former trappers Ceran St. Vrain and Charles Bent and alcalde Cornelio Vigil of Taos in 1843 and encompassed approximately four million acres of land. The records on actual ownership and exact boundaries have never been clear. Several parcels of the original grant were either sold, traded, or given to various comrades and were primarily used for ranching. This grant was also known as the Beaubein or Maxwell Grant. Given the approximate location of the Miranda and Los Animas grants, I have taken the liberty of assuming they were located in the general area of the fictional Empress Valley, which I have placed in the Sangre de Cristo Mountains in southern Colorado.

I've also fudged a little on travel times between Valverde and the Empress Valley, the Empress Valley and Raton Pass, and the valley and Mesa Verde in order to expedite my story. As in the forced march of the Colorado Volunteers, travel times varied widely, depending on circumstance and necessity.

Connie Rinehold